I0556498

INVITATION

A novel by

Don Miller

Dr. Dennis Hensley, Director of the Professional Writing major at Taylor University says:

"In one respect, *INVITATION* is science fiction. In another, it is a love story. It also has elements of adventure. It should appeal to a wide readership."

Also by Don Miller

Commonguy.com

Published by Don Miller

No part of this publication may be reproduced, stored in or introduced into a retrieval system, or transmitted in any form, or by any means, without the prior written permission of the author.

This book is a work of fiction. Names, characters, places, and incidents are the product of the author's imagination or are used fictitiously, and any resemblance to actual persons, living or dead, business establishments, events, or locales is entirely coincidental.

ISBN # 978-0-9839612-0-8

Cover design by Leah Henderson

ACKNOWLEDGEMENTS

My special thanks to:

Dr. Dennis Hensley and Beth Rose for their expert editing services and words of encouragement.

Leah Henderson for the knockout cover.

Most of all to my wife Nancy for her support, insight, suggestions, and understanding from the beginning of the effort to the end.

INVITATION

Prologue

Bill Holden, steward and loadmaster for Air Force 1 during the summer of 1963 reported that he asked President John F. Kennedy while aboard Air Force 1, "What do you think about UFOs Mr. President?" He said Kennedy became quite serious and thought for a moment before replying, "I'd like to tell the public about the alien situation, but my hands are tied."

Nazi engineer Rudolph Schriever claimed to have designed a flying disc, which was constructed in 1944. Drawings of this saucer published by Rudolph Lusar in 1959 show the saucer as a ring of separate disks carrying adjustable jets rotating around a fixed cockpit. The craft had a height of 150 feet and could fly vertically or horizontally depending on the positioning of the jets.

Apollo astronaut and retired Air Force Colonel Gordon Cooper wrote the following in 1985 in a letter addressed to and read at a meeting at the United Nations on UFOs. "I believe that these extraterrestrial vehicles and their crews are visiting this planet from other planets, which are obviously a little more advanced than we are here on Earth." Cooper also states, "There are several of us who do believe in UFOs and who have had occasion to see a UFO on the ground, or from an airplane."

The following excerpt is from a CIA report dated May 27, 1954. "A German newspaper recently published an interview with George Klein, famous German engineer and aircraft expert, describing the experimental construction of 'flying saucers' carried out by him from 1941 to 1945. Klein stated that he was present when, in 1945, the first piloted flying saucer took off and reached a speed of 1,300 miles per hour in 3 minutes."

Retired Colonel Philip J. Corso, US Army, stated the following in his book *The Day After Roswell*, published in 1997: "My boss, General Trudeau, asked me to use the army's ongoing weapons development and research program as a way to filter the Roswell technology into the mainstream of industrial development through the military defense construction program. Today, items such as lasers, integrated circuitry, fiber optics networks, accelerated particle-beam devices, and even the Kevlar material in bulletproof vests are all commonplace. Yet, the seeds for them all were found in the crash of the alien craft at Roswell...."

Colonel Corso also stated the following regarding Lieutenant General Nathan Twining's comments about the Roswell crash: "Twining had suggested the crescent-shaped craft looked so uncomfortably like the German Horten wings our flyers had seen at the end of the war that he had to suspect the Germans had bumped into something we didn't know about. And his conversations with Wernher von Braun and Willet Ley at Alamogordo in the days after the crash confirmed this. They didn't want to be thought of as crazy but intimated that there was a deeper story about what the Germans had engineered."

A March 22, 1950 office memorandum to J. Edgar Hoover from the special agent in charge of the FBI's Washington office stated the following: "An investigator for the US Air Force stated that three so-called flying saucers have been discovered in New Mexico. They are described as being circular in shape with raised centers, approximately 50 feet in diameter. Each one was occupied by three bodies of human shape but only 3 feet tall, dressed in metallic cloth of very fine texture."

Questions and opinions relating to the existence of alien life abound. Five years from today, will the public have more accurate knowledge regarding intelligent extraterrestrial life than we have today?

Chapter 1
Saturday, January 19

"Dozens of UFO sightings were reported over New Mexico, Arizona, and Utah this morning between two and four a.m.," reported attractive, blonde news anchor Rachel McNary. "Many were from official sources trained in observation: state troopers, deputy sheriffs, and airline pilots. Our Albuquerque affiliate station even received a call from an Air Force pilot. Lieutenant Patrick Herner chased one of the objects near Kirtland Air Force Base."

John Resnic, sluggish from last night's partying, wondered how the media had pulled *that* assertion out of a military pilot. Lieutenant Herner would undoubtedly be immersed in a thrashing from his commanding officer this morning.

Tidbits from last night's revelry wafted through John's head. It had been a small affair, just the Jarretts, Megan, and him, here at the house for his thirtieth birthday. There had been plenty of booze. Megan had kept him awake long after the Jarretts had gone home. His mind toyed with that party, the later one with Megan, and he couldn't keep from smiling.

"The night sky was clear and moonlit over most of the Southwest all night," McNary continued. "We now take you to an eyewitness account in Green Valley, Arizona."

The screen switched to an outdoor predawn scene of a lanky young news correspondent in a tan sport jacket and dark tie standing beside a swarthy man in a deputy's uniform.

"Waaall," the deputy drawled, "I was gettin' in my cruiser t'go back to the station after an accident cleanup on Continental Road when I heard somethin' up there and looked up and saw two objects hoverin' in the sky, 'bout a half-mile away.

'Bout the size of passenger jets, except round. Light shined down, like they was lightin' up something, and they had flickerin' rings 'round 'em. I radioed in a report, then one of 'em zipped off to the east so fast it seemed like it just disappeared. 'Bout ten seconds later, the other one did the same thing."

"What do you think the two objects were?"

"I never seen anything like it. I reported unidentified flying objects 'cause I couldn't identify 'em."

"Did the Sheriff's Office receive any other reports of UFOs overnight?"

"I'm told more'n twenty."

"Do you think you saw craft that didn't come from Earth?"

The deputy looked down at the rookie reporter with an almost imperceptible shake of his head. "Don't see how I could know the answer to that."

The screen switched back to McNary in the network studio. "We'll bring you more eyewitness accounts as we get them. We're attempting to contact Air Force pilot Patrick Herner. We're also receiving reports of other sightings from around the world and will report on those.

"When we come back, we'll talk to Dr. Bartholomew Swartz about how governments around the world are doing in the effort to reverse rapidly increasing cancer rates."

Wearing a sloppy green tee shirt, a faded pair of jeans, and loafers, John sat on a bar stool with his elbows propped on the high-top round table and sipped from a steaming cup of coffee. His gaze was drawn to the full-height bay window and its view of the Sandia Mountains rising above the grassy knolls to the west. This scene never failed to awe him. The mountains weren't huge. They were austere, sparsely vegetated at the upper elevations, and almost bare at the top, exposing sandy purplish red rock. John felt as if they were his. The main reason he'd bought this southwestern ranch-style house near Sandia Park, New Mexico four years ago was for this view of the mountains. He watched the mountains change hue as the rising sun illuminated them, coloring the dark patches as undulating shadows crept across the slopes.

His mental mix of half-focused contemplations of the mountain, recollections of last night with Megan, and lame attempts to plan his day's activities was intermittently intruded on by the TV. The UFO segment piqued his interest. Sightings were usually whisked under the rug with a variety of commonplace explanations or official denials, but once in a great while, a sighting would occur that was hard to discredit. He hoped this one wouldn't get swept away. He always hoped that.

Space had fascinated him for as long as he could remember. In grade school he'd devoured books and articles about the planets and nearby stars. His high school senior physics project had been to build a transmitter to send a message into the universe via radio waves. He'd broadcast the story of his life on Earth and described his fascination with the possibility of life elsewhere. His teacher had been impressed, but it had generated a lot of ribbing from classmates.

"Hey, pretty boy," came a playful voice from behind as Megan, clad in an oversized Arizona Wildcat football shirt, slipped her arms around his chest. Her lean five-foot-six-inch frame pressed against his back, and her long, dark hair tickled his neck as she kissed his cheek. "Gonna get us some space invaders today?" She drew him tight to her.

"Morning, baby!" He looked around and grinned at her. "What're you doing out of bed? It *can't* be after noon already."

She leaned over and whispered in his ear, "Bite me."

"How do you always know *exactly* what I'm thinking?"

"You're bad. I don't know why I keep hanging around."

"It's 'cause I'm so damned handsome. Want a cup of coffee?"

"Yeah. I need one."

"I'll get it. Sit here and look at the mountains. They're mesmerizing. Besides, it's gotta be tough for you to find your way around in the morning haze."

"Get my coffee, klutz." She watched him go – six feet tall and stocky with short cropped blond hair and soft blue eyes – with a sparkle in her eye. When he came back, he set her cup on the table and leaned over and kissed her, a long, soft kiss that hinted *let's go back to bed*. Instead of pursuing that urge, he sat down, brushing lightly against her, and their smiles exchanged the message: *Later*.

They heard Dr. Swartz say, "Skin cancer diagnoses are up seven percent from last year, which were up four percent from the year before. We've made less progress on reversing ozone depletion than our governments would have us believe. Although thinning of the ozone layer is most pronounced near the poles, it's now significant at lower latitudes, where there is greater incidence of the sun's rays on the Earth's surface. Skin cancer caused by ultraviolet radiation is on the rise from the equator up to the forty-fifth parallel. All of the United States is impacted. Melanoma diagnoses are on the rise for persons who spent significant time in direct sunlight years, even decades, ago. The ozone layer was thin enough ten years ago that we're now seeing thousands of cases caused by exposure at that time."

"But," McNary replied, "we've been told the proactive measures implemented after the Montreal Protocol back in 1987 resolved the ozone depletion problem."

"Reports on ozone levels over the past twenty-five years have varied, depending on who publishes the information. Current *independent* scientific studies indicate the ozone layer is thinner than ever, and the distribution of the thinning is much broader than just at the poles.

"The main cause of ozone depletion," Swartz continued, "is the release of chlorine-containing chemicals, CFCs, into the atmosphere. The world must abandon the previous meager program to reduce the manufacture and use of ozone depleting substances and go cold turkey. Right now. We must prohibit any further manufacture of CFCs worldwide and reclaim and neutralize all of these substances in existence. Even if that were to be accomplished this year, the problem would continue to worsen for many years due to releases over the past decade. No one knows what will happen if we don't fix the problem."

"There's a lot of on-going debate on this issue, Dr. Swartz. Many scientists and government officials insist the problem has been solved. They say the increasing cancer rates are due to the time lag required for the ozone layer to build back to its mid-twentieth-century levels. They allege that skin cancer caused by UV radiation is at or near its peak rate and will soon begin to decline."

"No. All of the *non-government* scientific organizations that measure ozone thickness report that the average thickness is still decreasing."

"So, what's your advice to the public?"

"First, protect yourself and your family. Our love affair with beaches and the sun is now so high risk that it has to end. Stay out of the sun. Second, make your voice heard. Contact your political representatives, and be insistent. Participate in demonstrations that promote cleaning up the environment and restoring ozone."

"That's a good segue to our next piece," McNary said to the camera as it faded to a commercial.

Megan glanced at John. "What do you bet *this* commercial will be for sunscreen?"

"Woof," came an insistent call from the back door. "Woof. Woof."

"Hold your horses, Rufus," John responded. "I'm coming. It's hard to tear myself away from this ozone and cancer stuff, but I'm coming anyway." He strode through the kitchen and into the small laundry room, where he opened the back door to allow their pet to enter.

Rufus was a three-year-old short haired Husky John had bought as a pup. The canine had grown into a powerful animal, but he had the friendliest, gentlest disposition of any dog John had ever known. Rufus offered a quick jump and paw touch to John's chest, and then trotted off to Megan for her morning greeting. He laid his head on her lap for the customary ear-scratching, tail wagging non-stop. The master then trotted off to lap at his water bowl in the laundry room before returning to the table to curl at the feet of his two human servants.

John kissed Megan again and sat as McNary reappeared. "Correspondent Ralph Nickerson is at the United Nations, where the topic of protecting and restoring our environment is center stage."

A round, red-faced reporter dressed in a heavy overcoat and fur hat appeared, his breath steaming as he shivered in the bitter cold. Behind him was a horde of bundled-up bodies. The throng pulsated and bulged beyond the boundaries of a frigid, sprawling plaza spotted with dirty snow and ice patches.

"Rachel, it isn't only Dr. Swartz who's confronting world decision-makers about ozone depletion. Despite the howling wind and the single-digit temperature, the crowd behind me is determined that their demand for environmental restoration be heard. They look cold, but a pot of rage is boiling beneath the surface. I spoke with one of the activists a few minutes ago."

The screen zoomed to a close-up of a fiery, belligerent face with shaggy, dark blond hair whipping out from under a University of Florida ball cap. "This is Tom York, of Panama City, Florida. Tom, it's *really* cold here. What drove you to leave the Florida warmth to be here today?"

"This is *my* fight!" York bellowed at the microphone over the gusting wind and the din behind him. "I don't care how cold it is. *Nothing* is colder than losing a wife and child to cancer, and I've lost both. These idiots making decisions about how to use and destroy our environment don't give a *crap* about the average human being or what this world will be like fifty years from now. All they care about is power and control and money!" York looked angrier and angrier. "They don't care if they kill *all* of us common people. Well, I've had enough. *Everybody* out here's had enough. There are better and simpler ways to live. We can all have comfortable lives without annihilating our planet. The corporate fat cats and their puppet politicians don't get to control us all just so they can keep getting richer. And if world governments are going to keep taking the wrong side, *by God, they're gonna find out the average guy is a force to contend with!* There are *way* more of us than them. We can stop their damned piece-by-piece devastation of our planet. And I'll tell you what, Mr. Nickerson, *I'm sure as hell gonna do my part!*"

The screen switched back to Nickerson, live. "Mr. York is out here in the cold, but he's really hot. We talked with dozens of people this morning, and he's actually *less* agitated than most. We taped several interviews that just weren't suitable for airing."

"Enough of that," John said, picking up the remote and flicking the TV off. "The end of the day yesterday was way more fun than starting today watching this stuff." He and Megan grinned at each other.

"Rufus and Brady sure had a ball," Megan said. Brady was the wiry, rambunctious, carrot-topped son of John and Megan's best pals, Randy and Kathy Jarrett.

"Yeah. It worked perfectly. They wore each other out. They must've played hide-and-seek for over an hour after it got too dark outside for fetch."

John had taught Rufus how to play hide-and-seek when he was a pup. Rufus knew every hiding spot in the house and had the concept down pat, knowing when it was his turn to hide and when he was to seek. He knew how long to wait before seeking and didn't cheat by watching the hider, which always impressed witnesses. With four-year-old Brady, it was wild sport. There were delighted squeals from the boy upon either finding or being found and raucous barks from the dog. The game was hardly fair, since Rufus had senses that more than made up for not watching the hider. However, the dog always put on a show of it being a difficult affair.

Randy was the information technology guru for Optics Solutions, the telescopic systems company that also employed John. They both had gone to work for O.S. when they had graduated from college seven-and-a-half years ago, and they had become fast friends. That same year, Randy and Kathy, who had been a couple through the last three years of college, had gotten married. Megan and Kathy had been best friends in high school and had maintained the friendship through college. Randy and Kathy had introduced John and Megan to each other.

Friday nights during the past two years usually found John, Megan, and Rufus, together with the Jarrett family. There was always card-playing, laughter, and no shortage of beverages. Recently, home-bound designated-driver trade off duty had changed in Randy's favor; Kathy was three months pregnant with their second child. Last night, the rest of the group had more than made up for Kathy's abstinence.

John smiled at Megan. "That was some birthday party."

"With Randy and Kathy? It's always a hoot."

"Well, yeah, that too. But, I'll tell you one thing: if I'd known how much you liked thirty-year-old dudes, I would've told you I was thirty the day we met."

"Three times between eleven-thirty and one?" She grinned at him. "You'd better be thanking your lucky stars you

7

only turn thirty once. You couldn't take many nights like that, boy. I figured *you* would be the one who wouldn't get out of bed before noon."

"You're nuts. I could've gone twice more. *Easy.*"

"Sure, you could've. And Rufus is gonna read *War and Peace* this afternoon. Out loud."

Even with the playful conversation, Megan couldn't shake the guilt she felt. It wasn't that she hadn't had a great time last night. They both had, but she knew she wasn't being honest with him. She tried to convince herself she really did have his best interest at heart, as well as her own. *But, still....*

Chapter 2
Sunday, January 20

Brian Betz sipped scotch as he stood inside the fifth-floor bulletproof window-wall and watched the Potomac flow gently past Alexandria, Virginia. He lived on the top floor of the recently constructed ultra-secure building, which housed three other occupants on the three floors below. Each floor was served by an isolated street entrance and a private elevator from the ground-level garage. The grade floor was compartmented, each garage space separated from the others by concrete walls. The building was surrounded by twelve-feet-high, reinforced brick walls that had four vehicle gates, one per side, all solid steel. Adjacent to each vehicle gate was a locked, steel walk-through door.

Betz had occupied the top floor of this building for twenty-seven months, longer than he had lived in any one place since his twentieth birthday. Though he had never seen or heard any of the other residents, he knew the three floors below him had been occupied continuously since he had been placed in his exclusive suite. The only fact about the other building inhabitants he was certain of was that they were not ordinary citizens who had simply decided to lease or purchase these living quarters.

Betz occasionally allowed himself a drink, never more than one, and only upon successful completion of a notable mission, or, rarely, when he acquiesced to a twinge of nostalgia. Today's mission had been successful, but not notable. Tonight, if his mind wandered into reminiscence, so be it. Betz stood a trim six-feet-two-inches tall and had an Aryan look: fair-complected, with steel-blue eyes and white hair, once blond, combed straight back from his forehead. He had removed his jacket but still wore a conservative dark-gray necktie. His white shirt looked freshly pressed, even after the events of the day.

The jacket, shirt, and tie triggered the musing in his mind. How different today's uniform was from those of the early days of his career. How odd this attire, considering the particular activities of the day, activities that had been unforeseeable to him, or to anyone else, before yesterday. Tonight, Betz didn't know what tomorrow's task would be or whether anyone had yet determined that. His life tomorrow would be a continuation of his unpredictable life of today, yesterday, last year, and the years before.

Not so for the unfortunate pilot he had met early this morning, the Air Force lieutenant who, forty hours earlier, had found himself in the unique circumstance of sighting unidentified flying objects and giving chase. Patrick Herner's life would not have changed so drastically today had he exhibited less penchant for bravado, or had he limited his discourse about that singular experience to his superiors. Lieutenant Herner had a tendency to discount the importance of following procedures, and he liked to be the center of attention. More accurately, he had possessed those personality traits before today.

Betz had received instruction electronically Saturday morning. Lieutenant Herner would arrive at the interrogation facility early Sunday morning. Betz was to interview him and ascertain every detail of the UFO encounter that could be extracted from Herner's mind. Then Betz was to ensure the brash young lieutenant would never divulge this information to anyone else.

Betz replayed the Herner episode in his mind. At 6:13 that morning, Betz had walked into the interrogation room. It was an expansive, bright clean-room with a polished white tiled floor, white epoxy painted walls and ceilings, and stainless steel furnishings. A patient procedure table occupied one corner of the room. Betz, dressed in his expensive business suit, had for the most part stood back and observed. His stalwart operatives, Lawrence Chirtle and protégé Duane Smith looked like doctors in their white lab coats. They were primed for the task, even though they'd had only one day to prepare. There had been no hiccups.

Herner had been surprisingly at ease at the beginning of the session. Most detainees, after having been subjected to the ordeal of being delivered for interrogation, were either spitting fire or shaking in their shoes. The havoc imposed during seizure and transport was intentional. Subjects never had a clue where they were. For all they knew, they could be on the east coast, west coast, or overseas. They were always blindfolded, cuffed, and manhandled for hours prior to arrival. The nightmare unraveled them. Anyone with any kind of agenda or plan always failed miserably if sufficiently distraught. Herner, however, was unexpectedly relaxed, cooperative, truthful, and unafraid … at first.

Chirtle had conducted the interrogation. "Lieutenant Herner, tell me about the UFO encounter you experienced yesterday morning."

"I was flying an F-22 Raptor solo from Edwards to Holloman early Saturday morning. I took off just after midnight. When I got close to White Sands, I saw some weird lights. I was cruising at ten thousand feet when I saw some lights below me and then some above. At first, I didn't notice any moving horizontally, but I saw vertical movement. So I slowed to get a better visual. I saw at least ten of them. Then I spotted two lights dead ahead and braked to avoid a collision. But, they didn't get any closer. They stayed ahead of me. So I decided to try catch them, you know, get a better look. But, the faster I went, the faster they went. I maxed out at mach two and started to close in. Then, bam! The one on the left shot straight up. I went after the other one and got to within a thousand feet. Then it turned right so hard I was past it before I knew where it went."

"Did you get a good look at it?"

"Pretty good. The moon was bright, and its lights were vivid. It was disk shaped, about a hundred feet in diameter and thirty feet tall, with flashing lights all around it."

"Did it have windows? Could you see anything inside?"

"I didn't get close enough to tell for sure."

The questions continued, but Herner offered nothing more of substance. Betz was certain Herner was being truthful and holding nothing back. However, he also knew there was more taken in by Herner's mind than the pilot was conscious of. That information remained to be extracted.

"Lieutenant Herner," Chirtle asked, "did you radio the tower at Holloman about the lights when you first saw them?"

"Yes."

That was the talkative pilot's first one-word answer. Betz could feel Herner's level of discomfort rising.

"What did they say?" Chirtle asked.

"They said there was nothing abnormal on their radar."

"Did you ask permission to approach or chase the objects?"

"No."

"Why not?"

"Well – and I know I'm in a lot of trouble for this. I've already been reamed by Colonel Johnson, and I guess that's why I'm here, wherever we are. Anyway, truth is, I didn't think the guys in the tower were being straight with me. I mean, the damn things were on *my* radar. How could they not be on the *tower* radar?" Herner was getting worked up. "Anyway, if they weren't being straight with me, they for sure wouldn't let me get up close and personal with these things. So, I didn't ask. I just did it."

"Who, besides your commanding officer, have you talked to about what you saw?"

Herner's shoulders slumped as he heaved air out of his lungs. Betz watched Herner's naturally hospitable disposition start to drain away. "God, I hope I don't get court-martialled for this. I hope this isn't a debriefing for that. The Air Force is my *life*. I *love* flying those birds."

"Who've you talked to?" Chirtle demanded.

"Man, I don't want to make trouble for anybody. Can I just tell you what I said and let it go at that?"

Chirtle turned vicious. "Herner! Answer my questions! I want complete responses to exactly what I ask. This is *not* a negotiation. I don't *care* how much it might torment you, or how much trouble you might cause your buddies or girlfriends. If you hold back on me, this interview's gonna get painful for you *right now*! You got it?"

Herner looked befuddled, obviously not used to being browbeaten. Most Air Force pilots would have spewed their tough guy persona at this point and exploded in a futile attempt at combat, despite being cuffed and chained to a chair. The result would have been that most pilots would have been beaten to the point of semi-consciousness. That wasn't in Herner's nature. He acted dazed, emotionally wounded. He mumbled, "I'll try, sir."

"*Bullshit!*" Chirtle yelled. "You'll do it! Who'd you talk to?"

"I ... I went to my girlfriend's house after I left the Base, at around two-thirty. We're night people. There was another couple. We ... we drank some beer. And talked."

Chirtle looked at Duane Smith, who was clenching his fists. He said, looking at Smith, "We'll give him one more chance." Then he asked quietly, still looking at Smith, "Lieutenant Herner, what were the names of the people you talked to?"

Herner looked at the floor and spoke quietly, hesitatingly. Betz saw shame wash over the valiant pilot's expression. "Jimmy Lorimar. Claudia Bayfield. And, and ... Evelyn Jackson." His voice cracked when he relinquished the last name. "Jimmy should've never called the TV station." Herner's rib cage made an involuntary convulsion as he struggled with speech. "That's what triggered everything. Half an hour after that, my cell phone rang. It was Colonel Johnson, ordering me back to the base for a face to face ... meeting. More like a mauling. He, he went *crazy* on me. I wish he would've just locked me up. Instead, I guess he sent me ... here." Herner closed his eyes and drooped his head.

Chirtle derided him. "Tell me what you told your pals, Jimmy, Claudia, and sweet Evelyn."

Herner choked out the same details he had related before.

When he was finished, Betz spoke for the first time. He was calm and deliberate. "Patrick, what else did you tell them? I know there is more."

Herner looked up at Betz meekly and replied, "What are you, clairvoyant?"

Betz bored his laser eyes into Herner and observed the impact of his invasive stare. Herner was finished off, completely unnerved.

"Okay. Yeah. Maybe I ... embellished. I, I told them I followed the one that shot off to the right and that I got close enough to see windows and something inside, but couldn't tell what it was. That's it. I've told you guys everything. What do you want me to do? I feel like crap. I wish I could go back to Friday night and never get in that damned plane. This is god-awful. I *know* I'm not supposed to talk about stuff like that. I never thought Jimmy would call the station." His hands and lips were trembling.

Betz had no doubt Herner was sick inside, worrying that his Evelyn would be subjected to this same treatment because of him.

"I don't care if I do get court-martialed," Herner moaned. "I, I deserve it."

"All right, Patrick," Betz said quietly, "we're going to step out of the room for a while and review what you've told us. Then we'll come back and talk more."

"Great," Betz heard Herner groan dismally under his breath.

The trio left Herner to give him time to stew over the events of the past six hours and fret about what the next few might bring. They returned two hours later.

Chirtle badgered him incessantly. "Tell us the rest of it! Stop holding back! You're lying!" He got louder and louder, more menacing by the minute, as Herner became almost whiny, pleading that he had told them everything. After harassing Herner for more than an hour, Chirtle yelled abruptly, "That's it you stupid, worthless piece of crap! I'm not puttin' up with another second of your evasive bullshit!" He jerked his head toward Smith and commanded, "Do it!"

Smith lurched at Herner and ferociously round-housed him in the jaw, cracking bones and knocking him senseless. Sudden, violent infliction of pain was part of the process. Sometimes shock, pain, adrenaline, and alteration of the subject's state of consciousness brought forth bits of memory that might not otherwise emerge.

After the blow to the jaw ended the second session, the trio again left Herner alone for two hours, allowing time for his psyche to reorient. Betz had little hope of obtaining more information from the third phase of the interrogation. Often, subjects who had withheld information at first no longer had the stomach for that after the beating and would spill their guts.

14

However, Betz was certain Herner had not held anything back and there would be nothing more to be drained from his conscious mind. He was right. Herner responded to Chirtle's questions no differently than he had before.

The interrogators left the room again, but only for a few minutes this time. The final phase required more people. Three heavy, muscular men accompanied Betz, Chirtle, and Smith when they returned. They forcibly transported a despondent Patrick Herner across the room to the patient procedure table and wrenched him to it. Now Herner's eyes were wide with terror, but there was little fight left in him.

Once Herner was bound to the platform, Smith brought forth a hypodermic needle and inserted it into the vein in Herner's right arm. After five minutes, Betz began asking questions. He would have a full hour to extract reliable information. Betz wasn't surprised that few new facts were elicited. The most notable detail was that Herner hadn't entirely made up his earlier admitted embellishment. He *had* made an effort to follow the UFO in a hard right turn. He had gotten close enough to see windows and blurred forms within, but the glimpse had been so brief that he hadn't believed he'd really seen it.

After an hour of pliable access into Herner's mind, the synapses within it began to misfire and cross-connect. After another hour, the young pilot would no longer be the person he had been before. His brain would flit in and out of reality. His recent memory would be gone, and his long-term memory would be confused. For the rest of his life, however long that might be, nothing he would ever say would be interpreted as meaningful.

The quality of Lieutenant Patrick Herner's future life was of no import to Brian Betz. Herner was nothing more than another assignment. Betz's life consisted of executing missions. Often those missions involved maiming or killing. Such acts were essential to some missions – the way it had to be. He didn't make the decisions. He followed orders. Whatever the consequences to other persons, so be it. Those persons had committed some act or other that had resulted in their becoming a threat. It was not up to him to determine who was a threat or why. His charge was to eliminate threats in whatever manner instructed.

Invitation

In some interrogation assignments, a second injection was part of the operation, an injection that would terminate the life of the subject. In other cases, as for Lieutenant Herner, that was not directed. Betz guessed Herner owned a motorcycle and would probably have an unfortunate accident on it later tonight, or maybe he had already had the accident, and the accident would cause the brain damage that would ruin his life. This follow-up action, whether it was to be a motorcycle accident or whatever, would be executed by others. Betz's talents were used for more intricate tasks.

Today's mission had been accomplished with relative ease. From time to time, Betz still received one-day assignments. He was sure this one had been assigned to him because someone had determined it to be highly sensitive for some reason. He still attained minor satisfaction from performing exercises in total control over another human being. However, over the years, Betz had executed tasks similar to this one many times, and there was little challenge left in such actions.

He lived for the impossible missions and their execution to utter perfection, for the sweeping, incomprehensible operations that required complex planning, coordination, and control from one focal point, that point being Brian Betz. He craved assignments requiring results that would catch the attention of the world but would have obvious and provable causes completely unrelated to the actual operation. Sometimes those missions took weeks, sometimes months. Betz's intuition told him that today's assignment was a prelude to one of those monstrous missions.

Betz was vaguely aware of the identity of the organization that engaged his services. He knew he was employed by an association of the richest and most powerful individuals who had ever lived. He didn't know how many persons belonged to the nameless group. He suspected it had coalesced over the past one or two hundred years and was fueled by inconceivable wealth and influence. Some members of the group likely possessed old money and power, maybe top-ranking Masons with lineage as far back as the Middle Ages and the Templar Knights. Some possibly descended from seventeenth

Don Miller

and eighteenth-century European and Asian royalty. Some probably held hand-me-down wealth from bigger-than-life nineteenth-century American tycoons. Maybe some were from the current crop of twenty-first-century self-made billionaires or conglomerate CEOs. Some even might be endowed with the untold secret knowledge of the formidable group of German Nazis who had survived and avoided capture or control at the end of World War II.

That possibility, that a Nazi remnant could be pulling strings, held special fascination for him. Brian Betz had been born Rudolph Heinrich in Lisbon, Portugal, in 1966. His father, Wilhelm, had been six years old in 1943 when Rudolph's grandfather, grandmother, and their seven children had been relocated there from Berlin. His grandfather and namesake, the elder Rudolph Heinrich, had led a life of mystery that had fascinated young Rudolph. He recalled being together with his grandfather no more than a half-dozen times before he'd been old enough to go to school. Notwithstanding his youth and the scarceness of time spent together, the bond he felt with his grandfather had been overwhelming.

Then, when he was six years old, his family had suffered an automobile crash that had taken the lives of his father, mother, older brother and sister, and his younger sister. Every member of the family, except Rudolph, had perished in that accident. He had been taken to live with his grandparents, who had immigrated to the United States.

His grandfather had been employed by the United States Central Intelligence Agency, beginning shortly before the Germans had been defeated in World War II. His father, who had become a history professor at a Portuguese university, had actively promoted extremist Nazi reorganization activities. The accident that had claimed the lives of his family members had been a collision with a train, followed by the violent explosion of their automobile – *not* a survivable event. Yet, young Rudolph, his grandfather's preferred descendent, had miraculously emerged unscathed. Even in the days immediately following the accident, young Rudolph had felt that neither the extinction of his family nor his own survival had been an accident. By the time he had reached his late teens, he'd no longer had any doubt of either fact.

Rudolph had lived with and been raised by his grandmother. He had been a dutiful child and brilliant student. He'd respected his grandmother but worshipped his grandfather, whose duties had kept him continually away from home. Grandfather and grandson had seen each other rarely, never more than twice a year. Yet, the connection between them had been intense, almost supernatural. When they were together, one could sense invisible tendons linking the two of them, stretching between them as they moved about. Rudolph had wanted nothing other than to be an international spy like his grandfather. When the elder Rudolph Heinrich had turned seventy-five, he'd told his twenty-year-old grandson he would retire, which for him meant disappearing. His last act as a high-ranking CIA official had been to offer his grandson an opportunity to become a special operations officer. Young Rudolph had accepted eagerly and with pride.

Rudolph had inherited two essential espionage talents from his grandfather. These two underlying faculties set them apart from their colleagues and propelled them to the top. Young Rudolph, Brian Betz, surpassed his grandfather in both. First, and most vital, was intuition. His grandfather's had been astonishing, but his was infallible. Second was the ability to ascertain other human beings' thoughts, invade their minds and souls, by simply looking into them and absorbing them. His grandfather had a keen ability to do this. Betz was astounding at it. No one felt comfortable when affixed by even a glance from Brian Betz.

Young Rudolph had progressed deftly through training and his early assignments, exhibiting prolific physical and mental toughness and command prowess. His brilliant performance had landed him in charge of an elite, deniable special missions force within five years. In that venue, he had developed an extraordinary reputation for audaciously executing the most difficult operations. Upon detailed scrutiny by top CIA officials evaluating his missions, invariably his operations were recognized as less audacious in action than they first appeared, but more outstanding in originality, concept development, planning, and control. After ten years in the agency, Rudolph had developed an unparalleled record of successfully executing impossible missions.

It was then that the CIA Director had informed Rudolph that more challenging positions, for more clandestine organizations, existed. Rudolph would be offered an elite position serving an omnipotent entity. The Director had explained that this organization was the most powerful in the world, more powerful than any national government – in fact, capable of controlling any national government. The identities of the persons controlling this organization were unknown to the Director. He had two contacts, emissaries from the organization, and he knew three of their operatives personally, but there were many others he did not know. The Director had told him that he had recommended Rudolph to fill a vacancy. He'd advised Rudolph that accepting this offer would place him in a setting where his particular talents would be utilized to their fullest potential. The assignments Rudolph would receive would be his dream missions.

Rudolph had accepted with no hesitation. He had never regretted it. Within three days of his acceptance, Rudolph Heinrich, grandson of the elder CIA officer Rudolph Heinrich, was officially dead, killed in the line of duty. In his place, Brian Betz was born at the age of thirty-one.

Neither young Rudolph Heinrich nor Brian Betz had ever jeopardized his career by falling in love. He had taken gratification in many women, always related in one of two ways to a mission. In one scenario, brief affairs without entanglement had occurred with collaborating female operatives. In the other scenario, the trysts had been with counterparts, and the illicit activities had been inherent to the espionage or operation being carried out. In either case, every sexual episode of either of his lives had occurred within the framework of executing lethal actions. The atmosphere of pervasive threat always intensified the experience. Never since he'd lost his family in the fatal crash had Betz permitted himself to feel emotional love for, or commitment to, any individual other than his grandfather.

After becoming a CIA operative, Rudolph had never again had contact with either his grandfather or grandmother. He knew his grandfather wanted it that way. He was sure they were both long dead by now. Brian Betz had no family, no loves, no confidants, no friends. He wanted none.

Invitation

Betz seldom thought farther into the future than his next mission. Although he had some curiosity about the organization he worked for, he doubted he would ever know much about the group or its membership. He was sure no one ever left this group except in death and that the only means of entering the group were through blood lines, limitless wealth, or limitless influence. He assumed the overriding goal of its members was the preservation of their individual lives and lineages and of their perceived ability to control their destinies along with the destiny of mankind as a whole.

Betz didn't care about their overriding goals or who they were. He didn't care whether this group promoted good or evil, concepts that had no meaning to him anyway. He didn't care how much money he was paid, although he was well-compensated. He didn't really care about anyone or anything except flawlessly planning and executing impossible missions. That, he craved.

Betz knew there were few like him. He was one of four agents in North America and one of thirteen worldwide. They all knew the organization they worked for had boundless resources. The thirteen operated independently. They didn't know each other's identities. They didn't know when any of their group was replaced, which did happen, but not often. These men, if indeed they were all men, received their direction through various channels, but there was never any doubt regarding the authenticity of their instructions. There was never any doubt they would have anything they needed at their disposal to accomplish whatever missions they were assigned. Each of these thirteen maintained a host of trusted operatives, all of whom had been set up or approved by the organization, and each of whom was known to only one of the thirteen agents.

This group of super-agents constituted only a small fraction of the means of influence that emanated from the tentacles of the organization. These agents were utilized only when covert force was essential to accomplishment of a mission. Usually, desired results were realized through the application of less clandestine pressure. Betz knew that virtually anything could and had been accomplished by this organization. Scientific and technological advances had been controlled, contrived, and obliterated. Governments had been toppled.

Guerilla and terrorist groups had been created and made successful ... and destroyed. Powerful world political leaders had been controlled. Betz was convinced the assassination of John Kennedy in 1963, the existence and direction of NASA and the Russian and European space exploration programs, and even the maintaining of tension between Islam and Christianity, were part of this organization's legacy. He was certain this all-powerful group could accomplish anything.

As Betz surveyed the Potomac, savoring the last swallow of scotch, his electronic encryption equipment signaled an incoming message. He walked through a passageway into the spacious office suite, sat at the message station, and decoded the instruction. He read it vigilantly, contemplating the exact meaning of every word, as he always did. When he had absorbed the entire message, he read it a second time, as he always did. After that, he read it a third time, which he *never* did. Betz felt an emotion, a stir of excitement. He forced the sentiment to die as swiftly as it had fashioned itself.

This mission would eclipse all previous ones. It would require cooperation – subservience – from the highest echelons the organization could tap. The deadline was April 15, twelve weeks from now. He would not sleep tonight. He would work all night, formulating the bones of a plan. He thought of his grandfather, and another emotion tried to worm its way into his psyche. How he wished he could share this message with the elder Rudolph Heinrich. This all-powerful organization had chosen him, above all others, to execute this blockbuster mission. He sensed the specter of the emotion struggling to rise. Pride. He squelched it.

Brian Betz leaned back in his chair and considered the possible circumstances that might have prompted the decision to undertake this particular action at this particular time. His unfaltering ally, his intuition, tied the momentous mission to today's simple assignment. There was nothing tangible connecting the two, no rational link between ascertaining details of alien craft sightings less than two days ago and the necessity for this action twelve weeks in the future. It wasn't logical that such a far-reaching exploit could be spawned so quickly from anything as commonplace as UFO sightings. Nevertheless, he felt the connection.

Invitation

The mission was staggering. Putting someone that powerful under control of the organization had no historical precedent. *Daniel Jamison!*

Chapter 3
Friday, March 28

Two and a half months after John's birthday, the Friday night get-together was at Randy and Kathy's home in Alameda. John and Megan sauntered hand in hand up the walk to the front door as the sun sank in the west, a big red ball on the horizon, shedding its last slanting rays on another warm, clear Southwestern March day. When they reached the door, Megan pushed the button, and they immediately heard Brady bounding and yelping, "They're here! They're here! John and Megan are here!" John opened the door, and they walked in. For this group, ringing the doorbell just served as notice that, "We're coming in."

"Where's Woofis?" Brady asked, looking out the door.

Rufus had already started the game of hide-and-seek, standing hidden to the side of the door. As soon as Brady poked his head outside the dog barked and jumped at him, drawing squeals of delight.

"Randy's out back, putting steaks on the grille." Kathy motioned to John. "Beer's in the fridge," she added after John had already reached the refrigerator and opened the door. "Help yourself," she said dryly, feigning aggravation.

"Don't mind if I do," John replied, pulling two out and twisting off the caps. He cheerfully held out one to Kathy, eyes on her tummy, puffing out in her fifth month. "You are lookin' *fine* tonight!"

Kathy was a striking woman. Both she and Randy had auburn hair, pale skin, and hazel eyes, but the resemblance stopped there. Randy was six-foot-two and stick-skinny with curly hair. Kathy was voluptuous, five-foot-six, and, at twenty-eight, still kept her wavy hair just past shoulder-length. Pregnancy enhanced her attractiveness.

Randy was the incessant clown of the foursome, and Kathy was the most practical and quick-witted, always first to grasp situations in terms of the lowest common denominator, instinctively discerning the pertinent factors. Her ability to ascertain the best course of action while everyone else was still trying to figure out the options always impressed the other three.

"You're a sadist," Kathy retorted. As she was speaking, John was already turning to Megan and holding out the beer to her.

"I think I'll pass. My stomach's been sort of queasy today."

"You okay, hon?" John asked.

"Yeah, I'm fine. Go on out and drink mine for me. I've seen you drink two before."

"All right. I'll make the sacrifice. But, I have to say, it's gettin' tougher and tougher, always picking up the slack for you."

"You'd better get your butt out of here!" Megan warned as he turned and scurried for the door.

"C'mon Brady, follow me. It ain't safe for guys in here."

"It ain't safe in here!" Brady yelled, running after John. "C'mon, Woofis!"

"Thanks for the English lesson for the boy," Kathy quipped as they disappeared out the door. "Not to mention the great example of etiquette and courtesy!"

"So, what's up?" Kathy asked Megan after the boys went out.

"Long day. I'm a little worn out."

"Yeah? Stomach queasy, too? No beer tonight? You look tired. But, there's a little gleam in your eye. A hint on your face that you know something the rest of us don't. Shall I start guessing? You realize I know you pretty well, right? Have you been nauseated in the mornings lately?" Kathy looked at Megan with raised eyebrows.

A room-brightening smile broke across Megan's face. "I never could keep secrets from you."

"Are you sure?" Kathy asked.

"Pretty sure. The home pregnancy test said yes, but I'm going to the doctor in the morning."

"How far along?"

"My best guess is the night of John's birthday party."

"Does John know?" Kathy queried. "I thought you were on the pill."

"Well, I've got some things to deal with." Megan looked sheepish. "I kind of decided on my own a baby would be the right thing for us. I'm sure John'll be great with it. I know he's been adamant he isn't ready for another marriage or a family, but I *know* it'll make him happy in the end. It'll be the best thing for him. You've seen him with Brady. And you've seen him with me. He just got so messed up the first time, he can't let go and risk it again."

"Ah, yes," Kathy said knowingly, "Miranda, the witch, still haunts. You really think he'll be okay with this?"

"I hope so. I've thought about it a lot. We've been together for over three years, living together almost two. In some ways, I know him better than he knows himself. I love him, and I know he loves me. He loves kids. He's thirty, and I'm twenty-eight, and neither of us is getting younger. I know I want a child, and I want it to be his. If I'm wrong about how he'll take it, I'll still want a child, and I'll still want it to be his. If I turn out to be wrong, I'd be willing to let him go if I have to and raise the baby on my own."

"Well, that's all pretty heavy. Maybe we can lighten things up. Do you think the medical sages are really right about drinking being bad for expectant mothers and their expecteds?"

"Yeah." Megan smiled at Kathy. "I'm pretty sure they're right about that one."

"Dang. So, you find out for sure tomorrow? Does John know you're going to the doctor? Is tomorrow the day you tell him?"

"Yes, yes, and yes. He's concerned about how I've been feeling. He wanted to go along in the morning, but I insisted on going by myself. I think that worried him even more. I'm not sure yet how I'll tell him, but I'll do it tomorrow."

The door banged open as Brady burst in. "Daddy says to get the plates on the table, Mommy, the steaks are comin' in!"

"Go ask Daddy who his slave was last year."

"He already told me to tell you *you* was his slave last year and the year before!"

Kathy winked at Megan. "And you think you're ready for this? You can see it'll be like having two kids – one will just be tall."

"I can hardly wait," Megan whispered with a grin as the big boys entered noisily.

Brady provided the entertainment during the meal. When the living room clock chimed seven times, he exclaimed, "Mom, it's seven bells! Can I watch *Sesame Street* now?"

"Come here. Let me wash your face and hands. Then you can watch TV."

Brady jumped off his chair and trotted to his mother for the mopping. Then he ran into the living room, grabbed the remote, flopped down on the floor, and hit the "on" button. Rufus lay at his side.

"What a live wire," Megan said as they all chuckled. "Hey did you all hear about the UFO sightings last night?" Megan was the only one of the group who worked where TVs were on all day. None of the others had heard.

"From the bits and pieces I caught, it was similar to the sightings back in January except earlier, between eight and ten in the evening. So far, I haven't heard of anybody other than regular people reporting sightings. I didn't see any cops interviewed this time."

"The last time, it all got swept under the rug," John said. "It was a big deal on the news that Saturday morning, with promises of more interviews, especially from that Air Force pilot. But then it just got dropped. I never heard another word about it."

"That's the way it always works," Randy said. "UFO sightings are all big news for about twelve hours, and then nothing more is ever heard. It's like there's a burst of information sprayed by the media on the day of the sighting, but by the next day, all traces of the information and any thoughts of follow-up have evaporated. It's all just gone, like nothing ever happened."

"I was testing the new Baldy Mountain Observatory last night," John said. "We flew up to Santa Fe Baldy by helicopter in the morning and didn't get out till after nine. The test showed some anomalies right around eight-thirty. The system reported background light flashes the software couldn't categorize. The oscillation frequencies in the flashes didn't match up with any patterns programmed in the software. It was late, so we didn't spend much time on it. We just noted it as a bug that would have to be traced out during commissioning. But if there was weird activity in the air, maybe it wasn't a system glitch." John grinned at Randy. "Hey, buddy, I'm getting a feeling our test crew won't be able to figure this one out, and we'll be turning it over to our techy guru."

"Gee, thanks. I'm looking forward to it already," Randy replied.

Kathy looked troubled. "I've been overhearing some pretty strange conversations at work the past few weeks."

John, Megan, and Randy glanced at each other around the table. Kathy was the executive secretary for The Crowley Group, a two hundred employee private research company that thrived by performing government investigations. Most of their projects were classified. Kathy was responsible for organizing and preparing reports for all executive-level meetings, including those that dealt with classified subjects. She had a high security clearance. She had worked for Crowley since graduating from college six years ago. None of the group, not even Randy, had ever heard her say anything significant about specific projects at work. Kathy took her security classification seriously.

Randy stared at her. "Uh, you *sure* you want to talk about that?"

"Well, I haven't really seen any documents or anything, and I haven't been involved in any conversations. I don't know that there *is* a project, and there hasn't been any hint of a classified subject. That's all strange in itself. Not that there isn't always project talk in the halls. But I've *never* heard this much talk on a subject where no project has been identified and no documents distributed to classify it. I'm usually near the top of the list to be told I'm not allowed to talk outside the office about a project, and I haven't been told a thing on this, whatever it is."

Randy asked, "Does that mean you're allowed to talk about it?"

John and Megan were staring at Kathy, waiting for what she would say next.

Invitation

"Like I said …." Kathy shrugged. "I'm not sworn to secrecy on this one. Not specifically. Not yet. The talk started a week or two after the January UFO sightings and has escalated ever since. We've had some pretty high-ranking Air Force officers coming and going. I overheard one of them talking about the old Roswell incident. It almost sounds like there are people in the know who believe the Roswell crash happened and is related to the January sightings. Today was *really* strange. No one was talking where there was any chance of being overheard. Most office doors were kept closed. Phone conversations were kept quiet enough to avoid being heard in the halls. But, even today, I still didn't receive any direction designating a classified subject. It's almost like the security level of this one is beyond my clearance, but no one realizes they need to keep their mouths shut around me. At least, it was like that until today. I had no clue there'd been more sightings till now. But I'm wondering if there isn't a whole lot more known about UFOs than is being let on."

Kathy noticed the other three staring at her, all at a loss for words. She gave her head a quick shake, as if to fling the unwanted thoughts out. "Okay, enough of that," she said as she rose to get a deck of cards to carry on the traditional Friday night activities. However, the rest of the evening wasn't quite as carefree and raucous as usual. Kathy, in particular, had difficulty shedding the feeling that something was amiss in the world and it was being covered up; being kept secret, even from her.

Later, with Randy asleep in bed beside her, Kathy lay awake, trying to work through the issues that had her stirred up. *Why was I so loose-tongued? Why did I want to talk so badly? Why is it so hard to get to the root of this?*

Gradually, she realized her own emotions were at the heart of it. She was being kept out of the loop, and she resented it – a lot. She was proud of her trustworthiness and valued the position her reliability had earned. Executive Secretary. She had risen to that position in six years. She had proven herself and did not deserve to be excluded, as if she couldn't be trusted. Kathy began to recognize that her resentment had been building since early February, as she had been continually guessing about the half-hushed talk and the meetings with the Air Force brass. Then, today, after all of the doors went closed and the hushed talk changed to silence, without comprehending what she was feeling or why, she had gotten really mad about it.

That's why I blabbed tonight. I was so mad at being kept on the outside that I violated my trustworthiness and gave them a reason to exclude me. I talked. I don't deserve to be part of the inner circle. However, even as she began to understand what she felt, why she had acted as she had, and the consequences her actions deserved, she still placed blame on the leadership at Crowley. *They <u>know</u> they have to classify projects. If my clearance isn't high enough for this project, why didn't they have the guts to tell me? And then keep it quiet instead of half-talking about it around me?*

What's this all about, anyway? On one hand, she thought she should talk to Jerome Schrader, tell him she'd overheard conversations not intended for her, and ask him to make sure to keep the discussions screened from her, if her classification wasn't high enough. *On the other hand, if this issue has a higher secrecy classification than anything I've ever heard before, then it must be really big.* She knew she should play by the rules and talk to Jerome, including disclosing her slip of the tongue tonight. However, she also wanted to know what was going on. And, if this was as big as it seemed to her late-night head, *I have a right to know. And so does everybody else.*

Invitation

Chapter 4
Saturday, March 29

Megan stood at the counter, signing paperwork at Dr. Sheila Griswold's office. The suspected condition was confirmed. The good-natured, middle-aged receptionist looked up, smiled, and said, "We're glad you showed up today. We were beginning to think we were being blacklisted by new moms. Usually, we have at least five, sometimes ten or twelve, initial visits every week. But you're the first we've seen in two weeks."

"That explains the extra-special treatment." Megan smiled back. "Don't worry about us," she said, placing a hand on her abdomen. "We'll keep coming back."

During the drive home, Megan wrestled with how to approach John. She had not played by the rules. John didn't have a clue she might be pregnant. He knew she was on the pill, and he knew she was not the kind of person who slipped up or forgot details. The decision to try to have a baby had been hers alone. She had monitored her body signs and had been sure the night of John's birthday was the perfect time. She had instigated the action. That, in itself, wasn't unusual, but there had been deceit on her part.

She had never pushed the subject of having a child with John. They had discussed it casually, and John had always been quick to make it clear he was not ready for a family. She understood why. The failure of his first marriage had cut deeply.

Her first few dates with John had been friendly but superficial. They had been attracted to each other, but he had consistently sidestepped personal conversation. Kathy had warned Megan his previous marriage had ended disastrously and he had spent the three years since avoiding relationships. Kathy had said she and Randy knew a few details about the breakup

30

and surmised a few more, but suggested it might be better for Megan to avoid the subject until John brought it up.

After three months of dating, Megan had cautiously mentioned she felt he was holding back. After that, bit by bit, John had revealed the story. As he'd divulged it, he'd begun to relax, and their relationship had blossomed. After a year of dating, Megan knew the whole story, and the two were falling irresistibly in love. Another six months and they were sharing John's house. Still, he couldn't escape paranoia at the thought of marrying again or starting a family.

It had taken months for the whole sordid story of John's first marriage to come out. Knowing it increased her understanding of and appreciation for John. He was a good man. He enjoyed life and people. He had a good sense of humor. He believed in living life, setting goals, making commitments, honoring them, and improving the world. He was not a quitter. He liked people and loved kids. Miranda had severely tested his outlook, but he had eventually rebounded. The lone holdover was his reluctance, to the point of panic, to consider remarriage and children.

Megan pulled into the driveway. *It's time to deal with our future and bury the past.* She wished she felt as sure of herself as she had yesterday.

*   *   *

John rolled out of bed just before Megan left for her doctor's appointment. He was concerned. It was obvious she had been having stomach problems for the past few weeks, not eating much, and not keeping down what she did eat. She had been treated for ulcers as an adolescent but had not experienced any recurrence. They had almost gotten into a fight last night on the way home from the Jarretts' haggling about John going to the doctor with her. He wasn't sure why, but Megan had been adamant: she would go by herself. Finally, after she had agreed to call him from the doctor's office if anything serious was found, he had given in. So, this morning, he sat in bed and kissed her goodbye as she left, threw on a pair of sweats, loafers, and a worn, oversized sweatshirt, and walked to his favorite spot at the window to absorb the mountain.

Invitation

He flipped on the TV after pouring his second cup of coffee and was transported to live coverage of demonstrations in Washington D.C. and San Francisco. The west coast crowd was peaceful, but the east coast mob was not. The familiar face of Ralph Nickerson appeared in front of a disorderly, sprawling mob.

"I'm at the Walter E. Washington Convention Center in Washington, where the Conference of Governors on Climate Change is scheduled to begin at nine o'clock. The streets for blocks around are packed with demonstrators. A permit was granted for a rally, but ten to twenty times more people than anticipated arrived overnight. Although the size of this crowd was apparently secretly planned by its organizers, local law enforcement has been caught unprepared and understaffed. The boundaries established by permit were initially roped off but were overrun before seven this morning. The protestors, incensed by lack of governmental response to increasing cancer rates and disappearing ozone, are unleashing their frustration on a vastly outnumbered security force. For the past hour, policemen have been jeered and bullied by this unruly throng, and it's getting worse by the minute.

"*Whoa!*" Nickerson exclaimed. "Guys! Get that action on the left! S*how the crowd!*"

The scene was of a cadre of police officers using clubs and Tasers. Their actions appeared to be in self-defense as the mob pressed in around them. The view zoomed out to show tear gas being fired into the crowd. Rocks and other projectiles were suddenly being hurled at police from all quarters. The camera abruptly swung and zoomed in on a violent group of twenty or more men overpowering four policemen, relieving two of them of their Tasers, and turning them on the officers.

John was absorbed in the melee for the next hour, the amount of time it took to get enough law enforcement on site to regain control. Lots of tear gas was used. Protesters were dragged off in cuffs, many of them bleeding. Dozens of police officers were injured. John had read about riots that had occurred during the late 1960s, but he had never seen video of anything like this in the United States during his lifetime.

As police regained control, live coverage was finally sacrificed for a few all-important commercials, and John turned the TV off. "C'mon, Rufus," John called as he headed for the back door. It was time to check out the clear morning sunshine and let Rufus romp. As much as John loved being in the sun, he remained under the porch roof. During the past few months, he, along with most other people, had found themselves consciously avoiding exposure to direct sunlight.

John and Rufus were coming back inside as Megan entered the front door. "Hey, babe, how'd it go?" She didn't reply immediately, and John caught the anxious look on her face. "Are you all right?"

"Can we sit down and talk?"

"What is it?"

"I'm okay. It's nothing serious. I just want to talk."

"Okay," he replied, not convinced. "Do you want coffee or juice or anything?"

"No, nothing." She took a deep breath as they sat at the table, and then blew it out as John watched her. "The right words," she muttered to herself, trying to start the discussion. After a few more seconds, she said, as much to herself as to John, "Okay, I just need to say it." She looked straight at him and said resolutely, "I'm pregnant."

John stared at her, disbelieving. Her face was not normally pale, but it was now. After a minute, he finally responded, eyes locked on hers. He asked softly, "How can that be?"

She gave an understated shrug of her shoulders and looked away from his stare. "I guess nobody's perfect," she uttered.

"What does that mean? The pharmacist gave you the wrong pills? The pills didn't work? You forgot to take them? You don't *screw up* on things that matter." His voice rose in pitch and volume. *"Did you forget?"*

"No."

"Then what?" He got still louder. *"How?"*

"Okay," she took another deep breath. "Please, hear me out. Let me finish what I have to say. Then I'll answer whatever you ask."

He didn't respond, but just looked at her, waiting.

"I love you with all my heart, John, and I know you love me. You're thirty and I'm twenty-eight."

John's mind went into fast-forward, drawing conclusions. *She knows exactly how I feel about this. Love and age don't have a damn thing to do with it.* He felt the rising ball of anger explode in the pit of his stomach. He was not a physically aggressive man, but rage overcame him.

"I know you always say you aren't ready for a family, and I know I don't have any right to think I know you better than you know yourself or that you really *are* ready and just don't see it."

John was visibly out of control, face crimson, fury blazing from his eyes. A tear slid down Megan's left cheek. She brushed it away.

"The thing is," she went on shakily, "I *know* I want a child, and I *know* I want it to be yours, and I'm pretty sure deep down inside you want the same thing."

"*God dammit, Megan!*" he erupted, stepping toward her. "You did this *on purpose!*" As he tensed, took another step toward her, and clenched his fists, something inside him grabbed hold and he was able to check himself. He felt sick. "No way in *hell* you could do this on purpose!" He glared fiercely at her. "You *know* what I've been through! You know *everything. You can't be doing this!*"

"John, please listen to me," she cried. "*Please*, let me finish."

He stepped back.

"Look, if you hate me for this, I understand." Now, everything began pouring out in a torrent. "I know what you went through with Miranda. I thought about this for a long time. I know for sure I want your child. I want it, even if you don't, and even if it means I have it without you. I want you. I love you, and I want you *desperately*. If I'm wrong about what you really want, that's just a chance I have to take. If you want out, you're free. There won't be any strings from me. You'll never hear from any lawyer. I'll make it on my own with our child if I have to. I want you with me, but I'll *never* force you." She stopped and looked up at him, searching his face. She was trembling.

"So, you decided to get pregnant, and never said a word to me 'cause you *knew* I'd say no." He felt drained and disoriented.

"Yes".

"How could you possibly *do* that?"

"I guess, if you look at it in the worst possible light, I did it for me. Maybe I was being selfish."

"You *think*?" he replied sarcastically.

"John, please, believe that I love you more than anything, and I want to spend the rest of my life with you. *More than anything!* You don't have to say or do anything right now. Let it sink in. We can talk whenever you're ready. I'm not forcing anything on you."

"*Bullshit!* There's a life inside you that's part *me*. You can say it's okay if I just walk away and pretend it doesn't exist, but you *know* I can't. *You know it!* And you say you aren't forcing anything on me? You *know* that's a lie!"

"John, it can be any way you want." She was crying softly. "We can be friends and live apart and share the parenting. We can get married. We can live together. You can leave if you want. I'll leave if you ask me to. But I can't make the baby go away. One thing you can be positive of is I *won't* make it go away. If I'm laying more on you than you can handle, I'm sorry. But I don't think I am."

"Okay, okay. Okay. Shit," John said to himself. "I'm goin' out. C'mon, Rufus." Rufus leapt up and followed John out the front door, more than ready for a change of karma.

John drove up into the Sandia Mountains, to a longtime favorite spot of theirs. He parked, and they hiked up a rocky path to a clearing with a panoramic view of both the town below and the crests above. Rufus knew the routine. If John wasn't ready to play, Rufus had the run of the area, so long as he stayed within sight. When John selected a perch on a cupped cut portion of rock bathed in sunlight and gazed off into the distance, Rufus bounded off to explore on his own.

Nothing had focused in John's head during the drive or the climb. A whirl of emotions and thoughts seemed to control his mind rather than be generated by it. Pieces of the heated conversation with Megan mixed with flashbacks of his short-lived marriage to Miranda. His chaotic thoughts were overlaid on the resurrected emotional roller coaster he'd ridden through the Miranda ordeal. He felt anew the culminating self-disgust –

self-hate – that had burned after that union had ripped apart. Those unearthed, devastating passions intertwined in his head and his heart with the more recent contentment from his life with Megan. This collage of emotions swam in the remnants of the anger and fraught disbelief he had felt an hour ago.

Relax. Let the sun soak in. Just relax. He tried to calm his emotions, to control his thoughts. *Relax.* It was warm in the late-morning sun. With no thought whatsoever about UV rays, or cancer, or the fracas he had witnessed two hours ago on television, John removed his jacket, leaned back against the curve in the rock, and wadded the jacket behind his head for a pillow. He closed his eyes, felt the wispy breeze on his face, and lay quietly for ten minutes, pushing out uncontrolled thoughts and feelings. He forced himself think about the past. He felt it crashing down on the present. *What really happened with Miranda? Where did I go wrong? What should I have done?*

John's best high school buddy, Smitty, had a younger sister, Miranda, who had been popular with older kids, especially older boys. By the time she was sixteen, Miranda's circle of friends was one where alcohol flowed freely. During her junior and senior years in high school, she'd delved progressively deeper into alcohol, drugs, and sex. After graduating from high school she had gotten accepted, barely, into Ohio State, where she'd quickly fallen into trouble both academically and socially.

When Smitty had asked John to check in on his loose kid sister, he had done so for his friend. Smitty had been at Florida State, far from their Circleville, Ohio, hometown, where his dysfunctional family had disintegrated just days after his high school graduation, when his father had left his mother. Miranda, two years younger than Smitty and already dysfunctional in her own right, had suffered from the loss of what little guidance had existed before.

At Ohio State the pace of her downward spiral had hastened. By spring of her freshman year, she'd seemed beyond hope. She had no longer attended class. She didn't eat, but only drank. She'd freely bartered whatever body she had left for whatever alcohol and drugs it could get her. She'd had a college dorm room and a roommate, but had rarely graced their presence, preferring the squalor of a group house occupied mostly by males looking more like gang members than students. A dozen people, more or less, including Miranda, semi-lived in this grimy house with seven bedrooms, none of which was Miranda's.

That was where John had found her, haggard, insensible, and reeking. It had taken an entire day to rouse her into consciousness, get her away from the filthy house, get her cleaned up, and have meager communication with her. Over the rest of the spring quarter, he'd coaxed her back to life. She had stayed at his shared apartment. He had given her his room, and slept on the couch. He'd seen to it that she ate, helped her resist alcohol and drugs, and tutored her.

That summer, Miranda had refused to go back to Circleville, so he'd stayed in Columbus with her. His two roommates went home for the summer, and it was just the two of them in the apartment, alone together. Within a week they'd succumbed to sex. He hadn't instigated it. Miranda had come to him while he was sleeping on the couch. But, neither had he resisted. During the summer they'd grown closer – in love they'd decided. Miranda got pregnant. In the fall, they got married.

Both families, his and Miranda's, had been furious with him – his family because he was throwing away his life, and hers because he was taking advantage of her precarious emotional state. In order to make ends meet, he'd taken a job. While he'd been busy with school and work, Miranda had had trouble coping with being alone, and she'd backslid. She had begun to spend time with one of her old friends, Natasha, and started drinking again. The marriage began to crumble under the stress. One December evening, when he'd arrived home late from work, Miranda had told him unfeelingly that she had miscarried. He was distraught. He couldn't fathom that this had happened without her even calling him – that he hadn't been there for her. Miranda had been detached, uncaring. Natasha had spent the tragic day with her.

After several weeks, a semblance of normalcy had begun to return. The stress in the marriage had dissipated, but so had Miranda's interest in it. He'd vowed to himself to make the marriage work. When he had graduated and gotten the job with Optical Systems he had looked forward to a fresh start for them.

In Albuquerque, Miranda had attempted and promptly failed at several part-time jobs, then enrolled at the University of New Mexico. She'd continued to slip away from him.

One Friday in early October, he'd made up his mind that he was going to rescue the marriage once and for all and had gone home in the early afternoon, anxious to take his wife on a long getaway weekend. What he'd found at home was his wife in bed, naked and intertwined with another man and woman. He'd been stupefied. Miranda had sat up in bed and gloated, seeing him looking incapacitated and pathetic at the bedroom door. Her words had been, "Now you know. Leave us alone. *Get out!*" He'd felt the world smash down on him and crush him.

He'd spent that weekend drunk, living out of a motel room. When he'd telephoned Miranda the following Monday night, she'd made it clear she was through with the marriage. He had moved out and she had promptly filed for divorce. At that point he hadn't cared about anything. He had shunned participation in the divorce proceedings. As a result, the judge's ruling had been disastrous. Miranda and her attorney, who he had to pay, had painted the same picture her family had perceived. He'd done nothing more than found a struggling girl with no self-esteem and taken whatever he wanted from her, plunging her even more deeply into hopelessness. He had been ordered to pay alimony for five years to allow Miranda to get a complete education and start a career. The alimony payments had ended last year. The whole affair had almost destroyed him; bequeathing an all-pervading sense of self-loathing he didn't fully recognize or understand.

"What should I have done differently?" he whispered to himself, leaning back on the rock, eyes closed. "Shit, what *shouldn't* I have done differently?" Who had he been anyway, to think he had the power, just by being around someone, to save her from herself? Why hadn't he tried to guide Miranda to professional help instead of pulling her to him, thinking he could propel them both into happily ever after? How could he have allowed himself to be drawn into a lifetime commitment with someone who had *no clue* what the concept of commitment even meant? How could he have pushed Miranda into a situation she couldn't possibly have understood or been ready for? *How could I have created a life I couldn't keep from being terminated?*

That last question was the killer. It had driven him crazy for the year after the divorce, after he had finally admitted to himself he had known all along there had never been any miscarriage. Over time, the rest of his psyche had mended. However, although he had masked this overpowering issue from himself, he had never gotten past it.

His eyes were moist as he forced himself to confront the problem. His real reason for avoiding all thoughts of marriage and children was his feeling that he had already been given that opportunity and had failed beyond redemption. He had stood by and allowed the life of his own child to be terminated. Simply ended. He had never forgiven himself for that. How could he? He had *proven* he was untrustworthy and unworthy of another chance to father a child.

"So, where am I?" He was still muttering to himself. Whenever he thought of the Miranda affair, which was almost never, he had always allowed himself to feel victimized. But, maybe he was more the *cause* of the whole mess than the victim. Were the failed marriage and the loss of the child really all Miranda's fault? What more could he have expected from her? She had been incapable of a committed relationship of any kind at the time. How could he not have seen that? She had needed help, professional help, not sympathy and some nonexistent easy way out. There was no easy way out of the mess she had already created for herself. Maybe the disaster that befell him had been of his own doing, no less than Miranda's personal disaster had been of her own doing. He shook his head. "What a mess."

So, where am I now? What about Megan? She is not Miranda. She's nothing like Miranda. Megan is rock-solid. I love her. She loves me. Nothing about this relationship is remotely like anything with Miranda.

He thought about Megan. They had met at Randy's twenty-sixth birthday party. It had seemed like an innocent enough outing, but it had been planned to appear that way by Randy and Kathy, who had been looking for the right opportunity to coax John and Megan together. The birthday party had worked perfectly. It had been a small affair, three married couples and John and Megan invited to a picnic at

Invitation

Chavez State Park for an afternoon of outdoor games, with some spiked punch for added interest. As hoped, John and Megan had hit it off well, at least as well as could be expected, considering John's protective shield. Over the next few months, Randy and Kathy had kept nudging them, not to the point of being bothersome but enough to keep the two crossing paths – a weeknight meal here, a Saturday evening movie there. After several weeks, the need for nudging melted away; the two were casually dating on their own.

Megan and John fit perfectly together. They liked each other. They had fun together. They had developed mutual respect for each other. Gradually John's shield had thinned and love had begun to take root. Within a year, passion had set in. Once it had ignited, the flame had rapidly become irresistible. By then, they knew each other well. Megan knew the whole story of his first marriage and was understanding of John's self-imposed limits. She had never lived with a man before, but after dating for a year and a half, she'd moved in with John.

Living together, their relationship had deepened. Megan had not pressed for marriage or a family. Regardless, after almost two years living together, neither of them had any desire to consider ever parting. They felt perfect to each other. The just didn't seriously discuss marriage or a family.

There was a problem, John knew, but it wasn't hers. It was his. The disaster with Miranda had been *so* bad. Everything had started falling apart as soon as they got married. It wasn't just that the marriage had begun to disintegrate as soon as it started. He had lost his best friend, her brother. Miranda's mother had gone from friend to foe. John's own family had been devastated at the news of the marriage, as if all their hope and pride in him had been sucked away. Then his life had collapsed with the loss of the baby. He had been able to live with that so long as he could deceive himself into believing it had been a miscarriage, but that lie could only stand for so long. And, the way it had ended, the legal disaster and the five years of alimony, the *god-awful* feelings of worthlessness that had tormented him for years, his powerlessness to move past it ....
No, the problem is not with Megan.

Megan was a beautiful person. She was bright and witty. She was healthy and athletic, a cross-country runner in

40

high school, who still kept fit by running two or three times a week. She was an achiever, organizing and leading groups and activities, always motivated to help or benefit anyone in need.

Megan had changed her career plan – most said lowered it – after her mom had died of brain cancer. That had happened during the middle of Megan's junior year in high school, five months after the cancer diagnosis. Shortly after that, Megan had changed her goal of becoming a doctor to becoming a nurse. She believed the shift was an upgrade. Doctors might make the bucks, make the decisions, shoulder the responsibilities, and get the limelight, but it was the nurses who had the patient contact, the day-to-day personal involvement where comfort, caring, and emotional interaction occurred. Her career as a nurse in the oncology unit at Lovelace Medical Center had its difficult times. Her patients' battles were intense, and many didn't survive. Regardless, Megan always strove to soften and improve the daily lives of her patients and their families. She had made a conscious choice to work in this difficult and sometimes disheartening environment because it brought the opportunity to help patients feel a little bit brighter, a little bit more alive, a little bit more contented, whether they were recovering or dying.

I don't have a clue what she sees in me or why she would want to stick with me. I won't even talk about marriage, and I unravel at the thought of having a family. I should be thanking my lucky stars for her. I can't believe she wasn't snatched up years ago.

So, how do I deal with this baby? She's right. I love kids. I want a family as much as I've ever wanted anything. I've been too scared of screwing it up again. It was my fault. It was Miranda's fault, too, but mostly mine. I created a child I didn't protect. Now I've created another. I didn't plan to, but I did. It's here. It doesn't matter how much guilt I feel about last time. It's too late. I have to be stronger. I owe that to Megan. She deserves way better than I've been. I owe it to our child. I owe it to me. People fail, sometimes miserably, but life goes on. Maybe everybody deserves a second chance. More than that, maybe everybody owes it to the world to set their failures right. Maybe the way to set right a disastrous failure is to learn from it and do it right the next time.

Now, he was sure. *I want Megan more than anything. If I lose her, I'll have lost the best thing that's ever touched me. I want this child as much as she does. She's right. She knows me better than I know myself. I have to cut loose my past. Let it go now, this minute. I will do it right this time. I will protect them both. No harm will come to this baby or Megan as long as I live.*

"Rufus! C'mon, boy, let's go!"

It was mid-afternoon when John and Rufus returned. The house was silent. Megan had been sitting at the table since they'd left, staring out the window at the mountains. She turned her head and looked anxiously at John.

"You were right," he said immediately.

"About which part?"

"All of it. Everything. Mostly about me. About you knowing me better than I know myself. You're the best thing that ever happened to me. All I want is to spend the rest of my life with you. You and our family. I've been so screwed up over the mess I made with Miranda, I wouldn't let myself even think of trying again. But, I'm way beyond that with you, and I didn't even know it. I just hope you'll still have me after I've been such an ass." His eyes locked on hers.

She walked over to him, put her arms around his neck, laid her head on his chest, and melted into him, tears streaming.

"I love you," John said gently. "I'm really sorry I was such an idiot this morning. You didn't do anything wrong. You just broke through and finally made me see what I really needed. If I could change anything, it would only be having you do it sooner." He wrapped his arms around her and held her tightly. "It's been an emotional day. How about spending the rest of it curled up on the couch, watching old movies? I just want to be beside you. Close to you."

She nodded her head against his chest. "That sounds perfect. We can deal with tomorrow tomorrow."

Neither of them could have imagined the nightmare the next month of tomorrows held in store for them.

Chapter 5
Monday, April 7

During the first week of April, John and Megan planned the wedding. They decided on a modest wedding over Memorial Day weekend, shared with immediate family and closest friends. So far, the only people who knew were Randy and Kathy. The official announcement would occur in a week and a half. That was the soonest John and Megan could arrange a trip, and they wanted to tell their families in person. They would fly to Ohio on Thursday night, April 17, for a long weekend with John's family and return to Albuquerque Monday morning. Upon landing, they would drive to the Stanforths' in Los Alamos and spend the rest of the day with them.

John couldn't keep from smiling whenever he thought about telling his family. They were well-acquainted with Megan and unanimously loved her. They would all have favored a wedding two years ago, but none of them had pressed the issue, painfully aware of the anguish John had experienced with Miranda. They would enthusiastically overlook the minor timing problem with the coming family addition and welcome Megan into the family with open arms.

Megan's dad, stepmom, and younger sister, Rally, would also be overjoyed. It had been difficult for Megan to keep the secret from them for the past week, but she wanted to be in their presence with John and see their faces when they heard the news. John looked forward to revealing the news to Megan's family as much as she did. They were both elated about the marriage, the wedding, their child, telling their families, and the promise of a fulfilling life together.

The ceremony would be an intimate one, in the large, tree-canopied backyard at John's parents' home in Circleville on Saturday afternoon, May 24. John would purchase flights for Megan's family, the Jarretts, Megan, and himself, and they would all travel together to Ohio Friday evening. Everyone would spend the holiday weekend at the spacious Resnic residence, which had three spare bedrooms and a pull-out sofa where Rally could sleep. John's brother and sister and their families would spend the weekend with the group.

It was a nontraditional wedding arrangement, but considering the people and personalities, the entire weekend would be a big hit with everyone. Settling on a plan like this before talking to everyone would be presumptuous for most groups, but not for this bunch. Everyone would see it as a great plan. As much as John and Megan were excited about a Gulf of Mexico honeymoon cruise, they looked forward to sharing the weekend with their most cherished loved ones more.

Their short-term plan was to remain in Albuquerque. Megan would continue to work through the pregnancy for as long as she felt like it. After the baby arrived, she would take a year off. Beyond that, their plans were less certain.

The whole country was stirred up about increasing cancer rates and disappearing ozone. John and Megan were more acutely aware of this issue now that they had a child to consider. Before, they had not been concerned enough to take action. Now, they had a vague plan to track the problem and the trends for the next several months while educating themselves about options to minimize risks.

One option would be to relocate to a safer location. The challenges would be to determine where the safest places to live were and then to figure out which of these locations might be less prone to being overrun by people with similar aspirations. For now, they were not close to making any decision to move away from Albuquerque. They liked life there. They loved the house and its setting in Sandia Park. Randy and Kathy were irreplaceable friends. They both had developing careers and no desire to abandon either, and they didn't know what they might do for a livelihood if they moved to some remote spot. Regardless, they had decided that, pending the progression of the environmental problems, relocation was a possibility.

Today, John worked late and arrived home after eight o'clock. They had just finished dinner and loaded the dishwasher. "I'm going to email my folks and let them know we're coming," he said to Megan, turning on his laptop.

There were seven email messages in his inbox. One was from Randy, forwarding a joke; two were mass blurbs from sites from which he sometimes made purchases; one was from his mother, which he would reply to; and three were spam. Two of these three were from China and Brazil, and he immediately deleted them. The third one caught his eye. There was nothing in the email heading that identified the sender or the time it was received. He didn't open the email but saw that the subject line read: "Would you like to visit another planet? If so, hit Reply and Send."

Crap. Here comes a virus. He quickly deleted the email, updated his anti-virus program, and ran a system check. No virus was detected. Then he opened his mother's email.

Hi, John! Hope your weather is making up for ours. It's April, for goodness, sake, and we still have snow on the ground! If this keeps up another week, I'm coming to live with you and Megan. How is that pretty girl, anyway? Don't you think it's about time to bring her around to see us again? Clay and Marsha and the boys were over yesterday afternoon. Ricky signed up to play tee ball, and practice starts in two weeks. He won't part with his bat. It goes to bed with him. It's a good thing it's plastic. He does enough damage with it as it is. I can't imagine what he'd do with a real bat. And what a handful Josh is. You should see your dad play with him. They'll go at it for an hour or two and then your dad will say, "Boy, I think this little rascal is plum tuckered out. I've got him ready for his nap." And that's true, but the first one to fall asleep is Grandpa, in the recliner. We're going to visit Lisa and Charlie this weekend. I can't wait to latch onto Tyler again. She's cute as a button, just started taking her first steps. Dad and I are doing pretty well, all things considered. Oh, well, at least in our heads we're still thirty. Come see us when you can. We miss you. Love, Mom.

John grinned at the thought of his growing nephews and niece. He worried about his dad, who had given them a scare three years ago when he had been diagnosed with skin cancer.

So far it had been controlled; a carcinoma that, although it had recurred, had again been removed. John didn't like it. Supposedly, carcinomas weren't serious, but cancer couldn't be trusted. John wondered briefly if the depleting ozone had been responsible for his dad's cancer. At least for now, the cancer appeared to be gone. He smiled as he pictured his mom reading the reply he was about to write.

> Hi, Mom! Sounds as though my youngest relatives are creating all sorts of mischief. Maybe you're right. Maybe we do need to come back for a visit and check out their capers for ourselves. In fact, I think we'll just do that. Truth is, we already have the flight set up. Megan and I will arrive at the airport in Columbus Thursday night, April 17, at 10:30. If you and Dad will pick us up, we'll spend the weekend with you. Otherwise, I guess we'll just watch TV at the airport for a few days. We're scheduled to fly back Monday morning. We can't wait to see you. Please let everyone know we are coming and set up whatever get-togethers you want. We'd love to have a whole day with you and Dad and Clay and Lisa and their families, if that works out. We both love you all. John

He smiled again as he imagined her wondering whether there might be some special reason for this trip home. Then he got up, poked his head in the living room, and said, "Hey, pregnant lady, you want me to take you to bed?"

Megan smiled. "I was beginning to think you'd never ask. Oh, by the way, it looks as if President Jamison might finally be getting serious about cancer rates and ozone. He scheduled an address for tomorrow night. Maybe that'll get you home at a decent hour."

"I'm not surprised," John replied, "after seeing how violent some of the demonstrations are getting. I'd hope that'd get *somebody's* attention. Yeah, I'll be home in time to watch. If we can get some straight talk about what's really happening and what can be done, maybe it'll help us figure out a plan."

*   *   *

It was almost midnight before Brian Betz was satisfied his trip plan was set. He would drive to Andrews Air Force Base late Wednesday night and sleep on his jet during the flight to Kirtland in New Mexico. The first meeting was scheduled for 7:00 in the morning at Kirtland with the two Air Force generals who would administer secret contracts with two private research firms.

Betz didn't often attend meetings with private companies executing portions of his plans. In this case, their roles were critical enough for him to do so. He would not participate actively in the discussions. His attendance would have two purposes. First, he would make sure the generals carried out their roles to the letter, that they conveyed the instructions *exactly* as directed and that their demeanor communicated the consequences of failure to deliver. Second, and more importantly, by being present, Betz would punctuate the requirement for complete and timely accomplishment of objectives. Without saying a word, he would put the fear of God into the corporate officers running these two companies: the firm in Albuquerque in the morning, and the one in Los Angeles in the afternoon.

Betz didn't yet know how the separate missions he was currently executing were linked, and he might never know. Regardless, he had no doubt both assignments fit into a larger scheme and his part had been initiated in January with the interrogation of Patrick Herner.

The plan for the extraordinary part entrusted to him, establishing control over Jamison, was coming together. Betz had done his research meticulously. He had identified the organizations and individuals he needed and put them in play. He had laid out the sequence of actions to be taken to make Jamison certain he had only one choice. All the technical equipment required was on hand. The date was set: April 14. Physical access to the necessary locations had been arranged – no small task. Everything was ready. After the trip to the west coast, Betz's entire focus for the next week would be on ensuring everything proceeded as planned with Jamison and reacting instantly to any hiccup, no matter how trivial.

Invitation

The first act in the Jamison plan, orchestrated by the organization rather than directly by Betz, would occur tomorrow evening. Immediately prior to Jamison's address, the network news would air a segment asserting the emergence of an absurd, unbelievable worldwide pandemic. The allegation would seem preposterous, but Betz knew there was at least some measure of truth to it.

Beginning tomorrow morning, the network would threaten to air a more forceful piece. Then, throughout the day, the network would play along with Jamison's people to negotiate down the segment's punch. The more benign news clip that would air would be exactly what the organization intended. It was already prepared. Jamison would erroneously think he had won a small victory in forcing the network to trim back the content. The impact of this exercise on Jamison would be to set him off-balance, a position foreign to him. *That* was the whole purpose of the play. That was step one.

Chapter 6
Tuesday, April 8

John and Megan finished dinner and watched the news, waiting on the President's address. Most of the newscast was devoted to skin cancer issues, the extent of public unrest, and speculation on the content of the address. The last piece before switching to the oval office featured young, blonde, shapely correspondent Tricia West, with a story about babies, or more aptly, the lack thereof. The scene was from Miami, Florida, and Tricia, wearing a light pink sleeveless blouse, stood outdoors in the shade of a grove of palm trees, cradling a baby in her arms.

"Here's a story from our trend-monitoring specialists that should motivate us all to action." Tricia smiled. "It seems the nation is experiencing a decline in pregnancies. Expectant mothers usually first visit their doctors within seven to nine weeks of conception. Recent trends indicate a noticeable drop in initial medical visits from expectant mothers, beginning around mid-March. Since the first of April, it appears initial visits have almost stopped. To date, no government agencies have confirmed this development. The apparent trend is not confined to the United States, but seems to be occurring worldwide. Now, baby Abigail here ...." She tilted the baby toward the camera. "She wants some little playmates. What do you think, America? *Surely* we can do better." She winked at the camera and smiled at the newborn. "I'm Tricia West, reporting from Miami and encouraging *everyone* to boost your efforts." She smiled again as the screen faded out.

"That's weird," Megan said. "When I went for my exam, they told me the same thing at Dr. Griswold's office. They said I was their first new pregnancy in two weeks. What the heck?"

"Really? Well, they can't say we haven't done our part." John patted her abdomen. "Sounds pretty farfetched to me. Surely, that wasn't based on any scientific evidence. They didn't quote any statistics or official sources, and it seemed like they were poking fun. I'll bet the Administration thought that was just great, though, right before the big speech: a little present from the network to the President to screw up the tone."

Then, the network tuned to the presidential speech. After several minutes of conjecture by various political analysts, President Daniel Jamison appeared on the screen from the Oval Office. "Good evening," he began.

*   *   *

Jamison was tall and fit, with a full head of well-groomed black hair graying at the temples, distinguished at fifty-three. The demands of his job had taken no noticeable toll since his election two-and-a-half years ago. He always appeared self-assured and confident. However, tonight, John thought, there was a hint of uncharacteristic uncertainty or anxiety in his manner. It was so slight, it was barely noticeable.

Dan Jamison was a lifelong politician, an expert at projecting whatever aura he wished at any given time. Now that it was time to start building momentum for reelection, portraying the desired image was critical. His ability to exude the required persona of the moment, regardless of whatever chaos might currently be center stage in his personal or political life, had been his strongest and most consistent quality. It was this signature characteristic that had vitalized his political career, eventually landing him the Presidency.

Today had been distressing. Although he thought he was controlling his demeanor effectively, he was having more difficulty pulling it off than he had ever had before. The cancer and ozone issues were truly challenging. He had a package to sell that he knew had some holes in it. He wouldn't talk about those holes tonight, but he would lay groundwork for making them seem inconsequential in the days ahead. Presenting any situation in whatever way he wanted it to be understood and accepted was typically a small order for him. Tonight, the growing public unrest made it more important, although not necessarily more difficult, to make the people see the issues as he wanted them to be seen.

Jamison knew there was an opposition group to his plan, and it wasn't a group to take lightly. Saturday, he had been informed of this group's snowballing strength and its intentions for discrediting the plan he was about to advocate. The opposition was not the other political party, but a coalition of consumer advocates with some prominent scientists as their spokespersons. This group, he had been informed, had obtained the details of the plan he intended to unveil Tuesday evening. Listening to his staff play devil's advocate with the shortcomings of the plan on Saturday, he had realized it would require a lot of smoke in the days after the address to undermine the criticism. Since Saturday, he had been battling a stubborn nervousness that had wormed its way into his psyche.

A 2:00 to 3:00 time slot had been set aside Monday to meet with the Secretary of the Department of Health and Human Services, Peter Richardson; the Director of the Center for Disease Control, Helen Kursch; and Jamison's chief of staff, Jim Hollingsworth. One purpose of the meeting was to polish up on the fine points of the science behind the plan he would propose. However, the main reason for the meeting was to create an opportunity for this core group to solidify Jamison's feelings of confidence in the initiatives he would champion Tuesday night. Over the years, such meetings had become an essential part of his routine in preparing for public appearances. Before taking a public stance on anything, Jamison needed to feel total conviction that whatever he was about to advocate was the best policy attainable. This small group exercise had been devised years ago to create a controlled venue conducive to Jamison convincing himself he was totally right.

Unfortunately, in the flurry of preparing for dealing with the opposition group's claims and rewriting parts of the address to make the future discrediting of those claims easier, Monday became jammed. The booster meeting, as Jamison had come to think of these sessions, had been rescheduled for 2:00 Tuesday. He hated scheduling a meeting like that so close to speech time and, late Monday afternoon, considered canceling it altogether, further heightening his uneasiness. Then, early Monday evening, his staff got wind of a planned network news segment on pregnancies. Jim Hollingsworth had informed Jamison one of the networks was planning to air a potentially disconcerting piece right before the address. The segment would make an absurd claim that there have been no new pregnancies in the world since January. Jamison's immediate reaction to Hollingsworth's ridiculous revelation was to direct his staff to squelch the story. As his comfort level deteriorated, he decided he could not afford to cancel the booster meeting.

By noon Tuesday, the effort to squelch the news segment had only partially succeeded. Hollingsworth had reported to Jamison that all the network's sources on the story were recanting; the Administration had been able to dissuade supporting statements from all respectable experts and had threatened dire consequences if the network reported anything as fact that later turned out to be false. By late morning, Hollingsworth himself had telephoned the network CEO to make certain he personally understood how displeased the Administration would be with the network if it continued to persist in airing this segment anytime Tuesday. That phone conversation ended with both parties frustrated and uncertain about what would be aired, if anything. Shortly after noon, Hollingsworth had learned and informed Jamison the clip would be presented in the vein of an amusing anecdote with no identified sources, but it was still scheduled to air immediately before the presidential address.

Jamison had long ago mastered control of his emotions. Fury *never* emanated from him, but Hollingsworth and a handful of others who knew how much effort had gone into squelching the story could see the irritation in the lines of his face. They knew how displeased he was.

The 2:00 meeting with Richardson, Kursch, and Hollingsworth didn't begin until 3:30 and its one-hour allotment was reduced to thirty minutes. It was a disaster. In Jamison's mind, the whole day had been a disaster. He absolutely *hated* presenting a national address, especially one as important as this one, after a day like today. Regardless, he knew it came with the territory. He had been in tough spots before and would be in more. When crunch time came, he had always been able to make ice cream out of shit when he had to.

Secretary of HHS Peter Richardson was a balding, large man, six-foot-three and two-hundred-sixty pounds. He was a shrewd career politician who knew how to maneuver through constituents and colleagues. Politically, Richardson was always more concerned with appearances than realities. He did care about increasing cancer rates and the depleting ozone, but he cared more about public perception of the Administration's approach to the issues. In private meetings, especially when all was not quite as he wished, he had a tendency to be too impulsive and loud. Jamison had selected him as Secretary of HHS to fulfill an unwritten agreement between the two men, in return for Richardson's efforts and ability to deliver voter support in several Northeastern states during the presidential primaries.

Helen Kursch, while also a political appointee, was a doctor and scientist first and a politician second. She had been kept on as Director of CDC from the previous Administration because she had proven herself impeccable in her performance and leadership of the organization. At fifty-seven, she was lithe and attractive, easily mistaken to be fifteen years younger. She exhibited a caring personality and had a reputation for honesty and genuineness. Kursch was a critical thinker, reached her conclusions carefully and with an open mind, and presented her opinions clearly and concisely, without coatings. Unfortunately for Jamison, the opinions she had developed on correcting the ozone problems were not much different than those being outlined by the opposition group. Facts were facts.

Jim Hollingsworth was the President's right hand man. The same age, they had been close friends since their early college days. Hollingsworth, at five-foot-ten, was two inches shorter than the President, and skinny, with thinning gray hair. The strain of the Office of the President was revealed much more in Hollingsworth's features than in the President's. Jim had played critical roles in every campaign Jamison had ever run and had served at the highest staff level of every political office Jamison had ever held. The two men knew each other's thoughts in advance. They liked, respected, and protected each other.

Although the battle to reduce cancer incidence and overcome ozone depletion was scheduled to be the topic of the booster meeting, it wasn't even mentioned until the last five minutes. Then, it was a rush conversation that left everyone feeling less settled instead of more. When the meeting ended,

Invitation

every one of the participants wished he or she had not been there.

The President inadvertently started the meeting on the wrong track. Stinging over the network's refusal to acquiesce, Jamison glanced at Hollingsworth and said, "I need to get past that ridiculous network piece on pregnancies. It's distracting." He said it softly and directly to Hollingsworth, but loudly enough that Richardson and Kursch heard.

Noticing in Kursch's eyes that she was taken aback by the comment, he explained calmly: "Helen, we became aware yesterday that one of the networks is planning to air a segment stating that human conception has dropped off dramatically in the past two months. I assume CDC is unaware of any such trend?"

"What a *crock!*" Richardson belted, although the question had not been directed to him. "I heard through the vine some reporters were trying to get anybody they could scrape up to offer some kind of comment they could hang their hat on for airing that piece of crap. They try to get some sort of confirmation from your people, Helen? How do they even dream up this stuff? They can't *possibly* have a shred of evidence to support such a stupid claim. Right, Helen?"

"Unfortunately," Kursch replied uncomfortably, "they *do* have some evidence."

"What do you mean?" Hollingsworth asked quietly, looking Kursch squarely in the eye.

"*What?*" Richardson exclaimed.

Kursch continued: "CDC noticed a slowdown in new pregnancies in the United States the first week of March. It was more pronounced by the week of March 17. During the week of March 24, we determined a drastic decrease in pregnancies was, in fact, occurring in the United States. That week, we expanded our research to worldwide but avoided contacting other national health agencies or the World Health Organization, due to potential ramifications of communicating such findings. On March 28, we issued a classified, high-priority memo to the Administration reporting on the issue. I'm surprised no one in this meeting appears to be aware of it. Late last week, we concluded the problem is worldwide. There've been few, if any, conceptions in developed countries since February 1, and

54

possibly not since January 20. The same's probably true for developing nations, just more difficult to confirm.

"We sent another classified memo to the Administration yesterday morning. It was marked, 'Urgent.' Pete, I've left *at least* a half-dozen messages for you since last Thursday. I've been trying to bring this to the Administration's attention, but I apparently didn't try hard enough. Frankly, although it's unprecedented, it appears to be happening."

Richardson bellowed, "*What a boatload of bullshit!*"

"No, sir, it isn't," Kursch replied. "It's difficult to believe, almost inconceivable, really, but *is* occurring."

Hollingsworth looked dumbfounded. Jamison was incredulous but didn't show it. He looked persistently at Helen Kursch. Finally he spoke: "What's CDC doing?"

"The extent of any definite plan was to speak to you, Mr. President."

The President paused, wheels turning. "All right, then, what action do you recommend?"

"Open up communications immediately with other countries' health agencies and the World Health Organization. Assign ample research resources to determine the cause. Work diligently at creating artificial conception. Compile all the information the world can generate and then create a definitive plan of action. Implement this recommendation immediately. Today."

"Helen," Hollingsworth asked, "are you saying you've known about this for three weeks and haven't experimented with artificial conception?"

"No, sir. We've been pursuing that in every way we could devise for the past two weeks. It's all detailed in the two memos we submitted. Regrettably, we've been unable to get any human sperm to fertilize a human egg."

No one spoke for a moment, each of them considering the implausibility of the situation Kursch had described. Finally, Hollingsworth asked, "What about animals?" "Other mammals?"

"We've found no reproduction anomalies with any species except humans."

"That's completely absurd," blurted Richardson.

"That's an understatement, sir," Kursch replied.

"Christ," said the President, feeling tugged further and further askew. "I have a public address to deliver in four hours." He looked at Kursch. "Helen, were you aware one of the networks was planning to air a story on this?"

She looked chagrined. "Not until about two hours ago, sir. That was when I first received notice reporters were questioning our staff about it. I don't believe any information has been offered by anyone at CDC. We limited participation in our investigation to the least possible number of people to minimize the potential for leaks."

"Well," Jamison said, trying to rebalance, "at least tonight is a set speech and not a news conference. I'll get through it. If we have to, we'll schedule another address in a week to deal with the pregnancy issue. Who knows, it might resolve itself by then. Jim, have you seen the spot that will air?"

"Just before this meeting, I previewed the clip they say they'll show. If they leave it that way, it's pretty innocuous. It's just Tricia West holding a baby, winking about an apparent downturn in new pregnancies and encouraging people to do what they can about it. They don't make any reference to evidence or sources. I don't think it'll make much of an impression, the way it's being presented. Not that their decision to run it doesn't piss me off. We'll definitely make that network understand *exactly* how disappointed we are in it. For tonight, I think we need to ignore it. Considering all the support that'll be trumpeted for your plan after the address, their little piece of crap clip isn't going to be the topic of much conversation in America tonight."

"Damn," Richardson said quietly, his robust manner having dissolved. Kursch and Hollingsworth glared at him.

The President was deep in thought. After a minute, he said calmly, "We need to move on to the topic of my speech. We're about out of time." He eyed each of them, pulling their attention back to the topic of tonight's address. "Let's run through a summary.

"This Administration has concluded the 1987 Montreal Protocol is not nearly aggressive enough. The world's been working toward compliance with it for decades and has made far too little progress. We all now face a crisis this Administration deems immediate, a crisis demanding emergency action. Every major government has committed to adopt measures similar to the United States' plan I'll describe tonight. Tomorrow morning at ten o'clock, I'll sign a six-part executive order implementing the following emergency actions.

"Part one will halt the production of all ozone-depleting substances in the United States. As of June first of this year, any entity in the United States manufacturing any products listed as ozone-depleting by the Environmental Protection Agency will have its assets seized by the government, and the business operation of the entity will be terminated."

Everyone in the room knew that before Saturday, the June first date had been June first of next year. For all of the other cooperating nations of the world, it still was. Also, the drastic terminology of seizing assets and terminating businesses had been added after Saturday. Before that, the penalty would have been fines enforceable only by court action. These two changes had been incorporated to undercut the opposition group's claims that the action was too late and had no teeth. There remained a question relative to the constitutionality of the executive order, but that would be dealt with later.

Jamison went on: "Part two requires all business organizations utilizing ozone-depleting substances to make any and all modifications to their plants and processes necessary in order to stop their use of those substances by the end of this year. All such substances on hand will have to be reclaimed by an EPA-licensed recovery contractor. These contractors will be required to neutralize the substances. Any business still utilizing ozone-depleting substances will be subject to fines of one percent of their year-end net worth per calendar day beginning on January first of next year."

Before Saturday, the deadline had been one year later, the fines had been significantly smaller, and court action would have been required for enforcement. There were holes in this item. It would require a monstrous effort by the EPA to train and license enough contractors to accomplish the reclamation. There was also the question of how the reclaimed material would be neutralized. The plan called for incineration, but scientists didn't agree on the effectiveness of that approach.

Jamison continued. "Part three requires all homeowners and residential rental property-owners to have any ozone-depleting substances on their properties reclaimed by the end of next year or be subject to a fine of one hundred dollars per day and imprisonment until the substances are reclaimed. For rental properties owned by corporations, the prison terms will apply to each of the company's officers."

Before Saturday, this requirement had also allowed for an additional year before implementation of fines, and there had been no penalty of imprisonment.

"Part four requires that, beginning January first of next year, the United States will prohibit any American company from exporting to, or importing from, any country that has not implemented actions that mirror the United States' initiatives. Additionally, the United States Government will not subsidize any government or its citizenry if that government has not adopted like policies."

Before Saturday, the implementation date had been a year later and there had been no clause prohibiting subsidies to underdeveloped countries. This provision still had no answer to the opposition's argument that the enforcement procedures for the import and export clause were vague. That was because enforcement of this provision would be so multi-faceted and difficult that no viable procedures had yet been agreed upon.

"Fifth, beginning in September of this year, the United States Government will distribute one billion dollars per month to help offset health care costs incurred by individuals suffering from UV radiation-related cancers and eye disease."

Before Saturday, the amount had been half a billion. The only answer the Administration would be able to give to the question of where this money would come from would be to state that Congress has committed to this plan and committed to finding the funds.

"And sixth, the United States Government will contribute an additional billion dollars per month, beginning this month, toward supplementing the Earth's natural means of ozone generation and toward research into better and faster ways to restore upper atmospheric ozone levels to pre-1970 levels."

Before Saturday, this amount had also been a half-billion, and this part of the plan had been the first point instead of the sixth. The problem with it was the lack of agreement within the scientific community on exactly how supplementing the Earth's natural means of generating ozone could be accomplished. The plan called for injecting specially formulated aerosols directly into the stratosphere. The opposition's claim would be that this was an unproven technique and might do more harm than good. The late adjustments to the plan included emphasizing immediate research rather than immediate implementation of action. The Administration viewed this change as the biggest hit to the original plan, since it shifted the bent of the message from decisive action to admission of uncertainty.

Sunday and Monday had been frantic for the Administration, due to the stupendous effort required to get Congress and a plethora of influential American corporations to stand fast behind the changes being made to the plan. However, that had been essential preparation in order to thwart the opposition, which focused on arguments that the plan was too slow, too soft politically, and too presumptuous scientifically, contending that those faults would douse any hope of achieving the drastic turnaround necessary for long-term survival of civilization as it currently exists.

The President finished the summary of the address: "The cost of implementation of this plan to the American Government, American businesses, and individual American citizens will be staggering. Regardless, we have reached a point where we, the American people and the people of the world, must realize there is no longer a choice. The political leaders of this country and of the world have been aware of this problem for fifty years and have accomplished woefully little to overcome it. As evidenced by the increasing incidence of skin cancers and eye disease, the situation continues to worsen. This executive order is bold to the point of being audacious. Many will say these actions are not affordable. Some will say they are not enforceable. But this Administration, this Government, makes the commitment today that we *shall* do this, we *shall* enforce it at home, and we *shall* ostracize any nation that does not follow suit.

"Considering the intense and frank international discussions held over the past month, the forceful language of the plan toward foreign countries is less harsh than it sounds. Over ninety percent of the nations of the world have already agreed to implement their own virtually identical plans. This is not a unilateral action forced on the world by the United States, but a deliberate, well-informed, and cooperative world-wide effort."

Jamison wrapped himself up in delivering this message to the small group gathered in the Oval Office as he knew he needed to. His three listeners were already thoroughly familiar with the message but knew that delivering the overview would help him drive it home to his audience tonight.

"I know we're out of time," Jamison said, "but I'd like to know from each of you personally and honestly how you feel about this plan. Pete, are you completely on board?"

"All things considered, I don't see how we could possibly do any better, Mr. President," Richardson replied. "We have unprecedented bipartisan support. The plan is extremely tough and will cause some alarm at first. But, with both parties, the business sector, and the international community all proclaiming overwhelming support on TV right after your speech, you'll prevail quickly."

Hollingsworth looked at Kursch. "Helen, what do you think?"

She spoke deliberately, choosing her words carefully. "We'll likely convince the general population in the short term. But, in my opinion as a doctor and scientist, I believe the opposition's points will have to be dealt with in the long run. A case can be made that we might have already passed the point of no return, and we'll need to prepare to respond to that. The biggest unknown relates to our technical capability to supplement the natural ozone replenishment processes. We need to make great strides fast on the research."

Hollingsworth looked displeased at the missing component of unwavering support for the President's plan. "So, what are you suggesting, Helen? President Jamison goes on live TV in four hours."

"I understand the predicament. Our proposed program and speech can't be revised by eight o'clock this evening. We all know technology development and testing take time. Unfortunately, time is a commodity we may not have. If I had to make a recommendation, it would be to soften our stance on aerosol injection. Leave more room for further study and development of alternatives, and commit to unrelenting resolve to finalize that portion of our plan within 30 days."

Hollingsworth replied, "You're suggesting we go on national TV and say we aren't sure we know a solution, but we're working diligently on it? That doesn't sound strong and confident. Strength and confidence are *exactly* what we have to project to get the full support of our citizenry and the world as we move into the years necessary to fix this problem. Now is *not* the time to say that we aren't sure what to do."

The President listened intently but didn't speak. He was thinking through the task at hand. In a matter of hours, he had to address a simmering citizenry and project strength and confidence, while proposing a plan he was not sure would solve the problem. And, he had to do that right after the airing of the disconcerting news clip claiming the wild notion that human conception was no longer occurring on planet Earth. His typically boundless energy and political savvy were stretched to their limits. Jamison felt drained. The events of the last four days were exacting their toll. He had slept little during that time. The next few hours would be the most politically challenging hours he had ever faced.

*   *   *

John and Megan listened attentively to the President's six-point plan. They now had a family to think about and protection from cancer-causing radiation was of concern. The Administration's plan seemed well-researched and organized. The President claimed unprecedented, multifaceted support. He sounded confident and committed to this plan, which would carry with it untold cost. As the address concluded, John felt satisfied the United States Government was finally aggressively pursuing a solution to the problem. The proposed plan seemed workable. He thought the President looked tired, which he had never perceived before in this president.

"That was interesting," he said.

"Did you think he seemed a little off tonight?" she asked.

"I thought he looked tired. But then, that job would make anyone look haggard. I think I'll grab a beer. You want anything?"

"Sure, bring me a soda."

When he returned with the beverages, the commercials were over, and the political responses to the speech were beginning to air. After watching for half an hour, Megan said, "Jamison's claim of broad-based support was an understatement. Have you ever in your life seen both parties, Wall Street, and Labor all in complete agreement on anything?"

"Nope. Never. It almost seems rehearsed. Even the other governments. All of them. Obviously, this speech wasn't the work of just this Administration all by itself. All the key players must've been knee-deep for weeks in working out this plan. Maybe the scope of the problem's really gotten everyone's attention. I hope so. It's a big deal."

"It still seems uncanny," Megan said. "There seems to be no opposition at all."

"There probably is. Give it a day or two and see if the other side surfaces. Surely not everybody agrees on all the details. I'm bushed. I need to check email. Then I'm turning in."

Megan continued to watch world leaders and political analysts discuss the address and offer total support and praise for the President's plan. John booted up his laptop. When his email came up, he stared at the first one for a few seconds before he said anything. "Hey, baby, come look at this."

Megan walked over to the table and looked over John's shoulder at the screen.

"I got an email like this first one last night. There was no sender listed and no message in the email, just a subject line."

She read the subject line: "John, do you want to visit another planet?"

"The one last night didn't mention my name, and it said to click reply and send if I was interested.

"Did you?" She grinned at him.

"No. I deleted it and updated my anti-virus program and ran it, which is exactly what I'm gonna do again."

"Did you find any viruses?"

"Nope," John replied as he initiated the process again. "You ever get any emails without a sender identified?"

"I don't think so."

"Me neither."

"Well," Megan said, "it'll take a while to get through your virus check and emails. I'm tired. Think I'll sack out."

"Okay, hon. I'll be in as soon as I'm done."

Megan headed for bed while John scanned for viruses. None. Then he finished checking emails. The only one he responded to was from his mom. She was thrilled about the upcoming trip. He wrote briefly about the President's speech, the trip itinerary, and how much he and Megan were looking forward to visiting.

A few minutes later, he was in bed lying next to his sleeping wife-to-be. As he drifted off, he wondered who in the world would be sending out emails about visiting other planets and why. *Is anybody else getting invitations to visit other planets? What possible purpose could anyone have in sending emails like that?*

Invitation

Chapter 7
Wednesday, April 9

Randy's task for the day was to wrap up his
investigation and report on the unexplained oscillation
frequencies the Baldy Mountain system had depicted on March
27. John had overseen inspection of the system wiring and
connections and had run the standard diagnostics on the installed
system. No problems had been found with the physical
installation. Over the past week, Randy had run all his software-
checking routines on the system. He had found nothing that
could explain a false system interpretation of observed data. The
system software and programming looked good.

The frequency data reported on the Baldy system had an
unusual twist. Software glitches typically generated data
showing that events had occurred that were not possible. In this
case, that could not be asserted. The indicated pattern of
oscillations was not technically impossible. Even though
nothing could be identified that was man-made, or was on record
as a natural phenomenon, that could account for these particular
oscillations, Randy could not certify that the occurrence of the
reported oscillations was not possible. The project engineering
team had reached the same conclusion in its findings. John's
preliminary report suggested equal likelihood that either the
system had erroneously reported an event that had never
occurred, or the system had accurately reported an occurrence
with no known precedent or cause.

Randy's charge was not to investigate the potential of
the event having actually occurred. His task was to assault the
system from every angle. If there was a system fault, he was to
discover it. He had read all the reports, run all applicable
diagnostic routines, examined the installation, and monitored
system operation for several days. Today was a free-thinking
day. He ran several simulations to try to recreate a similar data

report that would point to a software or system glitch. At the end of the long day, he concluded there was a sixty-percent probability the reported data had been unexplainably erroneous and a forty-percent probability the oscillation patterns had actually occurred.

*   *   *

Shortly before 7:00 a.m., Megan entered the oncology unit at Lovelace Medical Center, where she was day shift charge nurse. The morning bustle was beginning. Three night-shift nurses were charting; Doctor Warrick was reviewing records; and Dr. Jansen was walking briskly toward the nurses' station, followed by Jennifer Wilson, Megan's assistant charge nurse. Inexplicably, Megan felt uneasy.

"Hi, Darlene." Megan smiled at the middle-aged, moderately heavy, kind-eyed night shift charge nurse. "How was the night?"

"Quiet," Darlene replied with a strained smile. "Rose isn't good. It'll be a tough day."

Megan winced. She knew the cardinal rule of nursing was to avoid attachment to patients. She was professional, but it was impossible for her to remain completely detached. "I guess we knew her time was getting short. Nobody expected her to go home last time."

Rose was a gentle seventy-four-year old black lady who had been diagnosed with melanoma six years ago. It was a testament to her fortitude and positive outlook that she had survived this long. Since her first stint in the Lovelace Oncology Department, she had returned for four operations. This time, cancer had invaded her pancreas, and there was no hope. Megan had been working at Lovelace for just two weeks when Rose had first been diagnosed. Rose, five-foot-three and frail, had impressed Megan as a kind, secure, good-natured lady with the quiet inner strength of an oak tree. Megan, who considered it her mission to brighten the day of every patient, found that to be effortless with Rose, who, with her ready smile and easy conversation, was often the one brightening Megan's day. Megan knew Rose didn't fear death and was ready, but Megan wasn't ready to lose Rose.

"I'm going to go see her for a minute," Megan said to Darlene.

"I know," Darlene replied. "Take your time. I've got paperwork to finish."

Rose lay quietly on her back, breathing shallowly. Megan went to her, lifted her hand, and held it lightly. Rose half-opened her eyes, squeezed the hand weakly, and whispered, "Hi, sweetheart."

"Good morning, Rose. How are you today?"

Rose managed a feeble smile and breathed, "It's a good day."

"You don't need to talk, Rose. Rest. I'm here for you."

"I'm glad." She closed her eyes. Rose's morphine drip helped with pain and rest. Megan held her hand five more minutes then laid it down on the bed, wiped a tear, and walked back to the station.

"You're probably right, Darlene. A bad day. Has Ruthann been called?" Ruthann was Rose's daughter.

"I called her half an hour ago. She'll be here any minute."

At 10:15 ICU called to say thirty-eight-year old Jack Verner was being transferred to Oncology. Jack, a construction worker, had been suffering intestinal issues for three months but had resisted seeking medical attention. Total blockage had eventually occurred, forcing him to give up and allow his wife to drive him to the emergency room. Exploratory surgery had uncovered stage-four colon cancer, a ruptured large intestine, and cancer spread throughout his abdominal organs. After a week in ICU, Jack had fooled the doctors by remaining alive. The prognosis had been that he would not survive the week. His wife, Bonnie, and three kids, ages eight to sixteen, arrived on the floor before he did. Megan's day was getting tougher.

She greeted the family at the nurses' station. "Hello, I'm Megan Stanforth. Are you the Verner family?"

Mrs. Verner nodded. "They said my husband would be transferred here."

"Yes, he'll be here shortly. Please, feel free to ask us for anything you need, Mrs. Verner. We'll do whatever we can to help you and your family be more comfortable. Do you know where all the amenities are? The cafeteria, snack shop, restrooms?"

"Yes, thanks. Call me Bonnie. We'll try not to be a bother. Are there restricted visiting hours on this floor?"

"Don't worry about visiting hours. You and your family can come and go as you like. So, who are the other members of this handsome gang?"

"This is Jim, our oldest, Jeremy, our second, and our daughter, Jody".

"Well, I'm very pleased to meet you all." Megan smiled. "Your dad will be in room ten-twenty-six. You can wait in his room or in the waiting room around the corner."

"Thank you," Bonnie said. "We'll go to the waiting room till Jack gets settled in."

Megan glanced at Rose's door at 11:25 and saw Ruthann drift out. Megan had seen Dr. Warrick walk into the room a few minutes earlier, and, seeing Ruthann's expression, knew Rose was gone. She walked to Ruthann and wrapped an arm around her. "We'll take care of your mother. Is there anything I can do for you?"

"No, I'll be okay. Megan, you've been a godsend. Mother loved you. She couldn't have received better care anywhere."

"She loved you, Ruthann. She talked about you all the time. Rose was very lucky to have you for a daughter. I'll miss her. She was the first serious cancer patient diagnosed here when I started and she's always been special to me." Megan brushed back a tear.

"I know. I expect you need comfort as much as I do. I want to thank you for everything you've done."

"You're welcome, honey. I go on break in a couple minutes. Can I go downstairs with you for a cup of coffee or anything? The staff will be with your mother for a little while. Then we can come back for her personal things." Megan glanced toward the nurses' station at Jennifer who nodded understandingly.

"I'd like that," Ruthann said.

Megan took a call from admitting at 1:25. Ten-year-old Terry Griffiths was on his way up. Usually, kids went to Children's Hospital, but Terry's case was special. And heartbreaking. His mother had fought cancer for three years, spending more time in the hospital than at home. It had been almost two years since she had succumbed. During her prolonged stays at the hospital, the family had developed a special affection for the oncology staff.

Six months ago, Terry had been diagnosed with melanoma, and his father, Cliff, had insisted Terry be treated at Lovelace. When Terry was discharged after skin-grafting operations, the doctors had been confident he was cured. Megan had fervently hoped she would never see him here again. Now, he was on his way up. After hanging up the phone, Megan took a deep breath to steel herself and looked at Jennifer. "They just admitted Terry Griffiths. *Bad* day."

"What a rotten deal," Jennifer responded somberly.

A few minutes later, an orderly wheeled Terry off the elevator, his dad by his side. Megan was at hand to greet them. "Hi, Terry." She smiled, leaning over to hug him. His eyes were moist as he put his arms around Megan's neck. He couldn't speak for a moment. Megan straightened up and looked at Cliff. "We all hoped we wouldn't see you two back here. I'm sorry."

"Well, we're back," Cliff said, trying to smile at her. "If a person has to be sick, this is the best place to be."

"Follow me, and we'll get you set up. You guys know the routine. We're here to try to make your stay as comfortable as possible. Just let us know how we can help." Megan could tell how hard Cliff was trying to convey an impression that this was just a minor bump in the road, but she also saw the stress in his eyes and knew it was bad. *He's just a ten-year-old kid, for Christ's sake. Why?*

Megan got through the shift change routine and was in her car at 3:45. She sat there for ten minutes and wept. She had become a nurse to help hurting people feel a little better. *But God, sometimes it's hard. If every day was like was like this, I couldn't do it.* She drove home, longing to be wrapped in John's arms.

*   *   *

Kathy was at her desk in the The Crowley Group's executive offices when the president of the company, Jerome Schrader, buzzed and asked her to step into his office. She opened the door and walked in to find senior project manager, Bill Johnson, seated across the desk from Jerome.

"Good morning, Kathy." Jerome smiled. "Please, close the door and have a seat."

"Mornin', guys." She smiled back and closed the door.

Jerome was a savvy but personable businessman. In his mid-fifties, he was tall, trim, and handsome, with gray-peppered dark-brown hair. Schrader had always been involved in politics behind the scenes, not seeking office but generously supporting those of his persuasion who did. The Crowley Group had been founded as a confidential research and information-gathering operation in 1952 by three retiring Air Force officers, all about forty at the time. Colonel Travis Crowley was the wealthy one, having inherited the fortune his father had made in aircraft parts manufacturing during World War II. Crowley had outlasted the other two, who had retired from the business at reasonable ages. In 1983, he had hired Jerome Schrader fresh out of college.

The Schrader family had long tentacles. At the time he was hired, Jerome had an uncle on his father's side who was a U.S. congressman and one on his mother's side who was a New Mexico senator. His father was the chief executive officer of a software development company specializing in simulation programs for military applications. Jerome had brothers and cousins who were career military officers in the Army, Air Force, Navy, and Marines.

Schrader had proved to be an impact player from day one. He had been hired to act as liaison between the company and its main client, the United States Government. His family name, his contacts, his captivating charisma, and his business savvy quickly resulted in an enviable increase in government contracts. He was soon Travis Crowley's top protégé. Crowley had stayed on long enough to place Jerome, at the age of 31, into the office of company president.

From Kathy's perspective, Jerome was an exceptional corporate leader. He knew and used all the ropes. The business was very profitable. Although Kathy had little involvement with corporate finances, she knew the dollar volume that poured in from government contracts was proportional to a significant percentage of dollars flowing back out, in various forms, to politicians. The flow was particularly heavy to those who were influential in deciding how Government contracts were doled out to companies involved in classified operations.

Since its inception, The Crowley Group's top client had been the United States Air Force. From the day Kathy had begun working for the firm there had been meetings every week with top officials from Kirtland and Holloman Air Force Bases and White Sands Missile Range. For years, Bill Johnson had been in charge of all of the most highly classified projects.

Johnson had none of Schrader's personal charm. He was five years older than Jerome, short and stocky with a thin shock of white hair and dark-rimmed glasses. His conversation was limited to communicating project information and instructions with those who needed to know. He wasn't sour or unfriendly, just professional, and careful to a level that exceeded common experience.

"Kathy," Jerome said, "you've probably noticed some unusual efforts at privacy around the office over the past couple of months." She gave her head a small nod as he looked her in the eye. "The Air Force has involved us in some highly classified investigations and has insisted on higher secrecy precautions than normal. Brian Betz is coming in this morning with two generals for a 10:00 meeting. We don't know if they'll bring anyone to create a meeting record, but we need to be prepared to do it if they don't. The issues to be discussed might be sensitive, but your security clearance is high enough that there shouldn't be any concern." He was watching her, hesitating.

She looked him back squarely in the eyes and said, "Okay."

"Needless to say, nothing of the conversation can leave the office. No talk with *anyone*, even within the company, except for Bill and me. And only then in secure rooms behind closed doors."

Kathy was not comfortable. This was obviously not a typical Crowley commission. Guilt gnawed at her from having talked too much last Friday night. Also, the thought of being in the same room with Betz made her shudder. She replied calmly, "You know I'll keep a lid on it."

"That's why we called you. This meeting won't be like any you've been in before. Some of the discussion might seem astonishing. If it does, keep your demeanor professional."

"Of course," she said. *What the hell?* "Is there anything I need to do or know to prepare? Do I need to know the generals' names?"

Jerome glanced at Bill. Kathy thought they were struggling to decide how much to tell her. After a moment, Schrader said, "They haven't been here before, and I doubt if their names would mean anything to you. Your task will be to take meticulous notes to create an accurate meeting report. Wherever the conversation leads, just perform the task. My guess is they'll arrive right at ten. The meeting will be in the secure conference room behind my office. You should be in the room at the keypad when they get here."

"Should I get the recorder ready?"

"No. They specifically directed no recording. You'll need to get it all on your own."

"All right. Is that it, then?"

"Yeah. But, after the meeting, you and Bill and I will need to stay in the conference room and decide how to draft the report. Can you skip lunch, or go late today?"

"No problem."

"Okay. That's it. Thanks, Kathy. Close the door on your way out."

Kathy went back to her desk. She guessed the meeting would be UFO-related. That seemed to be the issue creating the unusual secrecy around the office. She felt uneasy and disappointed in herself for the mention she had made of the topic to Randy, John, and Megan Friday night. What was done was done. At the time, she'd officially known nothing and had not been involved. She had not told Jerome of her slip or her concern with overhearing unintended conversations. With any luck, this meeting would have nothing to do with UFOs.

At 9:50, as Kathy was getting up to go to the conference room, Bernie Ricardo – half-Hispanic, with black hair and dark eyes, jovial, and eight months pregnant – burst though the main entrance. Bernie worked in Crowley's communications technology research group on the second floor. "Hey, Kathy, I've got to go back out in ten minutes, and I've got twenty minutes worth of prep before I go," she blurted breathlessly. "Is there a free desk close by I can use?

"I'm headed for a meeting. Use mine."

"Great! I'll be long gone before you're back, and I won't touch a thing. Thanks a million."

"No sweat," Kathy said, walking away. "Make yourself at home."

Kathy walked into the secure conference room, closed the door, seated herself at the keypad, and made sure the transcription system was on and working. She sat calmly, waiting for the meeting participants to arrive. Brian Betz had been to the Crowley office twice before. Kathy was one of a handful of people who had seen him and knew who he was. That was to say, she knew his name. She doubted if anyone knew who he really was. His visits were not advertised, and he never signed in. He seemed invisible arriving and leaving, and he never spent a moment waiting or talking in corridors or reception areas.

Kathy had met Betz face to face once at a meeting to review intelligence gathered on a terrorist group's level of access to missile technologies. He *unnerved* her. She couldn't put her finger on exactly why. It might have been his eyes. When he had looked directly at her, which had been for not longer than two seconds, she had felt he was looking *inside* her. His glance had made her feel as if he knew her thoughts. She had never heard him speak. Betz was apparently associated with the Government, but Kathy had no clue what agency he worked for.

At 10:01, Bill opened the door and Jerome walked in, followed by Betz and two Air Force generals Kathy had never seen before. For a split second through the open door, Kathy saw Betz glance back at Bernie, who was gaping at him, a wildly disoriented look on her face. Johnson followed them in and closed the door. The three visitors immediately focused their attention on Kathy.

Jerome quickly introduced her. "Gentlemen, this is my executive assistant, Kathleen Jarrett." He added hastily, "Her security clearance matches Bill's."

Betz's fleeting glance at Kathy felt as though it penetrated to the depth of her soul. He turned his head and locked eyes for a brief moment with one of the generals.

The general asked brusquely, as if Betz had telegraphed the words into his brain, "Why is she here?"

"To take notes and generate a record," Jerome replied.

"There is to be no record," the other general stated. "She'll leave the room."

"Certainly." Jerome was taken aback. "I'm sorry, Kathy. Would you please leave us?"

"Surely," Kathy replied, and she abruptly rose and walked out of the room, closing the door behind her.

"*My God!* Who *was* that guy?" Bernie whispered, gathering her papers to leave. "I looked up and saw him when they walked in, and I thought he was going to *kill* me with his eyes … just for seeing him." Then she saw Kathy's expression. "What're *you* doing back out here?" Bernie was still whispering. "Did they kick you out?"

"Yes," Kathy replied, feeling as bewildered as Bernie had looked a minute earlier.

Bernie stared at Kathy for a second, shook her head hard, and said, "I've gotta go. Thanks for lettin' me use your desk." She was out the door as fast as she had burst in.

Kathy didn't see the five men the rest of the day. There were three exits from the secure conference room. They could have all left at any time without her knowing. She was off balance all day. *What the hell is going on that has to be so secretive? Is there some kind of threat being concealed? Is it all about the UFOs?* The top brass at Crowley was obviously uncomfortable, but everyone was keeping tight-lipped. When she left the office shortly after 5:00, she had no clue whether the meeting was still going on in the conference room, whether the five of them had moved to other quarters, or whether the meeting had adjourned 15 minutes after it had begun. As she drove home, she was spooked by the whole affair. During the six years she had been employed at The Crowley Group, she had *never* been so conspicuously excluded from *anything.*

*　　　*　　　*

Invitation

John spent the day checking a telescope OS had refurbished two years ago at an observatory in the highlands near Los Alamos. The observatory director, Sam Barnes, had called last week reporting erroneous readings, and had asked OS to send someone to take a look. After performing diagnostics on the system, John told Barnes he had found no irregularities. He also told Sam the logged data was similar to that reported by the new system on Baldy Mountain on the same night. Even the time the data had been generated matched the Baldy system. John was becoming convinced an actual physical disturbance had created the unusual data. Regardless, John would take the data back to OS for more detailed evaluation, and OS would issue a findings report.

John and Sam went to lunch, along with Rick Greer, a part-time observatory assistant completing his senior year at the University of New Mexico, studying astrophysics. They ate at the Long Branch, and little of their discussion related to telescopes.

"Did you guys see the President last night?" John asked.

They both nodded. "Who didn't?" Sam replied. "It sounded more like politics than science, but the plan sure has strong support."

"I'm not so sure about it," Rick said. "The ozone problem might be more drastic and getting worse faster than we're being told. Jamison's plan might not be enough to reverse it, and if we don't reverse it, like right now, it could be too late."

"Are you saying they're all too optimistic?" John asked. "All the politicians, governments, and scientists?"

"Maybe too political … or maybe too influenced by forces that aren't seen by you and me. I'm no expert, but I'm not sold on the plan."

"You might have a point," Sam said. "There's something suspicious about both parties, both houses, and huge corporations *all* having a united front. I haven't heard of any dissent from other governments at all. Even the media seems all gooey-eyed over it. It does make you wonder."

"Megan and I had the same thoughts last night," John said. "When has that kind of agreement *ever* happened in the United States? It doesn't feel right. Speaking of not being right, did you catch the clip right before the speech? Tricia West and the pregnancy thing?"

"Yeah," said Sam. "What a faux pas to allow that as a prelude to a presidential address."

"I was listening to news on the way up here this morning," Rick said. "They're saying most of us bought into the President's plan, and ozone isn't much of a hot topic today. The thing everybody's talking about is baby-making."

"Well, either there's bogus data out there," John said, "or Megan and I just slipped in under the wire, uh, no pun intended. She's two months pregnant."

"Hey, congrats," Sam grinned. "You two could be famous if you have the last baby on Earth!"

"Aw, Tricia was probably right. Maybe we all just need to try harder," John said.

Rick quipped, "I wonder how many people've made that comment today?"

"Probably not more than a million or so," John replied.

John pulled into his driveway at 5:30. As he got out of his pickup, he saw Megan, wearing a light jacket and head scarf, walking up the road with Rufus. He slipped on his own jacket and hat, and then scurried off to meet them.

"Hi, baby!" He kissed her. "Nice afternoon for a walk."

She held onto him after the kiss. "It was a pretty rough day at work, and I thought a walk might help. But, what I really need is this." She pulled him tighter.

"You want to talk about it?"

She told him about her day, not releasing the embrace.

"Woof." Rufus jumped, putting his front paws on John's side. He had waited long enough to be acknowledged.

"Hey, Rufus." John tussled the dog's head and ears. "How was your day, buddy? Better than Megan's?"

The dog barked a happy response. Satisfied, his paws returned to the ground.

"You want to walk some more?" John asked Megan.

"Sure." They walked three-quarters of a mile to Kokopelli's Kantina, a small tavern that was pretty quiet at 6:00 on Wednesday evening.

"Stay here, Rufus," John said when they reached the front door. Rufus lay down by the sidewalk near the entrance. He would wait at that spot until John and Megan emerged. They went in, ordered salads, and talked of the trip to Ohio, of marriage, of names, and of their future. They walked back home at twilight, arm in arm, with Rufus trotting alongside.

They passed their neighbors, Marty and Brenda Black, walking the other way and stopped to chat. The Blacks, who lived across the road an eighth of a mile from their house, were in their late fifties and had two children, both married and both living in Colorado. Marty was short and wiry, his black hair having a touch of gray. Brenda was matronly, white haired, and taller and stouter than Marty. John, Megan, and Rufus were their locally adopted family.

"Megan," Brenda said, "you looked so sad this afternoon when you walked by the house, but you look happy now. Does John always have that effect on you?"

"Always." Megan smiled at them.

"It's been a while since we've had you over for an evening," Marty said. "Do you two have a free night this weekend? You know you're invited anytime."

"We're flying to Ohio to see my folks next Thursday and won't get back till the following Monday night," John replied. "We've got a lot to do before the trip, but how 'bout the Saturday afternoon after we get back? What would that be, the twenty-sixth?"

"That'd be great," Brenda said. "Say, mid-afternoon? We could play some cards, throw steaks on the grill, and then have a rematch."

"And toss down a few brews," Marty added.

"We'll look forward to it," John said. "See ya then."

When they got home, Megan threw on a robe, and John checked his email. The one that jumped out at him read: "John, do you want to visit another planet?"

All right, that's enough. Let's see who you are. He clicked the reply button and typed: "Who are you?"

He clicked "send," and the message disappeared. Then he opened the sent items screen to see who it had sent to. It wasn't there. John clicked back to the inbox screen, and the email he had replied to was also gone. "Shit," he whispered, and again updated his anti-virus program and ran a system scan. No virus was found. He reopened the inbox to see if his email had been replied to. Nothing. *Baffling.* He turned off the laptop, got in bed, wrapped his arms around Megan, and drifted off to sleep.

John slept soundly for an hour, but then fitfully for the rest of the night, dreaming nonsense. He dreamt of reaching inside his laptop to grasp for information it kept hiding from him. He dreamt of standing in a light beam and being levitated up into a flying saucer. He dreamt of Rufus, Megan, and him outdoors, running helter skelter, dodging magnified neon blue UV rays pounding down all around them. He dreamt of planets and moons hurtling past him; Mars, the moon, Venus, IO, Titan, Saturn; of space beings, unseen and without form, watching him, drawing him in. His dreams were fraught with anxiety: they had an undercurrent panic but were somehow devoid of fear. Dreaming, dreaming, dreaming.

*   *   *

Jerome Schrader and Bill Johnson arrived at Schrader's secluded residential mansion twenty miles outside of Albuquerque shortly after 1:00 in the afternoon. Their morning meeting had ended at 11:30, and the five men had left through the back door. Betz and the two generals departed in their waiting limousine. Jerome and Bill went to lunch and discussed personnel allocation for several new commissions signed in the past week. They avoided speaking of staff assignments for the undertaking assigned them at this morning's meeting.

That discussion was deferred until the two were seated in the secure "Situation Room" behind Schrader's private home office. This room constituted Crowley's most secure and technologically advanced facility. Jerome reserved its use for intense technological research or conferences requiring absolute secrecy. The Situation Room had every state-of-the-art communications device available, each with the most impenetrable security protection money could buy. For commissions where the consequences of information leakage or speculation by staff were intolerable, meetings were held here.

"This commission looks like it'll be the most lucrative we've ever had," Jerome said to Bill, "but I'll tell you, Betz makes me more uncomfortable every time I see him. This morning was the third time he's been at our office in four years, and I hope to hell it's the last. Does he make you feel like he knows everything you're thinking and will see every action you take?"

"Yes. Without saying a word, he unravels everybody he's around. Even Bernice, at Kathy's desk this morning. Did you get a glimpse of her? From the look on her face she probably had to change her pants after he just *walked past* her."

Schrader shifted uncomfortably in his chair. "He hardly ever speaks. He controlled every word from those two generals without sayin' a thing. The only words from him during the whole meeting were the question he bored into us right at the end. 'Do you comprehend the consequences to you if any information related to this assignment finds its way into unauthorized hands?' Not just 'the consequences' but 'the consequences *to you*.' It felt like he was ordering us to maintain absolute control over all information or *die*."

"That's *exactly* what he meant. He obviously got our attention. We're here."

"Yeah," Schrader said, chagrined. "Well, we both took a lot of notes since he kicked Kathy out. All things considered, Kathy's way better off for not having been there. Anyway, let's compare notes and make sure we're both dead certain exactly what we have to do."

"We have identical missions for two targets," Bill said. "We find out everything there is to know about the people involved in two disappearances: Patricia Laurent, Medicine Hat, Alberta, Canada, and Jeremy Gilmore, Johannesburg, South Africa."

"Right. We'll start with Web research this afternoon from here, just you and me. We'll find out everything we possibly can from here. Then we'll choose two-person teams to investigate and develop a complete dossier on each target. The two teams have to be totally independent, not even aware of each other. They operate covertly and develop the dossiers without allowing *anyone* to suspect an information-gathering operation's in progress.

"After today, 'after midnight exactly,' we can't even talk to *each other* about either assignment, not one word." Schrader shook his head as he spoke. "You take Gilmore and communicate only with General A, and I'll take Laurent and communicate with General B. Hell, they wouldn't even give us their *names*. This is the most unsettling commission we've ever had. I'll tell you, I was tempted to turn it down, regardless of the payoff."

"Except you knew as well as I," Bill said, "as soon as we saw Betz, there was no option to turn it down."

"Shit," Schrader said, accessing the sophisticated equipment. "Let's start the research. We've gotta use today to the best possible advantage, while we can still work together."

Bill Johnson walked out the front door of the Schrader mansion at three minutes before midnight.

Chapter 8
Thursday, April 10

John was in the office to catch up on reports and paperwork. The first thing he did was buzz Randy.

"Hey, buddy," Randy chimed, seeing John's name on the phone display.

"Morning, Randy. You busy for lunch?"

"No plan. What's up?"

"I've been having some pretty weird email issues at home. I'd like to run it by you over lunch, see what you think."

"Sure," Randy said. "How's 11:30?"

"Great. Across the street at Monroe's? You give the advice, and I'll buy lunch."

"Deal."

John was knee-deep in drafting reports, reading memos, and responding to emails all morning, so 11:30 came quickly. He arrived at Randy's office a few minutes late, and they headed out the door and across the street. A pretty young waitress appeared and asked for their drink orders as soon as they sat down. They both knew the menu by heart and ordered sandwiches and coffee.

As she left, Randy asked John, "Did you catch any news last night or this morning?"

"No. Megan had a tough day yesterday. When I got home, we walked down to Kokopelli's and spent the evening there. This morning we … uh … enjoyed the morning and didn't get out of bed till the last possible minute. Then we had to rush to get to work." They grinned at each other. "Why, what's up?"

"Everybody's goin' nuts over the baby strike. That's what the media's calling it: a baby strike. Nobody in Government has made any comment, but the media's hounding them. The activists who were already going off the deep end over ozone are making a stink. They say increasing radiation is causing mass infertility and, of course, the Government's covering it up. I'll bet Jamison's fit to be tied. As if it wasn't enough to have to deal with the ozone issue while positioning for reelection, now he's got this crazy-assed media blitz stirring up everybody over a baby strike! Ha!"

"So, what do *you* think about it?" John asked. "I mean, there must be *something* behind it. From what I've heard, they're claiming almost *no* conception has occurred since about the time Megan got pregnant. Has anybody said anything about artificial insemination? That's pretty common anymore. Is that a problem, too?"

"I haven't heard anything about that. I don't know *what* to think. But, I'm like you. Why would the Government allow the media to keep up the charade, if it's easy to show there's nothing to it? The next few days'll be interesting. The economy's been a roller coaster for months. If there really is anything to this, it could become a disaster. If the roller coaster comes off the track, who knows what'll happen? Anyway, you said something about email problems? If you're buying lunch, I'd better keep up my end of the deal."

Lunch arrived, and the conversation continued between bites. "Have you ever received emails where the sender wasn't identified?" John asked. "Emails with the 'From' line empty?"

"Nope. You been gettin' some?"

"Yeah. Last night and the two nights before, I got emails from an unidentified sender. Is there an easy way to find out where they're coming from?"

"Maybe. Is your virus protection up to date?"

"As soon as I got the first email, I deleted it and ran my anti-virus program. Everything was good. Same deal Tuesday night. Last night, I thought I'd outsmart whoever the sender is. I replied and then went to my sent emails to see where it went, but my reply wasn't there. So, I went back to my inbox, and the original incoming email was gone. I did the virus scan again and got the same thing. No problems. Is there some kind new virus going around doin' stuff like that?"

"No. And if there was one that started Monday, I'd know it by now, unless it was a really selective virus making very few hits. So, you opened the last one? What'd it say?"

"More craziness. None of them had anything in the email body. Everything was in the subject line, and it wasn't much. The first one said ...." John hesitated and shook his head before spitting it out. "You'll think this is bull, but it said, 'Would you like to visit another planet? If so, click reply and send.' The second one said, '*John*, would you like to visit another planet?' The one last night was the same."

"And you *answered* that one? So, what'd you say? Are you *going*?" Randy grinned.

"Funny, pal. I said, 'Who are you?' and sent it off. I don't know where it went. Somewhere out in the ether, I guess."

"Did you get a reply?"

"No," John said. "Not before I shut down, anyway."

"That's a new one on me." Randy laughed. "Friday's our night to come to your place. Maybe we can play around with it then. That is, if you're still here and haven't got zapped up in outer space."

"Who knows? The world's running amok."

"Speaking of running amok, you're receiving crazy emails, and you said Megan had an extra-bad day yesterday. So did Kathy. You know she doesn't talk about work, but she was really upset last night. She'd been scheduled into a meeting yesterday and was requested by the client, I presume the Government, to leave. I don't think it could've been a security clearance issue. Hers is as high as anyone's at Crowley except their president's. Crowley must be involved in something big, probably for the Air Force. Anyway, it looks like I'm the only one of us getting along just fine." He laughed.

John got home at 6:00 as Megan was setting dinner on the table. Instead of their usual conversation over dinner, tonight they flipped on the news. It wasn't pretty. They heard first there would be a press release by Chuck Williamson, the President's press secretary, at 7:30. The rest of the newscast showed the beginnings of public hysteria.

Demonstrations were occurring, not just in the United States but also in Europe, Russia, Australia, Japan, and even China. The protest issues were jumbled and incongruent, even within individual demonstrations. The majority of the protesters were incensed over the ozone, cancer, and infertility problems, but there were other fringe topics thrown in: the worldwide economic downturn, social inequities, government cover-ups, even UFO visitation and potential space invasion.

Watching was disconcerting. The media was feeding on the unrest, mixing it around and stirring it up. John and Megan didn't talk, their attention glued to the scenes of disruption. They wondered what kind of world they were bringing their child into.

At 7:00, they took a break and took Rufus for a walk. They were back in front of the TV by 7:30 for the press release. Chuck Williamson's always-red face was redder than normal as the cameras focused on him at the podium.

"Good evening, ladies and gentlemen. I have a statement to read, prepared jointly this afternoon by President Jamison, Senate Majority Leader Sharon Eubank, and Senate Minority Leader George Cleary:

"The President's six-point plan to restore the stratospheric ozone layer has been adopted by an unprecedented majority in both the House and Senate. Virtually every economically developed nation on Earth has adopted a similar plan. Measurable results in the form of increased ozone layer thickness are expected within one to two years. The President's Ozone Restoration Plan represents an historic step toward the preservation of the environment and will benefit mankind for centuries. World leadership has never before been confronted with such an all-encompassing challenge as we currently face. The United States Government is proud to be taking a leading role in the responsible actions now underway worldwide.

"Another issue of growing concern relates to economic conditions around the globe. All national economies have performed erratically for the past several months, with the overall trend being downward. A significant contributing factor to this instability has been the erosion of public confidence in world political leadership because of a perceived inability or unwillingness to tackle the deteriorating ozone and health issues. We expect this perception to dissolve in the wake of the actions now being implemented.

"Even so, the leaders of the most productive nations of the world, including all those ranked among the top twenty-five in gross national product, have scheduled a week-long summit in

Stockholm in June. The purposes of the summit will be to analyze the performance of the global economy during the months of April and May, and to propose measures to supplement recovery, if insufficient improvement has occurred during that period.

"Here in the United States, the Federal Reserve Board has indicated it will reduce the prime rate by at least a half-point to ease the credit crunch for small businesses and families. In addition, the President and Congress have agreed on a plan that will be implemented in July if inflationary pressures do not diminish before that time.

"The President and both Leaders call upon all Americans to keep faith and remain positive, calm, and steadfast, and once again to manifest the inner strength that has always defined the spirit of America. Peaceful demonstration always has been, and always will be, a vital part of our American heritage. However, it is important that demonstration exhibit a positive goal. Beyond that, it is imperative that demonstration remain peaceful. Demonstration is welcomed and encouraged by this Administration, but we must all understand how essential it is that demonstration remain orderly and lawful. Violence and chaos cannot be tolerated. The law-abiding citizens of the nation can rest assured the United States Government will protect them and won't abide violence at demonstrations.

"The President and Leaders also wish to inform the public that the Center for Disease Control has confirmed a downturn in the rate of new pregnancies reported during the months of February and March. There is no reason to suspect this downturn is anything other than a temporary incongruity. CDC is continuing to monitor and investigate this temporary anomaly.

"Thank you, and good night."

"What's your take on that?" John asked Megan.

"Unsettling. The point on demonstrations staying peaceful seemed threatening. That, and the part about inflation control makes me wonder if Jamison's considering some form of martial law in the back of his mind. The add-on at the end about pregnancy was *way* understated, compared to the media claims. And addressing fertility and demonstrations and inflation in the same press release as ozone and cancer detracts from the environmental plan, which seemed really solid before."

"I know," John said. "I'm almost wondering if the United States is the best place to raise a family. I mean, I don't have a clue where the best place is, but I'm not sure anymore it's here."

"I don't know, either. We'll do some research. I'm glad we've got some time to think about it. There's no push to settle on where we want to live till after the baby's born."

"Oh, by the way, I almost forgot to tell you," John said, changing the subject. "I got another email last night inviting me to another planet. I replied and asked who was sending the emails. I thought I could look at my sent emails and see who it went to. Instead, the damn thing *disappeared*. It didn't show up in my sent emails, *and* the original email disappeared from my inbox. I talked to Randy at lunch today, and he's never heard of anything like that. You want to see if anything came in today?"

"Sure. Let's see if we can find one more thing in the world that's gone mad. You told Randy you were invited to visit another planet? What'd he say?"

"He asked if I was going." John laughed as he opened his email.

A response was there, and it seized their attention. "We are from Bremo, a planet similar to Earth, orbiting a star you call Alpha Centauri B, four light years from your sun. John, would you and Megan like to visit our planet?"

They stared at the screen and then at each other. Finally, John said, "This has to either be somebody who knows us or some idiot Internet-spying on us. What do you think of *this* response?" He clicked "reply" and typed. "Bullshit. Who are you?"

He looked at Megan, eyebrows raised.

"That's the response I'd send," she said.

He clicked "send" and then checked sent emails and the inbox. Neither the email received nor the one sent was there. "Let's turn this damned thing off."

Chapter 9
Friday, April 11

John and Megan were in the kitchen when the front door banged open and Brady ran in yelling, "Woofis, Woofis!" Simultaneously, Rufus tore for the door, barking incessantly. A joint tackle occurred in the middle of the living room before Randy and Kathy entered.

"What the heck?" Randy exclaimed with a grin. "Is it safe in this place?"

"It's safe now," Megan replied. "The disaster crew is fully occupied."

"Beer?" John asked, looking at Kathy.

"Eat dirt, worm," came the quick reply.

"Sure, I'll have one," Randy piped up. "Don't mind her. Hormone issues, you know."

"I never do," John replied while Kathy scowled at them both.

"Can we go outside?" Brady asked, out of breath.

"Come here, and I'll put sunscreen on your face," Kathy said. "Then you can go, but leave your jacket on. And take it easy on poor Rufus. You don't want to wear him out."

The youngster scurried to his mother for a quick smearing. "Woofis never wears out! C'mon, boy, let's play tag," Brady squealed gleefully as they ran for the back door.

"There's a glimpse of what you're in for," Kathy said to Megan with a glint in her eye.

"Bring it on," Megan replied, carrying two tall glasses of iced tea to the table.

John sat down with a beer in each hand and handed one to Randy. "What sounds good to everybody?" They settled on pizza, and John called in a delivery order.

"Did you guys hear about the market?" Randy asked.

"Yeah," John replied. "I caught it on the news on the way home. Dropped seven percent today, fifteen percent for the week. Lucky for us, we're too young to be rich and haven't got much invested."

"I'll bet the brokers are glad it's Friday," Randy said. "With any luck, it'll rebound Monday. At least our jobs all seem safe. I don't know why, but big system orders keep coming in. And Crowley always gets busier when the chips are down. Megan'll always be in demand, so I guess we just keep bringing in paychecks and don't worry about retirement accounts."

"I don't know," Kathy said, shaking her head. "The whole country seems on the verge of blowing apart. I'm starting to wonder where it'll lead. The politicians are spewing bravado, but I have a feeling they're not convinced themselves where it's heading."

"Yeah, John and I are wondering if the USA's really the best place to start a family," Megan said.

"All I have to say about that is, if you get serious, you'd better include us in the discussion," Kathy replied. "I'd sure hate to see our foursome break up. And I'd really hate to lose Brady. I'm sure he'd go wherever his pal Woofis goes."

"You know," John broke in, "iced tea's the downside to pregnancy. Beer is better for lightening up conversation." He held up his bottle. "Let's make a pact right now that if any of us go, we all go together."

"Hear, hear!" Randy raised his. Two bottles and two iced tea glasses clinked in a toast of commitment. "All for one and one for all!"

The pizza arrived, and the dining entertainment came in from the backyard. Brady was a nonstop source of action and words. He sat, more or less, at the table, yakking it up between bites, jumping down intermittently to feed Rufus his fair share of pizza. After ten minutes, Brady and Rufus scampered back outside.

As they ran out, Kathy kidded John, "Oh, talking about going away, Randy tells me you're going *interplanetary*! That must be exciting."

"Well, now it seems we've both been invited," Megan chimed in. "But, we haven't accepted yet. John says he and Randy are gonna pin down the extraterrestrials tonight. I hope

Randy doesn't accidentally hit the wrong button and get us zapped out on the spot. I'm not ready yet."

"This might be fun," Randy said. "Why don't we bring the laptop out here and play with it?"

"Okay, I'll grab it," John volunteered.

After it was started up, John asked Randy if he wanted to check anything on the system before going to email.

"Nope, let's see if we have any messages."

John opened his email, and there it was. Randy read it out loud: "'John, we invite you to ask questions you would like to know answers to that would help you and Megan make a decision.' Looks like they wanna get right down to business. Can we look through all your emails from this week and your sent and deleted items? Will this message stay here?"

"I think so," John said. "So far, none of the messages have disappeared until I either deleted them or replied to them."

"This email doesn't have a time tagged to it," Randy observed. "Did the others? Do you know when they arrived?"

"None of them had time tags. I can tell you about when I deleted them or replied, if that helps."

Randy spent five minutes searching through this week's inbox, sent items, and deleted items. "On the surface, it looks like none of the emails you are talking about ever existed. Have you tried to save any of them?"

"Nope. The thought never occurred to me."

"Okay, let's save this one." He clicked on 'File' and 'Save as.' "Let's call it 'Space Garbage' and save it to your desktop," he said as he typed. He hit enter and opened the desktop. "Crap, it's not there. I hope we didn't lose it." He went back to the inbox. The message was still there. "Okay, let's forward it. How about forwarding it to Megan? Hey, Megan, can you turn on your computer?"

"Okay." Megan went to the study, soon to become the nursery, and turned on her computer.

"I'll wait till you're up and have your email open before I send it." After Megan said she was ready, he sent it. "Yell when it comes in."

"Yell when you send it," she replied.

"I sent it 30 seconds ago."

"Well, it isn't here yet."

"I'll send you a test email." He typed in "TEST" and sent it to Megan.

"Got that one," Megan said after a few seconds, "but not the first one."

"This is nuts," Randy muttered. "I'm going to do some IT magic on your laptop, if you don't mind. It might take half an hour or so. You're all welcome to watch, but it'll be boring. How 'bout if I take the laptop to the study and you guys play a game of cards or something?"

"Play a game and leave you out?" John jibed. "How could we? What would I do with your beer? And your woman? Oh, go ahead, I can figure out something for your beer, but I don't know about the woman." Kathy displayed the middle finger of her right hand to John, who grinned at her.

"I'm sure you'll find a way to deal with both, buddy," Randy said as he carried the laptop away. "If you want to have some fun and make yourselves useful, why don't you figure out some questions to ask your space friends while I'm working on this? Maybe we'll be able to guess who is sending this junk from their responses ... if they respond."

"Good idea," John said. "Let's do that." During the next half-hour, the trio came up with a list of questions:

1. How would we travel to Bremo?
2. How long would it take to get there?
3. Have you contacted others? How many? Can we communicate with any them?
4. Why did you choose me to receive your message?
5. How do you make emails disappear and why?
6. How many people do you want to take to Bremo? Both John and Megan? Can our dog, Rufus go? Can our friends Randy, Kathy, and Brady go?
7. What would happen here if we go? Would we be levitated up to a spaceship, or just disappear, or what?
8. After we go, would we be able to communicate with anyone on Earth?
9. What would we find different on Bremo than Earth?
10. Could we come back to Earth? Anytime we want?
11. Have you been on the Earth?
12. Where are you now?

13. Do any governments on Earth know you exist?
14. Why are you inviting Earthlings to visit Bremo?
15. Do we get any assurance we won't be harmed?

It took half an hour of bantering to come up with the list. The trio made plenty of noise honing the questions but didn't hear a peep out of Randy. "Hey, Randy, you still alive in there?" John asked.

"Yeah, I'm bringing the laptop back. I didn't get anywhere at all. This is different than anything I've ever seen. Sounds like you guys were having a grand time with your questions. Are you ready to type 'em up, send 'em off, and see what happens?"

"Let's do it," John replied.

The back door banged open, and Brady and Rufus dragged in, huffing and puffing, both worn out. "Woofis wants to watch TV. Can we, Megan?" Brady asked.

"Sure. Come on in the living room, and I'll turn on whatever you want. You look thirsty. I'll bring you in a glass of milk, but don't let Rufus spill it."

"Okay. I won't let him."

John clicked on "reply" and typed in the questions. He sent the email, and they all stared at the screen, waiting for a response. Nothing happened. "Maybe we scared them off."

"I hope not," Randy replied. "But, we might as well set the laptop over on the counter and do something besides stare at it for the rest of the night."

"Right," John said. "There's still beer to be dealt with." He set the laptop on the counter beside the refrigerator and returned with two fresh bottles.

"There's really a lot of weird stuff going on," Kathy said.

"You mean the baby strike and all?" John asked. He glanced down at her midsection and added, "You don't seem to be having much trouble with that. Megan, either, as far as that goes."

"That *is* weird," Kathy answered. "But it isn't the only thing. Everybody's going nuts over ozone and cancer – I mean, rightly so – but we've also got demonstrations getting out of control. The economy's nose-diving. It just seems like a lot."

"Some of it probably feeds off the rest," Randy said. "Ozone depletion has to be partly to blame for cancer rates, and both feed the demonstrations. All of it influences public confidence and turns the market on its ear."

"It's the *crazy* stuff that's weirdest," Kathy said. "I mean the pregnancy thing. Even if the media's completely off-base, how could anybody ever come up with something like that? But they did ... *and* it didn't get laughed out of coverage. And the UFO talk isn't just melting away like it usually does."

"Ooooh-weeeou-ooooh-weeeou-ooooh," Randy mocked with a raucous grin.

"Well, think about it for a minute, you ding dong!" Kathy retorted. "There's something to these sightings. Neither of you guys have any explanation for your little pulsating light problem. And I don't know *what* to think about Crowley. I've *never* seen it like this before."

The other three stared at her. This was the second time in a week Kathy had brought up conditions at Crowley.

"I got tossed out of a meeting Wednesday. You can call it sour grapes if you want, but I've *never* been asked to leave a meeting before, no matter *how* sensitive the topic. I didn't get much prep for the meeting, but what little I got was disturbing."

"Are you sure you should be talking about this?" Megan asked.

"I don't *know* anything. Yeah, now I've been officially told not to talk about it. But, talk about *what*? Nobody ever said a single word about what the issue is. Jerome told me I was to be available in case the government didn't bring anyone to record the meeting. He made a *huge* point about staying composed and professional, even if the discussion was unbelievable. They didn't give me a clue what it was about, only that no matter how shocked I might be, I couldn't show it. Then, as soon as this Betz guy walked in the room with two generals, they looked at me like I was *poison*, said there would be no meeting record, and told Jerome to get me out of the room. I mean, *what the hell?*"

"Really, honey," Randy said quietly, "You could get in a lot of trouble. Don't say any more."

"What? Like any of you guys are gonna run to the cops and turn me in? If I can't trust you three, then I *really* wonder what the world's coming to."

"Well," John said, trying to lighten the conversation, "You don't have to worry about us, but look in there at Rufus. He's looking right at you, ears perked up, taking in every word. I've been trying everything under the sun since he was a pup to get him to keep a secret, but I can't break him. He is the biggest freakin' gossip dog I've ever seen. He uses everything he hears, even exaggerates it, just to impress all the neighborhood lady dogs he wants to nail."

"Hey! Woofis is a great dog!" Brady interjected, jumping up from the living room to defend his pal. "He don't zajurate, and he don't hammer other doggies!" They all got a good laugh out of that. Even Rufus seemed to be laughing.

"You do have a point, Kathy," Megan said. "There's never been so many crazy things happening. Not the least of which is John's invitation to visit aliens." She winked at John.

"Well, I think that's one we can shut the door on," John said. "I don't know who's emailing this crap, but, for sure, it's somebody whose feet are planted here on the good ole Earth. Actually ...." He glanced at the laptop. "It looks like all we had to do was fake taking them seriously to scare them off. No reply. So, how about reorienting the evening? Cards? Guys against girls? I know that isn't fair, considering it's four of you against two of us, but me and Randy, we're not scared of you or your broods!"

The rest of the evening reverted to their typical Friday night romp at the card table. Brady and Rufus were soon fast asleep on the living room floor. At one point during the festivities, Randy suggested the laptop be restarted. John rebooted it and reopened his email, but no new messages appeared.

At midnight, the party came to an end. As John reached over to shut down the laptop, he said, "Well, Kathy, I think we got rid of some of that weirdness you were worried about. No emails from space tonight. It looks like that little episode is behind us. But it was fun thinking up questions for the space trip!" With that, Randy gathered up Brady the Feed Sack, and they bade each other goodnight.

Had they received the email that John would find in the morning, none of them would have slept.

Invitation

Chapter 10
Saturday, April 12

It was a good start to a Saturday morning. John rose early to let Rufus out then sank back in bed and wrapped Megan in his arms. They slept on and off, snuggled together, for two more hours. Finally, they both woke feeling well-rested, warm, and comfortable. John lay on his back, staring at the ceiling.

"What's on your mind?" Megan asked, lying beside him, her hand lightly touching his chest.

"I was thinking about places we might live if we decide to move."

"So, where we going?"

"I don't know, maybe some small town in the Canadian backwoods. They're saying the worst places in the northern hemisphere for UV penetration are below the fiftieth parallel or above the sixtieth. There's a lot of open territory in Canada in between. There are thousands of little towns in that belt that'd be pretty isolated. They might not have high-paying jobs, but making a lot of money isn't high on my priority list right now."

"I don't care about the money, either. I thought I would when I started a family, but I don't. I want us to be safe, close, and healthy. I'm all for being comfortable, but I don't care about rich."

"We're on the same track. I'm not sure what Randy and Kathy would think." John grinned at her. "And we do have to consider them, now that we have a sealed pact. Randy likes IT work, and there probably isn't much demand for that in the Canadian north woods."

"They might agree with us. I know they're as concerned about the health and safety of their family as we are. If we decided seriously to consider a move like that, I think their problem would be the same as ours. It'd be really hard to leave

94

our families, especially if getting back and forth turned out to be difficult, and it might."

"I've thought about that, too," John said. "If we found a really great place, maybe some of them might go, too. It could depend on how bad it gets here."

"Whatever happens, we'll be fine as long as we have each other. I love you, John," she said, gazing into his eyes.

"I love you, too, Megan." He pulled her tight against him.

Half an hour later, they lazily got out of bed, showered, dressed, and made their way to their tableside view of the Sandia Mountains for coffee and a mid-morning breakfast. John turned on the news. It was more of the same. The worldwide attack on ozone depletion was expected to stem the tide of public unrest soon. However, for now, the markets were tanking, cancer rates were still up, and angry demonstrations were everywhere. Fringe religious sects were proclaiming the end of the world.

Rachel McNary appeared on the screen to contribute her part in the media's penchant for intensifying the agitation. "The state of public unrest is expanding into deeper angst over the drop in worldwide fertility. Demand for adoption is experiencing a sharp increase. There are signs that child black market activity is escalating. Reports are coming in from underdeveloped nations in Africa, Asia, and South America that the incidence of mothers selling newborns is increasing sharply, stimulated by higher payoffs. In the past week, hospitals in Bangkok, Nairobi, Mumbai, Cape Town, Buenos Aires, Rio de Janeiro, and Mexico City have reported multiple abductions of newborns. Our sources indicate healthy white babies less than one month old have been bought in the past week for over one hundred thousand dollars outside of the United States by U.S. citizens. Official statements from all leading national governments and health organizations have admitted only that a slight, temporary reduction in fertility rates has been observed. Our own research shows that the reduction is drastic, possibly a complete halt in conception worldwide."

John turned the TV off. "This day started off too well to get dragged down by this crap. You'd think, once in a while, the media would ease off its nonstop effort to rile people."

Megan turned on their favorite music selections. "Is that better?"

"Much. We should check email to make sure the aliens got scared off for good."

She teased him. "I hope not. They're kind of fun to talk to."

John carried his laptop to the table and opened his email. They saw the reply and leaned in close to read it.

John and Megan, here are the answers to your questions. What else would you like to ask?

1. If you decide to go to Bremo, at the moment you instruct us, you would immediately be teleported to our ship. After a few days of orientation, you would be teleported to Bremo.

2. The teleportation process is instantaneous.

3. We have contacted one thousand people. It would be unsafe for you to communicate with any of them, because your governments would be likely to discover the communications and create difficulties for you and your contact.

4. We did not choose you to receive our invitation. You chose us, twelve years ago when you broadcast your message into space.

5. We don't communicate by sending emails over your Internet. It appears we are emailing, but the process we use transfers communications by direct implant into and retrieval from your computer. It could be unsafe for you if our communications were discovered, and we avoid endangering those we contact.

6. John, Megan, Randy, Kathy, Brady, and Rufus are all welcome to visit Bremo. The two unborn would be safely teleported.

7. At the moment you instruct us to teleport you, you would disappear from your location on Earth and arrive on our ship.

8. After teleporting, you would have the ability to communicate with anyone on Earth by the same process we use to communicate with you. However, if your government discovered evidence of the communications,

it would likely make the lives of those you contact difficult.

9. Much is different on Bremo than Earth, but much is also similar. The air, water, gravity, and temperatures are similar. The species of life that have evolved on Bremo are different.

10. You would be permitted to return to Earth at anytime you direct.

11. Bremoians have physically been on the surface of Earth many times.

12. We are currently operating from our vessel several thousand miles from the Earth.

13. Many national governments on Earth are aware of our existence.

14. We are inviting humans to visit Bremo in an effort to ease dialogue between your species and ours to promote the development of mutually beneficial dealings. Our first goal is to convince a select group of humans that we are real, that we desire only mutual benefit, and that we intend no harm to your species. We anticipate the members of this group would then assist in expanding dialogue.

15. The only assurance we can offer that you won't be harmed is our word.

Megan gasped when she read "the two unborn." After reading all the responses, John and Megan stared at each other.

"How do they know we're pregnant?" Megan demanded. "This *has* to be somebody who knows us all. But they blew it on five. How could you have sent a message to them *twelve years* ago?"

John shook his head slowly and didn't say anything for a minute. Then, looking chagrined, he said, "Twelve years ago, I was a senior in high school. For my physics project, I built a communicator and transmitted a message into space to anything that might be listening."

Megan gaped at him. "How many people who know the four of us know *that*? I didn't." She paused. "Actually, that should help narrow it down. Who do you know who knows that and also knows Kathy and I are pregnant?"

"I can't think of anybody," John replied hesitantly. "We haven't told anybody you're pregnant, except Randy and Kathy. They wouldn't have told anyone. Well, I guess I let it slip at lunch with a client a week ago. I told two people. They know Randy – at least, one of them does – but they don't know you or Kathy. There's no way either of them could know about my high school senior project."

"Does anybody at work know about it?"

"I don't know. I've been there six years. I don't remember ever talking about it, but who knows? Maybe I did somewhere along the way."

"This has to be somebody from work or some Web-spy fanatic. If it's somebody who knows us, we should be able to figure it out. If it isn't, then I guess we're just the unlucky dogs some jerk landed on."

"I'm racking my brain about people at work," John said, "and can't come up with anybody. I s'pose Randy could be doing it, but that just doesn't make sense. We joke around a lot, but this'd be absurd. I don't think he could've faked being as perplexed as he came off last night if it was all a setup. I can't believe it could be Randy."

"I can *guarantee* you Kathy wouldn't have been in on anything like that," Megan said. "And I can guarantee you Randy couldn't have pulled it off without her knowing. I'm *positive* it isn't Randy."

John's mind cranked as he talked: "They said they contacted a thousand people. Maybe there's something to that. We're probably not the only ones they're pulling this hoax on. I wonder if we'd have any luck searching the Web for others. Sharing information might help find the culprits."

"So, how do we go about finding others? Go to UFO chat rooms and blogs and web sites and look at postings?"

"That's as good as anything. We could also send another reply, asking questions set up to get answers that might give us a clue. Before we do anything, we should get the last message on paper, so we don't lose it. I'll print it." He hit the "print" button. The printer didn't respond. He selected a different email and clicked "print," and the printer purred into action. He tried printing the Bremo message again. Nothing.

"Well, let's take the laptop to the study and type a copy on your computer."

Megan typed it. "I'll get a CD," John said. "We might as well save it on something we can carry around. We'll want it with us next time we see Randy and Kathy. If there turns out to be more, we can keep adding the whole mess to one CD."

Megan saved the document, put the CD in its case, and put the case in her purse. "I'll keep it with me, so I won't forget it. We can add to it from Randy and Kathy's computers if we need to."

"Okay," John said, "let's get on the Internet and see if we can find anybody else dealing with this crap."

They spent the next few hours searching the Web. There was no shortage of sites and postings dealing with UFOs and aliens, but they found little that bore any resemblance to their emails. Most of the entries seemed crazy.

One guy described his personal experience with a civilization living on the far side of the moon. One had visited Venus. Many described their abduction experiences, complete with brain implants, sexual encounters, visits to other worlds, and transmutations of body. Everything imaginable could be found, along with some things that were not.

Around mid-afternoon, they were scrolling through a web site that invited postings of personal experiences. They found an anonymous posting:

> On April 6 we began receiving emails from a source claiming to be from another planet. The emails are strange. They don't identify a sender and both incoming and reply emails disappear from our email record. Is anyone having similar communication? If so, and if you would like to compare notes, send a brief description of your experience to our temporary link below. If we think your experience seems genuine and similar to ours, and if you include an email address, we will reply to you.

"That's the one we've been looking for," John said. "Should we email them?"

"Let's do it."

Invitation

John clicked on the link and typed.

> We are John and Megan from the southwestern United States. I received an email from an unidentified source on Monday, April 7, asking if I would like to visit another planet. Suspecting a virus attack, I deleted the email. It happened again Tuesday night, and I deleted it again. I found no viruses. On Wednesday, I received another and replied, this time asking, "Who are you?" After I sent the reply, both the incoming email and my reply email were gone from my system. Thursday, they responded that they were from the planet Bremo. Friday, they invited questions, and we sent them several. Their responses were unsettling. Aside from being far-fetched, they know enough about us that we are concerned and want to figure out who is sending the emails. We decided to start by looking for someone else having similar experiences. Searching the Web, we ran across your posting. Yours is the only one we found that matches our experience. We hope you might be able to help us identify the sender. Thank you. John and Megan.

"Does that look okay to you?" John asked.

"Yep. Let's send it and then figure out what we want to ask our space agitator."

Half an hour later, they had a new list of questions typed.

1. How could we be teleported instantaneously? That would violate the physical laws of nature.
2. Why do you think our government would care about us communicating about contacting space creatures and going off with them?
3. What do you mean by the development of mutually beneficial dealings?

4. Tell us of some times and places where your species have physically been on the Earth.
5. When did you start making contact with humans for this endeavor?
6. Has anyone accepted your offer? If so, how many, and can you give us any names?
7. Is there a deadline for us to make our decision?
8. How would we inform you of our decision? There are six of us: four who could make decisions, one who is too young to decide, and a dog who can't understand the question. How do you control who decides for themselves and who decides for others?

Megan said, "If this idiot answers four and six, there should be something in the response we could shoot down. If we've found an Internet collaborator, maybe we can compare notes; see if the emails are consistent. If nothing else, the answers might give us a clue to how smart the bastard is. Maybe with some Internet help, we'll be able to piece the puzzle together and pinpoint him. Before we send it, I'd better type a copy for the CD."

After it was retyped and saved, John said, "I hope this gets us somewhere." He sent the email and shut down the laptop. "I've had enough. We've been at this all day, and I want to get my mind off it. Besides, it's been a long time since breakfast, and I'm starved. I could go for a steak and a glass of wine. Or two."

"Yeah, me, too, but I'll have to settle for just the steak. Do you think there's much chance we'll talk about anything else during dinner?"

"Maybe not, but I'm not gonna try."

*   *   *

United States Secret Service Officer Darryl Kirkwood sat alone at the thirty-seat table in the plush conference room, waiting. He had arrived ten minutes early. Tardiness would not have been tolerated. After he waited an additional ten minutes, the elevator doors opened into the conference room, and the person who had ordered him to this meeting walked purposefully to the table and sat across from him.

"I need to be certain you understand your assignment precisely, Darryl." Kirkwood *felt* the eyes dissecting his brain as the man spoke quietly and directly.

Kirkwood knew his mission inside out. He was Secret Service, assigned to protect the President, but his ultimate loyalty was to neither, nor to the United States of America.

President Daniel Jamison's nineteen-year-old daughter, Vanessa, a student at Duke University, was fiercely insistent that she be allowed live a normal college life. She would not be enclosed in a cocoon of protection. So, her bodyguard detail was camouflaged – veiled from her – and they operated from a distance that distressed the Agency.

Vanessa had agreed to carry signaling devices. She had three of them, all three always within reach. Kirkwood was to make certain that, when she woke Monday morning, all three would be missing, along with her cell phone. She would report the missing devices and have new ones delivered before leaving her suite. The point was not to rob her of her ability to send an emergency signal. The point was to show her, and her father, that she was vulnerable.

"You will ensure she sleeps too soundly to be wakened between the hours of two and three o'clock Monday morning," Brian Betz directed Kirkwood. "You will gain access to her room during those hours, and you will confiscate every wireless signaling device she has. You will not be observed. You will deliver the devices to the attendant in this room at four o'clock Monday morning." Betz's eyes had not disconnected from Kirkwood's since the elevator doors had opened. Betz had not blinked.

"Yes, sir," Kirkwood replied. "I understand my mission and will execute it."

Betz rose, turned, and walked into the waiting elevator. Before closing the door, he turned around, locked once more onto Kirkwood's eyes, and spoke quietly and precisely: "Do not fail." The ocular X-ray penetrating Kirkwood's mind broke off when the elevator doors closed.

Kirkwood sat motionless for five minutes. He was a professional. He carefully considered and visualized every detail, and assessed every contingency of every mission, over and over, before putting a plan into action – this particular assignment more so than any previous mission. Before this meeting with Betz, he had been positive there was no way he could become more one with this mission, more committed. However, before this meeting, he would never have imagined *fear* could be instilled in him to heighten the intensity of the ultimatum for perfect execution of a plan. Before this meeting, he'd had no clue that three words, spoken in a singular manner, by a singular person, could generate such bone-chilling trepidation. *"Do not fail."*

Chapter 11
Sunday, April 13

John intended to sleep in, but he woke before 6:00. After half an hour of lying awake in bed, he gave up, got up, and made coffee. He wanted to check email but knew Megan would want to read them with him. He turned on the news instead. It was disturbing.

The first story was from a village in Spain, near Madrid. The scene was of a small house cordoned off by police. Middle-aged British correspondent Emily Wharton, fighting a stiff wind and light rain, stood in front of the crime scene, describing the gruesome incident. "The couple who lived in this house was entertaining another young couple last night when they were attacked. Both women were more than 8 months pregnant, and the visiting couple had a two-year-old child. Authorities believe four henchmen broke in and immediately shot the two husbands to death. They then drugged both women, slashed their abdomens, and extracted the unborn children. The murderers abducted the child and both babies and left the women to bleed to death. The police have not stated whether or not any suspects have been identified. Except for officers at the scene, no authorities or government officials have been willing to comment."

The picture changed to the entrance of Mercy Chicago Hospital and Ralph Nickerson. "This hospital was the scene of a double crime last night. At the 11:00 shift change, two newborns were abducted from The Birth Place. So far, no one with any information on the crimes has come forth. The outgoing shift nurses reported that all babies were accounted for. The incoming staff realized two were not in the nursery and assumed the babies were with their mothers. The babies were apparently gone for ten minutes before anyone realized a kidnapping had occurred. No names have been released.

Hospital and police authorities have declined to be interviewed, saying only that everything possible is being done to recover the newborns, and they believe both babies will be returned to their mothers soon."

The screen switched to the studio and Rachel McNary. "The two previous reports are ominous and horrifying. Governments and health organizations the world over continue to discount the seriousness of the conception decline. However, it's become distressingly obvious there are those who feel otherwise. Authorities have offered no information on either the scope or the cause of the fertility crisis. This morning, our medical consultant, Dr. David Strauss is here to offer his insight and opinions. Good morning, Dr. Strauss."

"Good morning, Rachel." Dr. Strauss was fortyish, distinguished, trim, and good-looking. He exuded competence and experience.

"Doctor Strauss, has the Government or the Center for Disease Control issued any meaningful information relative to the apparent nosedive in fertility rates?"

"To my knowledge, *no* information, instructions, cautions, or explanations have been issued by any Government agencies. But, after the events of last night, the medical community will be as demanding of information as the public has been."

"Based on your personal medical experience and knowledge, do you believe a crisis exists?"

"From reports and information generated from within the medical community, a fertility crisis exists and may be nearly total and worldwide. Truthfully, *I* am having difficulty comprehending the situation. Evidence suggests human conception on Earth might have simply ceased sometime in late January."

"How could that be possible, Doctor?"

"Had you asked me that question a month, or even a week ago, my response would have been, quite frankly, it *isn't* possible. But, as evidence continues to accumulate, it looks more and more like the impossible is happening."

"*Surely*, artificial insemination and fertilization techniques are still being practiced. Why do you think the

Government, or CDC, has not come forth with this as proof conception is still occurring?"

"The word beginning to leak indicates artificial methods have also been unsuccessful. It seems likely that our political leaders have not come forward with this argument because they can't back it up. It's possible they've had little to say about the crisis because they don't know what's causing it, or what to do about it."

"That's incredible, Doctor Strauss. Are you saying it's possible that after the end of this year, no more human beings will be born *anywhere on the Earth*?"

"No, I'm not going that far. It's difficult to believe conception has come to a halt. But, if it has, with our vast medical and scientific knowledge, given time, we'll *surely* determine both a cause and a remedy."

"What about animals, Doctor Strauss? Many species have a lifespan of only a few years, or in some cases, only a few months or even weeks. Some species could become extinct quickly if conception within the particular species simply stops."

"All indications suggest that *only humans* are experiencing this malady. I'm aware of no evidence that any other species have been similarly inflicted."

"The recent reports of baby and youth abductions make it painfully obvious that black-market trafficking in young children is intensifying. What do you foresee relative to the social impact of this crisis?"

"That is of grave concern. What must occur immediately is a *total* crackdown by *all* governments to put an immediate stop to kidnapping and murder. This abomination *must* be checked and checked *right now*. *Today.* Otherwise, panic will take over, and severe government action will be required just to maintain order."

"Do you mean *martial law* might have to be imposed, Dr. Strauss?"

"Let's hope it doesn't come to that."

"Yes, let's hope not. What would the impact of a pervading military presence be? The world economy's already fragile."

"It isn't possible to predict the full impact of instituting martial law. The United States Government and citizenry *must*

106

step forward and take a leading role before it comes to that. We must espouse the virtues historically exhibited by the American people. Time and again, throughout the past three centuries, we have demonstrated our ability and willingness, our unfailing commitment, to overcome obstacles of all kinds. Our greatest scientific, political, and social minds *must* step forward boldly and discern the path."

"Well said, Doctor Strauss. Let us all work diligently to contribute to the solution, rather than the problem. Thank you for visiting with us this morning, Doctor. We'll return shortly after this commercial break."

"Jesus," John breathed. *How could civilization become fear-driven so fast? And who does McNary think she's kidding? Let's all contribute to the solution? The only thing she and her media cohorts ever do about anything is contribute to the problem.* He turned off the TV, poured a second cup of coffee, and said, "C'mon, Rufus. Let's go out and enjoy some early morning air." As soon as he said it, he thought that a few months ago he would have said *sunshine* instead of air. Rufus took off for a romp around the yard, and John stretched out on a lounge chair under the porch roof. Try as he might to think upbeat thoughts and improve his mood, he could not shake the apprehension that had swept over him while watching the disturbing newscast.

He closed his eyes and eventually drifted in and out of fitful, dreamy sleep. He started when Megan touched him lightly on the shoulder. "Oh, man," he mumbled, waking up. "What a lousy dream."

"What?"

John shook his head and grunted. "You've seen the old movie ET, haven't you?"

"Sure."

"Well, this stupid dream was that movie in reverse. I woke up in the middle of a whole world of ETs. *I* was the ET. All I wanted to do was go home, and I couldn't find my damn cell phone. I was terrified. Really stupid."

She needled him. "So, your emails are gettin' to you, huh?"

"Watch yourself, girl. You'll pick on the wrong guy and wind up on the bottom."

"Of what?"

"Of you-know-*exactly*-what. You've been there before."

"Why do you think I keep jerking your chain, boy? That's my favorite place." They smiled at each other. "Let's go in. I'll make you some toast. You can watch me slave for you in the kitchen while you recover from your trauma."

As Megan set coffee, juice, and toast on the table, she picked up the remote. "You wanna see what's going on in the world?"

"I had it on earlier. It's more trash and getting worse. Believe me, you'll enjoy your day more if you leave it off."

"Why, what's up?"

"Nothing with any direct impact on us, just more depressing crap. It's a little disturbing. You can turn it on if you want, but you'll have a happier day if you just let the TV keep it all to itself."

"Okay, I'll take your word for it." Megan laid down the remote. "So, what do you want to do today? I mean, besides pinning me on bottom."

"Well, that sounds like the best potential action of the day. I'll make sure that gets fit in somewhere. I guess we should check email. Then how about you, me, and Rufus pick up a picnic lunch and heading out to Sandia Park? It's going to be a beautiful day. I'd like to lie in the shade this afternoon and read a book."

"Sounds great, Johnny. At least, the second part. Shall we check email, and get that out of the way?"

When they opened John's inbox, they saw that both of the emails they had sent Saturday had been replied to. "What do you think?" John asked. "The Earthly email first?"

"Sure."

Hello, John and Megan. We're Elizabeth and Ben from Australia, near Sydney. We've received dozens of emails, but yours is only the third one that seems enough like our experience to reply to. One of the other two was from Ireland, and he believes his emails are a hoax. The second was from Thailand, and he's convinced the communication is from a race of space beings. We're skeptical, but beginning to think it might be possible the emails could be what they claim, crazy as that sounds. Feel free to reply to us. We'd like to know more about your communications. Here's a summary of ours and what we have heard from Ireland and Thailand.

The only reason Ireland contacted us was to gain ammunition for turning in the perpetrator. He was angry that whoever was emailing him knew so much about him and even more irate that the emails disappeared. We posted our response invitation on Tuesday, after receiving three messages supposedly from space, and replying to the second two. We received Ireland's first email on Wednesday and replied back to him the same day. He emailed back on Thursday, and we replied again. During that time, we were also sure it was a hoax. We haven't heard from Ireland since Thursday. He was going to report everything to the authorities, and we assume he did.

Thailand was just the opposite. He was excited about accepting the invitation. He had experimented with the communications and found he could get immediate replies to his emails by shutting his system off and starting it back up. Rebooting doesn't work. It has to be a complete shutdown and restart. We tried it and were astounded by the reply speed. No matter what we ask, as soon as we power down and back up, complete answers are there. That's one more unexplainable piece adding doubt.

Thailand told us of some responses to questions he'd asked that we hadn't. He said their intent is to develop a liaison group of humans who will visit their planet, Bremo, and report back to the rest of humanity, with the goal being an eventual complete trade of planets between the two species. They say the trade would benefit both species. The aliens have already determined they'll move to Earth and won't commit any violent actions in the process. They say they're dedicated to nonviolence. They claim responsibility for the fertility stoppage and say they can be patient. If it's fifty years or more before they can peacefully move in, they'll wait, but, in the end, they will move in. The current action is an effort to expedite the plan in a way that would be best for both species.

Thailand is excited about playing a part. He responded to our posting late Wednesday, and we emailed back and forth on Thursday and Friday. His Friday evening email said he was going to accept the invitation, and we haven't heard from him since.

We no longer know what to think. We're skeptical but can think of no reasonable explanations. How can they know so much about us? How can they send logical and consistent responses within seconds to questions that take us hours to compose? How can they make incoming and outgoing emails disappear from our systems? How can some of their responses be so outlandish, yet impossible to disprove? We hope you, or someone, can point out fallacies in their claims. Ireland was so upset that none of his views seemed rational to us. Thailand was as bad the other way. Neither of them offered any truly objective points.

Here is some of the information the "aliens" have given us. They've been visiting and observing our planet for thousands of years. They were involved with the pyramids and have created crop circles. They have lost some of their members in attacks on their small reconnaissance crafts visiting Earth. They've been conversing with some of our governments for the past fifty years. They can teleport over distances of light-years instantaneously. They won't transport any of us against our will. They believe our species on Earth is doomed to self-destruction and, as part of the planet trade, humans would have to adopt nonviolence as a prerequisite for survival. Ben and I fear we're succumbing to an irresistible hoax, and we're groping for a life raft. Maybe we can help each other. Ben and Liz

They read it again, more slowly. John said, "I'm not sure I want to read the next email. Let's throw this laptop in the trash and forget we ever heard of any of this."

Megan didn't say anything for a minute. "Open it."

He clicked on it. They read.

1. Teleportation does not violate natural laws. There are many forces at work in the universe that are not understood by humans. The transport process is instantaneous.
2. Some departments and persons in your government and other governments on Earth know we exist. Some are fearful that, should we choose, we could destroy human life. They believe knowledge of our existence by the populace would result in panic and chaos. That could be correct. It is possible some governments would take all conceivable actions to keep our existence from becoming public knowledge.
3. The most mutually beneficial dealing that could occur between our species would be trading planets. The Earth's atmosphere and oceans have evolved into a more hospitable environment for our species than exists on Bremo, and Bremo has become more hospitable to human habitation than is the Earth.
4. Our most highly publicized recent visit to Earth was the downing of our small craft at Roswell, New Mexico, in July of 1947. Lesser known is our 1957 landing in Utah, where we abandoned one of our craft, which was ultimately recovered by the United States Government. There have been several unpublicized visits involving face to face meetings with some of Earth's world leaders.
5. We initiated our current endeavor to contact humans for the purpose of establishing a liaison group on April 6.
6. Twenty-seven people have accepted our offer. They are on our craft now. We will give you three names but caution you against openly investigating. Your government is likely to deal with any activities related to us as treasonous. Jeremy Gilmore of Johannesburg, South Africa; Patricia Laurent of Medicine Hat, Alberta, Canada; and Yergi

Sepmanlov of Kiyev, Ukraine, are all currently on board our vessel.

7. The deadline for transporting humans to our ship for this effort is midnight April 30 of this year.

8. We consider there to be eight of you, counting the two unborn. Rufus will come if John comes. Brady will come if Kathy comes. Teleporting of multiple transports will be simultaneous. We will consider any message transmission saying, 'Bremo, take me,' as your direction to us to teleport you. We will know who is sending. Teleportation will be immediate upon sending the message. For John, Megan, Randy, and Kathy, your current status is that each of you must individually transmit your request to be taken. Should you want to go in pairs or as an entire group, you must each first send a message indicating who among you has the authority to request teleportation for each other individual. We will not teleport anyone who has not authorized transport.

"Unbelievable," Megan muttered, shaking her head.

"I think we'll send two more emails," John said, "one to Bremo, whoever that is, and one to Liz and Ben. We need to give some thought to what we want to say and ask."

"What do you really think? You don't think there could be anything to it, do you?

"My head is screaming 'no,' but doubts are creeping in. What do you think?"

"I think I'm getting scared."

"Let's compose another list of questions," John said. "Then another email to Australia. We'll send 'em out then turn this damned thing off, and get out of here for the rest of the day."

"Okay. Should we see if we can find out anything on the Web about the names they gave us?"

"It's worth a try."

They found two Jeremy Gilmores in Johannesburg, one Patricia Laurent in Medicine Hat, and no Yergi Sepmanlov anywhere. They found web pages for two Johannesburg Saturday newspapers and found no reports of any strange occurrences or any mention of a Jeremy Gilmore. Next, they found one newspaper in Kiyev. It was viewable but was printed in Russian, and was no help. They checked *The Medicine Hat News* and stared at the front page headline: "No Clues in the Disappearance of Patti Laurent." There was a picture of a pretty young woman beside the heading. They read the story.

Police remain clueless in the Tuesday disappearance of 18-year-old Patricia Laurent from her mother's home. She was reported missing at 7:33 Tuesday evening by her mother, Gretchen Pierre. Mrs. Pierre arrived home from work at approximately 5:15 Tuesday afternoon to find empty house. Ms. Laurent's computer had been left on with her email page called up. Mrs. Pierre stated that, whenever Patricia went out, she always left word, saying where she was going and when she expected to return. Considering the absence of any note, the computer left on, her purse on the desk, and all vehicles accounted for, Mrs. Pierre assumed Patricia had gone out on a quick errand or for a short walk. By 7:00, Mrs. Pierre became worried and began calling her daughter's friends. When no one reported having seen or talked to Ms. Laurent since noon, Mrs. Pierre contacted the police.

Medicine Hat Police Chief Charles O'Riley stated no clues have turned up to Patricia's whereabouts. Police have found no evidence of foul play. No explanation has been given for why Ms. Laurent might have left without her purse, which contained all of her identification, credit cards, and money.

The last person who saw Patricia was her mother, Monday evening before retiring for the night. Mrs. Pierre did not see her Tuesday morning before going to work but believes Patricia was in bed asleep at that time. No witnesses have reported seeing Patricia at her home or anywhere else on Tuesday. Mrs. Pierre asks anyone knowing anything about Patricia's whereabouts to come forward with information.

"This gets worse and worse," John said quietly. "Let's try to think about our questions from a point of view of believing the Bremo communications, even though we don't." After much discussion and after typing and saving a copy of the previous response, John clicked on "reply" and typed their new list of questions:

1. When did your species first visit Earth?
2. What do you want of us?
3. Have you caused any of the current Earth problems: ozone depletion, cancer rates, or infertility?
4. Was Bremo involved in the January 19 and March 27 UFO sightings on Earth?
5. How would you be able to tell whether or not the human race as a whole would be agreeable to trading planets?
6. Is there a possibility of an Earth attack on your ship?
7. Could you take over the Earth without human consent? Would you do that?
8. Does the United States President know about you? Have you communicated with him? Does he know you wish to trade planets, and what is his position?
9. Have any of the people you contacted been harmed by their governments? Can you and would you do anything to protect them?
10. Have any humans ever visited Bremo?
11. Is there a chance that humans could not survive or survive well on Bremo?
12. Are there circumstances whereby you would decide to leave Earth alone and go back to Bremo or go somewhere else?
13. If we go to Bremo, could we ever come back to Earth and live normal lives?
14. If we go with you, would the friends and family we leave behind be safe? If they wanted to, would they be able to be transported to Bremo?
15. Is it possible for us to communicate with Patricia Laurent?
16. Has anything ever gone wrong in the teleportation process?

Megan typed a copy of the email, and then John sent the reply and typed an email to Australia.

Elizabeth and Ben,

We may not be much help to you. We're beginning to feel like you. Our emails and research are impossible to believe, but we have no other explanations. We asked Bremo for the names of people who've accepted their invitation. They gave us three, and we were able to find information on one of them, Patricia Laurent of Medicine Hat, Alberta, Canada. She disappeared mysteriously Tuesday. No one saw her disappear. She was home by herself. All her belongings, identification, and money were left behind. She disappeared with her computer turned on. The police have no clues.

Have you asked how or why they chose you to contact? They told us they contacted me because I sent a message into space twelve years ago, which I did, when I built a communicator and transmitted a message. I can't think of anyone who would know that plus all the other information about me that Bremo knows.

They claim to have been the species involved in the Roswell, New Mexico, alien craft crash.

Have you asked about a deadline for accepting their invitation? They told us midnight, April 30.

They say several governments know they're real and they've had face to face meetings with some. They also say the US Government is likely to come after us if they find out we've been in contact with them. Do you have concerns over safety from your government? Are you sure you won't send an email agreeing to accept the invitation?

We're drained. We may leave our computer turned off for the next couple of days and just think through all this, and try to make some sense of it. We'll send a follow-up email later this week. Sorry we're not more help. Good luck.

John and Megan

John sent the email and turned off the laptop. "Let's grab a blanket, pick up some wings and beer, and take Rufus to the mountain. Sorry you aren't eligible for the beer. I'm sure you're as ready for it as I am."

"Okay. But, before we completely chuck this for the day, let's do one more thing."

"Turn the laptop back on and check email?" John asked hesitatingly.

"Yes. Let's find out about their turnaround speed."

"All right." John breathed out heavily and turned the laptop back on. He opened his email. The reply was there.

1. We first visited Earth over ten thousand years ago.
2. We want to show the people of Earth it would be in their best interest to trade planets, which we know to be fact. We want to do this with as little disruption to human life as possible. We believe the best way is to prove it to a small group and ask that group to help convince the rest of your population. We would like for you and your friends to be part of that group.
3. We caused the loss of fertility. That is our means of ensuring we will eventually be able to inhabit Earth without resorting to violent action. We have not created other adverse situations on Earth.
4. A fleet of small craft operates from our main vessel. As part of our efforts in implementing our Earth plan, we carried out several reconnaissance missions, including those on January 19 and March 27.
5. We will continue to pursue a one-at-a-time process for inviting and transporting humans to Bremo. Only individuals requesting to go to Bremo will be transported. The planetary trade would be gradual over a period of many years, possibly decades, with some cohabitation by both species on both planets for a number of years. No humans would be forced to go against their will and none would be harmed.
6. It is not possible for Earth to attack our main ship.

7. Bremo has the capability to take over the Earth and eliminate the entire human population in a single action. There are no circumstances under which we would resort to such a violent act.
8. We don't know whether or not your President Jamison has been informed of our existence. If not, he will be told soon. We have not communicated directly with him and we don't know how amenable he would be to trading planets.
9. Some of the individuals we have contacted have been harmed by their governments. Our commitment to nonviolence does not allow us to intervene. If notified that any person wants to come with us, immediately upon receiving notice, we transport the individual from whatever situation he or she might be in.
10. No humans have ever visited Bremo.
11. We believe humans would thrive on Bremo, but that isn't proven by experience.
12. The civilization on Bremo is committed to inhabiting the Earth. It will happen, and there are no circumstances whereby this decision will be reversed or changed. It is a matter of timing.
13. You could return to Earth at any time you would choose to do so. However, it would be impossible for you to resume living as you are accustomed to after having experienced life with us.
14. We don't know what your governments might do to the family and friends you would leave behind. We would not be able to guarantee their safety on Earth. If they would choose to follow you to Bremo, we would transport them off the Earth upon their request.
15. We will present your request to communicate with Patricia Laurent to her. The decision on whether or not to communicate will be hers.
16. There were a few transport failures when the process was new, but failures have rarely occurred in the past five hundred years and never in the last one hundred years.

They both read the response twice. "Let's turn it off," John said tersely.

"Do it," Megan replied. "C'mon, Rufus. Let's go."

Chapter 12
Monday, April 14

It had been only a week since his previous televised address, and it was distressingly clear to Jamison he would have to perform another very soon. One week ago, the issues that had necessitated the address were increasing cancer rates and depleting ozone. The economy had been lurking on the periphery but hadn't yet reached front and center. Jamison was comfortable with the impact of the previous address on public perception of government action on the ozone problem. Maddeningly, even before that address, the *inexplicable* dilemma of worldwide infertility had surfaced. That crisis, coupled with the multiplicity of other issues, was now threatening to wrest control of domestic order away from local law enforcement agencies.

The past week's crashing economy, growing protest momentum, and news media denigrations had resulted in exploding public volatility. Chuck Williamson's press release last week had only made matters worse, planting suspicions that his Administration might consider implementing martial law. The economy and the concern about demonstrations becoming deadly were difficult issues. Both had potential to get out of hand quickly, but both could be dealt with. The trick was to do it decisively and quickly, and in a way that would be seen in a positive light. That was all possible.

The stumbling block was infertility. This was untrod territory, and public perceptions had already developed that would be difficult to redirect. The effort to downplay the issue had been counterproductive. His Administration appeared inept and impotent, first implying there was no serious problem, and then seeming to ignore it after virtually everyone believed it was real. To make matters worse, *not even a hint* of either a believable cause or prospective solution had yet been proposed

Although it appeared to the public that the political leadership was ignoring the issue, every major government, including that of the United States, and every national and international health organization had been pursuing this problem at a frantic pace for the past week. Nonetheless, to the chagrin of all, little progress had been made. No convincing theories had been forthcoming. No laboratory experimentation had resulted in successful insemination of an embryo. All the vast resources of the top scientists and health organizations around the world had come up with nothing. Not one single government had confessed to its citizenry that a serious fertility crisis *even existed*, let alone that it was a worldwide *total stoppage* in human conception.

The situation was fast going beyond Jamison's personal political concern over re-election and becoming a significant threat to political stability worldwide. The ensuing bedlam could result in much worse than just tumbling political leaders from power. Advisors to world leaders were warning that this circumstance implied the foreseeable end of the human race, and *that* implication, when taken seriously by free-thinking and free-acting citizens, could lead to total chaos everywhere. Entire national governments could crumble in the very near future. Jamison was no longer sure any one individual, group of individuals, or government could wield enough control to avert catastrophe. Regardless, as leader of the most powerful nation in the world, it fell on him to step up to the plate and find a path through the minefield.

He had an 8:30 meeting scheduled, five minutes from now, with his Chief of Staff, the Secretary of Health and Human Services, and the CDC Director. This one had to be a hard-nosed working session. At 11:00, he had a meeting with the directors of CIA and NSA. This would be a highly unusual meeting. The directors had jointly requested the conference, which was to include only the three of them. No topic for the meeting had been stated. The conference had been scheduled for him. Jamison's calendar had been cleared before he had even been notified. This would be his first private meeting with just these two individuals since he had assumed the presidency. It was sure to be memorable. Jamison hoped it would result in a foundation for some sorely needed crisis solutions.

His direct line from the Secret Service rang. He picked it up.

"Yes?"

"Mr. President, this is Officer Harold Tallyrand. I'm required to inform you of an incident that occurred overnight involving your daughter, Vanessa."

Jamison's adrenaline level jumped. This wasn't the first time he had received a call from the Secret Service about a family member, and every call was disconcerting. "Go on," he said, maintaining composure.

"Vanessa contacted us by land phone at eight-seventeen this morning, when she woke. She reported that all three of her emergency call devices and her cell phone were missing from her room. Vanessa said she had not come into contact with anyone or seen anyone since retiring last night. All of the devices were in her suite when she went to sleep, and they were all gone when she woke. The suite was locked and secured all night. We swept the suite and found no evidence of any break-in or entry, but the devices were gone."

Jamison was instantly angry. "How can that be, Officer Tallyrand? Was Secret Service watching the suite all night?"

"Yes, from a distance, as directed. No one was observed entering or leaving, sir."

Jamison was exasperated. Vanessa adamantly refused conspicuous protection. Everything had to be concealed and distant. He *hated* it. The Secret Service hated it. Without saying it openly, they never let him forget they were being inhibited, by him, from providing the necessary level of protection. He was mad at Tallyrand. He was fed up with Vanessa's independent streak.

Finally, Jamison spoke. He wanted to say it was *unacceptable* for the Secret Service to have allowed this breech and that the Director, and Tallyrand, were *fired*. He demanded, "What's the assessment? What was the objective of stealing communication devices knowing they'd be immediately replaced?"

"Our assessment, sir, is the objective was to send a message that the perpetrators can get to Vanessa anytime they want. They want you to know that. Mr. President, it is imperative we abandon the policy of protecting Vanessa from an unseen distance."

"Bring her to the White House. Now," Jamison ordered. "She'll have to stay there today. I don't care what she says. I'll talk to her before the day's over."

"Mr. President," Tallyrand continued, "Vanessa isn't the only one the Secret Service has been required to protect too loosely. Until we determine exactly what happened last night, why, and who was behind it, security should be tightened on everyone."

Jamison wanted to wring Tallyrand's neck, snap it in two. He wanted Secret Service to do its damned job *right* and not be a pain in the ass for him. He did *not* need this problem today. He said, "Get *everybody* into the White House. Right now. I'll deal with them tonight. And I'll deal with Secret Service tomorrow morning."

"Yes, sir," Tallyrand said as Jamison hung up on him.

His secretary's voice announced, "Mr. President, everyone is here for your eight-thirty meeting."

"Send 'em in.

"Sit around the table," Jamison commanded as they walked in.

"Good morning, Mr. President," came the cautious replies.

Jamison took a minute to shake off the distraction of the conversation with Tallyrand, regroup, and gather his thoughts before speaking. "I'm sure you all realize it's necessary for me to deliver another address. Soon. Wednesday or Thursday at the latest. The sooner the better." The three sat motionless, eyes glued to the President.

"The economy and public restlessness are challenging, but we can deal with that," Jamison continued. "The crucial issue we have to resolve is mounting fear over the infertility issue. So far, I've heard nothing from the three of you, or your organizations, or any other people or organizations, that could be of *any* use in that effort. Regardless, I *have* to address it. It can't be put off any longer.

"We already look incompetent for downplaying the problem. I can explain how much effort has actually been put forth on the problem over the past few weeks, and especially during the last week. But, without a reasonable explanation of a cause and some kind of planned course of action, my speech won't help. The public temper is intense and deteriorating. I have to know everything there is to know about the problem, and I have to be sure what I say won't end up turning sour on me. What does CDC have, Helen?" The President's commanding eyes fixed on the Director.

"Mr. President, we believe there is nothing abnormal with human sperm or embryos. It appears to be the fertilization process itself that's being inhibited. The problem isn't occurring in any other species, only humans. We've done some experimenting with laboratory crossbreeding of similar species. Conception in the non-human primates and other mammals is not impeded, but all efforts using either human sperm or human embryos have failed." She looked at Jamison guardedly, waiting for him to respond.

"I'm not going anywhere *near* your crossbreeding comment," he said, looking squarely at her. "What do you mean, exactly, by saying the fertilization process is being inhibited? Being inhibited by what? How?"

"In all our artificial insemination efforts, the instant the sperm cell touches the embryo, both die. It's as though there's a force causing it, something in the air or the environment. We've been unable to determine, specifically, what that might be. We don't believe it is related to radiation levels, environmental contaminants, solar flares, or anything else that could be considered a natural cause." She stopped again, twisting uncomfortably in her chair.

"What're you saying, Helen?" Jamison asked with uncharacteristic sarcasm. "That you've ruled out natural causes but not *unnatural* causes?"

She looked uncharacteristically tense. "We haven't ruled out natural causes. We just haven't been able to find, or postulate, a natural cause. The fact that inhibition is occurring only with humans and no other species is very perplexing and problematic to rationalize. What in nature could be so selective, and so instantaneously total, as this? We've come up with nothing natural, so far.

"Consideration of other possible causes," she continued, "call them unnatural or supernatural, is precarious activity for

CDC. We deal in science, in matters that can be investigated and proven using scientific methods. Nonetheless, we realize there is much that our scientific body of knowledge cannot explain. There's strong evidence that various forms of extrasensory perception exist. We don't know how that works and can prove little about it. The human mind has many facets we don't fully understand. We simply don't know the limits, or potential, of the power of the mind. Could a person, or group of persons, be causing infertility somehow, using the power of the mind? We believe that's highly unlikely but can't unequivocally say it's impossible.

"Are there... unnatural forces... that exist in the universe?" Kursch became noticeably more uncomfortable. "Forces we don't understand and can't describe or quantify in scientific terms? Certainly. What are these forces, and what are they capable of? We don't know. Could they be responsible for imposing human infertility? This would seem very unlikely, but we can't say it's impossible.

"Are there alien life forms in the universe, possibly even in our solar system, that could be capable of impacting life on Earth? Probably. Mr. President," she continued, now meekly, "you might know more about this possibility than CDC does. Could an alien life form attack the human race in this way? If so, we don't understand how, but, again, we can't say it would be impossible.

"Is there an all-powerful being, a creator? Are there multiple gods? Demons? Most people would answer yes to at least one of those questions. If so, it's conceivable he, she, it, or they, could do anything they want, and we might be powerless to do anything about it." She stopped abruptly, unable to look at Jamison or the others.

"Christ, Helen." The President exhaled. "Are you suggesting I go to the public with *that* kind of crap?"

"No, sir. You asked me what CDC has. We have nothing. We're researching fervently and keeping our minds open. We're considering everything fathomable."

"All right." He calmed down and considered what she had said. "Do you think there's anything to be gained in considering any unnatural cause? Are there *any* real possibilities you think we could figure out and do anything about?"

Don Miller

"Maybe two," she replied hesitantly. "It seems unreasonable that any hypothetical forces in the universe would be selective to humans on Earth. This doesn't seem like an avenue that merits expenditure of vital resources. If the problem is being caused by a supreme being or beings, it would also seem pointless to expend effort to try to identify or overcome that. The two more logical areas of concentration are in realms you might know more about than we do, sir... or that you have the power to know more about if you demand to know."

She drove her point home: "It's likely the more clandestine arms of our intelligence agencies know much more about the extrasensory powers of the human mind than CDC does, and about the existence and nature of alien beings than we do. Our suggestion is that seeking input from the agencies most knowledgeable about such things might return more useful information than will come forth from the scientific and medical communities."

The President thought about his next meeting with NSA and CIA and wondered. "All right. In my two-and-a-half years as President, I've had very little discussion about those topics. I'll become knowledgeable fast." On several occasions, he had tried to have conversations about both subjects but had never gotten far. He had been led to believe government agencies had spent considerable effort in both areas and had concluded nothing of any substance was there. However, he had always felt these conversations evasive. It had never mattered much. Until now.

"What's HHS' assessment of the infertility issue?" Jamison focused on Peter Richardson.

Richardson was more reserved than usual. "We've spent most of our energy and effort evaluating public reaction under various scenarios. For the most part, we've left the scientific and medical evaluations to the experts in those fields." He glanced disapprovingly at Kursch as he spoke. "Our hope is certainly that a *natural* cause can be explained to the public very soon, within the next day or two. We don't feel that proposing a solution is as critically time-sensitive as convincingly explaining the cause."

"Peter," Jamison broke in, "Helen just told us they have nothing on a natural cause. Has your department been

125

communicating with CDC? They work for *you*. Have you evaluated public reaction under a scenario wherein we admit we simply don't know the cause?"

"Yes, sir. Our projection of public opinion based on not giving a believable explanation of a natural, scientific cause, very soon, doesn't paint a pretty picture."

"So, what *is* that picture?"

"Extreme loss of public confidence in the abilities of the Government to perform its function." Richardson directed his eyes on Kursch rather than on the President. "A dramatic and immediate surge in crimes involving black-market demand for young children. Bedlam, riots, chaos. Control of the populace would become manageable only by imposing civil obedience by force."

"Shit, Pete," Jamison rebuked him. "These are the citizens of the *United States of America* you're talking about. These are the most resourceful, ingenious, industrious people the world's ever seen. Don't underestimate their capacity to deal with catastrophe. What do you think they're gonna do? Overpower local police agencies, requiring intervention by the National Guard and military to subdue them?"

"We believe that's a possibility, Mr. President."

"So, do you have any suggestion on what I should tell these American citizens?"

"If we can buy some time, it might allow for the scientific and medical communities to solve the problem. Tell them something, *anything*, that has plausibility. Buy some time to allow our brain trusts to solve the problem."

"Do you have a suggestion for a plausible explanation?" Jamison asked disdainfully.

"Sir, everyone is well aware of the ozone problem and high UV levels. The world has never seen that problem to this extent before. The fertility issue could be an unexpected consequence of that. We think that could be believable."

"Do you think it could be *true*?" Jamison was now openly sarcastic.

"Who knows? Maybe."

The President looked at Kursch. "What would CDC think of that approach?"

Don Miller

"We have nothing to offer to back up such a claim." Kursch glared at Richardson, open disgust emanating from her expression. "We've researched that possibility in depth and found no evidence whatsoever that ozone depletion or high UV radiation levels could result in instantaneous worldwide infertility to humans, with no impact on any other species."

"*Goddammit*, Helen," Richardson exploded, "the scientific probabilities are *not* the issue here. The crucial issue is *maintaining political stability in the United States of America!*"

"How long, sir," Kursch replied indignantly, "does the Department of Health and Human Services believe the American public can be misled before their government is forced to confess the truth they've known all along? How much time can we buy? Three days? One week? Two weeks? If we can't develop a better answer than we have now, how much better off are we when our citizens discover their government has intentionally misled them all along?"

Richardson, red-faced and belligerent, shot back, "Our course *has* to be considered in terms of the best interest of the public. *Bedlam* is *not* in their best interest."

The meeting was deteriorating fast. Jamison spoke softly. "So, your suggestion, Pete, is that the United States Government lie, cheat, and do whatever else might be necessary to convince our people that things are as they are not, based on our assessment that we think that's in their best interest?"

"We know *without question* that political stability *is* in their best interest!" Richardson now displayed disregard for deference due the President of the United States.

"This is getting us nowhere," Jamison resolved. "I know the current status of information at CDC. I know the short-term recommendation of the Department of Health and Human Services. *Nothing* brought forth at this meeting is of any help to me in trying to lead our country through this crisis. That's all. This meeting is over. Keep availability in your schedules. We may need to meet again tomorrow. Jim, I need you to stay for a couple minutes."

Unlike the booster meeting last week, Chief of Staff Hollingsworth had remained silent, listening while the President led this discussion. "Yes, sir."

"Thank you, Mr. President," Richardson said as he rose.

127

"Thank you, sir," said Kursch. "I'm sorry we don't have more."

"Both of you keep your organizations running full-tilt. We desperately need a break. *Find one.*"

"Yes, sir," they replied in unison as they turned and left the office, glaring at each other.

After they had gone, the President turned to Hollingsworth. "Do you know who my 11:00 meeting is with?"

"I was told you'd cleared your schedule. I assumed there was someone you wanted to meet with after HHS and CDC, but I don't know who."

"I didn't clear my schedule. It was cleared for me. I was informed by the directors of CIA and NSA that I'm meeting with them at 11:00. Just the three of us in a secure meeting room. I don't even know where. They're to let me know what room a few minutes before the meeting."

"That's highly unusual. Do you think it's prudent?"

"I'm not sure I have a choice, which seems strange, what with me being the President. Unusual or not, this meeting might shed light on the infertility fiasco. Considering that possibility, I can't afford to balk at going."

"Do you think there's any need to increase security around the meeting room?" He sidestepped openly suggesting the possibility of threat to the President of the United States.

"No. I can't imagine a security risk to the President from NSA or CIA in the middle of the White House. Give me up to an hour with them. At noon, if I'm not out of the room, send word it's essential for you to have an immediate five-minute conversation with me. I'll come out."

"All right. Anything else?"

"Yes. Have you been told Vanessa's emergency pagers and cell phone were stolen from her bedroom last night, while she slept? They were taken without her or the Secret Service seeing a thing"

"*What?* How could *that* happen? Is she all right? When did you find out?"

"She's fine. She never had a clue anybody was ever in the room. Tallyrand called and told me about it, right before you three walked in. I can't fathom how it could happen. Tallyrand says they think it was done to let me know how easy it is to get to my family. It also speaks to me of the competence level of the Secret Service."

"I don't like any of this, Dan," Hollingsworth said, involuntarily dropping formalities. "I sure as hell don't like the infertility problem. I don't like Richardson and Kursch at each other's throats instead of teaming up. I *really* don't like a breach of Vanessa's suite – while she's in it, no less – or the President's presence being compelled at a secret, unscheduled meeting behind closed doors ... all in the same morning. *Way* too many things going awry at the same time, Dan. This isn't right."

"Hopefully, the meeting with CIA and NSA will be the beginning of the solution," Jamison replied reassuringly. "Let's meet in my private office tonight at eight to sort out the day's events and sketch a plan for an address for later this week. Thanks, Jim."

"I'll be there. And I'll get that message to you at noon if you're not already out. Thank you, sir. And be careful." Hollingsworth rose and left the Oval Office, looking worried.

At 10:57, the President's executive secretary delivered a message identifying the secure room to which Jamison was to go. Although irritated by the circumstances, he left immediately. There was an armed guard posted at the door. The guard opened the door for him and the President went in, appearing confident and in full control but feeling uneasy.

"Good morning, Mr. President." Both directors spoke in unison and extended their hands. The Director of the National Security Agency, Air Force General Gregory Carrington, squat and balding at 57 years old and wearing horn-rimmed glasses, was apparently the lead for the meeting. He said, "We apologize for the circumstances of this meeting, but we're sure you will understand the necessity after our discussions."

"Good morning." Jamison nodded coolly as he shook hands with both men. The three of them sat around the end of a large conference table.

Carrington opened the conversation. "Mr. President, you're aware the highest levels of security clearance in the United States allow access to information in topic-specific fashion. There is no level of clearance that gives anyone access to any and all classified information. The nation's most highly classified information is accessible to properly cleared individuals only as necessary for them to perform their required functions. The highest clearances – even the President's, sir – allow access to the most sensitive information only on a need-to-know basis. Most matters of international security are fully briefed to the President because the President needs to know. However, there are many instances of activities, research, or information a sitting President never gains knowledge of unless a situation develops wherein the President needs to know."

Jamison listened intently, controlling his facial features to conceal his irritation. He made no attempt to speak; neither did Carrington pause to invite the opportunity for him to respond or ask questions.

"NSA and CIA," Carrington continued, "are well aware of the efforts being undertaken by governments around the world, including the United States, in searching for a cause and a solution for the fertility pandemic attacking the human race. We *know* the cause. We've not yet devised a solution, but, be assured, one will be found. Unfortunately, the solution will require time to develop and time is not a commodity that will be available unless the world population remains under control. Maintaining that control will become a *very* delicate process.

"You are in this room because you, sir, are in the unique position of being *the individual* best suited and best situated to lead the world through the crisis that's coming. And you can't do that without having full knowledge of the issue and its background. In other words, you now need to know some highly classified information that, until now, you did not need to know."

Jamison was fuming. There was no deferential tone or manner being offered by either of these two individuals, no acknowledgement that the President of the United States was their *boss*. They acted as if they were totally in charge and he was to do their bidding, regardless of his elected office. He didn't speak but glared at Carrington, his eyes demanding, *Go on*.

"Since the inception of the Air Force, our Government has conducted extensive research related to intelligent extraterrestrial life. Through that research, we've discovered, with certainty that such life exists."

CIA Director Norman Case, tall and fit, a veteran of immersion in many CIA missions, scrutinized the President. No outward signs divulged what was going on in Jamison's head.

Carrington went on. "Everyone has some awareness of UFO phenomena. The vast majority of reported sightings are easily explainable in terms of either natural activities or hoaxes. However, some sightings have been genuine. There *is* intelligent life from other places. They have physically been on the Earth. This isn't just a recent occurrence. They visited Earth thousands of years ago. They continue to visit.

"We have communicated with some of these beings." Now Jamison flinched. "There have been periodic communications between a group of aliens and a handful Earth representatives over the past forty years. We know these aliens have a desire to inhabit the Earth. However, we also know they are committed to nonviolence. They could take the Earth forcibly, but they haven't, and they won't. They won't attempt to settle in among us, because they know we'd resort to violence against them, and they'd be unwilling to retaliate. So, they *know* they can't coexist with us.

"*They* initiated the action to stop human conception. It's their nonviolent approach to eventually inhabiting the Earth. We haven't yet unraveled the science behind it, but we will. The agencies of the United States government have limitless capabilities. Given time, we *will* fix the conception problem."

Now, Case spoke up. "Your job, Mr. President, will be to keep the American public and, by guiding other world leaders, the entire world population under civil control during the interim. While we go through the process of finding an antidote, or vaccine, or whatever it takes to fix the conception problem, *you* will be the focal point for world order. You won't have to trouble yourself in figuring out what to do. It will be figured out for you. You won't have to worry about the politics of getting re-elected. You *will* be re-elected; it's already done. You won't have to worry about other national governments being uncooperative. They'll be at your service. Your job will be to lead the populace and lead them *robustly*. You know how to do that. You can do that excellently, better than *any other person* considered."

General Carrington spoke. "Few people know what you've just been told. Those who do arrived at the knowledge over periods of months or years. You've just been smacked in the face with it. It'll take some time to sink in. I'm sure you're questioning the factuality of what we've told you. It's all true.

"Regardless of what you might be feeling, or what your inclinations might be toward honesty and openness with the American people, you *absolutely cannot* devise your own agenda for dealing with this. Hundreds of brilliant scientific and political minds, building on each other's insights for decades, have devised the course of action to be taken in dealing with alien threats. Our ultimate goal, Mr. President, is *survival of our species* in the context of civilization as we know it.

"You have to keep in mind that this is an unprecedented, volatile situation. There's as much destructive danger from within as from without, maybe more. Please, don't interpret this as a threat, sir, but no one individual, *regardless of position*, can be allowed to undermine the course of action already devised to secure the survival of our species and civilization. Any political leader who believes he or she can devise a better path than the most brilliant minds in the world over the past sixty years is simply wrong. Any such belief would be arrogant and irrational, and could not be permitted to be acted upon."

Case broke in: "Mr. President, our course, your course, has already been determined, and there's nothing any of us can do about it. Due to the extreme intricacy and urgency of the circumstances, effective this minute, your every move and every communication will be monitored. Hopefully, this control will not continue indefinitely. However, until your commitment to follow the predetermined course of action has been demonstrated to be unquestionable, any chance that you might act on your own rather than in concert with the plan cannot be risked."

Jamison listened, motionless, expressionless, fire raging within.

"We understand the personal impact monitoring will have on your private life and we apologize for that," Case said. "But we can't do anything about it. The surveillance will ease up after the election, if you've satisfactorily demonstrated your commitment. The boosted security around you will be presented as being due to the high level of civil unrest. You may tell whomever you need you're being monitored by the CIA, but you *must* say it's a result of heightened concern for your safety. You will not be permitted to speak of any details of this meeting beyond saying the topics are classified and can't be divulged. You *cannot* discuss it with your wife, Jim Hollingsworth, the military chiefs, or anyone other than Gregory and me."

Carrington took over. "We'll need to meet with you often, daily for the next few weeks. These meetings will be with you alone, without anyone from your staff present. The meetings won't take long. Ten to twenty minutes. Pass them off as meetings to discuss classified security issues. Let's set the first few meetings at the start of your day, six-fifteen, beginning tomorrow. You'll be informed of our meeting location at six o'clock each morning. Do you have any questions?"

The President finally spoke, working hard to control his rage: "My first question is exactly what you should expect. I am the President of the United States of America, the highest office in the land, the most powerful office in the world. How can two government agencies that are subservient to my office – even more, how can two individuals who *I appointed and can dismiss at will* – presume to tell me what I shall and shall not do?"

"Sir," Case responded, "the answers to those questions are more obvious than they might appear. The person filling the office of the President is transient. The office is not. The office is a powerful office. The person filling it is just a person. The same is true of the offices of the directors of CIA and NSA. There are constraints controlling what each of us can, cannot, and must do. In this particular case, the constraints placed on General Carrington and me are that we are not permitted to allow you to act on your own tangent in this matter."

"Not permitted by *whom*?" Jamison demanded.

"There are people and organizations and procedures that place constraints on us all," Case replied. "The long and short of it is you will not be permitted to go against the grain."

"And if I decide to do just that?"

"Sir," General Carrington said, "you would not survive one week, maybe not one day... and there is nothing either Norman or I could do about it. Even knowing in advance, there is still nothing *you* could do about it. Your termination would not be the doing of CIA or NSA, but you would not survive.

And, sir, that would be almost as bad as if you were allowed to survive and devise your own course of action. You – *specifically you*, with your personality, your history, and your political abilities – provide the human race its best opportunity to overcome this threat to civilization and emerge better off on the other side. Should you decide not to cooperate, it would be more than just a personal catastrophe for you and your family. It would be a disaster for the *entire human race*.

"Unfortunately, it is you and your family we must discuss next. I said you wouldn't survive a week. What I haven't said but am required to tell you is, should you take *one step* out of concert with any direction you're given, one or more members of your family would perish within one hour."

Jamison could contain himself no longer. "*You bastards!*" he exploded. "I appointed you both, and I can walk out of here and dismiss you both in ten seconds. Who in the *hell* got to you sonofabitches and twisted you into monsters that could *even conceive* of having this discussion with the President of the United States?"

Two doors away, alone in a smaller room within the secure area, listening on a headset, Brian Betz's normally expressionless face revealed a trace of a smirk. No one was more able to remain emotionless than he was. Hearing this President, so expert at controlling his own emotions, lose it was satisfying. Betz glanced out the one-way glass into the adjacent sterile room and saw two doctors in white lab coats, seated, silently awaiting their task. Betz personally witnessed only the most crucial actions of his missions. Converting the President of the United States from a strongly independent individual into an obedient servant of his organization was as crucial as it got.

Betz was positive neither he nor any of his counterparts knew the full scope of the operation that was underway. Regardless, he was certain the installation of Jamison at the center of power, and the controlling of his actions, had to be *the* major act of the scheme.

In addition to implementing control over the actions of the United States President, he had been assigned responsibility for seventeen actions around the world to obtain comprehensive information fast on unexplainable disappearances, like the two cases he had delegated to Jerome Schrader and Bill Johnson. Betz realized the actions he was taking, the things he was witnessing, and the words he was hearing, were nothing more than a glimpse into the actual state of affairs. He had no way of knowing, any more than Jamison, whether or not the claims these men were making were true or were a setup. His best guess was there was at least some truth to their claims about aliens.

The coming weeks would be fascinating, no matter what.

"Mr. President," Carrington said, adopting a more deferential attitude, "this is a very unpleasant task for Norman and me. Had either of us had any inkling when you first approached us about filling our positions that we would one day be required to have this conversation with you, we'd have both run away as fast as possible. But, that doesn't matter now. The situation is what it is. We have no choice, and, sir, you have no choice, either."

"So, how do you intend to monitor my every action?" Jamison challenged icily.

"Norman and I will escort you into the room beyond this door, where a monitoring device will be implanted under your skin. Two doctors are waiting there for you now. Your exact whereabouts, your every action, your every utterance, will be monitored around the clock. Every written document you execute will be screened before you receive it. You will not be permitted to write any of your own documents for issue without authorization. I'm sorry, sir, but there is *no* alternative and *no* escape."

"What happens, Greg, if I just get up right now and walk out the same door we came in?" Jamison asked, back in control of his demeanor.

"That door is locked, sir," Carrington replied quietly. "There's an armed guard outside. You can't get out, and no one's coming in. Sir, you don't want to see what will happen if you rock this boat. You don't want to see it on a personal level, or national level, or world level. There simply are no choices."

The conversation ceased. After thinking for a few minutes, Jamison looked squarely at Carrington and said, "This feels like a coup."

"It's not a coup," General Carrington replied even more quietly. "The same people are in control who have always been in control."

Jamison didn't respond to Carrington's statement. Finally, he said, "An address to the people is desperately needed. How do we plan that?"

"It's already written," Case said. "We'll give it to you tomorrow morning. You have more than enough to absorb for today."

"The understatement of the century," Jamison retorted.

"You have a full schedule this afternoon," Case said. "Let's get the implant done and get you on your way. I must ask if you are committed to go along with our request."

"I have no choice but to say yes."

"You understand, sir," Case continued, "how quickly we would know if you were to act or speak in contradiction to the directions you receive? You understand the ramifications of such actions?"

"Yes," Jamison replied. *What are the capabilities of the implant about to be inserted in me, the President of the United States?* "Greg, I want to ask you one question."

"What is it, Mr. President?"

"Are you aware my daughter's bedroom was broken into while she slept last night?"

"I was informed of that at eight-twenty-five this morning. I had Officer Tallyrand call you."

"Did you know this breech would happen before it did?"

Carrington looked Jamison squarely in the eyes. "No, sir."

"Was that breech orchestrated to put me in the desired frame of mind for this meeting?"

"I have no way of knowing the answer to that question, Mr. President. All I can tell you is that I had no part in it and no foreknowledge of it. However, all three of us would know I was lying if I said what you're suggesting was not possible."

Case interjected, "We need to finish our task here, and President Jamison needs to get back into circulation."

Case led Jamison through the door into the adjacent room, and Carrington followed them. The President noted the wall with the reflective glass and wondered who was watching from the other side. No one in the room spoke. The doctors began their work.

Brian Betz watched from behind the one-way glass as the delicate procedure was performed. When the doctors were done, he turned on the monitoring system using his pocket remote control. He watched as the remote device confirmed that the satellite-based system that was communicating with the implant had executed all setup routines and was fully operational. The most powerful politician in the world, the President of the United States of America, was now controlled. Monitoring Jamison and giving him instructions would be handled by the organization. Betz's responsibility from here on would be to take immediate, decisive action, should he receive orders to do so.

The tiny implant was inserted into Jamison's scalp behind his left ear in less than three minutes. No trace of it was visible. "You are free to go, Mr. President," Carrington said. "The door has been unlocked, and the guard will allow passage. Carry on with your scheduled activities for the day. Your only mention of our meeting will be that you discussed classified information with the directors of NSA and CIA that you're not at liberty to reveal. You can tell Hollingsworth you're working in concert with us to plan an address to the nation. Don't engage in any discussion with anyone about the fertility situation, except to tell them you're working with CIA and NSA, and it's classified."

President Jamison walked out of the secure conference room. *Controlled. Free an hour ago. Now, controlled. Who do I work for? What'll I have to do? Will I facilitate good or evil? How much truth was I told? Any? How much truth will I know in the days to come?*

Chapter 13
Tuesday, April 15

John and Megan had made a pact Sunday while driving up the mountain. They would not discuss Bremo the rest of the day or Monday. They would check email Tuesday. They both knew they wouldn't be able to push Bremo out of their minds, but they would at least avoid making it a topic of conversation. Tuesday, they would take a vacation day, get up leisurely, and go out for breakfast. After a relaxed start to the day, then they would check emails again and try to make sense of Bremo.

Since Sunday, they had done surprisingly well at forcing the vexing emails from their thoughts. They wished they would never hear anything more of Bremo, but they both had the ominous feeling the situation would get worse before it got better. Tuesday morning, they took a slow drive through Placitas to a small diner in Bernalillo for breakfast and made it last, not wanting to leave. Now it was late morning, and they were back home, turning on the laptop.

Among the emails, two squelched any hope for an end to thoughts of Bremo. Like it or not, those were the two that sucked them in. One was from Liz and Ben, and the other had no sender identified. Megan took a long, wary breath. "Let's read the one from Liz first." John opened it.

John and Megan,

We sympathize with your need to get away from this. We get more frazzled every day. Here's what we can say to your questions. Bremo says they contacted me for reasons like they gave you. In college, I studied astrophysics. I led a student team that transmitted messages into space. They received the messages and put me on their list to contact. They gave us a deadline of midnight, April 30, also. Instantaneous teleportation

138

is a tough one to swallow, but who knows? At this point we are certain of little. When we emailed you last, we would've said we probably couldn't bring ourselves to type, "Bremo, take us," mostly out of disbelief, but a little bit out of fear. We're no longer sure.

To bring you up to date, we received another email from Gwan Chow (Thailand). If it can be considered authentic, he's on their ship now, preparing for transport to Bremo. The email has only the best to say about them. Nothing specific. He and the others, more than fifty now, are being treated royally. The hosts, he calls them, are kind, understanding, helpful, and even playful. The email urges us to join him. He also says Morgan O'Riley (Ireland) reported the Bremo contacts to the police and, shortly after, was taken into custody by government officials and hasn't been heard from since. What little research we've been able to do confirms that. Gwan says we're in danger because of our email contacts with O'Riley.

We're still not completely convinced this isn't all a well-played hoax contrived by some group with tremendous Internet savvy. Regardless, there must be some purpose for anyone to go to that amount of effort. Real or hoax, we've become concerned about the threat to our safety. We're also concerned that our contact with you and Megan has now put you in danger. We're going to delete all emails and then destroy this computer. This is goodbye. We're closing down this email account, so please don't reply. We wish both of you the very best. Who knows, maybe we'll meet in the near future. Take care, and be very careful.

Liz and Ben

Megan was glum. "Not good."

John clicked on the other email and scrolled down to the bottom. It said it was from Patti Laurent.

John and Megan,

Our hosts passed on your request to communicate to me. I'm guessing you're wondering if all this is real and maybe wondering what convinced me to go. It's real. I'm here on the ship, but it's still hard for me to believe, even though I was only half-skeptical before I was ever contacted. I understand how inconceivable this would be for anyone more rooted in earthly realism than I am. If you find yourselves on the fence, I hope this contact might sway you to to join us.

It's exciting here. There are more than seventy of us now, and the number grows by the hour. We're being treated very well by our friendly hosts. We like them, and they like us. They look a little strange, but, in their own way, they're kind of cute.

It was hard for me to decide to disappear and leave everyone I care about and who cares about me. As soon as it's safe, I'll get word to them I'm alive and well. There were two main reasons I decided to go. First, I've always been fascinated by space and what's out here. I don't know why; I just have. I've attended UFO conventions. Some of those events offered opportunities to send messages out into space. The Bremo beings picked up on my message and put me on their list. I was probably one of their easier sells.

The second reason I went was that my life in Medicine Hat had its problems. I was engaged, but he broke it off several months ago. Jobs and money have been scarce and I lived with my mother. Not that everything was bad. I love my mother and have some friends, a couple of them very close. I just wasn't finding my life very fulfilling or promising. Now, I feel like I'm participating in the opportunity of a lifetime. Of a thousand lifetimes! I've never been so excited to be alive!

If you've checked out my disappearance story, which I'm guessing you have, you probably would like to contact my mother almost as much as I want to. I need to ask you not to do that, for both her safety and yours. I'll find a way to let her know I'm fine without leaving a trail.

I hope you decide to join us.
Patti Laurent

John closed his eyes and rubbed his forehead, slowly shaking his head. Finally he said, "Well, at least that one wasn't depressing. Neither of them makes anything easier. You know, Liz might've had a point. Maybe we should copy everything from her emails onto the CD and delete them from my laptop. And Patti's email and Sunday's Bremo email. Maybe when we get that done, *then* we'll know what to do." He tried half-heartedly at humor. "I'll try printing Patti's, but I'm guessing it won't print." It didn't.

After Megan had everything typed and saved to the CD, John deleted it all from his system. He breathed deeply. "Well, baby, what do you think?"

"I'm scared. This stuff can't be true. It *can't* be. But, how else can you explain it? What I really wanna do is throw away the computer and forget every bit of it. Decide it's ludicrous and it can't be real. Decide it for sure, once and for all, and *believe* in that decision. We could even send an email saying we're not interested and leave us alone, before tossing the computer. Do you see any way doing that could turn out bad?"

"No, not really," John replied quietly. "Unless Bremo actually exists. At least, it doesn't seem like there'd be any harm to us if we just left it behind. If Bremo isn't real, then shutting it out right now couldn't make anything worse than it's gonna be anyway... which could be pretty bad. If this infertility problem doesn't go away, and go away soon, we, especially you, could become a target. Kathy, too. *Everything's* coming apart. Fast. I guess I'm saying, if none of it's true, our best move would be to cast it out of our lives right now. Just turn it off and get rid of the extra stress. Life here will be what it'll be, danger or no." He made a brief attempt to stop with that sentence but couldn't. "*But*, in the inconceivable possibility that it might be true, turning our backs on Bremo could mean turning our backs on our best shot at an unimaginable, beautiful future together."

"Great, John," Megan said dejectedly. "How much possibility do you really think there is it could be true?"

"How much of a possibility do *you* think there is, Megan?"

"*Quit it.* I asked you first."

"*I don't know!* Half my brain says there's no possibility. *None.* The other half says there's no possibility there isn't intelligent life on other planets. More intelligent than us, and capable of doing way more than we can understand. That half says this is just as likely to be true as not."

"All right. Let's take this track. What would you think about packing up and going to Canada now? Just get out of this whole mess and start living our downsized lives right now?"

"I'm thinking that's not a bad idea at all. I'm getting more convinced by the minute the *worst* thing we could do is stay right here and keep going like we are. I'm afraid it's going to get too dangerous, maybe really fast. If Bremo is real, the Government *might* come after us. Whether it is or not, the longer the fertility crisis goes on, the more dangerous it's gonna get."

"Okay," Megan said. "Let's hold that thought and switch gears. Are we going to send out any more emails?"

"Well, we won't be emailing Liz and Ben. I don't know about Patti. I'm not sure asking her more questions helps us figure out whether Bremo is real or a hoax. Probably no more emails to her. That leaves the question of whether or not to email Bremo again. Does more emailing back and forth with them help us, or make any difference in our decision? If it doesn't, are we ready to make a decision now?"

"I don't know. I agree about Liz and Ben and Patti. I'd like to communicate with Ben and Liz. They're in the same predicament we are. But we can't. I don't know about Bremo. I'm *really* stressed out." She paused. "You know what I think?" She laid her hand in his lap. "I think we should go to bed and work on tension relief. Who knows, maybe inspiration will come."

"Good idea. Keep first things first." He smiled at her, turned off the laptop, took her by the hand, and led her to bed. The lovemaking was fast and intense, with a touch of desperation. It did indeed relieve their stress, at least temporarily. They stayed in bed for two hours, much of it napping, wrapped in each other's arms. When they were both awake, Megan said, "I think I've got an idea for our next step."

"Good. I was hoping one of us might think of something."

"Why don't we call an extended family meeting with Randy and Kathy and talk it over with them? Lay everything out in front of them. Maybe that'll make it clearer."

"Sounds good to me. I'll call Randy. We could be at their place by the time they get home from work. We can make it a pizza and aliens night. Maybe Randy can find a way to make it fun."

At 5:30, Rufus raced in the Jarretts' front door to engage in frenzy with Brady. *No signs of undue stress there*, John thought as he carried in the pizza. As usual, Brady provided the dining entertainment. After the pizza was scarfed down and Brady and Rufus had galloped off to be heard but not seen, Randy asked, "So, what's up with the family pow-wow? Did you find out Megan's having quads?"

"Hmm," John replied, "I hadn't thought of the situation like, 'things could be worse,' but maybe that's a good point of view. Actually, this damn alien stuff is getting spooky, and we thought maybe some more rational heads might do us good."

Megan had printed copies of everything from the CD, and she laid it all out on the table. It took an hour to bring Randy and Kathy up to date. After everyone had the whole picture and Megan had explained where she and John had ended in their thought process, Randy said, "I don't think rational heads'll be worth crap for this. You want another beer?"

"You bet." John looked at the women. "Too bad about those pregnancies."

Megan, ignoring him, looked at Kathy. "What do you think about all this? What would you do?"

Kathy answered slowly. "Well, crazy as this might sound, to establish a perspective, I'd be inclined to think of everything in the emails as true, rather than not."

They all looked at her, but no one said a word.

"Not exactly what you expected me to say?" she asked.

"It's not exactly what I *wanted* you to say," Megan replied. "You know, if you think it could be true, you and Randy and Brady, and your 'unborn,' would be as involved as we are. You'd have the same decision to make."

"Not quite," Randy quipped. "From everything I read, we're only invited if you guys – well, specifically, John, I guess

– decides to go. So, we don't really have to decide anything. We can just screw with you two." He grinned at her.

"Men are all jerks," she replied.

"Thank you." Randy grinned. "I pride myself on always finding the lighter side."

"I'm talking to Kathy," Megan said. "Kath, if it were you and *clunk-head* here in the driver's seat and *you* had to make a decision, what would your next step be?"

Kathy replied with no hesitation. "I'd force myself to think of it as real, try to think of everything I really needed to know, and send another list of questions. Real questions looking for real answers. Then I'd send the questions out, turn off the computer, and turn it right back on. Part of the process would be to look at their response speed and logic to a difficult list of questions. Then I'd give the four of us a couple days to think it over. Then have another family meeting and list all the pros and cons each way. After that, make the decision as a group. For me, I'd vote all or none. Keep us all together. The worst that could happen is it wouldn't be real and we'd all feel really stupid. But, at least we'd all be stupid together, each one of us just as guilty as the others, and nobody else would know. Well... maybe that's the worst that could happen. If Bremo's real, I assume it'd be better to go than to stay, but I guess there is no guarantee of that."

John looked at Randy. "Somehow, that sounded rational. So, I guess that must mean I've had too many beers."

"No. It means too *few*," Randy replied. "Unfortunately, I've had the same number as you, which puts me at the same place. It sounded rational. *Crazy*, but rational. That means the task at hand is to come up with another list of questions. This is gonna be a long night. I guess we could call in sick tomorrow. Actually, if there's a chance we might be leaving by the end of the month, I've got a bunch of sick leave I need to use up. I think I'll call in sick, regardless. You know, thinking about the whole picture, there is always a dang downside. How would we get our final paychecks? Does the space shuttle deliver mail to Bremo?"

Kathy looked at him disdainfully and shook her head. "What an idiot."

"What an idiot," Brady chirped from the living room, giggling. Rufus barked.

The mood got more serious, even for Randy, as they compiled the questions. It was after midnight when they finished.

1. Is there any sensation to the transport process: any pain, disorientation, or discomfort?
2. If we come as a group, is there any risk we could be forced to be separated at any time?
3. What would we eat and drink? Would food be similar to ours here? Would we have water? Would this be the same on your ship and on Bremo?
4. How would medical emergencies be handled on your ship and on Bremo: heart attack, cancer, or infections? What medical care would be available for delivery of babies?
5. What would time be like? Is there day and night on Bremo? How does it compare with Earth's 24-hour day? Is there a pattern of sleeping and waking hours on the ship?
6. Does Bremo have a cycle like an Earth year? Would our aging process be different than on Earth?
7. Does Bremo have land, sky, rain, rivers, and saltwater oceans like Earth? Are the colors similar to Earth?
8. Would there be health hazards to humans, such as high levels of radiation or toxins? Would there be other dangers?
9. What is the environmental condition of Bremo? Are there pollutant problems as on Earth? Are pollutants worse than on Earth?
10. What would our accommodations be like on the ship and on Bremo? Would we have private family quarters, or does everyone live in an open community? Would we find the ship and existence on Bremo comfortable?
11. Are there facilities for dogs and children on the ship? Are there any other Earth dogs or children, or Bremo counterparts, on the ship?

12. What would be expected of us? What are your plans and intended tasks for us?

13. How would we spend our time on Bremo? Would there be restrictions on or requirements for our activities? Would these be forced on us, and, if so, how?

14. Once on your ship, we would be completely at your mercy. If we wanted to return to Earth, what would we need to do to make that happen?

15. You have told us that our extended families and friends could come to Bremo if they want. How would that work?

16. What do members of your species do on Bremo? What is daily life like? Does everyone work? If so, doing what? Are there entertainment and relaxation activities? If so, what?

17. Is the life process on Bremo similar to that on Earth? Is there conception, birth, and death? How long do individuals usually live?

18. Does your species live together in family units as we do on Earth? Do you pair off with permanent mates and establish homes?

19. Is Bremo crowded with your species? Compared to Earth, are there more or less members of your species using the available space on the planet? Is there travel on Bremo similar to Earth using powered vehicles?

20. Are there other species on Bremo with intelligence levels similar to your species? How does your species relate to other species?

21. Does your species speak? Are there multiple languages on Bremo?

22. Are there social problems or challenges on Bremo? Is there significant variation in the standard of living? Are there multiple races or variations of your species? Is the entire planet governed by a single political body, or are there multiple competing nations like on Earth? Are there certain individuals or groups in charge of governing, and are they in place for life, or do the individuals serve for a period

of time and then relinquish offices to other individuals?

23. How is civil peace maintained or enforced? Are there laws or customs that are rigidly adhered to?
24. Do you anticipate having to resolve tension among humans or between humans and your species and, if so, how?

John typed the email on his laptop as the group honed in on the list. Kathy typed a copy to save on Megan's CD. "This is a pretty good list," John said as he finished typing the last question. "Are we ready to button it up and put 'em to the test?"

"Let's do it," Randy replied. "Anybody want to add anything?"

They looked around the table at each other. "It's a go," John said and hit "send." Then he turned the laptop off and powered it back up. The reply was there. Kathy read it aloud.

1. There is no physical sensation during the transport process. Although the process is instantaneous, you would feel as if you slowly closed your eyes on one scene and opened them up to another. Your physical position would not change. If you left standing, you would arrive standing. If you left seated, you would arrive seated and be supported as if by the chair you had been sitting on, although there would be no physical chair. You would feel calm, but mildly surprised.
2. Your group would never be forced to be separated.
3. Your food and drink can be anything you want, both when on our ship and on Bremo. We can pull the constituents of anything out of the contents of the surroundings, out of space, even though it seems void. We can fill a glass with water or create a steak or green beans, whatever is desired.
4. Your medical care would be much better with us than on Earth. Delivery would be painless, with no complications. We can repair internal body damage without invasive incisions. Malfunctioning parts can be repaired. Sickness is rare and easily treated.

5. Bremo has day and night, although night is brighter because we have three moons. Days are 27.2 Earth hours long. We sleep, but more intermittently than humans on Earth, usually one to two hours three to four times during the night or day. The humans who are here with us are adapting to match our sleep patterns.

6. A Bremo year is 497 days long. Our bodies do wear out. Although we have the capability to extend life almost indefinitely, we can't completely stop the physical aging process. We choose to allow the natural death cycle to continue so new life can come into being without overcrowding our planet. We remove physical pain from the death process.

7. Bremo has fewer extremes in climate and geology. Life is water-based, as on Earth. There are clouds, rain, and freshwater lakes. Saltwater oceans are smaller, constituting about half of Bremo's surface, and they are less salty. The sky is pinker.

8. We believe humans would be in no danger from radiation, toxins, or any other hazards. Conditions on Bremo would be healthier for humans than those on Earth.

9. Although Bremo is a younger planet than Earth, civilized habitation developed earlier. A few thousand years ago, our pollutants were worse than on Earth. Since then, we have cleansed Bremo's environment, and pollutant levels are now much lower than on Earth.

10. Each Earth family on the ship receives a small suite containing a sleeping space, entertaining space, a bathroom, and a dining space. Dining is also accommodated in a large community space. On Bremo, each Earth person or family will be provided living quarters about three times larger than on the ship. We believe you would find existence on the ship and on Bremo pleasing.

11. There are three Earth young and five Bremo young on the ship. There are play areas for youth and for pets, and there are education and training programs.

There are seven Earth pets on board. We have domesticated pets on Bremo but do not have any on the ship.

12. Our intentions for the humans we will transport are for them to become familiar with life and the potential for living on Bremo. The task we would request of you would be to learn to know Bremo well and then communicate your knowledge to the human race on Earth in the most expedient and effective manner possible.

13. You would spend your time on Bremo learning about the planet and existence on it. You would tour the planet in groups, with guides knowledgeable of Bremo's history, geography, geology, and society. The tours would be educational. You would be expected to be interested and learn. You would be expected to exhibit civil conduct. You would be expected not to be lazy or consumed with self-interest. Discipline is not the correct concept for control of unacceptable behavior on Bremo. Counseling is more descriptive. Much personal and societal benefit results from industriousness and from interest in others, in natural surroundings, and in life. Much personal and societal harm results from self-interest, laziness, greed, and similar counterproductive attitudes. Through counseling, it is easy to show the truth of this and, thus, convince individuals to willingly adjust behavior.

14. Should any of you desire to return to Earth, you would need only request to be transported back. If you would like to discuss options, we would openly do that. If you have made up your mind and do not want to discuss it, we would send you back at your request, immediately, if that is your desire.

15. The process of inviting and transporting family members and friends to Bremo would be similar to the process you are going through now, except, instead of communicating on their computers with us, they would communicate with you. The request procedure is the same. Any invited individual need

only type and send, "Bremo, take me," and transport to the ship would be immediate. There would be a short orientation on the ship, as you will receive if you come, and then the transport to Bremo.

16. Everyone on Bremo, except those too young to be away from their families, participates either in productive work or in receiving education for one-fourth of each day. Work is similar to service work on Earth but more effortless and more productive. We have designers, artists, health care workers, researchers, and many other service occupations similar to those on Earth. Most of our entertainment and relaxation activities involve group activities and visitation. Most of those activities are outdoors, where our environment can be enjoyed and our star's energy absorbed.

17. The conception, birth, life, and death cycle on Bremo is similar to Earth. The average life expectancy for our species is eighty-six years, which is one-hundred-thirty-three years in Earth hours.

18. Our species mate for life, usually at around the age of twenty years. Mates usually establish a home near their parents' homes.

19. Our land population density is about 80% of the Earth's current human density. Travel is common, but powered vehicles are not necessary. We walk or teleport.

20. Our species is the most highly advanced on Bremo. Many other species exist, similar to Earth. The difference in intelligence level between our species and the second most developed one on Bremo is greater than the difference on Earth between humans and other primates or dolphins.

21. We communicate vocally and have spoken a single language across the entire planet for over two hundred years.

22. There are few social challenges on Bremo. In Earth terms, we would be considered socialistic. Counseling works well for maintaining attentiveness to civic responsibility. The standard of living is

similar for all individuals. We all share in production and consumption. There are slight variations in appearance and dialect within our species over various parts of our planet, but we are all of a single race. Our entire planet is governed by a single body. Five percent of our population works in our government. That equates to about four years of each individual's life. Typically, each individual participates in governing when he or she is between fifty and fifty-five years of age.

23. We have laws and customs. Law enforcement is an outdated concept on Bremo. Individual counseling and encouragement are all that is necessary to maintain order.

24. We don't anticipate difficulties with tension among humans or between transported humans and members of our species that can't be resolved with counseling.

There was no lightheartedness left in the group.

"Unbelievable," was Randy's astounded comment. "Let's read it again."

John read it this time. When he was done, no one said anything for a few moments, all occupied with their own thoughts.

Then John said, "It doesn't seem possible the reply could've been contrived. Way too fast." He looked at Randy. "Could responses like that be automated if the system is sophisticated enough and the people behind it had thought it out well enough?"

"You mean, could they be preprogrammed responses?" Kathy asked.

"Man, what a humungous effort that would take," Randy said. "The receiving computer system would have to understand and categorize the questions and assemble responses that couldn't be just canned statements. At lightning speed. The level of sophistication would cost a fortune. And the planning and programming would be staggering. Possible? I don't know. Maybe. Not by any outfit I've ever heard of."

"I'll type the response tomorrow night and email you guys a copy," Megan said. She glanced at her watch. "It's after one. We should go home."

"When do you want to get back together?" Kathy asked.

"We fly to Ohio Thursday to see my family, and then Monday morning when we get back we drive from the airport to visit Megan's folks," John replied. "How about our place next Tuesday, say six?" Then he added, "For another night of pizza and aliens."

"That works," Randy said.

"I almost wish we could do it sooner," Kathy added.

"Aw, honey," Randy said, tempting fate, "what could *possibly* happen in one short week?"

Chapter 14
Wednesday, April 16

When Megan got home from work, she typed a copy of the previous night's last email, saved it on her CD, emailed a copy to Kathy, and then deleted the document from her computer. By then, John was home. Thursday, they planned to go directly from work to the airport for the flight to John's parents, so they packed. The President had announced a special address to the nation for 8:00, and they wanted to watch. They finished packing in time to order Chinese delivery and catch some news before the address.

The news was frightening. There were riots in Washington D.C., New York, Chicago, Atlanta, and San Francisco, as well as around the world in London, Paris, Sydney, Tel Aviv, Moscow, and Copenhagen. Police control looked like military action, even in the United States. There had been gunfire and casualties on both sides in Paris and Moscow. Everywhere, projectiles hurtled from the mobs, and police used tear gas and Tasers.

The bottom had dropped out of stock exchanges around the world. There was speculation that markets would close Friday and Monday for a four-day holiday to allow an opportunity for stability to be injected. There were reports of marginal banks recalling open-ended loans to small businesses and individuals. Consumer spending was skidding to a halt, sparking layoffs by manufacturers and retailers.

Kidnapping and selling babies was becoming epidemic in developing countries. There were dozens of reported kidnappings in the United States, from shopping areas, day care centers, and maternity wards. In New York City, three women in late pregnancy had been murdered last night and had their babies extracted in the process by individuals who knew precisely how to do it.

Invitation

As if events weren't terrible enough already, a new cause for panic was thrown into the mix. There were a half-dozen reports from around the globe of people *vanishing into thin air*. Two involved circumstances that were difficult to dispute. In Frankfort, Germany a ranking court judge and his wife and daughter had been at home watching television while their twenty-one-year-old son had been typing on his laptop in the same room, and he had evaporated before their eyes. Another case had been reported from Sydney, Australia, from a crowded Internet café where two dozen people claimed to have witnessed a couple instantaneously disappear.

The Internet was reportedly jammed with traffic on web sites related to UFO's and alien encounters. There were hundreds of videos posted of spacecraft sightings. A news segment showed several clips of faked videos to explain what to look for in identifying fakeness in Internet postings. The media slant was that fanatical believers in space invaders were having a heyday exploiting the escalating frenzy around the world. Playing on heightened levels of fear, these groups were spouting demands for governments to come clean with what they were calling a highly organized and long-lived misinformation conspiracy on space phenomena.

Further adding to the incitement of panic were fringe religious groups and charismatic personalities espousing the end of times. There were worshippers of Osiris, Isis, the devil, the sun, and a myriad of other deities, in addition to mainstream religious groups, all pointing out their own preordained signs and predicting the end would come within days.

John and Megan were astounded. The speed with which civility was unraveling was horrifying. Megan said, "I am *really* rooting for the President tonight. Somebody *has* to get a grip on this. He might be our best hope. Everything seemed to be falling into place so well after his last address. That was only a *week* ago. What *happened?*"

"It's unbelievable," John said. "I'm worried about flying home, but I'd *hate* to cancel now. Just when things should be getting really solid for us, society's disintegrating. A couple at an Internet café in Sydney, *disappearing in thin air?*" He was thinking of Liz and Ben, and he knew Megan was, too. "Can this really be happening?"

The doorbell rang, signaling the arrival of dinner. John went to get it thinking that eating Chinese delivery during this ludicrous newscast and the presidential address added one more layer of absurdity.

John and Megan watched President Jamison stand tall at a podium, looking serious, presidential, in complete control, and sure of himself. If there had been an aura of nervousness or weariness about him during his previous address, whatever might have caused it had been conquered.

"Countrymen and women," he began, "over the past several weeks, the United States of America and the entire world have been beset by a succession of difficulties and challenges, some appalling and unprecedented. Tonight, I affirm that we, the citizens of the United States, will, without question, meet the challenges and overcome the difficulties. The United States Government is working diligently with the international community and is committed to leading the way through each and every threat to our civilized existence.

"We have multiple dilemmas to resolve, and I will address each of them tonight. We have a worldwide economy that is rapidly approaching bankruptcy. We have riots taking place all over the world. We have a black market dealing in, of all things, *our babies*, swiftly expanding out of control. We have a radiation problem causing a cancer crisis. We have fanatics shouting in the streets and on the Internet about the end of times, alien invasions, demonic possessions, and vanishings. Most absurd of all, human conception worldwide has been brought to a halt.

"For the past several weeks, while research was being performed and information was being compiled and analyzed, it might have appeared that American leadership was lacking. That was not, and is not, the case. The time for action is *now*. We don't yet know every detail about each quandary, but we are in possession of sufficient hard evidence and information to initiate action while we continue to solidify our knowledge and perfect the most effective plan of attack. Americans, believe that we shall take control and that we shall begin *right now*.

"The actions we are undertaking will not come without pain. They will be forceful actions. Some will say these actions usurp the peacetime limitations of our Constitution and our American way of life. However, and it is not possible to overemphasize this fact, we *are not* at peacetime. We are at war. War that has the potential to destroy our nation and to destroy civilization as we know it. Ladies and gentlemen, the United States of America will not allow that to happen. As long as we, the American people, live and breathe, we will not allow that to happen. As long as *I* live and breathe, as the leader you have chosen, *I will not allow* that to happen.

"Today, we are beset with problems that would have been unimaginable one year ago. This is the most daunting set of evils the United States and the world have ever faced. But, let no one question our resolve. As we have proven time and time again, we *shall* overcome. We are not here to give this our best shot. Look me in the eye, America. I know you, and you know me. There will be no middle ground. We shall overcome. *Period.*

"One positive result that will rise from the battle we're about to undertake will benefit us all. We will witness the nations of the world come together as never before. We will all unite to win this war. When it's over, we will truly be brothers and sisters around the world, whether Australian, Egyptian, Chinese, Israeli, European, Indian, Russian, or American. When this war is over and won, we *will be* a worldwide brotherhood.

"Over the past month, secret planning and negotiations have been under way in Geneva involving virtually every nation, large and small, on the face of the Earth. We are all together. The vote on every action has been, for all intents and purposes, unanimous. There is no power contest between nations. We are of one mind, with one common goal. We *shall* overcome.

"I'll speak of the toughest issue first. It is inconceivable that human conception could cease overnight everywhere in the entire world. Yet, that is exactly what happened on January twentieth of this year. Conception has not occurred since that date. The problem is paradoxical. There has been no lapse of fertility in any species on Earth other than humans. Artificial as well as natural conception has halted. It's insidious.

"Through intensive research and espionage, we have identified the cause of the infertility. We are diligently pursuing elimination of this cause and making progress. We have every reason to believe that, within two months, we will achieve complete success in this effort.

"We know who caused it. Yes, I said '*who.*' *Despicable* does not come close to describing the individuals and organization responsible. But, before I delve into that, I'll explain what happened. We have discovered that every species of mammal on Earth has certain genes susceptible to specific frequencies of electromagnetic flux. Electromagnetic flux of various frequencies occurs throughout the Earth all the time, but the frequencies occurring naturally are random and varying. On January twentieth, devices called magnetic inducers, placed deep underground in thousands of locations around the globe, were activated. These inducers caused a condition called resonance for two narrow frequency bands of electromagnetic flux everywhere on Earth. One of these two frequencies causes the human egg to die upon contact with any other living organism, and the other frequency affects human sperm cells in the same way.

"It's encouraging that we've had some success with artificial insemination when conducted in specially constructed shielded rooms that block electromagnetic flux. The fix for the conception problem will require disabling all of the thousands of inducers that have been planted. In the past week, we located, unearthed, and disabled the first three.

"Now, who could dream up and carry out such a vile plan, and why? Let's start with why. Assume five hundred men believe themselves to be the best of the best human civilization has to offer. Further, assume they believe they should be the procreators of all future human life on Earth. They are convinced they should be the supreme rulers of mankind, and to them the rest of the inhabitants of the world are insignificant. They have secrecy, intelligence, time, and their own distorted sense of history and destiny that they believe to be in their favor.

"Does such a group exist? *Yes.* Who are they? They are the remnants and progeny of the upper echelon of the World War II Nazi regime. At the end of World War II, many of the most brilliant Nazis either escaped or were recruited into the scientific communities of the most powerful nations around the world, including the United States. After the war, many of these individuals kept in contact with each other and gradually gathered in the jungles of Argentina and at a secret subterranean base in Antarctica. They and their descendents have been there for decades, performing research and experimentation, developing multiple technologies to use against the world in one fell swoop. Where are these people today? Many of them are dispersed throughout the world, safeguarding their entombed magnetic inducers.

"What are we *doing* about it? The forces of every covert agency of every government in the world are tracking down these individuals and their inducers, one by one. We *know* who the people are. We *know* what they've done. Through a World Court tribunal in Geneva, all of these persons have already received their trial in absentia, and all who have been convicted of terrorism have been sentenced to immediate death. That sentence is being carried out on sight. There are no captives being taken and no interrogations being performed. The blight is being obliterated, piece by piece, in accordance with the judgment handed down by the World Court.

"In addition, top scientists and engineers all over the world are locating all sources of magnetic induction so each inducer can be found and destroyed. The solution to the infertility problem is well into the implementation phase. We anticipate one hundred percent success within two months.

"The next problem I'll speak of requires a higher level of human compassion than does dealing with terrorists. For better or worse, some of us have more heightened emotional sensitivities than others. People can be overcome by emotions generated by charismatic speakers or by aroused masses. Currently, the scale of this psychological reaction is contributing to a social environment bordering on mass hysteria. Persons caught up in emotion don't necessarily deserve to be punished. However, when emotionally driven actions or hysteria endanger public safety, it is the *duty* of government to protect the citizenry.

"The United States Government will not interfere with anyone's right to free speech or to assemble in peace. However, peacefulness *must* be the limiting factor to our tolerance level. The emotional climate worldwide and here at home has become so volatile that force must and will be used to the extent necessary to maintain order and protect the public.

"The National Guard has been activated and assigned primary responsibility for maintaining peace within our borders. I issued a directive today implementing a plan, effective at eight o'clock this evening, transferring ultimate authority at every local and state law enforcement agency to the National Guard. This plan has been developed as a contingency over the past month, and the Guard has readied itself. By midnight tonight, every law enforcement agency in the nation will be contacted by the National Guard official designated to provide direct executive control of the forces of that local department.

"This action will not supplant the local sheriffs or police chiefs across the country. They will work in conjunction with the Guard to maintain order. We anticipate virtually all decisions would be the same, whether ultimately made by local officials or the National Guard. The difference will be that local law enforcement agencies will not be limited by their current staffing levels. The primary goal of activating the National Guard in this manner is to coordinate the supplementing of manpower wherever help is needed to maintain domestic peace and safety.

"The plan stipulates that, while the right to demonstrate peacefully will be respected, there will be *zero tolerance* for violence. Wherever assemblies are gathered, sufficient forces will also be gathered to maintain peace. Individuals releasing projectiles, throwing punches, or participating in violence of any kind will be arrested immediately, forcibly removed from the premises, and incarcerated. Anyone found carrying a weapon in public, whether it is legally registered or not, will have the weapon permanently confiscated and will likewise be incarcerated.

"Incarceration will be overnight for a first offence but will carry an automatic and immediate sentence of thirty days for a second offence. Offences will be computer tracked by the National Guard. Persons incarcerated without having proper identification will be incarcerated until proper identification is produced. Incarceration will be in local cells and will *not* be pleasant. Overcrowding could occur, as well as rationing of food. If local penal facilities become full, fenced, tented facilities will be set up. Any action perceived by National Guard personnel to be life-threatening is authorized to be halted by use of lethal force. Anytime and anywhere the maintaining of control exceeds the capacity of the National Guard, the United States armed forces will be called in immediately for support.

"This action is drastic. The reaction I expect to see from the United States citizens is that demonstrations will voluntarily remain peaceful and will likely reduce in number and size. We're *all* in this together, and we *all* have a common threat against us that must and shall be defeated. Law and order *must* be maintained. And, we must all realize that the effort required to ensure domestic tranquility directly detracts from the resources and energy available to defeat our true common enemies and the dangers they have set upon us.

"I believe the American people, by and large, are patriots. Peaceful demonstration is not unpatriotic. However, under current conditions, demonstration may not be entirely safe or advisable. Your Government must maintain order. Should you become involved in a demonstration alongside one or more people who exhibit violent behavior, it's possible you may find yourself receiving the same treatment they receive, although you might not truly deserve it. I urge *everyone* to give a moment's pause before deciding to attend gatherings that could become dangerous and could detract from the resources needed to the fight for our lives and civilization.

"The next topic I'll address is the world economy. Although I am committed to free market economics, one cannot argue with the fact that severely destabilizing world events have the potential to *decimate* the global economy. It's happened before. There remain a few among us who lived though the events of nineteen-twenty-nine and the ensuing worldwide depression. Economic advisors to governments around the globe agree that the current crisis has the potential to far exceed the disaster of the depression of the nineteen-thirties. A depression of the magnitude that appears possible, if allowed to occur, could result in political chaos, the toppling of every legitimate government on the face of the Earth. The potential result would be *anarchy*, with health, safety, and life itself protected by no one – world order reduced to rule by *brute force*.

"We – you, me and all of your public servants within the Government – shall not allow that to happen. However, again, drastic circumstances require drastic action. Before explaining the actions that will be taken to prevent this denigration, I want to advocate that the day-to-day activities of the people of America and the world should carry on as normally as possible. Worldwide, jobs and incomes, as well as business financial solvency, *will be protected.*

"All major national governments are taking steps simultaneously to prevent economic collapse. All are delivering the same message to their people right now, as I am delivering to you. All stock-trading venues worldwide were closed ten minutes ago. Stock values have been frozen at their closing values for thirty days. After thirty days, controlled simultaneous reopening of stock exchanges will occur. The control will be the imposition of limitations on the percentage of change in value of every stock on any given day. Initially, the limiting percentage of change will be very small. Once that percentage has been reached for any particular stock, the trading of that stock will be terminated for the remainder of that day. Gradually the value variation limitation will be relaxed until the control is no longer necessary.

"Similarly, for the next thirty days, banking interest rates have been frozen at their current levels. New loans will be on moratorium, but so will loan recalls. For thirty days, United States banks, backed by the National Treasury, will finance the continuation of business and personal financial activity on a status quo basis. Businesses and institutions are required by executive order to continue their current practices in issuing payroll checks, with no changes in pay rates over the thirty-day period. Business, industry, and private individuals are requested to carry on with current spending patterns. After the thirty-day period has transpired, a ninety-day interval will be set aside for controlled adjustment and gradual balancing out of financial activities that occur over the initial thirty days.

"I understand how extreme this measure is, along with the other actions being taken. These actions are necessary to save this country and the world from a debilitating and potentially civilization-destroying economic depression. We cannot go *one more day* without implementing these controls. The best support that can be provided by every individual and organization across the land is to go on with your normal activities. Don't hoard, and don't try to take advantage of the situation. The more each of us carries on business as usual over the next thirty days, the less painful it will be for *all* during the ensuing ninety-day adjustment period.

"I must now speak of the most *hideous* issue we have to deal with, a problem resulting from the ugliest of human traits: greed and selfishness to the point of *utter disregard* for the lives of other human beings. The kidnapping of young children and the murder of expectant mothers for the purpose of harvesting and selling their unborn children are actions I personally am unable to come to terms with. I struggle to comprehend the willingness of otherwise law-abiding citizens to offer exorbitant payoffs for the delivery of babies to them with no regard for the methods employed to achieve such deliveries. I realize that hardened criminals exist in our society. But, how hard would a human being have to be to attack a young expectant mother, slice open her abdomen, extract her unborn child, and leave her lying prone, bleeding to death in physical and psychological agony? Although I cannot fathom how any individual could carry out such an atrocity, I can *damn well* fathom what I'm going to do about it.

"If I was not bound by due process, I would issue an executive order tonight, making this crime punishable by an immediate, unappealable death sentence. But, whether for better or worse, I cannot legally require that such an executive order be implemented. I am taking the most proactive action available to me. I've sent a bill to Congress for immediate action and have been assured that this bill will become the *number one* congressional priority. I believe this bill will become law by noon tomorrow and will become effective the following day under emergency provisions.

"Under this law, the National Guard forces being deployed throughout the nation will double every law enforcement staff in the country. The additional personnel will be on continuous patrol, with the highest priority being to watch over the safety of children and expectant mothers. The bill will give trained National Guard soldiers the authority to use deadly force on the spot if necessary to protect these mothers and children.

"In addition, the FBI will immediately be assigned every case of kidnapping or murder of expectant mothers.

Apprehending the perpetrators of these crimes will be their highest priority. The bill requires a trial to begin within two days of apprehension, by a three-judge panel or, if requested, by jury. Either way, the trial will be time-limited to an additional three days. Insanity pleas will *not* be admissible. Persons aiding and abetting will face the same criminal process and punishment. Time allotted for consideration of verdicts will be twenty-four hours. In the event of a hung jury, retrial with a new jury will begin within two days. If the verdict is guilty, the mandatory sentence will be death by lethal injection. Executions will be carried out by the National Guard within 48 hours of the rendering of the verdict. Within fifteen days of passage of this bill, every state and territory in the union will be required to have an injection facility ready. This bill is proposed to be retroactive to all such actions occurring on or after March first of this year.

"In addition, persons found illegally transferring money or other consideration in the trade of children, either to receive a child, or in any chain of transfer of a child, will be subject to this same process and penalty. However, the law would not be retroactive for these accessory individuals but instead would go into effect seventy-two hours after passage of the bill. Crimes involving transfer of value for the trafficking of children occurring between March first and the effective date of the new law will be pursued just as vigorously by the FBI, but the legal process currently in effect today would be applied to those cases.

"As much as I personally want this law to result in immediate apprehension, prosecution, and execution of persons of such immoral, evil character, my primary goal in proposing and seeking the passage of this bill is not retribution, but deterrence. My intent is that by attacking this atrocity aggressively, this criminal activity will be brought to an abrupt halt. Pursuing and prosecuting *all* parties involved in transferring consideration in the trade of children, rather than only the actual criminal perpetrators, should give all parties great pause in deciding to act against this law. And that is my supreme goal, to stop this criminal activity and stop it *overnight*."

*   *   *

Invitation

Brian Betz watched ten television screens simultaneously from his personal war room, thirty feet underground below the garage of his residence. He knew he and his twelve counterparts around the world had been instrumental where necessary to induce political leaders to act together in this coordinated effort. The top officials of all major nations on Earth were giving simultaneous televised addresses, announcing the coordinated actions being taken by all their governments.

Betz watched the ten most powerful men in the world, one on each screen. What he and all his counterparts, whoever and wherever they might be, had been instructed to look for was any evidence of weakness, any flinching, any look of uncertainty in any leader's eyes. None would be tolerated. So far, everything was coming together flawlessly. Betz was in awe of the degree of perfection to which the organization could orchestrate its magic.

Jamison was delivering his message as if it had come from the very depths of his soul, even though he'd had no input whatsoever into its content. Betz marveled at his performance. Jamison was, without doubt, the ideal choice for leader of leaders, the man who would rally the world, the central figure who would pilot the populace through the nightmare to come. The people would follow him. He would do exactly as he was told. The stratagem was a thing of beauty.

*   *   *

Jamison continued his address. "I hereby issue a directive to *all* Americans tonight to avoid creating situations wherein these heinous crimes could occur. Parents, do *not* let your young children out of your sight except under the proper care of your trusted schools and care providers. If you have children six years of age or younger or are an expectant mother, do *not* be out alone after dark. I urge you to follow this practice during daylight hours, also. Beyond that, watch over one another. Report any and all suspicious activities. Call 911 immediately if you witness suspicious activity in the vicinity of children or expectant mothers.

"I must address one more unprecedented phenomenon tonight. In the past few days there have been a handful of reports of persons vanishing instantaneously. Almost all of the cases reported have been either erroneous or fraudulent. However, I must affirm that, in a very few cases, two or three, there is factual basis to the reports.

"Covert agencies from many nations, working together, have discovered the cause. This is the work of the same Nazi group that's behind the fertility crisis. This accursed group has been experimenting for many years with chemicals that, when introduced into a human body, will result in subsequent spontaneous dissolution of the body. The chemicals spread through and saturate the cells in the body and, when a critical saturation point is reached, instantaneously dissolve all of the body's cells into their component gaseous molecules and atoms. Upon dissolution, these gaseous molecules and atoms quickly mix with surrounding molecules and atoms in the air and dissipate. Due to the surprise and unexpectedness of the event, nearly total dissipation occurs before witnesses fully comprehend that the person has disappeared.

"We don't yet fully understand the disintegration process or how the perpetrators initiate it. Yesterday, a joint international crack force raided the laboratories where the Nazis performed their research and experimentation. We now know, with *certainty*, who the responsible organization is. We also know the chemicals required for the process are rare, and the Nazi group cannot possibly have enough of it to attack more than a few people.

"The United States military, along with the forces of many other governments, is in deadly pursuit of the organization and individuals responsible for both the fertility crisis and these insidious vaporizations. Again, several of the approximately five hundred guilty individuals have been apprehended, and some have already been executed in accordance with the legal order of the World Court. We expect to have half of these individuals incapacitated within one month.

"The request I want to leave you with tonight sounds absurd after everything else I have spoken. I ask you to live the coming days and weeks of your lives as normally as you can, with the exception of being more vigilant and wary of danger to expectant mothers and children. Please, continue to go to work, worship, entertain, eat, and shop as you're accustomed to. I make this request not only from human compassion, but also in the interest of maintaining the economies of the world, the United States, your own cities, towns, and counties, and your individual families. The more we withdraw from our habitual activities over the next thirty days, the more hardship we will all incur afterward, when we tackle the process of digging out from under impact of the sacrifices made in overcoming these crises. Be assured that, working hand in hand, we *will* preserve our cultures. But also, be mindful that we can help to ease the process considerably if we strive to live normally in the meantime.

"In saying goodnight, I admit to you that I am as shaken by the events of the past days and weeks as all of you are. Many of the recent occurrences are mind-boggling. Be that as it may, these events have occurred. Our key to averting worldwide catastrophe is *'We, the people.'* *We* are the people of the United States of America and the people of the world. We *shall* overcome. Don't doubt it for an instant. *Together*, we shall overcome. You have my fervent pledge, to my dying breath. Let us meet these challenges now, head on, and *together*. God bless and save us all. Good night."

John and Megan stared at the television, dumbfounded. Eventually, they looked at each other and John breathed, "Jesus."

Megan's reply was, "Turn the damn thing off. I'm not listening to any political analysis of *that*. At least not until it's had time to sink in. Nobody could *possibly* analyze that off the cuff."

John clicked off the set. "What're we supposed to believe *now*? I must've gotten more convinced than I realized that Bremo might be real. I mean, it's probably possible this Nazi group really is out there and has the ability to stage the whole alien thing as a front. On the other hand, it wouldn't be the first time our Government put out a line of bull to hide the real facts. But, this is our President. We elected him. I *like* him. I've thought all along, as politicians go, this one seems particularly trustworthy. He's been in office for almost three years, and that's been a consistent strong point for him. But there's *so* damn much happening, and his explanations were *so* wild. I don't have a clue what to believe."

"All I know is I want to escape. Right now, I want to escape from the TV and all the talk that'll be flying around tomorrow. I want to escape from this rat race of a life and live like human beings in a place where it doesn't matter what's happening in the insane cities. I don't want to wait to move out of here. I want to pick a spot. And if it turns out that speech was all bullshit, I'd be tempted to go to Bremo. I can't believe this is all happening right before we tell everybody we're getting married. How will we be able to make this a happy time?"

"Are you worried about flying to Ohio tomorrow?" John asked. "We don't have to go."

"I don't know. The good girl in me says I should do just what the President asked. Go on with my day to day life as normally as I can. Our plan is to fly to Ohio tomorrow. That part of me thinks it's the right thing to do. My defiant side says the same thing. I'm not cowering down and living my life in fear that something bad might happen to me. But, in the end, the most important thing is this is family, and it's a big deal. We're getting married, and we're having a baby. We're probably moving to someplace where it'll be difficult or impossible to see your family. I think it's really important to make this trip."

"Yeah. Me, too. If you're still in, it's a done deal."

"I'm in."

"Okay. Tell you what. There won't be anything on TV we want to see. We *damn sure* won't be able to sleep. Unfortunately for you, you're pregnant and forbidden alcohol. Being your weak partner, and not pregnant, I'm not. I'm having a beer, and it'll probably be the first of several. Why don't you pick out one of our old favorite movies? I'm game for staring at movies all night if we don't fall asleep. Anything to keep my head occupied. If we're awake all night and don't feel like going to work till nine or ten, we'll call in and go late. Or just screw it and don't go at all. I'm sure we wouldn't be the only ones staying home."

"Done," said Megan, opening the DVD case.

Chapter 15
Friday, April 18

Rays of early-morning sunshine streamed through the east bedroom window between the lower half-curtain and the valance as John's eyes drifted open. He always felt nostalgic when waking up in his old room. This was the third trip he had made home with Megan, and sleeping in this bed, in this room, with a girl lying by his side, added a twist of waywardness to the feeling. He grinned, rolled over to Megan, and snaked his arm around her. She stirred and pressed her back against him. After a few minutes she turned to him. "Sleep okay?"

"Like a rock." He kissed her on the nape of her neck. "You?"

"Great." She smiled. "We were exhausted."

Wednesday night, after watching the President, they hadn't drifted off to sleep until after 3:00 a.m. What little sleep they got had been fitful. They had gotten up before 5:30 Thursday morning and had showered, picked at breakfast, and loaded their luggage in plenty of time to arrive at work early. Neither of them had looked forward to facing the din they expected at work. Regardless, even though feeling like zombies, they had been unable to sleep in and had felt more obligated, more pulled by a sense of duty, to go to work than either could explain.

Their workplace atmospheres had not been what they had expected. Like John and Megan, everyone seemed to want to avoid a gossip fest. There had been virtually no talk about the President's speech. Moods had been somber, but kind. It was as if everyone was steeling up resolve to move forward into whatever their families, the nation, and the world might face in the days and weeks ahead. There had been no grumbling about politics, no moaning over shrinking retirement accounts, not even any bitching about the unusually stormy weather or the price of gas. There had been no negativism. It had been a most unusual and unexpected aura.

In a brief phone conversation from the airport Thursday evening, Randy had said he and Kathy had experienced similar ambiance. John had gotten the same feeling from his mother when he'd called her in the morning to tell her they were still coming. She had expressed only slight concern for the flight and had been happy they hadn't cancelled.

Activity and attitudes at the airports had been a continuation of the calm, kind, and professional experience of the day. The flight left on time in spite of the heavy rain and arrived a few minutes early in Columbus. One of their topics of conversation on the flight had been their wedding. The Memorial Day weekend gathering they had looked forward to would be scrapped. They'd never even gotten the pleasure of telling anyone of that plan. They would have a private wedding sometime before April 30 with three witnesses, Randy, Kathy, and Brady – and maybe Rufus. The late-night arrival, their lack of sleep, the full day, and the psychological upheaval of the past 30 hours had congealed to exhaust the two travelers by the time they landed.

Despite their fatigue, the reunion with John's mom and dad at the airport was spirit-lifting. His mother, Clare, looked matronly at 59, six inches shorter than John, her brown hair streaked with more gray than he had noticed before. Clare's hazel eyes were shining with love, her face a picture of contented happiness. His dad, David, two years her senior, displayed a middle-aged paunch and thinning white hair. John's deep blue eyes were inherited from him. David had the air of a businessman whose success derived from both competence and charisma. John was surprised by how good it felt to see their broad smiles and hug them. Megan was greeted as one of the family, and John could see the warmth in her eyes.

They talked of friends and family during the forty-five minute drive to Circleville. Clare asked Megan about her family. They talked of Randy, Kathy, Brady, and Rufus. John and Megan got the scoop on his brother's and sister's families.

When they arrived at the big, square two-story home, John and Megan carried their bags in, set them down at the bottom of the staircase and shared in another group hug. "Boy, I can't tell you how good it feels to be back home with you," John said.

"It feels even better to us, having you both here," replied David grinning happily at them. "We're especially delighted to have Megan back!"

"Well," John said, "as much as I'd like to stay up all night visiting, it's way after midnight, and we're beat. We're gonna hit the sack and look forward to breakfast and a day of catching up."

"We love you both," Megan added, initiating another round of hugs. With that, goodnights were said, and John and Megan hauled their bags upstairs to John's old room.

John's dad was one of five partners in the most prominent accounting firm in town. His mom had taught second grade for the past twenty-four years, since John had started school, and still loved teaching young children.

His brother, Clay, six years older than John, had always been the rock-solid big brother, successful at everything. John had always looked up to Clay and, in his younger years, had tried to follow in his footsteps. However, things had never clicked into place for John as easily as they had for Clay, with the most notable example being the Miranda disaster. Clay and his wife, Marsha, had enjoyed a great relationship from the start that had only gotten better with time. Clay was Vice President of Investment Accounts at a Columbus-based bank with subsidiaries and branches in nine states. Marsha taught twentieth-century history classes two nights a week at Ohio State. Their two sons, Ricky and Josh, were six and two, and were perpetual motion machines requiring constant surveillance.

John's sister, Lisa, and her husband, Charlie, were settling into the new house they had just built. Lisa was four years older than John and had always been the mischievous child in the family, exercising her own mind when it came to following the guidelines Mom and Dad established. She had never been spiteful, always loving, but more interested in experiencing life than following rules. She had been only nineteen when she and Charlie had wed after a two-year high school passion.

Charlie was a year older than Lisa and had a year of college behind him when they had married. They had both worked their way through college, struggling with time and finances and, at times, with each other. Regardless, they had stayed together, and their relationship had grown stronger and interdependent by the time they'd reached their thirties and their daughter, Tyler, had arrived. Charlie had completed medical school and was now employed in the medical research department at Ohio State. Lisa was a newspaper editor for the Circleville Herald. Tyler was just past one year old, toddling, and irresistibly attracted to any object within reach.

John and Megan felt well-rested for the first time this week as they lazily rolled out of bed. John felt lighter, and he could tell Megan did, too – as if everything weighing them down had been left behind, in Albuquerque. He eyed his bride-to-be and smiled. "You know, that skinny little bod of yours is developing a bit of a pouch. It's a good thing we didn't wait another week or two to come home. Our secret would have escaped before we said a word."

She grinned back at him. "That little pouch is gonna get a lot bigger before it goes away. What do you think your folks'll say about this out-of-wedlock mishap?"

"They'll jump for joy. I'm sure they'll be real happy there's a wedding in the works, but with what they've seen me go through, they'll be ecstatic to see my life finally falling in place. They love you. You're perfect for me, and they see that plain as day."

"Okay, you can lay off now. It's almost eight-thirty, I'm already out of bed, and I'm sure your mom has breakfast on the stove, just waiting for our first sign of life. I'm *not* jumping back in the sack with you, and your schmoozing isn't going to sway me."

"Oh, yeah?" he retorted, darting toward her across the room. She squealed and skirted out the door, down the short hall, and into the guest bath. By 9:00, they were both showered and dressed and descending the stair to the homey aroma of bacon, eggs, toast, and coffee.

"It sure smells good down here!" John said. "Breakfast just like Mom used to make."

"Your mom can still work her old magic," Clare replied.

"That's great! And I get to be the beneficiary," Megan chimed in.

"Well, you know, *I* did all the *real* work," David added. "I gathered the eggs, made the bread, and slaughtered the pig, all before seven."

"Uhuh," Megan replied dryly. "Now I know where John got his implacable honest streak."

"Yup," David said, "everything that boy got, he got from his ole dad, including his good looks and boss build."

Clare cheerfully served breakfast as they enjoyed visiting. After breakfast, they sat and talked over another round of coffee.

"Well," John said eventually, "we *do* have a little news for you."

"Do tell," said David while Clare's eyes sparkled in anticipation.

"There's gonna be another wedding in the family." John beamed, watching them.

"*Well, hallelujah!*" Clare cried out, jumping up and rushing to Megan to sweep her into a bear hug.

"Wait, there's more," John said. David was grinning broadly, looking as if he already knew what was coming next. "You get another grandkid in the deal."

Clare was already wiping tears. "You have no idea how much I've been hoping for this. You two are *perfect* together. I don't even care about the order of things. I should, but I don't at all. I'm just happy for you."

David was up and hugging them both, too. "She's also a bit happy for herself, in case you couldn't tell. You know she has a soft spot for grandkids."

"Now, that's a *huge* understatement, Gramps, and you know darned well your soft spot is *every bit* as big as mine!"

"Before we all get too carried away, I have some more news that isn't quite as fun," John said. "There's so much crap going on in the world that we feel we have to do something to protect our new family. We're really concerned about ozone and radiation. Also, unless things change fast, just being seen pregnant or having a small child, could get dangerous. We've been thinking about moving to the boonies, somewhere away from the rat race, somewhere not so prone to cancer and violence."

"I'd be thinking the same thing in your shoes," David said. "If this means it would be harder for us to visit, that'd be painful, but it might be the smart thing to do. Where would you go?"

"We're still researching," John replied, "but there are a ton of small towns in northwestern Canada that might fit the bill."

"I'd guess most of them don't have a lot of jobs for telescope engineers or nurses," David posed.

"They can probably use nurses everywhere. They might not get paid much, but Megan could probably find work if she wants. And yeah, I might have to learn a simpler trade, but that'd be all right. In fact, I'd kind of look forward to it."

"You know, when it's all said and done, I might be envious of you," David said.

"Let's talk about that for a minute." John took advantage of the opening. "When Megan and I get carried away, talking or dreaming about it, we wonder, if it turns out to be a good place, a happy place, if we might be able to entice our families to join us."

"Wow, John," Clare said, "when you come home, we really need to brace ourselves. It'll take a few days for all this to soak in. You know wherever you two go with my grandchild, just the fact that you're there would be half the enticement I'd need. How soon do you think you might move?"

John winced. "It could be within a month. It's possible we could be in a pretty remote spot. We've been talking with Randy and Kathy, and they might go, too. You know, Kathy's six months pregnant, so they might be in more danger than we are."

"Yes, they're probably very concerned right now. Speaking of being pregnant, I guess you guys just beat January twentieth?" David queried. "Not that I'm prying. It's just that right now, everything seems so ...." he trailed off, seeming unsure of how to finish the sentence.

"That points to part of our concern, Dad. It was January nineteenth. If you can believe the crap we're being told, our baby's scheduled to arrive on the last day of births. We don't feel a bit safe about that."

"What in the world is *happening* on this Earth?" Clare blurted. "How can all this even be possible? It just seems like what they're saying can't really be true. *Surely* they'll get it fixed fast, like President Jamison said."

"All the trouble going on, along with some problems at work, has made the past two weeks pretty tough for us," John said. He and Megan had wrestled with how to explain the danger their communications with Liz and Ben might have created. They had agreed discussion of Bremo was out of the question and had settled on a vague white lie. They would insinuate that John and Randy were involved in a secret project at Optical Systems that couldn't be discussed but was putting them at risk.

"Megan and I wanted to try our best to avoid thinking about all that while we're here. I don't think either of us has been very successful so far, but we want to have a great time with everybody. We probably can't completely avoid talking about some of the issues, but we'd like to stay away from television and the news.

"We – Randy and Kathy and us," John continued, "aren't sure how tough things might get in the next few weeks. There's a chance we might leave on short notice. I don't want to worry you, but we could just disappear, and you might not hear from us for a few weeks. We'll be okay, and we'll contact you as soon as we can and fill you in on everything. The longest it would be till you'd hear from us would be two months."

Clare's alarm was plain on her face. "There's more going on than you're telling us. You guys aren't in trouble, are you?"

"No, we aren't in trouble, but, yes, there's more going on for us than everybody else has to deal with, if you can believe that. Unfortunately, I can't talk about it. I've already said more than I'm supposed to. Whatever happens, keep the faith. We'll be in control and okay, and will be in touch. Don't worry about us. We won't let more than two months go by without getting in touch."

David looked worried, too. "What can we do to help? Will you need money?"

"No, we'll be fine. The one thing you might do, if it happens this way, is think about whether you would join us if we say we've found the most perfect place in the world to live. I'm pretty sure we'll be making that invitation. Before this weekend is over, I'll bring up the possibility of moving to Clay and Marsha and Lisa and Charlie, too."

Megan had been silent, watching everyone. Now, she spoke up: "I think that's enough heavy stuff for now. Clare, would you like to come over here and greet your newest grandchild?"

"I'd love to," she said, eyes watering.

Megan took Clare's hand and placed it on the little bulge in her abdomen. "It isn't big yet, but your grandchild is right there."

The rest of the day's conversation was lighter. They retrieved old picture albums and led Megan through John's childhood. They played cards. They sat outside on the covered porch and sipped iced tea and beer. They went to a restaurant for dinner and enjoyed steak and seafood. Not once did they glance at a TV or pick up a newspaper. Although they all thought about these things, not once did they speak of moving to distant places, or of a world without babies, or of threats to their lives.

Chapter 16
Saturday, April 19

The gang began arriving shortly after 9:00 Saturday morning. John and his dad were playing chess on the expansive covered porch overlooking the tree-canopied backyard. David had just put John in check when Clay, Marsha, and the boys pulled in, and the game came to an abrupt halt. Clare and Megan were hurrying out the back door by the time the boys were unbuckled. Out the youngsters scrambled. Ricky yelped, "Uncle John! Aunt Megan!" as he raced toward John, followed by Josh toddling as fast as he could go, "Papaw! Mamaw!"

"Hey, buddy!" John said, catching Ricky in a bear hug as he jumped up on the run. "Where's your bat?"

Ricky didn't bother to answer. The hug was done, and he pushed down to run and greet Megan. "Aunt Megan, Aunt Megan! Here I come!" The "Aunt" was Ricky's personal contribution. He and Megan had instantly fallen in love on her first visit to Circleville over a year ago. She had tussled with him and, even though she'd been introduced as just Megan, Ricky had immediately tagged "Aunt" in front, to Megan's embarrassment. It was old hat by now, and besides, it would soon be true. Ricky bowled into her, attempting to knock her to the ground. Megan played along, and the two sprawled in the grass. Meanwhile, David had scooped up Josh and the two were tickling and poking each other. Clare was beaming.

Clay and Marsha reached the group well behind the boys, laden with child paraphernalia. John wrapped an arm around each of them and squeezed. "It's amazing how much these kids change in six months. Look at Josh, even Ricky."

"You miss a half-year, you miss a lot," Marsha said, smiling warmly. "It's wonderful to have the two of you back."

"It's great to be back." John reached out to Josh, who was wriggling in Grandpa's grasp. Josh let out a yelp and stretched his arms out to John, seeming to remember the teasing and play they had shared on the last visit. John drew him in, gave him a hug, and set him down for a game of tag.

A few minutes later, Lisa and Charlie arrived. John and Megan marveled at curly dark-haired little Tyler. On their last visit, she hadn't been crawling yet. Now, with a little assistance from a supporting hand, she showed off her walking abilities, her wide brown eyes bright and her round face gleeful. She and Lisa made their way as quickly as her little legs could stagger to Grandma, where she was immediately lifted up into a loving squeeze.

Megan and Ricky were still frolicking, but Josh and John's game of tag had expired, and John was carrying Josh. As he took in the scene, a thought whisked through his brain: *How could I possibly leave this behind?* In the middle of a rollover, Megan's eyes met his for an instant. He could tell she knew exactly what he was thinking.

There was little adult conversation during the morning. Ricky's favorite games were set up on the porch, and he constantly had one member or another, usually Megan, playing one of them or a round of catch under the shade of the huge, blooming crab apple trees. Josh bounced from lap to lap, keeping two of the adults busy most of the time. Clare toyed at preparing lunch but mainly concentrated on toting Tyler around, leaving most of the fixing to others. Clay and Charlie tended the grill while Marsha and Lisa prepared a salad bowl, a cheese and cracker tray, and an assorted fruit mix. By 12:30, lunch was on the table in the screened-in portion of the back porch, and everyone was ready for it. John and Megan saw that picnicking with three young kids was great fun but didn't promote talk of anything except the kids. That was just fine with them. It felt great.

By the time lunch was consumed and the dishes were cleared and cleaned, Josh and Tyler were worn out and napping. Even Ricky was tuckered out, lying back in a chaise lounge, eyelids drooping. For the first time of the day, all the adults were sitting around the table, free of demands, each with a favorite beverage in hand.

Clare couldn't contain the secret any longer. "Okay, John and Megan, it's time to spill the beans."

All eyes turned expectantly to them. Megan watched John, her eyes gleaming. John looked at his mother and said, "*What* on earth are you talking about?"

She threw a dish towel at him, trying to look stern, although her eyes were dancing. "You'd better start talking, or *I will.*"

"So, what would be any different about *that*?" Everyone grinned at the banter. "Oh all right, all right, I'll come up with some kind of story to entertain everybody. Let's start with this. You've all met Megan, here. Well, I've known her for a while now, and she seems like a decent kind of girl. And she seems ripe for male leadership."

Megan rolled her eyes. Everyone else, except Clare, was chuckling. "Oh, *cut the crap!*" Clare blurted. "They're getting *married!* And I have to say, I'm concerned for Megan and what she'll have to put up with. But, I intend to make darn sure the rest of the family makes up for all *John's* shortcomings." She glared reproachfully but lovingly at John.

The table broke out in cheers and congratulations, everyone welcoming Megan into the family. John got up and put an arm around Clare. "Now, did you really mean all of that nasty stuff you just said about me, your youngest and most loving child? You're breakin' my heart."

"Well, you've gotta admit, you *are* taxing. But, like your father said last night, we all understand where you got it from, and we love you anyway." She smiled up at him.

John looked around and said, "Oh, by the way, there's a bit more news. Megan's three months pregnant. I realize the order of events might create a question or two, but we're pretty sure it's mine."

"*John!* You're an absolute *rat!*" Clare punched him in the gut.

Lisa chimed in, "*Megan*, throw him back, before it's too late! Don't go through with it."

"I'm afraid it's already too late," Megan answered. "I'm thoroughly hooked. You're all gonna be stuck with me."

"I don't know," Lisa replied. "Unfortunately, I think *you're* the one who got stuck." Then she murmured, feigning bashfulness, "No pun intended."

They spent the next half-hour in lively conversaticn, catching up on each other's lives over the past few months. Much of the talk was about the kids. Everyone avoided the subject of current world events. No one wanted to be the first to mention any concern for the safety of Megan and her baby. The effort to avoid those topics added a touch of strain to the conversation.

Eventually, John brought it up. "There *is* something else I want to mention. We haven't talked about all of the crap going on in the world, and I like it better not talking about it. But, it does impact Megan and me, and there are a couple of things I need to tell you. I'm sure you all watched the President Wednesday night. It's hard to know if what he said about everything's really the way it is.

"Anyway, it seems like there've been no new pregnancies since late January. Right now, the so-called civilized world doesn't appear to be the safest place for pregnant women, babies, or anybody else. We're pretty sure, real sure actually, that Megan conceived on January 19. That makes our baby possibly one of the last that would be born if things don't change before then.

"On top of that, there are some other issues we and our friends, Randy and Kathy, are dealing with, stuff at work, that make our situations worse than most. We've decided the four of us are probably going to dump civilization and move to a more remote location, some place where our families will be more protected from radiation and other threats.

"Here's the thing," he continued. "We're still researching the safest, best locations to raise our families. We might choose a small town in western Canada, but we haven't decided for sure. We'll probably make the move soon, maybe within a month. I guess what I am asking you all to think about is, if it turns out we think it's the best move we ever made, we'll invite you all to join us."

Everyone stared at John. After a minute, Clay asked, "What kind of stuff from work? Are you guys in danger because of something you're working on? You really think you'll quit your jobs and move away? That soon?"

Lisa asked, "Is there anything we can do to help or make it easier?" She was talking to John and Megan but looking at her mother, her concern showing.

"We talked to Mom and Dad yesterday," John said, "so it's not quite the surprise to them it is to the rest of you. We're not in immediate danger. The issues at work aren't cloak-and-dagger, but it *is* classified, so I can't really talk about it. Besides, our main reasons are radiation and the jump in child black market crime."

Marsha looked at Megan. "Honey, are you okay with this?"

"It was a joint decision. Not that I wouldn't follow John anywhere, or for that matter, that he wouldn't follow *me* anywhere, regardless of how chauvinistic he might act. Deciding to move was hard for both of us. I've been watching John this morning and last night. I know he's wondering if he'll be able to do it. I also know how much he loves me and wants his own strong family and how committed he is to providing the safest and best life he can for us. We agree our lives won't and can't be about money. It'll be about family. And that doesn't mean just the little piece of family we create. It's also about the families we come from. That includes all of you and my family. You all made us who we are. We love you all. We don't know where we'll be in five years, but our greatest hope is, wherever we live, we'll all be together."

John picked up the conversation. "There's more you should be prepared for. It's possible that, when we move, we might go on the spur of the moment, without contacting anybody. I told Mom and Dad last night not to worry about us. We'll be in control. But it could be as long as two months that you won't hear from us or know where we are. If that happens, don't worry. We'll be fine. And I promise, we won't be out of contact for longer than two months."

"*Damn*, John," Charlie broke in. "What the hell's goin' on?"

"Randy and I both work for the same company. Kathy works for a government consultant. Things are happening that could impact us that we can't talk about. All I can say is it could become important for us to get away from these situations."

"You say you aren't in danger and we shouldn't worry, you'll be fine," said Clay. "Then you say you might need to *get away* from somebody or some thing, maybe like the *Government*, and you might be out of touch for two months. Somehow, that doesn't sound all that safe."

"Well, look around," John replied emphatically. "We don't have enough ozone right here, and it's causing cancer. We can't even be outside without being smothered with sunscreen. Children are being kidnapped – from *hospitals*, for God's sake – and pregnant women are being cut open and left to die in order to steal their unborn babies. Both of the girls are pregnant. We aren't safe *anyway*. Unfortunately for the four of us, we just have an added factor, and we plan to deal with everything in one fell swoop.

"In some ways, Jamison's explanations sounded plausible, and maybe things *will* get better fast," John continued. "In other ways, it sounded far-fetched. Megan and I haven't picked up on much news since the speech. Actually, we've avoided TV and newspapers, trying to not spend every minute dwelling on how bad things are or might get. But, we are interested in hearing what you guys think about it all... what you think about everything Jamison said. Marsha, you teach history – what do you think? Is it really possible a group of holdover Nazis could be behind the madness?"

"Well," Marsha responded, "his claim that a few hundred Nazi extremists and their progeny carry on a secret faction, with lots of money and scientific prowess behind them, is certainly possible. People who know more about that than I do have been arguing the same thing for years. Several of the highest Nazi officials disappeared without a trace when Germany went down. There's always been speculation about a covert, advanced Nazi organization in Argentina and in a subterranean refuge in Antarctica.

"The Third Reich's most secret weapons development projects were controlled by a guy named Hans Kammler. The last known photograph of him was taken in nineteen-forty-five in Prague, in front of a huge German freighter plane, preparing for flight. No trace of Kammler or the plane exists after that. They just disappeared. He was hunted after the war, but he was never found.

"The Nazis were fanatics about protecting their weapons development secrets. There's a theory that their most important secrets, including documents on a super aviation propulsion system and advanced aircraft, were transported by long-range aircraft to Argentina. The propulsion system supposedly utilized magnetic field systems, and the advanced aircraft involved flying saucers.

"Other high Nazi officials who some say escaped include Martin Bormann and Josef Mengele. And a lot of top Nazi scientists were recruited by several countries, including the United States and Russia, at the end of the war. Operation Paperclip brought the cream of Germany's rocket scientists and engineers, over a hundred of them, to the United States.

"Kammler's top assistants working on his most secret projects included Wernher von Braun, who became the top scientist at NASA and then Director of the Marshall Space Flight Center; Walter Dornberger, who became a vice president of Bell Aerosystems Company after his days at NASA; and Kurt Debus, who became Director of the Kennedy Space Flight Center. The Nazi allegiance of these guys and the other space exploration scientists imported under Operation Paperclip has always been questioned by a lot of people."

Marsha went on as the others listened, awed by her knowledge of the subject: "The President's claim about a secret Nazi group capable of doing extensive damage to civilization is plausible. Whether or not it's true is hard to know. Not everybody is convinced, but it appears the majority of the public is buying into the President's story. A tremendous wave of anti-Nazi sentiment surfaced Thursday and is sweeping the world. If you think we're not safe here, I'll bet anybody known to be a Nazi is crapping his drawers, especially those in the popular Neo-Nazi movement. That movement doesn't even have any connection to a bona fide surviving hardcore Nazi faction, but the average person doesn't know that. Those people have to be running for cover.

"Is the scenario Jamison painted true? Well," Marsha summarized, "I'm not privy to Government secrets, but as for me, I'm not convinced. At least, not yet."

No one spoke for a minute. Then Megan asked, "You're saying you don't think President Jamison is being *honest* with us?"

"I guess it sounds unpatriotic at a time like this to say it like that," Marsha replied. "I'd put it more like this. The American public hasn't always received the straight scoop from our political leaders. There've been national security concerns that required discretion in disclosure. There've been people or groups, at times, who've had more power than the President and who controlled messages delivered to the public. There've been times when the President was only aware of part of the total story, when he was intentionally kept uninformed about some particulars of a given situation. In circumstances like that, the public has been told what the President believed to be true. It just wasn't. And, of course, there have been times when presidents have just plain lied to the public to advance or protect their own political or personal interests. It's well-documented that all these scenarios have occurred many times in the United States over the past two hundred years.

"In forty-five, Truman told the American public Hiroshima was a military base and we dropped the bomb there to minimize the killing of civilians. That was a *blatant* lie to mislead the public about the humanitarianism of his decision, if dropping the bomb really was his decision. And who can forget Richard Nixon in seventy-three saying, 'I have never obstructed justice,' and 'I am not a crook'. Lies *under oath*. In eighty-six, Reagan said, 'We did not trade weapons or anything else for hostages, nor will we.' What really happened was that he approved the sale of over two thousand anti-tank weapons to Iran in return for promises to release those American hostages. And, of course, Bill Clinton's good ones. About the Vietnam draft, he told the Washington post in ninety-one it was just a pure fluke that he was never called. Actually, he did receive an induction notice and pretended to join the ROTC to evade it. And the whole world knows his most famous lie from ninety-eight: 'I did not have sexual relations with that woman, Miss Lewinsky.' *Bald faced lies*. Even Kennedy, in sixty-one said, 'The United States intends no military invasion in Cuba.' The next day, an American pilot was shot down on a bombing mission over Cuba and Castro *froze the pilot* to prove to the world what happened.

Invitation

"Anyway, could something like that be happening now? Could the President be misleading, even lying, to us? It's happened before."

John winced. "That isn't exactly a confidence booster, Marsha. But it is impressive you can just rattle off facts like that, even if you do teach college."

"Unfortunately, it's realism," David weighed in. "There are also doubters about where the national and world economies are headed. Locking up worldwide financial markets and stock trading is so unprecedented it would've been *inconceivable* a month ago. It's possible some markets might never recover. Many, maybe *all*, stock exchanges could be completely closed out of existence by the end of the year, unless they get artificially supported by some faction.

"I don't know who that faction could be," he continued, "but my guess is, three months from now, we might have a pretty good idea. It's possible a year from now the entire world economy could be controlled by a handful of very rich and powerful individuals. And it'd be anybody's guess what they might do with all that wealth and power. Clay, what do you think? What's banking's take on it?"

"About the same as yours," Clay said. "Whether or not a controlled adjustment period could return us to normalcy after thirty days of total control depends on how much change in wealth distribution occurs in the thirty-day period. If auto manufacturers, retailers, the housing industry, and other segments of our economy are forced to continue their current cash outlays for thirty days without anybody buying their product, which could happen, the financial blow to many companies and whole industries could be fatal.

"It's possible the banking system worldwide could be dragged under and never recover. The result could be like Dad said. The national and world economies might not survive unless artificially supported by an inconceivably wealthy group, who would then become inconceivably powerful. From where I sit, that's a possible outcome.

"There appears to be nothing the banking industry can do about it," Clay continued. "Before eight o'clock Thursday morning, every bank in the country had been served legal notice by the Federal Government that it couldn't change operating

184

hours, had to honor all withdrawal and transfer requests, couldn't change interest rates, and couldn't recall loans. We've been informed federal banking service teams will arrive at the main offices of every bank in America Monday morning. Their charge is to ensure that all banking actions comply with all provisions of the temporary emergency regulations. So, as of Thursday morning, all decision-making power of every bank board of directors in the United States was usurped by the Government.

"But, who knows? Maybe this *really is* the best option. Maybe it'll all turn out fine. It's impossible to know. Apparently, for the next thirty days, I'm at least guaranteed my position and salary. During the ninety days thereafter, I don't expect drastic changes, but that's less clear. The only sure thing is that *all* control has been wrested from us. I tell you, John, when you talk about getting away from civilization and inviting us, you might be surprised how tantalizing that proposition might be to Marsha and me. The hardest part for us could turn out to be waiting these two months you're talking about."

Clare joined the conversation. "Well, I'll say one thing for *sure* about that. If you guys all go, you won't see Grandma and Grandpa staying around here by ourselves."

"That *is* heartening," John said. "Whatever happens, we'll do our best to get in touch with you as soon as we can. But, please, don't get worried if it takes the whole two months. Charlie, you work in medical research. What do you think about Jamison's explanations about infertility and vaporization?"

Charlie looked nervous. He glanced at Lisa and hesitated before speaking. "Thursday morning, every member of the Ohio State medical research staff was notified that mandatory attendance was required at a one-thirty video conference. And they were serious about meaning everyone. Anybody who wasn't at work that day was called in. Anyone out on travel, or even on vacation, was contacted and told where they had to report to attend the video conference.

"The whole first hour of the meeting was spent distributing non-disclosure forms to everybody and getting statements signed and collected. They told us we were about to receive information impacting national security, and we were required to sign the declarations on the forms. The forms stated disclosure of anything related to the video conference was an act of treason against the United States, and anyone disclosing any information would be prosecuted. Everybody was required to sign that we understood the statements and that we would not disclose any information."

"Jesus, Charlie," David said incredulously, "don't say anything else."

"It doesn't really matter," Charlie said. "I've already disclosed. I told Lisa everything."

"That's different," Clare said. "She's your *wife*."

"No, it isn't. They made it absolutely clear the restriction on disclosure included everybody. Parents, brothers, sisters, even spouses."

"So, how many people refused to sign and got up and left?" John asked.

"Not an option." Charlie paused. "We were told no one could leave, and everybody was required to sign. There were *armed guards* at every exit. Each signature had to be witnessed by the person in the next seat with full names, addresses, and social security numbers printed for each person and each witness. After all of the forms were collected and signatures were verified, we were treated to a film detailing the criminal prosecution process and punishment for treason."

"*Charlie, stop it!*" Clare cried. "We don't want to hear any more."

"What? You think I'm worried one of *you* will turn me in? You'll all be *way* more careful to keep it to yourselves than I will."

David looked sternly at him. "Charlie, we don't want to hear more. If anything happened to you, every one of us would think we'd let something slip."

"Okay. I won't tell you anything they said. I *will* tell you a huge effort was made to gather every medical researcher in the country to listen to the Secretary of Health and Human Services. I'll also tell you some mild personal opinions I have relative to human infertility and vaporization. Just speaking my opinions can't be treason.

"There's never been much, if any, research on either issue. I'm sure there was no suspicion in the medical community before this year that either worldwide human infertility or human vaporization was even possible. I doubt if any qualified medical research organization that isn't government controlled is legitimately researching either of these issues even *now*. Personally, I'm not convinced infertility is related to magnetism or instantaneous vaporization can happen."

"Thanks, Charlie," John said softly. "None of us need to know any more than that."

"Thanks for letting me talk a little," Charlie said to the group. "I needed to. For me. So, now I'm guessing none of you'd be all that surprised to hear that Lisa and I are every bit as anxious as Clay to hear from John and Megan about their Canadian utopia. We'd be tempted to go with you right now, if we thought it wouldn't make things harder for you."

"I guess I might as well add my two cents' worth to this conversation," Lisa said, glancing at Charlie and taking a deep breath. "Now, Mom, I don't want you to get all crazy about this, 'cause it's over and everything's fine. And I guarantee you it'll *never* happen again." She closed her eyes and shook her head before continuing. "Thursday night at seven-thirty, we made a trip to the grocery. Charlie dropped Tyler and me off, and he made a quick run to the hardware store.

"I came out of the grocery with a cart and Tyler riding in the seat about eight, when it was just starting to get dark. Charlie was back and catnapping in the car, waiting for me. When I got close to the car, I heard something behind me and turned and saw two men with sock hats over their faces running at us. I screamed as loud as I could for Charlie. He saw them about the same time I did, and he was already jumping out of the car. He yelled, and a man a couple of rows over yelled back that he was calling the police on his cell phone. Everything happening all together scared the goons off. They ducked out between cars and were out of sight in less than a minute. Charlie started to run after them, till I screamed at him to stay with us because there might be more of them."

Everyone stared, wide-eyed, at Lisa. Clare looked mortified.

"Anyway, we locked the groceries in the car and went back in the store with the guy who called the cops. We explained what happened to the store manager, and by the time we got the story told, the police – actually, two National

Guardsmen – were there. We filled out a report. The strange thing is, the incident hasn't been made public.

"Being a newspaper editor and all," Lisa continued, "I've been watching for the press release. But, so far, it hasn't been reported by the police at all. Other crimes have been reported, but we haven't received any police reports on any kind of attempted kidnappings since the President's speech. As far as I can tell, the national news agencies haven't reported a single kidnapping attempt since then, either. No news agencies are making a big issue of saying these crimes have stopped, but, by not reporting any, people think the speech and the extra policing effort have worked."

"*Lisa*, you *can't* be going out alone with Tyler! *Ever!*" Clare finally blurted, unable to contain herself any longer.

"I know, Mom. I won't. I really didn't that time. Charlie was right there." Lisa glanced at Charlie. "And, boy, am I ever glad he was. I was shaking for two hours after we got home. Don't worry. That won't happen again.

"Anyway, Friday afternoon, I called a couple contacts in Chicago and New York and asked them if kidnapping crimes had just stopped overnight. They both told me the same thing. As far as they could tell, there was a slowdown, but kidnapping hadn't stopped. The police were not making any kidnapping reports public, they claimed, to protect the identity and safety of the victims.

"They also said their newspapers weren't printing any crime reports not substantiated by the police. At both papers, the direction to take this approach came from top management. The reasons given were that downplaying these events would discourage other would-be attackers. The insinuation is the press is doing its patriotic duty by *not* printing reports on kidnapping crimes. Apparently, the whole news industry is handling kidnapping reports that way."

Megan asked, "Why would the entire media gang together to suppress news, important news that could contribute to public awareness of danger? Why would the Government go to such extremes to mute medical researchers? What's really going on, here? Is there some kind of huge misinformation campaign underway?" She looked warily at John. "I'm trying my best to feel good about Jamison and our Government, but it's getting harder and harder to believe what I really want to believe."

"I know, honey," John said. "All we can do is keep our eyes and minds open and make the best decisions we can based on what seems most likely to be the truth. I'm more and more sure we won't be living in Sandia Park by the end of this month."

"What would you do with your house?" David asked. "You surely can't sell it that fast, and it's sounding like you might not leave a forwarding address for rent checks."

"I don't know yet what we'll do with it. I'm not sure it even matters. We might just walk out and leave it for whatever happens. Maybe we'll deed it over to a charity, if you can do that with a house that's half paid for. Maybe we'll just give it back to the bank. I don't know."

"Give what back to the bank, Uncle John?" Ricky asked, stirring sleepily.

"Oh, look. *Sleepyhead* is waking up!" John chided him. "Well, I was thinking about getting all of your money out of your piggy bank and giving it to the Bank of Uncle John."

"*Hey!*" Ricky got up and thumped John in the side. "You keep your mitts off my piggy bank."

Josh woke up from his napping spot on a blanket on the floor and rose to toddle sleepily toward Grandpa. Tyler, hearing the commotion ratchet up, stirred in the playpen.

"*Good!*" Clare said. "I've had enough of this conversation. I'm ready to get back to the things that make *my* world go round."

"Well put, Mom," John said. "We have the whole family here. Let's have as good a time as we can the rest of this weekend. Whatever'll happen next week will happen. Let's do now, right."

As John said, "Whatever'll happen next week will happen," the hairs on the back of Megan's neck pricked to life.

Chapter 17
Monday, April 21

John and Megan passed through airport security more quickly than anticipated. They found a snack bar with news on the television and, for the first time in nearly a week, sat down to catch up on world events. The segments revolved around the issues the President had addressed the previous Wednesday night and the activities related to those issues. John and Megan had avoided the clamor over the weekend, but now it was time to pay attention. They had decisions to make and would need to be informed.

The media painted a positive picture. Economic controls had been imposed worldwide last Thursday. All evidence pointed to successful implementation of suspension of free markets. Everything appeared to be working in a thirty-day status quo mode. No unforeseen problems were reported. The governments of all nations were acting in concert.

The news anchor affirmed the laws enacted last Thursday to deter black market kidnapping activities were achieving amazing results. Although a few incidents had since been reported overseas, the rate had diminished by an order of magnitude and, in the United States, no kidnappings at all had been reported. John and Megan glanced at each other.

The President had held a brief press conference early Monday morning to emphasize that the world economy was maintaining stability. He appeared on the screen responding to a question about the infertility crisis. Jamison stated that normal conception had been achieved in shielded conditions. He added that good progress was being made in locating and beginning to unearth and disable magnetic inducers.

John said quietly, "I wonder what 'normal conception in shielded conditions' is."

There was a piece addressing the Nazi group whose evil actions were behind the calamity. "Unnamed government sources say almost half of the Nazi perpetrators have been apprehended and about half of those caught have already been executed. Our sources state the Nazis are on the run and in hiding, fearful for their lives, and giving up hope of succeeding in their vile mission."

Then came another clip of the President stating, "I wish to extend my thanks and the appreciation of my Administration to all the outstanding citizens who work for the United States Government, and to the American people, who've reacted to the current threats as they have to all threats in the past, with quiet confidence and unconditional commitment to their country."

The screen switched to show peaceful demonstrations in New York and Washington DC. The signs captured by the cameras were in support of the Government and the actions being taken. There was no mention in the press conference or on the news of anything related to the thin ozone layer or to human vaporization.

"Well," John said, "they're painting a rosy picture."

"Yeah," Megan replied. "I want to believe it's mostly true, but I'm having trouble overcoming my instincts telling me it isn't."

"Ouch. I can usually count on you to take the optimistic path. So, you think it's more likely Jamison's lying than telling the truth?"

"I'm not ready to blame it on him, at least not yet. It just doesn't feel like we're getting the whole story. It feels like they, whoever 'they' are, know more than they're telling us. I can't shake that feeling."

The airport speakers announced John and Megan's plane was preparing to board. As they got up, John said, "I feel the same way. I was hoping you'd talk me out of that."

The flight was less than half full. John and Megan found themselves with several empty seats around them, affording them the opportunity to talk freely so long as they spoke softly. Once in the air, Megan said, "I don't think either of us is convinced Bremo exists, but we have three hours to kill, and we probably need to go through this exercise anyway, so let's pretend we *are* convinced. What would you be thinking about right now?"

"This might be a fun game. Maybe conjuring up stuff out of nothing. How cool would that be? Well, let's see, I'd like a medium-rare fillet mignon about right now. Okay. *Zap!* Here it is. It sounds almost like, 'Anything you want, anytime you want'. What a different outlook on life that'd create. It'd completely change what we think's important. It wouldn't take long to figure out life's about way more than just creature comforts."

Megan grinned at him. "Okay, my turn. I wonder what kinds of life forms we'd see and how different they'd be. Our 'hosts'... I wonder what they *look* like. I wonder, when we got to Bremo, what strange plants and animals we'd see. Or if things could even be classified as plants and animals? And there probably are life forms from other planets besides Bremo. I wonder if we'd get to see any of those."

"I wonder how different Bremo would be from Earth," John said. "The sights and colors are hard to imagine. Things we don't even notice here would probably rivet our attention there. Sounds, smells, the difference in gravity, in the air. The difference in lengths of days and years. Three *moons*? That'd be cool. What would their buildings be like? I wonder if they have storms and how violent they'd be. Actually, the whole idea's fascinating."

"I wonder about teleporting," Megan took over. "You know, is it like we disintegrate and then reassemble? What if not everything reassembled, or didn't reassemble quite right? What if some brain cells or something got lost each time? What if some cells didn't reassemble in exactly the right place? I wonder if we'd become any different each time we transport, even unnoticeable, subtle changes. I don't know. Your turn, I guess."

"Okay. I wonder how communication would work. All we've seen so far is email... in English. They said they all use one single language on the whole planet. I wonder what it sounds like and how we'd communicate with them. I suppose we'd have to learn their language. I wonder if the sounds would be hard for us to make."

Megan raised her eyebrows. "You know, this is beginning to sound like a pretty laughable conversation. I want to know if we'll get put back together right? You want to know how hard it'll be to make the right sounds to talk?" John started laughing and so did Megan. As they eyed each other, they laughed harder and harder until it became uncontrollable. The stress that had been building up over the past weeks, coupled with the absurdity of the conversation, was cracking them up. They laughed until tears came, drawing the attention of most of the small crowd on the flight. Soon others were joining in at the sight, laughing for no reasons other than getting caught up in the hilarity of the young couple sitting by themselves in the rear of the plane, and involuntarily giving in to their own need for release of tension. After several minutes of the contagion, the cabin finally quieted down.

John could see Megan trying hard to force composure on herself as she chanced another comment. "I can't imagine what social life would be like. I mean, what's the norm for Friday and Saturday night? Heck. I wonder if the concept of weekends even exists." They started snickering again, trying hard to control themselves. "I don't know. Interracial relations have been a mess here. How in the world would interspecies relations work? Do you s'pose we'd get together with our Bremo friends for an evening of cards, beer. and, like, *pizza*?" John had to look away from her to keep from bursting out again from the mental images in his head. "We probably wouldn't stand a chance of winning at cards," Megan continued. "They're probably way more advanced than we are. Do you think we'd end up feeling really *stupid* all the time?"

"I don't know," John replied after taking a minute to settle himself. "They made it sound like we'd be ambassadors. It seemed like a function they think's important. But, are they really just experimenting or toying with us? It could be the greatest history-making opportunity man has ever seen. Or, we might be like mice in a maze going after the bait, just dumb pawns in their game. I'm not sure we'd even know the difference."

"Well, if we make a misstep or two, it sounds like we'd go to counseling," Megan said, grinning again. After pausing a minute, "That could probably be anything from getting fatherly advice to having our *brains* altered. Once we were there, we might lose all control over our lives – not that we really have much, anyway. I'll tell you one thing, though, if this thing really turned out to be happening, pushing the button would require a *huge* leap of faith. I wonder, if we *knew* it was true, would we be quicker or slower to actually type 'take me'? I'll bet slower. If we don't know for sure, I think deep down, we believe when we click 'send,' nothin'll happen. Part of the draw to push the button is that we really want to know if it's true. Just talking through this, I'm convincing myself maybe we really are stupid experimental creatures."

John stepped in for his turn. "The emails from Bremo and Patty Laurent make it sound like we'd be in some kind of utopia. But, you're right. What a leap of faith. They say any of us could return any time we want. Really? Maybe we should ask if anybody's already asked to return and how that worked out. But, I guess that wouldn't resolve the trust question unless they told us yes and gave us details. If they said nobody has asked to return, and if they aren't trustworthy, their response wouldn't confirm a thing."

"The same goes for getting our families transported," Megan said. "They tell us that's a sure thing. All they have to do is ask. But, how do we really know they'd follow through on that? Faith and trust... in something completely foreign and unknown. I'm getting more convinced, if we were sure it was real, we wouldn't go. But, not knowing for sure, I could be tempted to let my finger make that little click on the mouse. The whole thing's *nuts!*"

"Talk about nuts," John said. "Think about the overall picture. I mean, the goal of the whole thing is to get our species and their species to *trade planets*? C'mon! That's mind-boggling. Way *beyond* mind-boggling. The distance. The numbers. The political and social upheaval. It's *crazy!* It brings up the whole question of trust again. How could that *possibly* be the real goal? What're they *really* trying to do?"

Megan became more pensive. "So, who do we decide not to trust? The Bremoians or our Government, along with the other governments around the world? We *know* we're being lied to by one side or the other, maybe both. Something in me wants to trust both, but I want more to trust our President and

Government. I'm just having trouble doing that. We know we have an infertility crisis that we can't understand. The Government's blaming a bunch of Nazis. The Bremoians say they caused it. Maybe we should ask them if it's magnetic and whether man can overcome it. Apparently, there are some puff-of-smoke disappearances that also get mutually exclusive claims from both sides. Bremo says they'll have our planet and they won't take it by violence. If they're really here, you'd think they could've had their way with us anytime over the past thousand years, but they didn't interfere with us. That might lend some credence to their trustworthiness ... if we were past the question of their existence. But, still ...." She shook her head. "What a freakin' leap."

"Well, if we decide to go, or at least to click 'take us' and see what happens, we'd have just over two weeks to do it. It'll be interesting to see what Randy and Kathy are thinking. It sounds like you're talking yourself into thinking Bremo might be trustworthy ... if they exist. And, no matter how much we want to trust Jamison, Marsha was right. If history means anything, the American public has been misled by our political leaders lots of times. Just on the question of extra terrestrial life, I'm sure our Government, or at least some of the people in control, has known for decades other intelligent life exists out there. And I'm sure we've been misled about it. So, I might be getting to the same point of view as you. If I had to bet my life on who was giving us more reliable information, our Government or some Bremoians that might or might not exist, I think I'd bet on Bremo. Insane."

Megan replied, "It seems to me there's moderate risk that, if we click 'take me,' we'd actually be transported. If that happened, then I think there'd be huge risk that we'd have little or no control over our lives from then on. If we stay and move to Canada, our lives would probably still be in danger. The slow threat is from ozone depletion and cancers we might or might not be able to protect our family from. The immediate danger comes from Kathy and me being pregnant and having what everybody will become more and more desperate to get. Regardless of whether the infertility problem gets fixed, what's the economic and political climate going to become? Is there anywhere in the world we could go to avoid catastrophe for our family in the long run? I don't know. There's plenty of risk in clicking 'take us,' *and* there's just as much, maybe more, in not clicking 'take us.' So, what do we do?"

"Maybe we should look at the other side of the coin," John said. "Either decision carries lots of risk. But, I'd also say either decision also has potential for adventure and reward. Canada is more predictable on what the adventure and rewards might be like, but Bremo wins hands-down on adventure and the potential to be a player in something that could be inconceivably huge for mankind. I can't imagine what we might do, see, and learn, if Bremo turned out to be real and we chose it. They tell us there's more at work in the universe than the physical laws that we understand. Imagine what it might be like to learn about all of *that!*"

"Good point. If it were up to me, right now, before I'd decide on Canada, I think I'd click 'take us.' I'm sure it's partly because I want to know if it's real. My instinct – there it is again – is telling me when we click 'take us,' nothing will happen. Then we'll go on to Canada, knowing we didn't have any other option."

"On the other hand, if we left for Canada this coming weekend, we could get there in time to check it out before taking the chance on clicking. And if we decided to click from there, we'd have a better chance of not being seen, of minimizing the risk of our families hearing we'd vaporized."

Their conversation turned to John's family. Sunday had been spent at Clay and Marsha's and then Charlie and Lisa's homes. The time together had been heartwarming and the goodbyes tearful. Sunday night, they'd talked until the early morning hours with David and Clare. Parting at the airport had been anguishing. John, trying to occupy his thoughts with a different subject, redirected the conversation to Megan's family.

Her small family had taken to John. He had been considered one of the family before Megan had moved in with him. They would be delighted about the marriage plans and ecstatic about the baby – and crestfallen at the news John and Megan would be going away. It would be harder on her family than it had been on John's. Her family was smaller, and the child they would be discussing would be their first and only grandchild. The conversation was going to be painful. Megan and John talked quietly for the remainder of the flight as it hit home how difficult it would be to move away, let alone to click 'take us.' As they talked, Canada sounded better and better.

Megan's dad, Branson Stanforth, was fifty-one, a freelance architect. He and Megan's mother, Charlotte, had married during his third year of college, and Megan had been born three years later. Her nineteen-year-old sister, Rally, had arrived eight years after Megan. Megan and Rally had been seventeen and nine when their mother had succumbed to brain cancer. Rally was now finishing her first year of college.

Two years after losing Charlotte, Branson had met Glenda Walker, divorced with no children. Glenda's first marriage had been bad. She had married her high-school boyfriend shortly after she'd graduated. They had stayed married for five years, each one worse than the year before. By then, Glenda had absorbed all the bad treatment by a heavy-drinking roughneck she could withstand, and she had filed for divorce. There had been a miscarriage along the way, but no children. The divorce had been a painful ordeal for her. Having been strapped for cash to pay lawyers, and with no legal savvy of her own, she had emerged with virtually nothing.

Since graduating from high school, Glenda had worked as a secretary for a construction company, which was how she and Branson had eventually met. Glenda had a big heart and loved Branson's daughters as she would have her own. She and Megan had become close friends over time, and the relationship between Rally and Glenda had blossomed from the day they'd met.

John and Megan left the airport at 2:00 and drove an hour to the Stanforth home, east of Los Alamos. The residence was a Southwestern ranch-style adobe house Branson had designed to meld with the surrounding countryside. The sandy brownish-red house was larger than it appeared, blending in with its foothill setting. Branson, Glenda, and Rally were sitting on the covered front porch, enjoying the pleasant afternoon and awaiting the arrival of the guests of honor. Like John's family, they anticipated that an announcement was the purpose of the visit.

Invitation

When John and Megan pulled in the drive, the welcoming trio strode out into the front yard, all smiles, and greeted their guests affectionately. "Hi, kids!" Branson said. He was a big, boisterous, good-natured man. "It's great to see you."

"It sure is," added Glenda, as petite as Branson was massive. The lines on her face conveyed the hard times of her younger years, but her bleach-blonde hair worked to make her look younger. "Let's walk around back to the patio. It's a beautiful afternoon. You're probably worn out from traveling and we've got just the refreshment to help you unwind and relax in the shade and breeze."

Rally, five-foot-five, naturally blonde, bubbly, high-spirited, and independent-minded, squeezed in between John and Megan and wrapped an arm around each. "Yeah, let's get back there and cozy up so you can bring us all up to date on any *newsflashes*."

They sat around the patio table, enjoying appetizers and drinks. Megan caught a glimpse of a knowing smile from Glenda when she asked for lemonade instead of a glass of wine. There were a few minutes of small talk about John's family and the trip to Ohio, but it didn't take long before Rally piped up, "Okay, enough of the chit-chat. Somethin' tells me there are *bigger* things to talk about." She looked at John. "If you've got something to say, big guy, spill your guts."

John grinned at Megan. "Do you want to give them the dour news, or do you want me to do it?"

"Oh, you go ahead," Megan replied. "I can't bring myself to drop this little bomb on these happy people on such a fine afternoon."

"Okay, if you say so. Well, here goes. You all know how much of a swell guy I am, right?"

"Oh, bullshit," Rally broke in. "Are you guys gettin' married or not?"

"Well," John replied, looking hurt, "would it really be *that* terrible if we were?"

"*You are!*" She shrieked, jumped out of her chair, ran over to Megan, and hugged her.

"Hey!" John cried. "What about me? *I'm* the one telling the story."

198

Branson and Glenda were both out of their chairs, too. "Settle down, lover boy," Glenda said. "I'll give you your hug."

"This is great news!" Branson exclaimed. "Terrific! We couldn't be happier!" He bear-hugged them both. "We thought this might be in the offing, but it's great to know for sure."

John and Megan left it at that for the time being. Later, after dinner was finished and they were all carrying dishes to the kitchen, Glenda turned and winked at Megan and said just loud enough for the others to hear, "So, is there *more* news to tell?"

Megan mocked her. "Have I ever told you you're wicked?"

"Well, now that you mention it, yes, I do believe I recall you telling me that on occasion."

"Uhuh. And I was right, you know."

"What are you two haggling over?" Branson asked.

"Bun in the oven, if I don't miss my guess." Glenda grinned at him.

"No way!" he replied, but everyone could tell from Megan's gleaming expression it was true.

"*Bullshit!*" Rally blurted.

"Careful, Rally," John said. "You're overusing your vocabulary."

"You know what, Beanhead?" she replied. "Normally, I'd pound you for that, but I'm gonna overlook it this time."

John and Megan let them bask in revelry for a while, but eventually, the rest of the story had to be told. During a pause in the regalia, Megan looked at Branson and said softly, "Dad?"

"Yeah, honey?"

"There's also some not-so-good news we have to tell."

"What is it, baby?" he asked quietly. Everyone was silent, looking at Megan.

"We haven't talked at all about everything going on in America and the world, but there's a lot of bad stuff. Unless things change, the day I'm due would be about the last day babies might be born. I mean, I … we … really hope things will change. And the Government seems sure the problem will get fixed soon, but who can know for sure? Anyway, there could be … we think there is … a safety concern. John's sister, Lisa, has a one-year-old, and there was an attempted kidnapping of her last Thursday night at a grocery store in Columbus. It appears the bad stuff is still happening, it's just not being reported on the news. And the ozone and cancer danger to our child isn't good, and we don't know for sure if that'll get better, either. On top of that, there seems to be some chance of danger we aren't supposed to talk about from John's job. Randy and Kathy are in the same boat."

Everyone was quiet, gaping at Megan as she took a breath and struggled on. "Anyway, it's almost sure we're going to move pretty far away from here, probably to Canada. We'd pick a spot that has the least danger from radiation and is away from any cities, where we could raise our families in better safety. It'd probably be a little town pretty far north." She let that sink in for a minute. "We might leave soon, maybe by the end of the month. And ...." she paused for a moment and took another breath. "And," she repeated, "I know how difficult this would be ... but there might be two months when you won't hear from us or know where we are, but don't lose faith. We'll be okay, and we won't let it go *any* longer than two months before calling you.

"But it doesn't have to be *all* bad. We hope we'll find a place we love ... maybe a place you all might love, too. If we think it's really good, we'll *definitely* invite you to move to us. I know you all have a lot to stay here for, and I'm not saying we'd expect you to move. Only that we would invite you and be really, *really* happy if you did."

John had watched the exuberance turn to anger in Rally's face and the exhilaration turn to distress in Branson's. Glenda was the one who spoke, looking at John. "Are you sure you're safe? Is there anything we can do to help?"

John replied, "We'll be okay. We've thought long and hard about this and talked a lot with Randy and Kathy. We're convinced we'll be a lot safer if we go. Leaving our families behind would be the toughest thing each of us has ever faced. In all honesty, we're not positive, no matter *how* convinced we are that moving's best, that we'll be able to bring ourselves to do it. But, we have to let you know it could happen and might happen soon. I *know* it's breaking Megan's heart to tell you this after the rest of the evening we've had." He looked at Megan. She wasn't moving a muscle or making a sound, but tears were streaming down her face. "We absolutely *hate* this. The situation isn't our fault, but, unfortunately, it is what it is, and all we can do is try to act in the best interest of our family."

"*Damn* them," Branson muttered.

"*They suck!*" Rally blurted emphatically.

"I know," John said quietly, "but we don't even know who 'they' are. The whole thing's a crappy deal, but it's the hand we've been dealt, and we can't change that. All we can do is make our best decisions and live with them. And, really, don't discount what Megan said about joining us. Think about it. My family surprised me. I think the whole bunch of them might do it if we land in the right kind of place. Looking through all the haze into the future, maybe a few years from now, this move could look like the best thing that ever happened to us all."

"The eternal optimist." Glenda smiled faintly.

"How else could we possibly face it?" John asked.

"Okay," Branson said. "I understand where you are, and I don't want to make it tougher for the two of you than it already is. I want to help any way I can. It's just so damned harsh."

Rally, sobbing, went to Megan, sank to her knees, and put her arms around Megan's neck. *What a sad state of affairs.* John said, "Okay, raw deal or not, one thing we know is we have the rest of the evening together. Except for this last ten minutes, it's been a fantastic afternoon. Let's find whatever we have to inside ourselves to get us past this bump and make the rest of the day one we'll all be happy to remember." No one said anything for a moment. "Branson – ha, uh, Dad …." John grinned. "You're the only person here who knew Megan before she was nine. I'll bet you've got some tales in your memory banks none of the rest of us have ever heard, well, except for Megan, and, really, I think you should just go ahead and embarrass her. Why don't you enlighten us?"

There followed two hours of stories and mild laughter as the group enjoyed being together. It was after 11:00 when John and Megan finally left for the long drive home. The mood in the car was melancholy. Megan tuned the radio to a soft music station and leaned over against John. There was little conversation. They were absorbed in their own mixed thoughts of family, their conversations on the flight, moving away, the decisions they'd have to make in the coming week, and the unknown but imminent ramifications of those decisions.

Invitation

Chapter 18
Tuesday, April 22

The alarm went off at 5:00 a.m., and neither Kathy nor Randy had any desire to get out of bed. Monday had been a disheartening day. They were looking forward to seeing John and Megan tonight to begin to plan more seriously. It had been a week since their last evening together and their talk of Canada and Bremo. Much had happened since then. The world was not the same place.

The President's April 16 address, along with similar speeches in other nations, had shaken the world. Randy and Kathy had observed similar reactions at both their workplaces. Thursday had been a day of uncanny serenity. Everyone had been models of calmness, kindness, and quiet resolve. There had been no evidence of fear or mistrust, no grumbling or complaining. Friday had been similar, but with an undercurrent of misgiving wafting beneath the surface – whispers not so much heard as felt, a feeling that people were questioning, even if only in their minds, whether the things they were being told added up.

Office demeanor was offbeat. Thursday, most people stayed busy at their work stations. There was virtually no absenteeism. Neither was there any bustle. Many who were usually on the go, in and out of the office to and from meetings or out on projects, were in the office all day, working quietly at their desks. Thursday became a paperwork catch-up day for everyone, getting reports written and submitted and documents filed. A missing element was normal office and business communication. Phones seldom rang, and when they did, the conversations were quiet and short. Email traffic was slower than any day either Kathy or Randy could recall. Everyone stayed the full day, but no one stayed late. Neither office conducted any employee meetings, although upper management at both companies spent much of the day in quiet meetings in closed conference rooms.

Friday was stranger yet. Both companies held mandatory employee meetings in the morning. At least, they were mandatory for those in the office. A few people called in sick Friday at both offices. Most had caught up on their busywork Thursday and seemed to have little to do Friday morning. There were 'make work' tasks going on: file-shuffling, sifting through old files sorting items to discard, checking for emails often while receiving few. Some people, appearing to be researching, were doing little more than staring at their computer screens. Nerves were more on edge. There was more office conversation, but most of it was small talk. Close friends periodically walked off together for five-minute breaks and talked in whispers out of earshot.

The meeting at Optical Systems was held in their auditorium-style training room at 9:30. The CEO, George Richards, stood at the podium as everyone somberly filed in and found seats. All the department heads sat at two tables, one on either side of the podium, facing the audience. When everyone was seated, Richards spoke:

"I'm sure you've all kept abreast of the news over the past two days. We felt it important to update you on the impact we believe these extraordinary events will have on Optical Systems during the coming months. Long-term, it's obviously difficult to predict what the business climate in the United States and the world will be. But, as is our customary vision, the management of O.S. will maintain an optimistic view of the future. We believe in the ingenuity and resolve of the United States Government, the American people, and especially the members of our family of employees at O.S. We are not anticipating either financial difficulties or any need to reduce staff levels this year or next. We're making no contingency plans in anticipation of economic hard times. We'll hold future meetings and communicate as necessary to keep you all informed about the short-term and long-term business outlook. Having said that, the primary purpose of this morning's meeting is to communicate short-term projections for the next six months.

"First, O.S. will comply fully with the dictates of the Federal Government. For the next thirty days we will not reduce staff, and paychecks will be issued regularly, regardless of receipts. During the ninety-day adjustment period thereafter, we fully expect to maintain this same policy.

"We are currently under obligation to more than a dozen clients to develop and design proposed optical systems, manufacture and install new systems, complete installations currently in progress, or refurbish existing systems. We anticipate no retractions on any of these contracts by any of our clients. Timely delivery on these commitments alone will require us to maintain current staffing levels for at least six months.

"We also have some positive news to share. And if there ever was a week that good news was needed, it's *this* week. Yesterday, we were contacted by an intermediary representing four large observatories, each either government-owned or subsidized, requesting us to upgrade their optical systems to outfit them with state-of-the-art technology. The existing equipment in these observatories is in the range of ten to fifteen years old. Three of the four are systems we originally designed and installed, and the other was built by a foreign competitor. We were told these projects are urgent, relieving the Government of the requirement for competitively bidding them. Contracts are to be negotiated, and we've already been selected. We have responded that we'll accept all four projects.

"We intend to begin setting up teams and start project planning next week. Some of the technology for these projects is classified, and many, if not all, employees working on these projects will have to obtain security clearances. It's possible everybody working at O.S. who doesn't already have a security clearance will begin the process of obtaining one next week. So, we should all anticipate lots of background checks.

"As surprising as it seems, considering the current state of world affairs, we'll likely be shifting into an extended overtime mode. We intend to start ramping up as soon as contracts are signed. After our conversations yesterday and earlier this morning, we expect that will happen early next week. Then we'll announce specific projects, team members, and schedules. At that time, we'll also establish overtime schedules that would become effective immediately.

"I also want to speak briefly about the dilemma we all found ourselves thrown into this week. The inconceivable events that appear to be occurring will be very difficult for many of us to deal with in our daily lives. Adding a heavy load at work might appear enviable to those less fortunate, but, for each of us, it could heighten already precarious stress levels.

"Beginning Monday morning, O.S. will open a chat lounge staffed by counselors trained to help cope with difficult and stressful situations. The chat room will be located in the third-floor conference suite and will remain open for as long as it's being used. We encourage each of you to stop by the suite for ten minutes, an hour, or more, whatever you feel is helpful, at least once each week. There's no need for any of us to feel we shouldn't lean on others who can help us cope with the unique impact these circumstances will have on each of us. This will be a difficult time and, truth be told, there won't be a one of us who wouldn't benefit from talking through some of the struggles we'll face. Everyone in management has already committed to at least one visit per week.

"In closing, we reaffirm that this management team cares about every one of our employees and your families, and that we will move forward optimistically. We hope each of you also maintains a positive outlook on your future and ours. I emphasize that we want to provide all possible assistance to help each of us cope with the unprecedented issues we'll face.

"Lastly, acknowledging that this is Friday of a very difficult week, and in advance of ratcheting up next week, we're asking everyone to take this afternoon off, paid. You're all free to leave at noon. Thank you all, and have a good and peaceful weekend."

The meeting at The Crowley Group began at 10:00 and was held in the massive group conference room, which could hold everyone if chairs were lined up three-deep around the table. Jerome Schrader stood at the front of the room and addressed the company's one-hundred-plus employees.

"Good morning. I called this meeting to update and prepare everyone for the activities that will begin next week at Crowley. I'm sure none of you will be surprised to hear the Government, in dealing with the current potential catastrophes, is retaining the services of every trusted and capable research agency available. It's a testament to the level of confidence the Government places in us that they've included The Crowley Group in the American team that will lead the world in overcoming the current threats. For the next several weeks, probably months, and possibly years, we're going to be very busy contributing to this effort.

"The security classifications of virtually everyone at Crowley will have to be upgraded. More stringent background checks will be coming. Due to the urgency of the crises, many of them will take place next week, beginning Monday. Due to the necessity of maintaining secrecy, the Government will piecemeal research assignments. The most sensitive activities will be accomplished by several different organizations, all of whom will have severe restrictions on who they are permitted to communicate with relative to their assignments. It's been mandated to us that the same type of piece-mealing and communications procedures must be implemented within The Crowley Group for the various teams and individuals working on these projects.

"It will be *essential* that each individual involved – and that will be everybody in the company – discuss their particular assignments only along the lines of communications that each of you will be given. It's been made *extremely* clear to us how much emphasis the Government is placing on information security. Our contracts with the Government will require that violation of specified communications procedures by any individual must result in immediate dismissal of the individual and, depending on the particular violation, could subject the individual to prosecution for treason.

"We've been instructed that we are required to relay these stipulations exactly to each of our employees. Further, we have to require any employee uncomfortable with this arrangement, or who doesn't want to agree to it, to submit his or her resignation. We've been given personal security contract forms we're required to distribute to every employee. These forms are in the boxes at each door for you to pick up as you leave the room. Each of you is assigned the task of thoroughly reading your contract form today. No one is permitted to copy any portion of these contracts, and the forms may not be taken outside the office.

"I ask each of you to consider carefully the content of the contracts before you come to work Monday morning. Monday, we'll have a signing and witnessing station set up in this room. If you agree to the terms, stop by this room between eight and ten Monday morning to execute your agreement. Anyone choosing not to sign will be considered to have submitted a resignation, be given an exit interview, and issued two months severance pay. If you choose not to sign, in order to receive the severance package, you must personally inform either Bill Johnson or me by ten o'clock Monday morning. Employees we haven't seen by noon will be considered to have resigned of their own accord and will be issued no further salary or severance pay until or unless they contact us and participate in an exit interview.

"We understand how astounding all of this might sound, especially when piled on top of the news of the past two days. We, in management, find it difficult to comprehend ourselves. Our assumption can only be the Government has good reason to require such extremes in security. The position of The Crowley Group is, as it always has been, that we shall place ourselves at the service of the American people and the United States Government. We're committed to contributing to solutions to the problems. We accept on faith the necessity for such tight security and the requisite that knowledge of the full scope of the program be withheld from those implementing it.

"In arriving at your own personal decisions regarding signing the security contracts, you may discuss this meeting and the contents of the forms with your families. Nothing I've said here or that is stated on the forms is confidential. We hope each of you will join us in our effort to assist our Government in overcoming the current threats, but we'll respect the decisions of anyone choosing not to sign.

"None of you should spend any time this afternoon on anything that can wait until next week. Everybody's sole assignment for the rest of the day is to read and understand your security forms. If you have any other commitments you feel must be met this afternoon, see Bill or me right after this meeting, and we'll review and confirm your assignment priorities. Bill and I will both keep open doors all afternoon. Anyone with any questions about the forms, please stop and ask one of us. You don't need to call or schedule an appointment. Just stop by. Responding to your questions is the only task Bill and I have on our agendas for the rest of the day. We'll both be available beginning at twelve-thirty, and we'll stay as late as anyone is at our door.

"That's all I have for now. We appreciate your consideration and efforts in advance. Thank you."

Everyone filed out quietly. Kathy picked up her form on the way out. She had been at her desk five minutes and was beginning to sort her planned afternoon tasks into a pile to transfer to next week when her phone rang. It was Jerome, still in the conference room.

"Kathy, could you step back in the conference room for a minute?"

"I'll be right there." She hung up and walked into the conference room. Jerome and Bill were the only ones left in the room and were seated at the huge table.

"Kathy, there'll be several reassignments made in adjusting staff to the new services we'll be providing."

A brief recollection of the meeting she had been ousted from flitted through her mind. She wondered uneasily if Jerome had concerns over her trustworthiness – if he somehow knew of her conversational looseness with Randy, Megan, and John.

Seeming to sense her discomfort, Jerome continued, "Don't worry, Kathy. You might get reassigned, but, if you do, it would only be to utilize everyone's talents to the fullest. In any case, we'll need the paperwork on your current assignments organized by the end of the day well enough to explain to someone who might move into your position."

"Are you saying I could be reassigned as soon as Monday?" Kathy tried to sound unconcerned.

"Things are happening fast," Jerome responded. "It's possible."

"Do you already know what I might be reassigned to?"

"No, nothing is certain yet. You might not be reassigned at all. But, if you are, depending on circumstances, it could happen fast."

Kathy tried hard to look calm and confident but knew she might not be pulling it off well. Jerome's choice of words had a hint of evasiveness about them. *What circumstances?*

"Oh, and Kathy, I'll be working some over the weekend and might need to look through your documents. If you would, when you get everything organized, just bring your folders to my office."

"Okay. Anything else?"

"No, that's it. Don't worry. Whatever changes might be made, I'm sure you'll find them to your satisfaction."

"All right. It'll take me two or three hours to get everything put together. Do you want me to do that before reviewing the security contract?"

"Yes, please. The contract forms aren't all that complex, and I've seen you assimilate information. You'll have the forms digested in half an hour."

"Okay, thanks, Jerome." She walked out. This was strange. In all the time she had worked at Crowley, no one had *ever* asked her to consolidate her documents and hand them over. She had an ominous feeling Jerome knew more about her impending reassignment than he was telling her. As she worked through the afternoon, she racked her brain, trying to recall anything she might have said or done to cause Crowley to be suspicious of her. Other than her lapse with John and Megan, she could think of nothing. And she was positive no word of that slip could have gotten back to Crowley.

When Kathy got home Friday afternoon, she found Randy's laptop open at the table with all of John and Megan's alien communications scattered around it. Randy, Brady, and Rufus, for whom they were dog-sitting, were in the backyard playing keep-away with a tennis ball.

"Hey, Randy, how long you been home?" she called out the back door.

"O.S. gave everybody the afternoon off. We've actually picked up some new work, and it looks like never ending overtime, starting next week. I guess they wanted to give us a long weekend to brace ourselves. We'll come inside in a minute, and I'll fill you in."

"Hi, Mom!" Brady yelled, waving wildly.

"Hi, sweetheart. How was your day?"

"Great!" he exclaimed, diving and rolling to scoop up the ball a second before a bounding Rufus could snap it up.

They came inside, and Kathy was treated to a kiss from Randy and a leg-hug from Brady. "What's up with all the stuff on the table?" Kathy asked.

"Oh, since I got home so early, I thought I'd look through all of the communications and do some Internet research on promising places to live."

"Did you find any?"

"Yeah, maybe. I kind of like western British Columbia. There are some small towns like Telkwa or Moricetown that look interesting, at what seems to be the ideal latitude. Poor old O.S. will crap if John and I resign as soon as they order all the overtime. Oh, well. That's life in the big city."

Randy told Kathy about his day, and then she told him about hers. "Wow," Randy said. "I thought my day was unusual, but I guess it didn't hold a candle to yours. I wonder what Monday'll bring for you."

"I don't have a clue. But, I'll tell you what, I'm ready to talk about the places you found where life could be simple, pleasant, and safe.

"I'm hungry," Brady interjected.

"Good point, kid," Randy answered. "Let's go grab a Happy-meal at the playground. Mommy and I can talk about this stuff later."

"Oh, boy!" Brady yelped. "Let's *go*, Mom."

Randy and Kathy spent most of the evening talking noncommittally about alien communications and places to live. The rest of their weekend was planned. Saturday was to be spent with Randy's family and Sunday with Kathy's. The family visits were intended to give warning that they were considering moving to a distant location.

Although both visits were lengthy, no conversations about moving materialized. Neither Randy nor Kathy had reached the mindset of urgency about the impending choices. Several times, one or the other of them was about to mention the possibility of an upcoming move, but neither of them took the step. They knew they didn't have answers to the questions that would inevitably follow. When the weekend was over, they felt guilty for not broaching the subject. But then, they agreed, what good would it have done to have gotten everyone worked up over a move that might not happen? If it turned out they really did decide to leave, there would still be two more weekends left to drop the bomb. In that event, it would probably be best for everyone to put off the discussion for as long as possible anyway.

Monday morning, as Randy and Kathy were leaving for work, Randy said, "I don't know what'll happen at your office today, but call me if you need me."

"I'll be all right. Don't worry. I'll fill you in on any excitement tonight."

When Kathy arrived at work, her phone rang the moment she sat down. It was Jerome.

"Kathy, could you call Bernice Ricardo to come to the conference room?"

"Sure, I'll call her right away."

"When she gets here, come in with her."

"Will do," Kathy replied, sounding relaxed but feeling uneasy.

Kathy called Bernie, and she appeared in a few minutes, looking every bit of her eight months pregnant. "Hey, Kathy."

"Hi, Bernie. Boy, don't you look like the picture of comfort."

"Thank you, sweetie," Bernie retorted with a wry grin. "*Your* day's coming."

Kathy followed her into the conference room, wondering what was to come. Jerome and Bill were waiting.

"Have a seat, ladies." Jerome smiled at them. "We've got some special news for you two. I think you'll like it. Like everything else this morning, this precipitated to us from above, but, after thinking it over, Bill and I can't argue with the sentiment behind it. Everyone is concerned about the current particular dangers for women in your condition. The Government's of the opinion the work we'll be doing carries a certain amount of risk to those participating. That risk, along with your obvious conditions, could increase the danger of your becoming targets. While Bill and I don't know a lot about our assignments or the additional dangers that might come with them, we have to accept the Government's assessment. As a result, we'll be offering you both sabbaticals. You should interpret this as a temporary stay of your duties, but not your paychecks. Out of concern for your safety, we'll be asking you not to report to work until further notice, until the danger no longer exists. You'll continue receiving your full paychecks and full employee benefits. You just won't have to come to work."

Jerome paused and watched them. Both women were dumbfounded. It felt like getting fired and winning a small lottery at the same time. Kathy spoke first: "Would we be allowed to still come in and just not work on anything sensitive? Maybe just work as receptionists? Just some small way to contribute and do something to earn our pay? And Crowley makes us all take that self-defense training. We all had to pass that, and we take those two-day refresher courses every year. Don't you think that would be enough to keep just a secretary safe?"

"We've already been told 'no' to the question of allowing you to work as staff secretaries," Jerome replied. "The concern is that the danger to you could increase too much, simply by being associated with the company. To the outside world, it needs to look as though your relationship with The Crowley Group has been terminated. It wouldn't be obvious to anyone that you'd still be receiving automatic deposits of your paychecks."

"When would this go into affect?" Bernie asked. "And aren't employee terminations supposed to be illegal right now?"

"Today would be your last day. We'd ask that you not tell anyone here before you leave. The official line will be you both developed pregnancy complications over the weekend and requested maternity leave. This morning, just organize your work in progress, so Bill or I can understand where you left off. Kathy, yours is already pretty much done, from what I could tell over the weekend. Really, neither of you need to stay all day. Whenever your information is compiled, you can go."

"Man," Bernice said. "You'd think I'd be feeling great about this, but it feels more like I got kicked in the gut."

"Please, don't feel that way," Jerome said. "You haven't been fired or even laid off. Your positions are being held, and you'll both be put back to work as soon as possible, assuming you want your jobs back. Neither of you has done anything wrong. You've both been exemplary employees and will be sorely missed. In all honesty, this is *only* to avoid risk to you and your babies. Please, don't feel bad about it. I encourage you to enjoy both your free time and the paychecks. It really isn't a bad deal."

"I s'pose you're right," Bernie replied. She looked at Kathy and attempted humor. "So, what are you doing all week? You wanna go shopping?"

"I don't have a clue," Kathy replied. "Maybe."

Jerome smiled. "See, there? The right attitude's developing already. If either of you want to talk, call me anytime. Is there anything else you want to ask or say?"

They both shook their heads and stood, sensing the conversation was over. They walked out of the room, and the door closed behind them. "Hey, Bernie?" Kathy uttered. "Let's *do* get together later this week. I'll call you Tuesday or Wednesday, and we'll set something up."

"I'd like that. Maybe we can figure out what just happened. I wonder if this had anything to do with the asshole who kicked you out of that meeting a week-and-a-half ago. That guy who tried to *kill* me with his eyes."

"I don't know." Kathy had been rolling that same question around in her mind. "I've seen him here a couple of times before, and I know he doesn't like to be noticed. He *did* have encounters with us both that day. I don't know." They exchanged phone numbers and went to their desks to consolidate their paperwork and clear out their personal belongings.

Having already organized everything last Friday, Kathy was done in less than an hour. She assumed that, at this point, no one cared what time she left, and her heart was not in staying, so, without saying a word to anyone, she gathered her effects and walked out the employee entrance of The Crowley Group, wondering whether she would ever pass through those doors again.

Kathy was curled up at one end of the couch, sipping hot chocolate and reading a book, when Randy got home from work at 7:00. Brady and Rufus were frolicking in the back yard.

Randy, worn-out, smiled at Kathy and asked, "How was your day, hon?"

Kathy got up, walked over to give him a hug, and started crying, which was completely out of character. She had felt she had a grip on herself, but it wasn't as tight as she had thought.

"What's wrong, baby?" Randy asked, returning the hug. "Are you okay?"

Kathy stepped back, wiped her cheeks, and looked up at him. "I'm all right," she said, sniffling. "Feeling a little silly, actually. It really isn't bad... I suppose I should be thinking its great."

"What are you talking about? What happened?"

Kathy explained how the first and only hour she had spent at work that morning had transpired. "I should be feeling great," she repeated. "I can do whatever I want every day, and I just keep drawing my paycheck. Most people'd think I struck gold. I don't know why it's hard for me to feel like that."

"Sure you do, honey. We both know why. You're a *doer*. You take pride in performing a productive function and doing it well. You've filled a key position at Crowley for *six years* and established yourself as a person who'd be tough to replace. And in one day, that part of your life's been pulled out from under you, in a way that completely masks the fact you'll be hard to replace. If it were me, I'd feel the same way you do. Well, except maybe I'd be more selfish, thinking how cool it'd be to keep gettin' paid and having all the time to do whatever I wanted." He grinned at her. "But then, I'm not nearly as virtuous as you."

"Yeah, I guess you're right – at least that last part about you not being as virtuous."

They shared a long kiss. "Mmmm." Randy exhaled. "I'm tempted to demonstrate my lack of virtue and take advantage of this situation."

"Keep that thought in mind, tiger. You'll get your opportunity later. So, how was your day, besides long?"

"Not great. Actually, you've got a lot better deal going than I have. In addition to my IT work, which is gonna get more demanding, I'm getting put on a project team. You'd think, with all the extra IT support that'll be needed, they would've at least put me on a team close to home. And maybe with people I actually like working around, like John's guys. But, for whatever reason, they threw me on a project in Australia, with Drew Tennison's dreary group. And, since I'll have to travel some, they're giving me an IT assistant that I'll have to guide and be responsible for, sometimes from long distance."

"That sucks. Maybe, with me being free, when Brady isn't in school we could go along on a trip."

"You know," Randy said, continuing on his own track and skipping over Kathy's suggestion, "with everything that's goin' on, my head's in a whirlwind. My job just got crazy, but the compensation will be impressive. I'll be way less available to share time with you and Brady at the same time you suddenly have all the time in the world. You're pregnant and it'll be harder on you to be left alone. You'll bear up, but I know it'll be hard for you. Add to that all the crap putting your safety at risk. Pile on everything John and Megan have going on. I'm *sure* they're serious about getting out of here. And I think, but am not quite so sure, we might go with them. Craziest of all, the choice of location might be – or at least the thought's been planted that it could be – somewhere off the damned *planet*. *Way* off."

They could see Brady out the window, running toward the back door, Rufus in hot pursuit. "Yeah," Kathy replied, "it is a whirlwind."

"The only thing I'm positive of right now," Randy whispered in her ear, "is I *really* want to take you to bed."

"Keep that thought," she whispered back.

"Daddy!" Brady yelled, banging the back door open. He raced across the room and jumped into Randy's arms.

"Hey, buddy!" I thought you were having so much fun out back with Rufus, you weren't even going to come in and say hi to your ol' dad."

At 5:00 Tuesday morning, Randy turned off the alarm, lay still for two minutes, and then, against everything his head and body were insisting on, started to roll out of bed. Before he moved more than a few inches, he felt Kathy's arm circling around him, pulling him back. He sank back against her. They lay close against each other in silence for a few minutes.

Randy said, "I'm glad we'll see John and Megan tonight. John and I will need to find some way to get out of the office at a decent hour. He's gonna be shocked. I know he was making special effort on this trip to avoid anything having to do with work. I'd be real surprised if he checked any emails or voice mails. He'll walk in around eight this morning and find everyone already knee-deep in work. He'll be immediately told he's on an overtime schedule and will have to adjust whatever else he has planned for the week. That'll be just about enough to push him over the edge."

"I'm glad we're going to see them, too," Kathy said. "Now, roll over here and kiss me."

Randy smiled and turned over. "Well, it looks like I'll not only be sneaking out early tonight... I'll be getting there late, too."

At mid-morning, Randy's phone rang. It was John. "Welcome back, buddy!" Randy chided him. "How do you like the new policies?"

"This is crazy. You should *see* the load of stuff I'm gettin' dumped on me."

"Yeah, I knew you'd be impressed."

"Do you think we can sneak a half-hour in for lunch and talk?"

"We can try. Our best shot'd be to duck out early, maybe a quarter after eleven. Will that work for you?"

"Let's make it work. I'll meet you at Monroe's at eleven-fifteen."

"You got it. See ya there."

They arrived at the same time, both five minutes late. "Boy, I'm glad to see you," Randy said. "How was your trip?"

"It was great to see everybody, but it was really tough, too. Having to tell them all we're probably leaving, heading for an unknown destination, and will be out of touch for a couple of months was crushing. How'd it go for you guys?"

The hostess greeted them: "Take a table anywhere, guys. The stampede won't start for fifteen minutes. Do you want to make it easy on us and have the special?"

"Sure," they replied in unison, and then headed for the most remote table they could find.

"Drinks?"

"Coffee," John replied.

"Two beers'd be better, but if he's having coffee, I will too."

"Gotcha covered, guys."

"Everything's fuzzy for us," Randy responded sheepishly to John's question. "It seems hard – no, almost impossible – for Kathy and me to adjust our view of reality. I mean, we know there's this possibility, maybe probability, we could be leaving our lives here behind us soon, but it's like it isn't registering in our heads. I think it's more real to you and Megan. I mean, I *know* it is. You've been in the thick of this thing deeper and longer than Kathy and I. Anyway, I'm sure we didn't come close to preparing our families for what might happen the way you and Megan did. We have a lot to talk to you guys about tonight. We have to find a way to get out of the office way before seven. How prickly will it be for you to leave early?"

"Screw it. Let's just scram at five-thirty. Our decision's made, anyway. I mean, Megan and I really, *really* hope you and Kathy come too, but we don't see much of a choice for us. We aren't sure *where* we're going, but we *are* going. If I get too much flack about shirking on the overtime this week, I'll give them my notice on the spot."

"Wow," Randy said, shaking his head. "Kathy's and my heads are spinning. You won't *believe* what happened to her at Crowley. She and Bernie Ricardo, the only other pregnant woman working there, they both got... well, there isn't any *word* for what they got. It's like they got put on sabbatical with no destination or assignment. They just got told not to report to work till further notice. They'll still get their full paychecks; they just don't go to work. Crowley got a bunch of new Government work, too, all top-secret. They claim their assignments would put pregnant women in too much danger, so Kathy and Bernie are just supposed to stay away. Oh, and by the way, I don't know if anyone told you or not, but I got assigned to *Tennison's* shitty Australian project team. *Plus*, I keep all my current IT duties ... *plus* overseeing a new assistant."

"You're kidding. So, are you guys thinking of staying here and just *dealing* with it all?"

Seeing the waitress bringing their food, they both stopped talking. It had taken the staff at Monroe's only one day to figure out the folks across the street at O.S. no longer had time to whittle away an hour for lunch.

When the waitress left, Randy answered, "Well, no, not really. But, so far, I don't think either of us has been able to convince ourselves that leaving – leaving *soon* – is real. I mean, we know it is, but it's like it just isn't sinking in. It's all happening too fast. It's like we're caught in a whirlwind."

"Yeah, I know. Maybe it'll help to go over everything tonight and sort it out. In the end, we'd never try to push our decision on you guys. We have to do what we have to do, and we know it's the same for you and Kathy. We'll get everything worked out so we can each take whatever path seems best. Whatever happens, there'll never be any problems between us." He paused for a minute, his head catching up, and said, "No shit? They told Kathy, with no notice at all, to leave and not come back, and oh, by the way, you'll keep getting your paycheck?"

"Yep. Crazy. She's been there six years, in a sensitive position, in possession of lots of secret information, and they give her like an *hour's* notice to clear out. It's unbelievable."

"Randy, there's a lot going on we don't have a clue about. How can we make any rational decisions about actions that'll completely reorder our lives? Unfortunately, my gut tells me we don't have much time to figure it out. Well, maybe my gut, plus the non-existent Bremoians' stupid-ass deadline." He shook his head.

"So, how soon do you think you'd actually leave?" Randy asked between bites.

The stampede was beginning, as everyone from O.S. tried to beat the noon rush.

"Well, today's the twenty-second, and the deadline, false or not, is the thirtieth. We haven't decided whether we should reply to Bremo after we make a trip to have a look at some spots in British Columbia, or reply first and then go to Canada after we see that Bremo didn't work." John heard himself rambling, as if he were talking to himself, trying to sort out the options. "That is, *if* we reply to Bremo at all. We're hoping after tonight we'll be able to decide. If we decide to drive north and leave ourselves enough time to contact Bremo, about the latest we could leave here would be Monday morning. Saturday morning would be better. *Man*, it's on top of us already. If we don't decide in the next day or two, we'll have to default to replying to Bremo first, if we decide to reply to Bremo. I guess if we decide not to reply to Bremo, or if we decide to reply to them first, then the departure date for Canada wouldn't be quite so critical."

Randy breathed a laugh. "Sounds to me like you don't have any friggin' idea what you're gonna do!"

"Thanks for the support, buddy."

The tables around them were filling, and their conversation had to be curbed. They quickly finished their meals, talking briefly about their assignments at O.S. As soon as the food was downed, they left money on the table, got up, and hurried back to work. Before parting, Randy said. "I'll find a way to cut out at five-thirty. We'll see you guys at your place as early as we can get there."

Shortly after 6:00, pandemonium erupted as Brady and Rufus burst in and went nuts. Rufus spun back and forth between greeting Megan and John and giving due attention to his pal, Brady. Pizza was ordered, and the two couples caught up with events that had occurred since their last meeting, choosing words carefully when Brady was within earshot. There was much to discuss. They hadn't talked as a group since before the President's speech last Wednesday night. Randy and Kathy described the subsequent events and atmospheres at work.

"It's like the whole world's in suspended animation," Randy said. "A week ago, people were rioting everywhere. Then Jamison and all the other leaders spouted their wild explanations and told us all the unbelievable actions they'd already set in motion. And, bang! Everybody in the world just dissolved into meekness."

"I took a college elective about how Hitler overran the Jews," Kathy said. "The atrocities the German people committed were horrifying, but the whole world just pretended it wasn't happening. Even the Jews themselves, in the process of being *exterminated*, acted like, 'Surely everything will be all right.' It was as if everybody in the world was wearing blinders, including the Jews. I mean, is that what's happening now? Are we all just thinking our governments surely know what they're doing, so we'll just wait and let 'em do it? Is anybody even thinking *at all*?"

After a glum silence, John said, "We are."

John and Megan relayed the conversations they'd had with John's family members relative to their take on world conditions. By the time everyone was caught up, it was after 8:00.

Kathy initiated the decision-making discussion: "If I'm seeing everything clearly, here's where we are. You two are almost certainly leaving, probably within the next two weeks. You're on the fence about signing on for Bremo. With any luck, tonight will help you decide. Randy and I and our families are way less prepared for us to leave than you and your families are. We've pretty much decided, if you go, we go, but we haven't realistically dealt with it. We're laying a lot on tonight, but, if Bremo is to stay in the equation, we have no choice. It's gonna be a long night."

John raised his eyebrows at Randy. "She has a way of cutting to the chase, doesn't she?"

"That's why I married her. I'm usually in a fog and need somebody to find a clear path."

"That's true," Kathy said. "I'm not quite sure why *I* agreed to the arrangement."

"Oh, come on, honey, we all *know* what you can't resist about me."

Megan quipped, "Do you think we could talk to Bremo about selectivity? Like take us all, *except* the adult males?"

"Sorry, babe," John replied. "You have to go through me to get to Bremo."

"Okay, gang," Kathy said, "as much as it'd be easier to while this night away, we have work to do. Should we start with Bremo? What do we know now that would influence us to push the button or not to push it? Are there more questions we need to ask?"

"I think this discussion is only meaningful if we assume Bremo is real and everything will happen just the way the emails say," John said. "If we decide to go, and nothing happens when we push the button, then we go to Plan B. So, if we assume the instant we hit the button, we disappear and our lives change drastically, I see several negative points." John took a notepad and started a list headed "Bremo Cons."

1. Risk of transport problems resulting in unknown circumstances.
2. Some risk Bremo is being dishonest with us, which could result in fates worse than death. Who knows what?
3. Small risk we might not survive or survive well after transport, either on the ship or on Bremo.
4. Some risk we aren't understanding each other. Maybe Bremo counseling is more like mind control or mind-altering.

John stopped and handed Megan the pad. She added to the list:

5. We would have to leave our families and aren't sure we would ever be able to contact them again.
6. Maybe we wouldn't like it and would want to return to our lives here, but be unable to return and live life as we do now.
7. Maybe we would feel really stupid and inferior among beings way more intelligent than us.

She passed the pad and pen to Kathy. Kathy wrote.

8. How do we prepare Brady?
9. How do we prepare his grandparents?

She hesitated, and Randy took the pad.

10. How would we receive Crowley's never ending paychecks to Kathy?

Kathy smacked him on the back of his head as he continued:

11. Where would we go for sex?

Kathy took the pad from him and pushed it over to John. John said, "Both good points, buddy," and flipped the page to start a new heading. He wrote, "Bremo Pros," and pushed the pad over to Megan, saying, "We can come back to the negatives if we want." She began the list, writing nonstop.

1. We would be away from the dangers that face us here.
2. We could have an opportunity to contribute substantially to the good of mankind.
3. We could have the chance to see wonders we can't even dream of.
4. There might be little or no sickness or suffering
5. We could find a better place for our families and get them there.

"Hey, honey, leave something for the rest of us to write." John grinned at her.

"Yeah, I guess I should," she replied, passing the list over to Kathy. Kathy took the pad and continued.

6. We think we would all stay together.
7. We could have the opportunity to interact with a completely unfamiliar, yet friendly society/species.
8. Our children might have opportunities open to them we can't imagine.

She warily passed the pad to Randy, saying, "I know this is hard for you, lover boy, but try to contribute something meaningful." He took the pen and wrote:

9. Conjuring up stuff would be amazing. Never ending free beer.

Kathy rolled her eyes, grabbed the notepad, and slid it to John.

10. I'd like to meet Patti Laurent and Ben and Liz.
11. The life experience opportunities and personal rewards could be phenomenal.
12. It could become the greatest gift we could ever give our children and families.

Kathy eyed the list. "Okay, here's the quick, short version. For the con list it seems to boil down to questions of whether or not we believe the Bremoians are trustworthy, whether they are technologically able to deliver what they claim, how well we would personally be able to cope, and how difficult it would be for us to leave our families."

Megan said, "Comparing those questions to the positives, except for the issue of leaving our families behind, the positives look phenomenal."

"I agree," Kathy replied. "The decision could be easy, if it weren't for leaving our families behind. I know for sure neither me or my mom are *anywhere near* prepared for a decision to leave. We'd have less than two weeks to get ready. I don't know."

"Okay," John said, "the question of leaving our families is going to be the toughest part for each of us. Let's think about the other points and come back to that. Except for that, I agree the pros outweigh the cons. But, we should be serious about the cons. I'm less concerned about the Bremoian points than about our own abilities to cope."

"I see it the same way." Randy was serious, now. "When it comes down to it, I'm sure we'd each have our own tough days. To me, the thing that makes that beatable is that we'd all be together. We'd definitely need each other."

"If the toughest issue is leaving our families behind," Kathy said, unable to move past that question, "let's think that through. If it turns out Bremo doesn't exist and nothing happens when we push the button, then the question of leaving our families isn't such a huge deal. If it turns out Bremo does exist, but they duped us, and we find out that going was the wrong decision, then we're lost anyway and, again, leaving our families behind wouldn't be the big issue. The issue would be the other items on the list, and we'd simply have been wrong in trusting Bremo and would have ruined our lives because of that. The other possibility is Bremo is everything they claim. If that turns out to be the case, the *only* thing bad about leaving our families behind – and for me, that means my mom – is there'd be a temporary period of anxiety till we communicate with them and give them the opportunity to join us. For me, that's a no-brainer. Mom would be with us *the second* she could transport. So, maybe the question of leaving our families isn't as big an issue for me as I thought."

"That seems like a good way to look at it," John said. "After our visit home and talking to everybody, I think my whole family would come. It wasn't quite as obvious with Megan's family, but I'm pretty sure they would come, too."

"I don't know about mine," Randy said. "I don't come from such a tight-knit bunch. Mom and Dad are divorced and remarried. None of my brothers and sisters have the solid marriage Kathy and I have. I don't know if they'd come. I don't think any of them would relish all being together in the same place. I'm not saying that makes it easy for me, but it makes this issue less central to me than the rest of you."

Megan looked at John. "I think John's right about our families. In the end, I think all yours and mine would follow us. Maybe the question of leaving our families behind isn't so much of a stumbling block."

"It's beginning to sound like we're all pretty much in agreement that, if this opportunity really exists, as a group, we don't want to let it pass us by," John said. "If we're sure, and if we're ready to put total faith in each other, then the next question would be, are we ready to email Bremo and tell them if any one of the four of us sends the message to take us all, we're agreed. Are there more questions we should ask them before we do that?

"I'd like to ask more about their counseling," Kathy said, "and whether we would consider it brainwashing."

Megan added, "I'd like to know more about communication with and transporting our families. We've told everybody we might be out of touch for two months. Well, I guess Randy and Kathy haven't gone that far yet. I'd like to know if there are time limits on how soon we could communicate or how soon they could be transported. I'd really like to know how much danger we'd be putting them in, but I don't think Bremo knows, or at least I don't think they'll say."

Randy added, "I'd like to know if anybody who's transported has changed their mind and asked to be transported back, and how that worked out."

"Those are the questions I had in mind," John said. "Maybe this won't be such a long email, after all. I'll start my laptop and type it up. I guess maybe we should ask them how each of the four of us can get a message to them. So far, everything we've sent has been from my laptop, sent by just clicking 'reply'." After his laptop powered up, he opened the previous unanswered email from Bremo, clicked on "reply," and began typing.

> We have a few more questions.
> 1. We would like to know more about counseling. Is this just rational discussion or could it be interpreted in Earth terms as mind control, mind altering, brainwashing, or hypnosis? Could we lose some control over our conscious thinking process?
> 2. Once we would transport, is there any time limit on how soon we could communicate with our families on Earth or how soon they could transport?
> 3. Can you tell us how much danger we would place our families in by communicating with them or by us transporting? What might happen to them?
> 4. Has anyone who has transported asked to return? If so, how has that worked out?
> 5. If we were to decide that any of the four of us could send the message to take us all, how would we communicate that to Bremo? So far, all of our communication has been from this laptop, and every email we have sent has been a reply with no addressee. We have just clicked "reply" and "send." How do any of us get a message to you if we don't have an email from you to reply to?

"How does that look?" John asked. Kathy had been typing along with John on her laptop to create their copy.

They all looked at the email and each other. "Send it," Randy said. John clicked "send," turned the laptop off, and then turned it back on. The response was there. They crowded around the screen and read.

> 1. There is no mind control or altering. There is little need for any counseling. It is apparent to all there is no need for anyone to want for anything, and it is in the best interest of each individual to contribute to

the good of all. It is rare for anyone to need counseled.

2. You would be free to contact your families on their computers immediately upon your arrival on the ship. They could agree to transport almost immediately, so long as room is available on the ship. We would request one day to evaluate the people you would like to invite. At this point in our effort, we would not invite individuals who have demonstrated aggressive personalities or lack of concern for others. If there is no space on the ship, they could not transport until after the current group transports off, scheduled for May 5.

3. The danger level cannot be predicted. We don't know what your governments will do. If you transport, there is likely to be some immediate risk of interrogation for your families. Once you would begin to email them, the risk to them would increase with each passing day, as is the case with your own current situation. Consider waiting a few weeks for investigations to become less intense and to allow time for you to assess conditions on Bremo.

4. One couple requested to consult with us about returning due to concerns about family members they left behind. After discussing options and risks, they decided to stay. We would have transported them back upon their request, but the danger to them from their government would have been significant upon their return.

5. After we would receive an authorizing email from each of the four of you individually, then any one of the four could send an email from any computer anywhere addressed only to Bremo and saying in the subject line, "Take us all," at which time all of you would immediately be transported. Each of your four authorizations must be sent to us in separate emails to 'Bremo' with the following in the subject line: "If any of John, Megan, Randy, or Kathy send a request to Bremo stating, 'Bremo, take us all', take me," and type your first name. We will reply to

each of the sending computers acknowledging receipt of your instruction. After you open your email and our reply is displayed, the reply will automatically disappear as you close your email display program.

"Okay," John said. "This is April twenty-second, and we have to request by the thirtieth. We should try to make our decision this week. When do we want to set a time to get back together?"

Kathy replied, "I'd say no later than Friday night. What do you all think?" The other three nodded agreement. "Okay, let's make it Friday night at our place at seven. How about the alternative move, Canada? Do we want to look at options now or wait till after we make the Bremo decision?"

"It's too much for me to deal with," Megan said. "Let's put that off till later, after we punch the button, if we punch the button."

"I agree," John said. "Megan and I already decided we're giving our two-week notices Friday. We're already too late to take a trip to Canada or anywhere else before pushing the Bremo button. Assuming Bremo doesn't work, we'll have a little time to mull over Plan B."

"I agree," Randy said. "But I've gotta say, we sound like *lunatics* sitting at the table talking about transporting to another planet."

"I know," John replied, shaking his head slowly. "Ridiculous."

They all sat mutely, looking at each other. Eventually, Megan said, "I don't remember a single time when the four of us ever sat around a table with nothing to say." After a pause, she added, "Or had so much to sort out and talk through."

Even Randy was at a loss for words. "Well," John said pensively, "it's been a long day and the alarm clock will have no pity in the morning ... except for Kathy." He smiled at her sympathetically.

"Yeah, we should be heading home," Randy said. "I'll gather up Brady."

Invitation

Sleep eluded Megan. She couldn't get thoughts of her dad, Rally, and Glenda out of her head, of the disappointment on their faces during the discussion of moving away. *God, I hope this doesn't all come down to me. I could <u>never</u> make it happen.*

Don Miller

Chapter 19
Wednesday, April 23

Megan had included Tuesday in her vacation request, knowing Monday would be a long, exhausting day. One Wednesday per month, she conducted training at Lovelace Women's Hospital, and today was the day for April. When she arrived, she saw that security had been beefed up. There was an armed guard watching the surface parking lot and one at the employee entrance. Looking back as she entered the building, she saw another posted atop the parking garage. Within the building everything seemed normal, but upon passing the main entrance she noticed another guard.

"Hello, Greta," she greeted the charge nurse at the oncology station. "What's up with all of the guards? The President's speech?"

"Hi, Megan," Greta replied. "Welcome back. No, nothing changed after the speech. This is all from yesterday."

"Yesterday? Why? What happened?"

"It's being kept under wraps, but there was an attempted baby kidnapping."

"You're kidding! *Here?* I never heard anything about it on the news."

"We've been ordered not to discuss it with anyone other than hospital employees. But you're an employee, and we're all supposed to be on the alert, so you need to know."

"Ordered not to talk by *whom*? They can't do that."

"By the administrator. I'm pretty sure he had no choice and was following somebody's orders. They told us any employee disclosing information would risk losing their job and could be prosecuted for public endangerment."

"That's *nuts*! What happened?"

"Just after noon yesterday, a woman dressed as a nurse wheeled another woman into the maternity suite. They picked

229

the perfect time. Half the staff was on break, and everybody else was busy with patient lunches. For a half-minute there was nobody in the nursery. The perpetrators must've had some way of watching the floor. They came in unnoticed, and the fake nurse went right into the nursery, picked up a baby girl, cut off the baby's ID bracelet and alarm sensor, and handed her to the woman in the wheelchair. They headed for the elevator, as if the mother and baby were being discharged."

"Fortunately, the baby's father was in his wife's room, visiting. He walked out of the room to have a peek at his daughter and passed the kidnappers on their way to the elevator with a baby. He didn't think anything about it until he got to the nursery. He saw that his baby wasn't there, but it took him a few moments to realize that his baby's bassinette *was* there and the ID bracelet and sensor were lying in it. As soon as he realized it was *his* baby he'd passed, he took off like a shot and *flew* down the stairs.

"When he got to the first floor, the kidnappers were halfway to the patient entrance, where a car was waiting for them with two guys in the front and the back door open. The dad yelled out to stop the women, they were kidnapping his baby. When he yelled, the one in the wheelchair jumped up with the baby, and both women ran for the door. A big man, who was just walking in, saw what was happening and stepped in front of the woman with the baby. She crunched into him, barely managing to turn enough to protect the baby. The woman dressed like a nurse ducked under his arm, ran out the door, and jumped in the car. The one holding the baby turned and ran the other way, but, with people closing in around her, she panicked. She turned back around and ran straight at the big guy, holding the baby straight out at him. She tossed the little girl at him. The guy had good hands, and as he reached out and caught the baby, the woman ran by him and out the door, and dove into the car just as it peeled out. It was *crazy*."

"Wow!" Megan was astonished. "It obviously got somebody's attention. Guards are everywhere. How could that not have made the local news? The *national* news? What's going on, Greta? Who decided this had to be kept secret? *Why?*"

"It doesn't seem like we're hearing the whole truth about anything. There's too much that doesn't make sense. Maybe they think everybody'll be better protected if we *don't* know what's happening. Who knows what they're really thinking?"

"The world's going mad, Greta. I mean, I'm truly grateful to be pregnant, but it's *such* an awful time."

"I'll tell you what, kiddo. You're beginning to show, and if I were you, I'd start wearing loose clothes that don't look like maternity wear. With any luck, by the time you can't hide it anymore, this whole thing'll be over. But in the meantime, you should do everything you can to not look pregnant."

"That's good advice. I'll take it."

When Megan left the hospital that afternoon, she found herself unable to walk carelessly ahead. She felt an uneasy pull to be glancing to the side, a want for eyes in the back of her head. *What a way to live.*

She was home for two hours before John pulled in the drive. He was still wound up from the hectic pace at work.

"My day was nuts," he told her. "No time for any break all day. No lunch. Not even *five minutes* for a snack from the vending machine. It seemed like it was still morning when I saw six-forty-five on the clock and said, 'Screw it, I'm leaving.' I'm not sure why I'm going along with this pace. I'm quitting Friday, anyway."

"Sit, and let me rub your shoulders."

"Deal," he said. plopping down in his favorite recliner as she stood behind him and began to rub. "Ahhh. That feels great. I think I'll just stay here tomorrow and opt for this all day. So, how was your day?"

She told him about the attempted kidnapping. "Maybe we should watch the news tonight."

"Yeah, it wouldn't hurt us to get an update, anyway. We should still be able to get the late-evening local news. Let's see if the kidnapping is mentioned." He clicked the remote.

There was nothing about any kidnapping attempt, no hint of anything unusual at the hospital or anywhere else around Albuquerque. John flipped to national news, and they ate as they watched.

The lead story was an upbeat segment about a thirty-something fifth-grade teacher in Waco, Texas, leading her students through a wind power construction project. The class had designed and built a working model wind turbine electric generator as part of an attempt to entice a consortium of companies to donate and build a wind power generation system for their school. The kids built the model, wrote the letters inviting various companies to participate, and were partnering with the company project managers in administering the project. It was impressive, but the story was uncharacteristically positive and benign, considering the world situation.

Then followed a segment bemoaning flooding along the upper Mississippi River. Iowa had been getting hit with torrential rains for the past week. The flooding wasn't particularly heavy, certainly not a disaster. This story was also weak news for headlines.

After several more mundane stories, there was mention that the economy was "holding its own through these trying times" and that progress continued on tracking down magnetic inducer stations for dismantling. There was no mention of violent crime, nothing about any attempted kidnappings in the United States or anywhere else.

The newscast closed with a report that signaled a warning. Internet oversight agencies were detecting rising levels of "potentially subversive" Web postings. The FCC had received direction from President Jamison to scrutinize the Web for traffic that would incite unrest or panic. The FCC had further been directed to identify sites that were conducive to such postings. Each identified site would be given one warning by the FCC to cease allowing postings deemed potentially hazardous to public peace and safety. Sites that did not demonstrate corrective action and control over postings immediately after receiving a warning would be closed and denied Web access for a period of one year.

Megan looked at John and said, "That newscast sounded controlled."

"It sure didn't sound like the irrepressible bulldog media we've come to know and love. Everything I see and hear makes me feel more and more like we are *not* being told the whole story. Maybe nothing even close to what's really happening.

Don Miller

Now the Government's getting concerned about on-line drabble? The Web *is* pretty free-wheeling. Maybe we should see what's going on there, before it gets censored."

All the explosiveness that was missing from the newscast was abundant on the Web. The most popular browsers didn't lend themselves to finding the volatility. However, once one offbeat site was found, it was easy to expand to others. As always with the Web, there were ludicrous sites and postings, but there were also some convincing ones. There were hundreds of claims of recent kidnapping attempts, many of them successful. There were an infinite number of claims that the Government was deceiving the public.

There were almost as many differing opinions about what was really happening as there were postings. The range of explanations was mind-boggling. The Earth is being sucked into a black hole. The second coming of Christ will occur tomorrow – or it happened yesterday. The sun is burning out. The President is taking over the world. The President of Chile is taking over the world. There were postings denouncing the negative sites, accusing them of being anything from unpatriotic to demon-possessed, for undermining their country and for skepticism of its leaders. There were hundreds of postings claiming alien invasion. John and Megan found a few that described a familiar scenario. Megan clicked on one of them.

"Wow, babe," she said warily, "listen to *this* one. 'All governments are going overboard to hide what is really happening, which they can't control. The Earth is going to be taken over by beings from a planet called Bremo. This will be a slow and nonviolent takeover. They have already begun by inflicting infertility on the human race. If we won't cooperate voluntarily, they will just wait it out, until we are no more, or at least until we are too few to resist, and then they will move in. Their ultimate goal is to trade planets with us. They have already convinced a few people to act as ambassadors and to visit Bremo now. These ambassadors are the ones who have been disappearing lately. Yes, vaporization is happening, although it is being heavily downplayed and covered up. Major governments have imposed censorship on the media. Expect them to usurp the freedom of the Internet soon in their effort to suppress dissention, which is counterproductive to their all-consuming effort to gain control over a situation that simply cannot be managed.'"

"Of all the crazy postings on the Web," John said, "two months ago I'd have said that one right there is the most ludicrous. How is it possible that now, I think it's the most *believable*?"

"Well," Megan replied, "the obvious answer to that question is that you're off your friggin' rocker."

"I'm beginning to wonder if that really *is* the best explanation," John said.

"There's only one consolation to that thought. I'm right there with you. So, however far off the deep end we go with this thing, we're going over the edge together."

"Let's go back to that webpage," John said. "There was a link on it I'd like to go to."

Megan clicked on "go back," but instead of opening the previous page, the web browser closed. "That was weird," she said, reopening the browser. She spent the next ten minutes trying to get back to the Bremo post, but she couldn't find it. "Do you think the page got pulled? Censored?"

"I don't know. Maybe. *Nothing* would surprise me anymore. Who are we supposed to trust? Our Government? The media? Law enforcement? Our employers? Anybody? I mean, *you* work for a nationally prominent hospital. They have an attempted kidnapping and order their employees not to tell anyone or risk losing their jobs? *C'mon!* They beef up security like crazy, and there's no hint on the local news that anything ever happened? And Charlie – Ohio State forcing all their professional medical employees to assemble, *under armed guard,* and making them sign nondisclosure statements, under penalty of *treason*? Lisa attacked by rogues trying to kidnap Tyler? And the police report being squelched? I'll tell you, hon, the more I think about it, the more wary I become of everything I've ever trusted." He shook his head, becoming agitated.

"Come on, John," Megan said. "You've had a long day. I know you're tired. Let's go to bed and try to get some rest."

"All right. I watch this crap, and it makes me mad. I doubt if tonight'll be very restful."

"Come on, I'll rub your back some more," she said, taking his hand to lead him off to bed. He followed behind her, unable to see the anxiety in her eyes as she wondered what the next few days would bring.

*   *   *

It was almost midnight.   Betz read the message confirming the two pregnant women who had so conspicuously noticed him at Crowley had been discharged. He had received this word Monday through the Air Force general communicating with Jerome Schrader.   His independent investigation now confirmed that both women had walked out of Crowley's offices before noon Monday and had not returned since. Betz did not like being out in public and was paranoid about being noticed. Those two had honed in on him and would not forget him. He would probably never make another personal visit to Crowley, but if he did, and if either of the two women were there, Crowley would be *done*. Its Government contracts would go up in smoke, and the company would dissolve.

His reception system signaled incoming instruction. On Thursday, he was to stay available to receive and digest multiple task assignments. Many seditious Internet communications had been intercepted during the past two weeks. A batch of them would be forwarded to him, along with instructions conveying how five of the communicators were to be dealt with.   On Friday, Betz was to develop an action plan for implementing seizure and interrogation operations and to set up the necessary support.   Execution would begin early on Saturday, and the entire operation would wrap up by midnight Sunday. Mission closure reports were to be submitted on Monday. The next four days would be busy.

Chapter 20
Thursday, April 24

"Hey, Mom, I'm hungry." The words floated hazily through her consciousness. "What's for breakfast?" The intruding chatter was real enough that Kathy cracked her eyelids.

"What time is it?" The words mumbled off her lips.

"Time to get up!" Brady climbed up on the bed and poked her shoulders.

"Okay, okay, monster. I'm getting up." She glanced at the alarm clock and saw it was almost 8:30. She sighed. She had been off work for less than a week and already had shifted from getting up at 5:30 to 8:30. Kathy was struggling to adjust to the change. She liked being home with Brady but missed the organized, controlled productivity of her responsibilities at Crowley. She knew Brady liked having her home with him, but she also knew he missed his friends and the routine at the preschool.

Randy had been wonderful. He was getting up early and working twelve-hour days. She had insisted on getting up with him the first morning, but he had talked her into just rolling over and going back to sleep each morning since. It was so easy. She had gone from barely six hours' sleep to almost nine hours. Kathy knew she needed to put more activity into her days to shake off the sluggishness.

Today, she and Brady were meeting Bernie for lunch, at McDonalds, of all places, and then going shopping for baby clothes. She was looking forward to getting out. Although she had never gone to lunch with Bernie, that was only because their paths hadn't crossed much at Crowley. It would have seemed absurd a week ago for either of them to have scheduled lunch at McDonalds; the thing was, there was an indoor playground there. Brady could finish his lunch in ten minutes, and then

Bernie and Kathy could sit and talk for an hour if they wanted, easily keeping an eye on Brady. Bernie, soon to deliver her first, had developed an interest in watching kids play.

Kathy sauntered to the kitchen and munched on toast and cereal with Brady. After cleaning up, she read for half an hour while Brady watched TV. They spent some time on alphabet and numbers games, and then it was time to make the two of them presentable for the day before picking up Bernie.

The first ten minutes of lunch was predictable: Brady wolfed his burger and fries as fast as his mother would allow and talked as fast as he could between bites. "I'm gonna go down that big slide real fast. Bernie, do you know John and Megan and Woofis? Woofis is a really big dog. We play tag and hide and seek. Do you have kids? My mom's gonna have a little brother or sister for me. I hope it's a brother. Do you have a dog? I used to go to preschool, but now Mom doesn't work, so I stay home. Do you work or stay home?"

Bernie attempted to answer a few of the questions, but by the time she started to speak, Brady was on to the next one. Mostly, she just smiled at Brady and Kathy.

As soon as Brady had gulped the last bite and slurped it down with his drink, he blurted, "Mom, can I go play now?"

"Yes, but be nice to the other kids. And don't be too rambunctious."

"I won't," he yelled over his shoulder, scampering off.

"Whew," Kathy said, grinning at Bernie and wiping her brow. "What a handful."

"He's really cute," Bernie said. "I'm getting excited about making this change from career woman to stay-at-home mom. I don't think I'd have made that decision without being forced, but I'm starting to think getting fired with pay might be the best thing that could've happened to me."

"I'm glad," Kathy replied. "The week's been tough for me. I mean, I like being home with Brady. I guess I like the thought of being that stay-at-home mom whose focus is family. But, making the adjustment from career woman to full-time homemaker overnight still has me confused inside."

"Yeah, I'm trying to deal with the suddenness of it, too," Bernie said. "It would've been easier if we'd had some time, even just a couple weeks, to prepare. We just need to give it a little time to sink in. One of the things I spent time on this week that I never did before is social networking on-line. Have you done much of that? It's zany."

"No. Never had time for it. I've done tons of on-line research, but never just poked around to see what people are spouting off about."

"I'm not sure it's a healthy pastime, at least not when society's in as much turmoil as it is now. Thousands of people are posting opinions that just seem crazy. All extremism in all different directions. Any voices of reason get drowned out. It's like the tabloids gone out of control. If a person spent too much time at it, I think the line between reality and imagination could blur."

"That sounds like a reflection of an unbalanced society. What kind of crazy stuff?"

"You name it. Anything you could dream up is being posted by somebody. Infertility postings are exploding. Every explanation you could possibly conceive of and more that you could never imagine in your wildest dreams. The same for human vaporization. A few insist the government is right on top of it all, and they're giving us the straight scoop. Postings like that get pulverized from all directions.

"There are even wild posts from here in Albuquerque. There was an anonymous one this morning claiming a kidnapping attempt was made at Lovelace. It went into elaborate detail. A fake nurse and fake mother wheeled into the nursery during lunch hour Tuesday and took a baby right out from under everybody's noses. The father happened to catch them in the act, and there was a huge ruckus when they tried to make their getaway. The posting claimed the perpetrators got away, but not with the baby. How and why would somebody make that up? But nothing's been on the news, and nobody who'd know is saying anything like that happened."

"My best friend's a nurse at Lovelace. She works oncology at the Medical Center, but she'd know if anything like that happened. I'll ask her."

"My bet is she'll say, if it happened, nobody told her anything about it. Anyway that post was one of the more sane ones. There are tons of them about government intrigue, aliens, terrorists, ghosts, alternate dimensions of reality, the end of time

– you name it, and it's there. If you spend too much time immersed in it, sorting what's real from what's fantasy gets confusing."

"So, what do you think about all of it, Bernie? What do you *really* think is behind the infertility crisis? And vaporization? Do you think it's really happening?"

"Well, last week, when I still had a job, I pretty much believed what I heard on the news. You know, I didn't really question what our Government was saying. Now, this week – with too much time on my hands, and becoming borderline out-of-touch with reality – now, I find myself suspicious of our Government." She grinned wryly at Kathy. "Even worse, I'm suspicious of the news media. *Backwards* suspicious. Not that the media's making mountains out of molehills, like always. Now I'm suspicious they're making *molehills out of mountains*. It seems like, right after the President's last speech, the entire media flip-flopped from over-sensationalizing everything to being meek, ignoring news that should be blasted from the mountaintops."

Kathy returned the grin. "So, why don't you tell me what you *really* think, Bernie? Actually, I'd like to know what you think is happening. What do *you* think is causing infertility?"

"I don't have a clue. Truth is, mainly I'm just scared. I – well, you and I both – could be having two of the last children to be born on Earth. If *that* isn't scary, I don't know what is. How would these children grow up if there was nobody coming along behind them? How could we *possibly* prepare a child for the kind of life they'd face, watching the slow extinction of the human race?

"Even scarier, what are we supposed to do now, next week, next month?" Bernie raised her hands in gesture of despair. "How much danger will we face? There might be some powerful, dangerous people willing to do *anything* to steal these children. I mean, *Jesus*, what if the stupid-ass Web post about Lovelace is true? And how the hell do we *know* whether it's true or not? When it comes right down to it, I'm too scared about the infertility thing to have an objective opinion. And reading all this Web crap only makes it harder to know what to believe. Vaporization? Shit, I can't get past kidnappings. I can't fathom vaporizations *at all*. Excuse my French, but this stuff's pushing me over the edge."

"Don't worry, honey, I understand. The whole thing's driving me crazy, too, and I don't have the added catalyst of having gotten sucked into the Internet. In fact, thanks for the warning. I'll avoid it like the plague. What about going to the mall? Are you worried about being safe?"

"Actually, I *am* a little bit," Bernie replied, "but I don't want to be. I don't really believe there was a kidnapping at Lovelace. Here in Albuquerque? In the middle of the day? If this was really happening here, or anywhere in America, it would just *have* to be big news. No, I'm not going to let myself be scared to live. We'll be fine. I'm ready, whenever you are."

Kathy motioned to Brady, who was waving to get their attention as he headed down the slide head-first into a sea of plastic balls. "Time to go, Brady."

Usually, there were plenty of people walking around the mall even on weekdays, but today it was deserted. Kathy noticed a shaggy-haired, tough-skinned, middle-aged man leaning against a pillar near the main entrance, wearing a mall maintenance uniform, apparently an employee with nothing to do. The only other sign of life outside was a stick-skinny young woman with shoulder-length, stringy brown hair, wearing a dark brown long-sleeved shirt, jeans, and sneakers near the next mall entrance. There were a handful of cars in the parking lot, but once inside the building, Kathy wondered if the cars all belonged to mall employees. There were no shoppers. They went to the biggest department store in the mall and headed for the infant clothing section. There was *nobody* there, not even a clerk.

"Look at these marked-down prices," Bernie said. "I've never seen anything like it." Most of the racks were marked seventy-five percent off. "I guess I should take advantage of this. It takes some of the fun out of it, though. They've obviously given up on selling any of this stuff, and they're trying to give it away. Oh, well, we might as well stock up."

They spent the next half-hour picking out baby outfits. When they had all they could carry, and had Brady loaded down, too, they went off in search of an open checkout counter.

Don Miller

Between them, they had bought almost one thousand dollars' worth of outfits for barely over three hundred dollars.

As they were walking out the main entrance, Bernie, looking very pregnant, said, "I feel like a friggin' duck, waddling along loaded down with all this stuff."

"Friggin' quack, friggin' quack," Brady giggled.

"Well, you little gopher," Bernie retorted, when we get in the car, I'll get you for that. I'll bet you're ticklish."

"Oh, no you won't," Brady replied. "I'm a *fast* one. You'll *never* catch me."

As Kathy looked right for traffic before stepping off the sidewalk, holding Brady back, she noticed the mall worker still leaning against the same pillar. Looking left, she noticed the same skinny young woman they had seen before, walking toward them, not far away. Leading Brady off the sidewalk, she thought how strange it was, being at the mall and seeing no people. The only three she had noticed were these two people, twice, and the store clerk who had checked them out. Then she saw a paunchy middle-aged couple walking hand in hand toward them in the parking lot several spaces beyond her car. They both wore hats pulled low and had their collars turned up, making it hard to get a view of their faces. *Where did they come from?*

Something didn't fit. There was no car beyond them that they were walking from. Kathy squinted at them. She saw that they were both concentrating intently on Bernie, Brady, and her. The hair on the back of her neck tingled. She glanced quickly at Bernie, who must have been experiencing a similar sensation and was peeking back at her. They both instinctively looked quickly around behind. The mall worker and the stick woman were hurrying directly toward them. Through clenched teeth, Kathy said, "The car. *Fast!*"

Kathy dropped all of her bags, scooped Brady up, and started to run. Bernie was already scampering toward the car, waddle style, hanging onto her bags. It was too late. The couple in front of them, no longer holding hands, was between them and the car. They obviously had been watching all along and knew exactly which car belonged to Kathy. The couple behind them was almost running now.

"Mom, what's going on?" Brady exclaimed.

Then Bernie screamed, "*Heeeelp!*"

"*Shut up!*" the man coming at them from the front hissed, pulling out a derringer and pointing it at Bernie.

"Mommy! He's got a *gun!*" Brady yelled.

"You shut that kid up. *Now!*" The man commanded.

Kathy cupped a hand over Brady's mouth, her own mouth gaping.

The woman who had been holding hands with the gunman spoke in a gravelly voice. "You girls can either stay calm and cooperate, and everything will turn out just fine for everyone, or you can cause a scene, and it'll turn out real bad for you in a hurry."

"What do you want from us?" Kathy challenged them, as if she didn't already know what they were after. She clutched Brady, wide-eyed, tightly to her. "You want money? You can have everything we've got."

"Honey," the woman replied sarcastically, "I don't have a clue how much money you've got, but it can't be anywhere near enough to interest us."

"What do you want?" Kathy spat.

"Come with us," the gunman said, "and be quick, if you don't want anything bad to happen to the kid."

Brady was clinging even more tightly to Kathy than she was to him. Kathy's eyes were slits as she glowered at the pair. She wasn't sure what she was going to do, but she and Brady were not going anywhere with these rogues. She looked at Bernie and said calmly, "Okay, we won't cause any trouble."

She hoped Bernie could read her mind, and that Crowley's self-defense training program, along with the element of surprise, would pay off.

Bernie looked at the man with the gun and asked calmly, "Can I put these packages down?"

"I don't give a shit what you do with that stuff, as long as you're quiet and cooperative."

Bernie dropped everything on the spot. The group of four attackers had circled closely around their three victims.

"Follow me," the gunman said as he turned and put his derringer hand back in the oversized pocket of his jacket.

As he turned and took his first stride, Kathy, sensing that now was their best chance, brought her right foot up with every ounce of force she could produce, driving the point of her shoe into his groin from behind. Even holding Brady and being six months pregnant, she maintained her balance. The gunman dropped like a feed sack. Bernie knew the fake mall worker was directly behind her and close. As soon as she saw Kathy's foot leave the ground she spun around and crammed her knee into his groin, and he crumpled. As the man with the gun fell, the woman who had walked up with him jerked around, but as she was turning, Kathy, holding Brady in her left arm, grabbed a handful of hair in her right hand and put all her weight into a downward yank. The woman had been slightly off balance from her quick motion, and she crashed to the pavement head-first. Then, dazed and bleeding, her whole body slumped down onto the pavement. Stick woman, standing behind them, was the youngest and most tentative member of the foursome. Bernie screamed at her, "*Get out of here now, or you're next!*" As Bernie, with her bulging belly, took a step toward her, the woman jumped back, turned, and ran.

"Run for the car!" Kathy yelled. "*Now!*"

They ran the thirty feet to the car. Kathy opened the back door, tossed Brady in, and slammed the door in one fast motion. The man with the gun rolled over on his side and pulled the gun out of his pocket. Kathy grabbed the keys from her jacket as she got in the car, jammed them in the ignition, and peeled out before the front doors banged shut. The gunman fired. Both the back and front glass cracked and splintered as a bullet smashed through between Kathy and Bernie.

"*Stay down!*" Kathy screamed at Brady, glancing back to make sure he was lying down in the back seat and unhurt. She swerved abruptly right, heard *another* gun shot, and then swerved back to the left, out of the parking lot and onto the street, without considering stopping for the red light. She knew the area. It was a half-mile through city streets to the nearest police station. She tripled the speed limit getting there, just in case the creeps had any intention of giving chase. Getting stopped by a traffic cop would be a godsend, she thought. There was no chase, either from the would-be kidnappers or the police.

When they scurried into the police station, all was calm and routine, except for Bernie, Kathy, and Brady. The girls were both shaking, and Bernie was crying. Brady was molded to

Kathy. Kathy explained quickly that they had been attacked at the mall and shot at, then asked if they could call their husbands.

John happened to be walking by Randy's desk when he heard Randy exclaim, "*What?* Are you and Brady okay?" That was enough to turn John around. "What station are you at? I'll be there in ten minutes." He hung up the phone and jumped into action.

"What's going on?" John asked.

"Kathy and Brady were attacked!" Randy replied tersely, rushing for the door.

"I'm coming with you," John said, running after Randy, leaving without bothering to tell to anyone.

They arrived at the police station as the women were settling at Sergeant William Mallory's desk, beginning the task of filing the incident report. Bernie's husband, Keith, came running in the door less than a minute behind them. The men introduced themselves, and the women began recounting the episode. Brady was becoming himself with his dad and John now present, and he added his viewpoint as the telling progressed. John listened quietly but intently. Randy and Keith were not so quiet as the story unfolded, sporadically blurting expletives.

Sergeant Mallory was a bull of a man, tall, fat, and bald. His manner was methodical, bordering on languid, and he spoke with a slow Texas drawl. The debriefing took almost two hours. When all of the questions had been answered and the note-taking was done, John finally spoke up: "Sergeant Mallory, was there an attempted kidnapping at the Lovelace Women's Hospital on Tuesday? Do you think these fiends could be the same people?" Everyone looked at John. The girls' jaws dropped.

Mallory stared at him. "Where did you hear that? On the *Internet?* You know, you can't believe *anything* posted on the Web these days. You'd do better to leave your computer turned off. The best source of information anymore is the news. And I'll tell you, *that* is a statement I never thought I'd make."

"So, you're saying there was *not* an attempted kidnapping at the hospital this week?" John repeated his query.

Sergeant Mallory's eyes narrowed. After a moment, he replied, "Not that I'm aware of."

"Would you be willing to check the files to see if there's any record of one?"

"John, what the...?" Randy asked.

"Look, Mr., uh... Resnic, right? You said your name was John Resnic?" Mallory scrawled on his pad. "We're busy here. We've got serious issues to deal with. We can't spend time looking for reports that might or might not exist for people who are just curious. Otherwise, we wouldn't get a *thing* done around here. If you have some kind of *legitimate* reason for needing to know, give me your address and phone and number. If anybody around here gets some free time in the next week or so, we'll check it out and get back to you. Anyway, if something like that happened, it would be big news, and I haven't heard anything about it on any of the local broadcasts." A hint of pink rose around his shirt collar as he realized the trap he had just set for himself.

John picked up on it instantly and pushed on. "So, there's *no way* that this incident with Kathy and Bernie, with *gunfire*, won't be in the news, right?"

"Look here, Mr. Resnic," Sergeant Mallory retorted curtly, "you're starting to get on my nerves. We have no control over what does or doesn't get reported on the news. How would *I* know whether or not this will be on? Now, I've got a ton of work to do before I can go home, and I'm gonna be an hour late already. I don't have time to deal with people snooping around, trying to stir up trouble. And it's obvious that's the only reason you're here. You are *not* related to any of the victims. If you're just trying to instigate, and that's the way it looks to me, we have ways of dealing with that. Now, do you have any more stupid questions, or are you *done*?"

"No. I have the answers to my questions," John replied coolly.

Mallory glared at John as the group turned to leave. John sensed the man daring him to continue the challenge, and decided to drop it and leave.

Outside, Randy said, "What was *that* all about?"

"I'm guessing this isn't a good place to discuss it. We can talk about it tomorrow night." John looked at Keith and Bernie. "My wife and I are having dinner with Randy and Kathy tomorrow night. Would you guys like to join us?"

"Thanks," Bernie answered, "but I've had an overdose of excitement this week. And, in my condition, I think home is the only place I want to be for a few days. But, I'd really like to know: did that *really* happen at the hospital? Do you know for *sure*?"

"Yeah. It really happened, and yeah, I know for sure."

"Thanks for telling us, John," Bernie replied. "Kathy, let's keep in touch. Let's compare notes on keeping ourselves and our babies safe."

"Okay. I'll call you." Kathy made a mental note to call Bernie no later than the weekend to give her warning that they might be moving away. Bernie would go nuts if they just disappeared.

Randy said, "Hey, John, would you mind driving Kathy's car?"

"No problem. I'll drive it home tonight, and we'll drive two cars to your place tomorrow night."

He didn't add that he'd damn sure be checking the news to see if this attempted kidnapping – attempted murder – was reported. That turned out to be a futile effort. Not a single channel made any mention of any kidnapping attempt or violence of any kind near Albuquerque.

Chapter 21
Friday, April 25

After leaving the police station Thursday afternoon, John drove Kathy's car, with its cracked glass, back to O.S. before going home. He met with George Richards to tell him what had happened and that he and Randy were done for the day. During the conversation, John decided there was no reason to put off giving notice of his resignation. Although he didn't know yet where they were going, he and Megan were leaving. He explained his concerns about starting a family here and that he and Megan had made a decision to move away. He tendered his two-week notice. Richards expressed both disappointment and understanding, and told John that, if he were to remain available for more than two weeks, there would be a position for him until his move date.

As John walked out the door, his emotions, more than his mind, succumbed to doubt. He and Megan had made this decision several days ago, but it hadn't hit home until now. Now that he had actually resigned, it felt surreal. "Shake it off, John," he mumbled to himself, walking back to Kathy's car. *Staying here would be the wrong thing to do.*

He arrived home a few minutes before Megan. "Hey, baby!" She smiled broadly as she walked in the door, surprised and happy to see him home. "How'd you swing getting off early?"

He told her about the attack on Kathy, Brady, and Bernie, and the afternoon spent at the police station.

"*Oh, God!*" Megan moaned as he related the event. "It's *my fault*. Kathy would *never* have gone out if I'd called her last night and told her about the hospital kidnapping."

John reassured her as best he could. She was not at fault. Everyone was fine. Maybe it was even best for this to have happened now, in the way it had. The experience today might avert a more disastrous event from happening to Kathy or Bernie in the future. His bolstering didn't seem to help.

Megan called Kathy, spent half an hour on the phone, and calmed down a bit. After she hung up, John told her he'd given his notice when he had returned to work.

"Wow, John! So, we really *are* doing this?"

"Thanks for the vote of confidence." John managed a wry smile. "That's pretty much the way I feel, too. But, there's no way around it. There's *no doubt* that staying here would be bad for us. The attack this afternoon proves it."

"I know, honey. At the very least, we need to move to a safer place, and move as soon as we can. But, the closer it gets, the harder it gets. I can deal with leaving this home we like so much, but look at the people we're leaving behind. That's going to hurt. A lot."

"Yeah, it's going to be tough," he said. "The only thread that makes it bearable is hoping our families might join us. And I *am* going to miss this house ... the view ... the Southwest. This is where our history is. You and me. Our memories are from here. You know what I wanna do? Let's go to Vernon's Steakhouse for dinner. It's our favorite restaurant, and this could be one of our last chances to go there. We can reminisce the evening away."

"I'd like that. I'll be ready in ten minutes."

Friday morning, the alarm went off on Megan's schedule. John had decided he was done with overtime. Megan would drop him off at work, and he would knock off early enough for her to pick him up when she got off.

When she arrived after work, they had time to kill before getting Rufus and going to Kathy and Randy's. They stopped at a bar and grille for an appetizer, beer, and iced tea. Choosing a dimly lit booth in the back, John slid into the seat beside Megan and slipped his arm around her shoulders. Last evening, their talk had been of the times they had shared. Now, they mulled over decisions to be made.

"You know," Megan said, "I'm convinced the best decision would be to say, 'Bremo, take us.' And, in my mind, I almost believe there's more chance that Bremo's real than not. But, it doesn't matter. I could be *totally* convinced in my head that Bremo is real, and still, deep inside, I wouldn't be able to comprehend it. Regardless of what I tell myself, everything I feel says the next thing that'll happen after we click the 'send' button is that we'll all sit there and stare at each other and say, 'Okay, so where do we want to move to?' How can I believe it, but still not *feel* like it's real?"

"It's the same for me," John replied. "If there's one of us who *feels* it could be real, it's Kathy. She seemed more that way from the start. Maybe the information she's been exposed to at work makes it easier for her to believe. So, you've made up your mind? You're ready to punch the button?"

"Well, I'm not going *anywhere* by myself, and we're all four committed to act together. I just have one vote. But, considering the pros and cons, saying yes seems like the obvious decision … to me, anyway."

"Then the two of us agree. I know we made a pact of four, but if you and I are convinced and Randy and Kathy vote no, there's nothing that would prevent us from going our own ways. It'd make it that much harder for us to say, 'take us,' though … by ourselves."

"I wonder how Kathy's ordeal yesterday will affect their thoughts," Megan mused aloud. "You'd think it'd be one more push to leave, but you never know. Sometimes an experience like that can make a person really feel the need for family. Maybe it'll make it harder for them to go."

"If we all decide to go, which one of us do you think will be the one to hit the 'send' button?" John asked. "We should plan that ahead of time. Maybe we'll talk about that tonight. This is the twenty-fifth. If we decide to go, we probably shouldn't wait until the thirtieth. That leaves Saturday, Sunday, Monday, and part of Tuesday, at most, before we would send our message. Man! It's *here*. What day would you pick?"

"I don't know. Probably Tuesday. Late Tuesday. Stay as long as we can. I don't think I could leave without one more visit home. But, I don't know if I could handle it. I don't know how I could *possibly* say goodbye. Telling them what we're really doing could *only* be a mistake. *Not* telling them seems unthinkable. Maybe it'd be better if I just called them. You could do that with your family, too. Maybe Monday would be a good day to call. No matter what, I guess we're not going to work Monday or Tuesday. I gave my notice today, but I didn't tell them I wouldn't be in Monday or Tuesday. I'll have to call and tell them I won't be coming back. *Ever.*"

"Right, you resigned today," John said. "How'd that go?"

"They thought I was off my rocker, quitting and just pulling up stakes and moving to some outback location we haven't even picked yet."

"I'll bet." John chuckled. "They'll really think it's crazy if they never see you again." He shook his head slowly, pensively. "Four days. This is *nuts*. There's a chance, maybe remote, maybe not, that in less than one hundred hours, you and I could be somewhere in space, on a spacecraft, *with aliens*. I can't believe it, either. You're probably right. We push the button, and then we all look at each other and say, 'What do you want to do now?' This is too much. I think you're right about Monday, though. We need to spend a *lot* of time on the phone. Oh, and there's one other thing we need to do Monday."

"What?"

"Well, do you want to take a chance on leaving this planet still living in sin?"

"Aw, man! We need to get married!"

"Yep." He grinned at her. "In your wildest dreams, did you ever think that'd be an afterthought? Forgetting about your wedding day? Three days before?"

"Never."

The usual chaos erupted as Rufus burst through the door. However, the aura among the adults was subdued. The experience of the previous afternoon still had Kathy shaken.

"The grill's hot and ready to go," Randy said. "Tonight calls for a feast of steak. Steak for the adult humans, and burgers for the kid and the canine."

"Sounds good," John replied. "Rufus will be impressed. What can I do?"

"I've got the steaks. Bring out a couple beers."

"Done," said John, heading for the refrigerator.

"Are you doing okay?" Megan asked Kathy, hugging her as the boys and the dog went out the back door. "I still feel *terrible* for not telling you about the attempt at the hospital as soon as I knew. I could've prevented *everything*."

"We went through all that last night. There's *no way* this was any fault of yours. Even if we'd known about the hospital kidnapping, I'm sure Bernie and I would still have gone. It was *broad daylight*. And there were two of us. Who would've thought it could happen here, in the afternoon at the mall? Anyway, the only harm done is I lost five hundred dollars' worth of clothes that I paid a hundred-fifty for and possibly won't need, anyway."

"Does it make the decision harder for you? Should we put it off another day or two to let everything settle down?"

"No. We'd pretty much made up our minds before. The attack just made us more aware of that. Have you and John decided?"

"Yes." The two women stood silently for a moment, looking at each other. "But, I'm not sure I want to say," Megan finally added. "I don't want what John and I think to influence what you guys decide."

"It won't. We're ready to say, 'take us.' We think the possibility is too phenomenal to pass up. And, although it shouldn't be, we think going would probably be the safest thing for us. *Especially* after yesterday."

"We decided the same thing. But, do you *really believe* it? What do you think will happen when we hit the button? You think we'll all just be sitting in one of our living rooms afterward, looking stupid?"

Kathy spoke slowly, looking squarely at Megan: "I think when we hit the button, we'll disappear from the face of the Earth and find ourselves looking at each other in amazement in a place we've never seen before."

"You *really* feel deep down inside that will happen?"

"Yes. I don't think Randy believes it, but I think that's what will happen."

"What if it doesn't?"

"Then I guess we'd play cards and have a good laugh. Then maybe a good cry. Then we'd probably get out the atlas and talk about where we want to live."

"How can this *possibly* be happening?" Megan wondered aloud, shaking her head slowly.

Brady, plastered with sunscreen, and Rufus had crashed out the storm door and run off into the backyard, followed in more civilized fashion by Randy and John. The steaks hissed tantalizingly as Randy placed them on the searing grill.

"So, how's Kathy holding up?" John asked.

"Amazingly well. That girl has her head screwed on straight. I married a strong woman. Oh, she's still shaken up, but she's got good perspective on it. Societies all over the world are neurotic right now, and there's no guarantee it'll get better anytime soon. Maybe never. Even after yesterday, Kathy can stay calm and objective. *I'm* having more trouble coping with it than she is. Mainly, what *I* want to do is find those assholes and rip their heads off."

"Yeah, I don't know what I'd have done if it'd been Megan. I'd probably be in jail right now for murder. Has it mixed everything up for you guys about Bremo?"

"Nah," Randy drawled. "We'd already decided the only answer is to go. Well, I mean to *type* that we *want* to go. Kathy's pretty much convinced that *deciding* to go and *actually going* are the same thing, but I just can't see it. My gut feel is that we type, 'Bremo, take us,' and then nothing happens."

"We're like that, too. Our heads tell us Bremo might be real, but we just can't *make* ourselves, or maybe *allow* ourselves, to really believe it. I mean, three or four days from now, us living with *space creatures*? C'mon. What a load of bull."

"That makes it easier to decide, though," Randy said. "It isn't quite so hard to think about leaving people behind if you don't really believe you're leaving. But, that makes it *harder* for Kathy. Leaving her mom is more real to her." Randy took a swig of beer and flipped the sizzling steaks. Then he watched Brady and Rufus for a minute. "Can you imagine *those* two on a spaceship? No way."

"It's crazy, all right. But, it's also the most *intriguing* thing I've ever thought about. Wouldn't it be something?" They were both lost in their own thoughts for a minute before he continued. "So, you're saying you and Kathy have decided?"

They were both watching the boy and the dog tussle in the grass. After a period of silence, Randy finally answered. "Yep. We're in, if you and Megan are."

John finished off his beer. "Well, it sounds like tonight's discussion isn't going to take long. We might spend most of the night playing cards."

"Nothin' wrong with that, buddy. Might relieve some of the tension that's built up over the past couple days. The steaks look about right." He surveyed the ruckus in the backyard and called out, "Hey, Brady, bring that ole mutt over here, so you two can eat your burgers."

"Okay, Dad, we're coming. C'mon Woofus, let's go eat *hamburgers!*"

It was a nice evening. The group ate on the screened-in patio, Brady and Rufus trying to outdo each other in gulping their food fastest in spite of the admonishment. As usual, ten minutes after sitting down they were off again, playing a racing game of tag.

When dinner was done and all had shared in clearing the dishes, the four adults sat at the patio table. After an awkward silence, Megan prodded, "I'm guessing we've made up our minds already, and it's just a matter of spitting it out?"

"I'm in," Kathy said simply.

"You mean *we're* in," Randy added.

"So are we," John said.

"Well, *that* was quick," Megan said dryly. "So, what other decisions do we need to make?"

"We need to decide when," John said. "And where. And, at some point we'll need to decide which one of us will actually have the balls to hit 'send'."

"I'll do it," Kathy replied. The others nodded, not surprised.

"Tuesday night?" Megan queried.

"That's what we'd have suggested," Randy replied.

"Would you guys mind if we do it from here?" Kathy asked. "We're going to need to prepare Brady, and I think it might be easier for him if it happens at home."

"That's fine," John said. Then he added, unsuccessfully attempting humor, "There probably isn't a whole lot we can do to prepare Rufus. Do you know what you're gonna tell Brady? He's going to think we're a bunch of really stupid adults if we're all about going to see the nice aliens on their spaceship, and then nothing happens."

"Well, then I guess he'd learn firsthand that big people don't know crap about what they're saying half the time," said Randy, also attempting unsuccessfully at humor.

Megan said, "Okay, so we go from here. Tuesday night. How 'bout if we come over at eight and do it at nine?"

"It'll be a weird night," Kathy said. "Waiting around would be nerve-wracking. If you get here at eight, I say we go by eight-fifteen. Even quicker, if we're just sitting around waiting for the clock to tick."

"I agree," John said. "We'll get here at eight, on the nose. I think we just turn on the computer, get comfortable, and let Kathy do her thing. I can't *imagine* what I'll be feeling, watching her finger press that key. What a trip. Maybe. Kathy, do you *really* think you can do it?"

"Don't worry, honey. I'll do it. *You* just get ready for a ride."

"Randy, you got more beer?" John asked. "I need more beer."

"Randy, baby," Kathy said, "you two might as well drink it all up. I don't think we want a *drop* left in the house when John gets here Tuesday night."

"One thing's for *sure*, "Randy replied, trying harder at humor. "If you aren't gonna let us drink it Tuesday night, we *are* gonna drink it now. I damn well ain't leavin' this planet with *beer* left behind in my fridge."

Kathy shook her head. "Always on top of the details."

"It's gettin' dark," Randy said. "Let's move this party inside. I'll retrieve the beer and fetch a deck. It's time to lighten up this party."

"Come on in, Brady," Kathy called. "We're going inside. Bring your pal."

"Okay, Mom. C'mon, Woofus. Let's go inside and play hide-and-seek."

As Randy went to the refrigerator, he said, "I'm allowing five minutes to wrap this up. Everybody get any leftover issues off you chest. Then, we're going to have ourselves one last normal, New Mexico, Earth, Resnic/Jarrett party night."

"Lover, for once, I think you're right on target," Kathy said. "What else do you guys think we should cover?"

"For this trip," John said, "we don't need to think much about what to take. We apparently take nothing. Everything we'll need, we can just *conjure!*"

"That's mostly true," Megan said. "But, I know I'll want to take as many family pictures as I can stow on me."

"And maybe a few mementos and letters," Kathy said. "I'm guessing we can't take anything more than we can hold in our laps and pockets. We won't take much, but there *are* a few things I don't want to part with."

"What about keeping in touch over the next three days?" John asked. "Should we get together again?"

"You know," Megan replied, "we're all going to be together for a long time. I'm thinking we need to spend most of the time we have left in touch with the people we're leaving." Her voice cracked.

"Let's at least talk by phone a few minutes every day, just to make sure we're all on track," Kathy said. "Even if it's only for a minute or two. Other than that, I think Megan's right. We each have people we need to spend time with."

"Okay, so we party tonight, and then we come back Tuesday night for the trip of our lives," John said.

"Yep," Randy said. "The allotted five minutes are up. Any more trip-planning will have to be by phone. It's time to game on. We've got *twelve* more beers in the fridge that now fall under the heading of "use or lose." John, ole buddy, you happen to be blessed with a designated driver. Consider yourself called upon to do your duty for the cause. Here's one to start with."

"*Woooohhh.* Wait a minute!" John exclaimed. "We damn near forgot the most important thing!"

"No, we didn't, nitwit," Randy replied. "Your *beer's* right in front of you."

"No. If we're gonna *do* this, we have to email our Bremo 'hosts' and *tell* them."

"Jeesh," Kathy let out. "How could we forget *that*? What would've happened? Good old reliable Kathy types in, 'Bremo, take us all,' and the only person who disappears is *Kathy*? *That* ain't happenin'. John, get out your laptop. Randy, make some use of yourself, and go get my laptop and turn it on. If we're gonna do it, let's do it."

Invitation

John went first. He typed, "Bremo," and then, on the subject line, "If any of John, Megan, Randy, or Kathy sends an email to Bremo, stating, 'Take us all,' take me. John." He sent the message.

Kathy typed her message on her computer and sent it. Then Megan sent hers on John's laptop, and Randy sent his on Kathy's. They turned the computers off and restarted them. Two messages were displayed on each computer. "John, your message has been received by Bremo," and, "Megan, your message has been received by Bremo," on John's. Kathy's said, "Kathy, your message has been received by Bremo," and "Randy, your message has been received by Bremo." They both clicked their computers out of email, and then back in. All of the messages had disappeared.

"Okay, that's it," Randy said. "The formalities are done. Turn 'em off."

Chapter 22
Saturday, April 26

John felt a sense of déjà vu Saturday morning, sitting at the table and looking out at his Sandia Mountains. It had been just over three months ago that he had been sitting in this same spot, at this same time on a Saturday morning after partying with Randy and Kathy on Friday night. That was the morning after Megan had conceived. *Everything* had changed since then.

He felt sluggish from over-indulging last night. It was 9:10. The hot coffee tasted good and was beginning to help. The morning he was remembering had Megan sauntering out of the bedroom to greet him about now. He wished she were here now, but she had an early doctor's appointment, maybe her last one on Earth. She had gotten up at 7:00 and left before 8:00. At that time, John was still lying in bed in a half-asleep haze. Megan had wanted to go by herself and then visit two of her friends after the appointment. He didn't expect her back before noon. They were scheduled to spend this evening with Marty and Brenda Black. They would tell their lovable neighbors tonight that they would be moving away soon and might be leaving on an extended house-hunting trip Tuesday.

Rufus was lying still and quiet at John's feet, head resting on crossed paws. Eyes wide open and looking wistful, even Rufus seemed to be feeling nostalgic. John was staring deadpan out the window at 9:30, when Rufus, uncharacteristically, let out a low, mean growl from deep in his throat.

"Hey, Rufus, what's *that* all about?" John leaned down and scratched his head. The dog, head perked up, looking intently at the front door, didn't acknowledge the touch. Suddenly, there was hard banging on the front door. Rufus shot up, barking ferociously, and ripped to the front door, hair standing straight up on the back of his neck.

"Rufus, stop it!" John commanded. Rufus stopped barking, but continued to growl menacingly, five feet from the door. There was another round of loud banging. *Geez, we have a doorbell.*

"Just a second! I'll be there," John called out.

"FBI. Open up," came the loud reply.

Rufus let out another round of threatening yelping.

"*Rufus!*" John yelled. "Go to the kitchen." Rufus backed a few steps, growling, eyes not leaving the door.

"John Resnic?" The voice yelled from outside the door.

"Yeah, I'm John. I'm coming."

"Open up *right now*, Resnic. We have a search warrant."

John unlocked the door and opened it. Three large men in suits barged in displaying badges. One of them shoved a paper at John as they entered. "Search warrant," he said tersely.

Fangs bared, Rufus' menacing growl became ferocious, terrifying barks as he crouched, inching toward the group. The man who had thrust the warrant at John pulled a pistol from his shoulder holster in one lighting movement and pointed it at Rufus. "You get that damned dog out of here *right now*, or I'm gonna blow his brains out."

John's jaw dropped. "*Don't!*" he started toward Rufus as the canine came another step closer.

"You've got five seconds to get that dog *out* of this house, or he's dead."

John stepped between the gunman and Rufus. "*Now!*" the man shouted.

John jerked into action, lunged at Rufus, grabbed his collar, and dragged the eighty-pound, straining animal through the kitchen. On the way out the back door, John grabbed a pen and slip of paper from the shelf, making sure the quick motion was hidden from the agents by his body. Outside, he quickly scrawled a note and wrapped it around the dog's collar under its neck. John tossed the pen into the yard and went back in the house. The three agents were making their way into the kitchen. Rufus was making an ungodly racket outside. John wondered if these three glorified thugs were really FBI. He had no way of being sure.

Don Miller

The man with the gun, the oldest and apparent leader of the trio, said, "I'm Jack Talbot. This is Clarence James and Dorian Clemson", he nodded toward the other two as he spoke. "We're special agents with the FBI. *Jesus!* Can't you shut that dog up? I'm telling you it had better not get back in here. I'll kill it if it takes *one step* toward us." He was still pointing the gun in the direction of the back door.

John was beside himself. "What the hell do you expect, crashing in here, looking like you're going to attack? The dog's doing what he *knows*. He's *protecting* his family. What do you want, anyway? Nobody's done anything wrong here."

"Cry me a river, Resnic," Talbot replied sarcastically. "You're in big trouble. If I were you, I'd keep a civil tongue."

"In trouble for *what*?"

"You're under suspicion of conducting activities subversive to the security of the United States of America," Talbot answered.

"*What?* That's *crazy*. *What* activities? What're you lookin' for?"

Clemson, built like a heavyweight boxer and emanating the aura of one in the middle of a fight, spoke up. "Read the warrant, smartass. *We* are gonna search these premises, and *you* are gonna cooperate, or we'll cuff your ass and haul you downtown."

Talbot looked hard at John and said, "Megan Stanforth lives here, too, right? Where is she?"

"She's gone to visit her folks in Los Alamos for the weekend," John lied, praying she wouldn't get home until long after these agent thugs had left. Thinking the fastest way to get them out of the house was to cooperate, John forced himself to calm down. "Look," he said, "I'm sorry if I seem defensive. You guys scared the crap out of me. I wasn't expecting any of this, and my dog's never seen anything like it. I'll cooperate. Just tell me what you want, and I'll show you where it is."

"'Bout time you wised up," Clemson grunted.

Talbot said, "The warrant gives us the right to confiscate any and all paperwork you have, and all electronic and communications devices – computers, cell phones, what have you."

John was taken aback. "Okay. I'll show you what we have. Could you explain to me exactly what it is you think I've done?"

"I thought you said you were gonna stop bein' a smartass and cooperate," Clemson harassed him, as the other two looked on. "We already *told* you you're under suspicion of conducting subversive activities. Our job here is to collect evidence, and that's *exactly* what we're gonna do. Now, show us your computers, cell phones, fax machine, and anything else you use for communicating."

John led them through the house. The men took John's laptop and Megan's computer and all peripheral devices. Clarence, the youngest of the group and the only one who seemed to have been introduced to the concept of human civility, loaded the confiscated property into the back of their unmarked white-panel van. They took John's company cell phone. John showed them his desk and file cabinets. They took every scrap of paper. He opened the safe, and they took all the paperwork and the lockbox key. At that point, John spoke up: "You guys are taking *everything*. Does this warrant give you the authority to take anything you see, or is it limited to just certain *specific* things?"

Clemson exploded. "Are you *stupid*, Resnic? *You* are gonna be charged with being a subversive. You've got no property. The way things are in this country right now, you've got no rights. If we find anything that connects you to those damn Nazis, I'll tell you what, you've got no *life*. Now, we've had all the *shit* we're gonna take from you. Do you have any *more* stupid questions?"

"Just a couple." John mustered all the self restraint he could find in himself. "Are you going to arrest me, and can I call my attorney?"

"Mr. Resnic," Talbot responded, "we are *not* going to arrest you. We *are* going to escort you to our headquarters for questioning. If you want to call an attorney, you can do that from there. You're not under arrest, and we're not reading you your rights. But, you *are* coming with us. You may *not* call anyone before you get to headquarters. You won't be asked any questions before you get to headquarters. When did you say

Stanforth will get back?" he asked, immediately contradicting his previous statement but obviously not caring.

"She'll get back Sunday night, probably around eight. And this process doesn't seem like the way American justice works."

"That's *it*, Resnic," said Clemson. "I warned you about your shit a half-dozen times, and that's all you're gettin'. Cuff him, Clarence."

"Place your hands behind your back, Mr. Resnic," Clarence said evenly.

John stood unmoving, in disbelief.

"*Do it now!*" Clemson yelled.

John put his hands behind his back. Clarence said, "You caught Dorian on a bad day, Resnic. That's never a good thing."

"Okay, let's go." Talbot said.

Rufus was going crazy at the back door.

"*Christ!*" Clemson yelled. "Can I go *shoot* that damn dog now?"

"No," Talbot said. "Let's go. *Move!*" he commanded John, who could not believe what was happening.

The unmarked panel van had a full bench seat behind the front seats. It had a sliding side door behind the driver's door for access to the backseat, but not on the passenger side. There were no side windows at the backseat, and behind the backseat was a solid partition, concealing whatever cargo was stowed in the rear. John, hands cuffed behind him, was positioned uncomfortably behind the front passenger seat. Clarence sat behind Clemson, who was driving. John wanted to ask if he could at least have his hands cuffed in front of him, instead of behind his back, but kept quiet to avoid further antagonizing Clemson.

Talbot glanced back at Clarence and said, "Blindfold him."

John wondered what the purpose of *that* could be, but he kept silent as Clarence placed dark goggles over his head and positioned them so that he could see nothing. There was little conversation as they drove. John said nothing, trying to figure out what might have brought about this assault and trying to project what the next hours might bring.

Invitation

The most likely cause, he thought, was that the Government might have discovered his Internet communications with Liz and Ben. Maybe his behavior at the police station on Thursday had pissed off Sergeant Mallory enough to cause trouble, but that didn't seem likely. It was possible these men might be thugs *impersonating* FBI agents. Clemson especially seemed to fit that scenario. But, what would a group of thugs want with him? They probably were Government agents. What were they looking for?

If this was the Government, something had pointed to John. The only thing he could think of was interception of the emails to Liz and Ben that someone had finally gotten around to reading. If that was the case, then this was *all* about Bremo, which would increase the probability that the aliens were real. If Bremo was the issue, what did the Government intend to accomplish by confiscating all of his electronic devices and his paperwork, not to mention his person? *How far will they go to get what they want?*

If this was about Bremo, then the Government probably knew what was really behind the infertility crisis and vaporizations. They probably knew Bremo's aims and were trying to obtain intelligence on how to mount a defense against what they would be considering an attack on Earth. John didn't think they would find any reference to Bremo in any of his papers. And, if Randy could find no trace in his computer of any of the Bremo communications, he doubted anyone else would. That would leave the Government believing the only sources of information they would have would be *his mind* and – he shuddered at his next thought – *Megan's.*

He prayed that Megan would come home, comprehend the situation, and get lost before they went back for her. To what extent would they go to extract information from him, information he couldn't give because he didn't have? How soon would the process begin? Where were they taking him? It was already painfully clear that he was to have no clue where he was going. Should he begin to concoct some sort of lie, some believable story, to tell them? Would that help or hurt? If things were going to become unbearable, would making up something buy him any more bearable time? *Will I be able to last long enough for Megan to signal Bremo?*

What about Randy and Kathy? And Brady? The trail will lead to them. They'll go for them, too. Maybe they already have. He shivered again. He could only hope it would be at least a day before that happened, and that he could stretch things out until then. And that Megan would understand the situation and act in time.

After what seemed like hours – which was actually forty five minutes – the van slowed, turned, and stopped. John thought they were going through a checkpoint or guard station. He heard Clemson's window go down, then back up. No one said a word, but it sounded like a gate opened, and then they were moving again, slower. After a few more minutes and several turns, they came to a stop. He heard Talbot get out and then heard another gate or large door slide open. The van pulled forward a short distance, and then Clemson braked to a stop and shut off the motor. John heard the gate close.

"Okay, Resnic, we're getting out," Clarence said. "Watch your step." Apparently, neither the cuffs nor the blindfold were coming off. Clarence took John by the arm and helped him out of the van. Then, he escorted John a distance of what seemed to be about one hundred feet. "We're gonna go up a steep stair, now. Go slow, and watch your step. I'll be right behind you and catch you if you trip. I'll tell you when you get to the top."

Wouldn't it be simpler to take off the blindfold? John tentatively found the first step with his right foot and began going unsteadily up, saying nothing.

When they got to the top, Clarence told John to duck his head and take three steps forward so he could follow John off the stair. Then he guided John a few feet to his left. "Okay, turn around," Clarence said. "There's a seat behind you. I'll help you sit."

Someone came up the stair, and John heard Talbot say, "Here he is."

A voice John didn't recognize said, "Resnic?"

"Yep," Talbot answered. "We've got his computers, cell phone, electronic storage devices, and every document from his house. Dorian's getting it all out of the van. Clarence, help him get it loaded."

"Where's Stanforth?" the stranger asked.

"She wasn't there," Talbot answered. "Resnic said she's visiting her parents for the weekend and will get home Sunday night."

"Post a watch on the place. Resnic, you wouldn't lie to your Government, would you?"

John's heart leapt. "I don't know who you are, but I have no reason to lie to *anyone*."

Silence for a moment. "Jack, stake the place out today, just as soon as you can get back there."

"Will do."

John tried to figure the time. They had left his house at about 10:30. It had to be at least 11:30 now. *It'll take them an hour to leave here and get back to the house. They're Government. Surely, they'll stop for lunch. Megan said she'd be back by noon. She should be gone before they get there. Don't be late, Megan! And get away from there!*

Fifteen minutes later, Talbot and his gang left. Before leaving, Clarence said, "You'll need this fastened, Resnic." He reached around John and fastened a seatbelt. Then he cuffed one of John's legs to something under the seat. "Lean forward and I'll uncuff your hands." John was grateful for that. "Now, hold your hands in front of you." Clarence refastened the cuffs, and then John heard him go down the stair. Shortly after he departed, John heard a door near the top of the stair close and latch. A few minutes later, he heard, and felt, two jet engines start up.

Megan pulled in the drive at 12:25. It had been harder to leave her friends than she had anticipated. She had tried to act normal, but they had perceived this was *not* a normal visit. In the end, she had admitted she and John were moving away and had personal reasons for not being able to say where. She had been unable to hold back tears. She was still upset as she pulled in the drive.

Something was amiss. Nothing looked wrong, but it *felt* wrong. *Get hold of yourself.*

"John, I'm back," she called out as she entered through the front door. "Sorry I'm late, honey. It was hard to leave." No response. Rufus barked from the backyard. *They must be out back*, she thought as she started through the front room.

Then she noticed the two file drawers in the desk were open and empty. "John!" she called out louder. Rufus barked again. From where she stood, she could see into part of the den, and she thought she saw the safe open. She ran down the short hall, looked in the room. The *safe* was open… and *empty*. *All* the file drawers in the den were open and empty. And her computer was gone.

"*John!*" She ran to the back door and went out. When Rufus saw her, he stopped barking and began to whimper. "Rufus, what happened?" she asked breathlessly, scared. Spying the note under his collar, she grabbed it and read. "Get away from here fast. If I don't call by 9 am Sun take us."

"*Oh, God!* Rufus, what happened?" She thought for a second, then said, "Wait here, puppy. I'll be *right* back. I'm going to Marty and Brenda's for a minute." As she ran out the front door, she found Marty scurrying up the driveway.

"We were watching and saw you come home, and I thought I should come over right away."

"Did you see what happened?" Megan cried anxiously.

"Part of it. We started watching when we heard Rufus making all kinds of racket. At first, we didn't see anything. There was a white panel van parked in your drive. Pretty soon, a couple of big guys started carrying stuff out of your house. It looked mostly like computer stuff and papers. Then they brought John out, *handcuffed,* and put him in the van and drove off."

"When?"

"They left around 10:30. We first heard the commotion about forty-five minutes before that. Do you have any idea what's up?"

"I don't have a *clue!* How many guys? What were they like? Police?"

"We saw three of them, wearing suits. Didn't look like cops. The van didn't have any markings we could see. Just a plain white panel van. The license plates had some sort of tinted plastic over them, so we couldn't make out any numbers."

"Oh, Marty," Megan breathed. "I've gotta get Rufus and get out of here."

"Are you guys in trouble?"

"I don't know. I mean we *shouldn't* be. We haven't done anything wrong. I don't know. The whole world's going *crazy*. Thursday, my best friend Kathy was attacked at the mall. She's seven months pregnant, and she and her son were with a friend who's over eight months pregnant, and they were *attacked*. It was kidnapping, but they escaped. John went to the police with Kathy's husband, and I think he got a little belligerent. I don't know if this has anything to do with that or not."

Marty saw her clutching the note tightly in her fist. "Did John leave you a note?"

"I have to leave, Marty," she responded abruptly. "I think they might be coming back for me. I've gotta go *now!* If they come back and ask if you've seen me, *please*, if you can find it in your heart, just tell them no." She gave him a quick hug, turned, and ran back into the house.

She ran to the back door to get Rufus. "C'mon, boy, let's go."

Rufus barked and ran after her. Megan took a quick look around the room to assure herself she hadn't rearranged anything, and hurried to the car, putting Rufus in the back. She looked back and said, "Lie down, Rufus." He did. She didn't know why she said that. Maybe instinct. She didn't know why he obeyed.

Where am I going? She backed out of the drive. *I have to let Randy and Kathy know. Go there.*

Talbot, Clemson, and Clarence were on their way back to the Resnic residence. Clemson said, "I could eat a *horse*, Jack. Let's get some lunch."

"We'll take care of your hunger pangs later, Dorian. Something tells me our boy would lie in a heartbeat to protect his woman. We'd better get back there and set up the stakeout first. *Then* we'll worry about your gut. There was a neighbor just down the street. We'll impose ourselves on their hospitality for a good vantage point. After we're set up, we'll send Clarence for food."

Clemson scowled but kept driving. It was 12:30 and they would be back at Resnic's in ten minutes. A mile before they got to Resnic's road, as they were rounding a curve,

Clemson looked over at Talbot and said, "What're we going to send Clarence for? I could do with two or three big-ass burgers. Saturday work should allow for a couple of beers, too, especially for stakeout work for some gal who isn't even *coming back* till tomorrow."

"Dammit, Dorian. Like you don't know any better than drinking on duty? Whatever put the burr under your saddle today must've been a whopper. Keep your eyes on the road. Did you even *see* that car we just passed?"

"What car?" Clemson grinned.

Megan's heart leapt to her throat. Rounding the bend in the road, coming straight toward her, was a white panel van. Two big guys in suits in the front seat, and somebody was in the back. The two in front were talking to each other, not even watching the road as they passed by. She thought they hadn't noticed her. As soon as the van was out of sight in her rearview mirror, she punched her speed up to eighty-five, but quickly decided it was crucial to avoid a police pullover. She grudgingly forced her foot to ease up on the pedal, slowing to the speed limit.

Randy and Kathy were not home. Megan knew where they kept the spare key, and she knew the alarm code, so she let herself and Rufus in. Then she went into the garage, opened the overhead door, drove her car in, and closed the door. She desperately wanted to call Randy and Kathy to alert them of the turn of events. However, she assumed they were visiting family, possibly for the last time, and she didn't want to put a damper on that. She would wait as long as she could before calling them. She turned on the television for no reason except to make noise to ease her nerves. She couldn't *begin* to focus on whatever was on. She paced. Rufus lay quietly and watched her, whimpering from time to time.

By 4:00, she could stand it no longer and dialed Kathy's cell phone. It sent her to voice mail. Trying to sound natural, she left a message: "Hi, Kathy. It's Megan. When you get a chance, give me a call on my cell. I really need to talk to you." Catching herself before she hung up, she added, "Don't call our house phone." Then she hung up and paced for another hour. *Maybe her battery's dead. It's not like Kathy to let that happen, but her life is stressed, too.* She tried Randy's phone and immediately heard it ring in the bedroom. *Oh, no! He forgot it.* That *wasn't* a surprise, considering it was Randy. She tried Kathy again, and again was sent to voicemail.

"Shit."

Calm down. Calm down and think. She sat at the dining table and looked absently out the window. *What's happening? What do I have to do? They've got John. Our computers. Our documents. How could it be anyone, except the Government? If it's the Government, this is about Bremo. About getting information. What will they do to get it?*

She trembled and tears came to her eyes as she whispered, "John, where *are* you?" She shook it off. *What do you need me to do?* She opened the note he'd left and stared at it. "Get away from here fast. If I don't call by 9 am Sun take us." *He didn't know what was going to happen. The note's a guess. I have to trust it. He'll do everything to make it till then.*

She would need a computer. Kathy's laptop had communicated with Bremo last night. There it was, at the computer desk. She turned it on to make sure it would boot up and didn't require a password. It worked.

I've got to talk to them. Surely they'll come home tonight. Make sure. She walked into their bedroom and on into the master bath. *No toothbrushes. No sign of Randy's shaver. No! Gone for the night. Probably at Kathy's mother's. Find the number and call.* She went to the house phone and checked its speed dial feature. "Mom" was there, and Megan entered it. The phone on the other end rang ten times before Megan gave up. No voicemail. *Dammit! They're just out to dinner. If Kathy doesn't call by nine, I'll try again.*

Nine o'clock. The thought of time struck panic in her soul. *Twelve hours before John's deadline. Is Bremo real? What if I can't reach Kathy? Could I send us? By myself? No. If Randy and Kathy don't even know? I'd have to. No choice. I couldn't do it! Kathy will be here. It won't be me. She'll do it.*

"John, what are they *doing* to you?" she cried, trembling. Rufus looked up at her. "Where *are* you? Are you hurt?" She didn't pray often, but she prayed now. Remembering she had left the computer on, she walked to it and turned it off. Then she turned it back on again and watched it boot up. Then she turned it off again. "You're a *wreck*," she said.

At 8:00 on Saturday night, Jack Talbot, Dorian Clemscn, and Clarence James were settled comfortably in the home of Marty and Brenda Black, intently watching out the living room picture window at the house down the street. At first, the Blacks had resisted allowing the use of their home for spying on their neighbors. However, it had taken less than five minutes for them to understand that their home was going to be used with or without their permission. They had answered a few questions.

Yes, they were acquainted with John Resnic and Megan Stanforth. No, they had never visited each other socially. No, they didn't really know their neighbors' habits, except that they were quiet and respectful. Yes, they had seen some of the morning's commotion. The dog had gotten their attention. Yes, they had seen property being confiscated and John being taken away in handcuffs. They'd been surprised and disturbed by what they had seen. No, they had not seen Megan Stanforth all day. No, they had not heard any barking from the dog since John had been escorted away. No, they had no idea what had happened to the dog. It had probably jumped the fence and run off after the disturbance.

Shortly after 6:00, Marty asked Talbot if he and his wife could leave and go to dinner. Yes, they could go. Talbot felt more at ease in the house with the owners gone, anyway. It was beginning to look to him like Resnic had been telling the truth. So far, there had been no sign of Stanforth.

*   *   *

Randy, Kathy, Brady, and Kathy's mother Bea arrived at Bea's house after their dinner outing, just before 8:30. Kathy planned to tell Bea on Sunday morning after breakfast that they would be moving away. She wanted tonight to be as normal as possible, especially for Brady and his grandma. On the way home from the restaurant, Kathy had tried to call Randy's dad to confirm their planned Sunday-afternoon visit. She had been giving Randy a hard time for forgetting his cell phone when, as she had tried to dial his dad, she discovered *her* phone was not working.

As they walked into Bea's house, Kathy complained. "I don't know what the heck's wrong with my phone. It was charged when we left home this morning, and I never used it. The battery must be shot." Her mother's house phone rang as she walked past it. "I'll get it," she said. Then, glancing at the caller ID, she said, "What in the world? It's *our* house calling!"

"Hello?" she answered, warily putting the phone to her ear. "Megan! Are you calling from our place?" She was silent for a long time, which caught Randy and Bea's attention. Worry etched onto her face. "Honey, are you okay?" Kathy finally asked. Another period of silence. "Right." More silence. "No, that's okay. My cell phone isn't working. We'll be there by eight in the morning. Are you sure you'll be okay tonight? All right. If you need anything, even if you just need to talk, call back. I'll take Mom's phone into our room tonight. Get some rest. Goodbye, Megan."

Randy and Bea stared at her as she struggled with what to tell them. "That was Megan. She and John had a big fight today, and she left. She went to our house because she didn't know where else to go."

Randy was quiet.

"John and Megan had a fight?" Brady asked. "Is Woofis okay?"

"Yes, honey, Rufus is fine." Kathy forced a tight smile. "He's at our house with Megan."

"That just doesn't sound like John and Megan, at all," Bea said. "What happened?"

"It sounded like it all started out pretty silly," Kathy replied, trying to be evasive in order to avoid making up more than necessary. "I really think it's just premarital jitters and hormones. I'm sure everything'll be fine tomorrow."

"Will we get to see Woofis?" Brady asked.

"Yes, we'll see Rufus in the morning. I told Megan we'd be home by eight. I'm sorry, Mom. I *really* wanted to stay for lunch before going to Randy's dad's, but I think Megan needs us pretty badly."

"It's okay, Kathy. We had a great time today. There'll be other days we can have lunch." Kathy, in spite of her effort, could not restrain a tear from rolling down her cheek. "This is worse than you're letting on, isn't it?" Bea said. "Are you sure they'll be okay? Do you need to go to her tonight?"

"No, Mom." Kathy hugged her. "I'm sure she'll be fine till tomorrow. We'll just have to get up and leave early." *How will I be able to tell her in the morning? No time.*

Invitation

Chapter 23
Sunday, April 27

Randy and Kathy had set the alarm in the spare bedroom for 4:45, tight for getting home by 8:00, allowing for the hour-and-a-half drive and for spending some time with Bea over breakfast. It wouldn't be a morning for skipping showers and shaving considering that it could be *the* day. The night was short and fitful. Kathy woke and glanced at the clock at 4:13, feeling as if she'd slept for ten minutes. She had a headache and felt sluggish to the point of being drugged. The thought that she should get up flitted through her mind, but instead, she closed her eyes.

In what seemed the next instant, she heard and felt Randy toss covers and leap out of bed. She heard him howl, "*Shit!*" She looked at the clock, which displayed 5:20. Kathy bolted upright and then almost swooned. Dizzy, she braced herself for a few seconds, regaining her steadiness, before rolling off the bed and stumbling to the bathroom. She cursed her defective cell phone and its unusable alarm. She cursed the clock-radio that apparently had not gone off, and she cursed Randy's cell phone for lying at home on the dresser.

Last night, they had made an exception and allowed Brady to stay up as long as he wanted, showing off for Grandma. By 11:00, he had conked out on the sofa, and Randy had carted him off to bed. Randy and Kathy had stayed up talking with Bea until after midnight, when her eyelids had drifted dreamily closed in mid-sentence. At that point, they had all gone to bed. Kathy had filled Randy in on John and Megan's predicament in bits and pieces during the evening. After going to bed, they had talked until 2:00.

Maybe John would get released, and they would all be together Sunday morning, allowing them two more days, as they had planned. They *desperately* needed the time. They were not

272

ready. John getting apprehended had convinced Kathy beyond any doubt that, when they clicked the "send" button, they would be gone. Randy didn't argue the point, but Kathy knew he still couldn't believe it. They didn't discuss the alternative. That scenario had its own dilemmas. What would happen to John? *What would happen to them all?*

While they'd lain in bed, Kathy's mind had recapped the day spent with her mom. She'd gone through her list of people she still needed to see or talk to. Her lips had moved as her mind flitted. She'd cried, which was way out of character. Randy had consoled her. They'd consoled each other.

There appeared to be no choice, if Megan didn't receive word from John before 9:00. He would do everything in his power to make it until then. Unless something unexpected happened in the next few hours, Sunday would be the day. Sunday morning. *Today.*

Kathy didn't know whether the alarm hadn't worked or they hadn't set it right or they had slept through it. It didn't matter. By 5:50 she and Randy were showered, dressed, and ready to spend their last minutes with Bea, over breakfast. Randy went to rouse Brady while Kathy helped Bea set breakfast on the table. They talked their way through breakfast. Kathy tried hard to be herself but made a poor showing.

At one point, Bea asked, "Kathy, are you okay? Is it just John and Megan, or is there something else?"

"No, Mom, it's just them," Kathy lied. "They're our best friends. I know how upset Megan is, and I want to help."

"I'm sure it'll all work out, honey. They really love each other. They'll fix it. John'll probably be there by the time you get home, and everything'll be fine."

"You have no idea how happy that would make me," Kathy replied, thinking how much of an understatement that was. She couldn't tell her mother what was going to happen. She didn't have the words. There was no time. She couldn't tell her, and she couldn't not tell her. She felt *awful*.

Cheating time, Randy delayed until 6:35 before saying, "Honey, you know how much I'd like to stay and visit, but we really have to get on the road."

"I know," Kathy replied, getting up from the table.

By the time they had everything loaded and ready to go, it was 6:40. Standing by the car Kathy said, "We're going to be ten or fifteen minutes late. I don't want Megan to worry about us on the road, on top of everything else. Mom, I need to run back in and use your phone."

Kathy ran back inside, cursing her cell phone for the hundredth time. And Randy's. She dialed Megan's cell phone. Voicemail. Megan probably had not thought to bring her charger in her rush to get out of their house on Saturday. "Damn cell phones," she breathed, hurriedly dialing her home phone. "Pick it *up*, Megan," she pleaded into the mouthpiece. Megan answered on the second ring, and Kathy quickly explained that time had been their enemy all morning, and they were just now leaving. "We'll be there," she glanced at the clock on the wall, "by quarter-after-eight." She hung up after the short conversation, ran out to the car, and hugged her mom tightly, trying to hide her tears. "We love you, Mom," she said as she entered the car and closed the door. "Goodbye." She had not even *hinted* to Bea that they might be going away.

"Mommy, are you crying?" Brady asked from the backseat as they left.

She sniffed. "I'm okay, Brady. I wanted to spend more time with Grandma, and I'm a little bit worried about Megan. Everything will be okay, though." She knew that, before they arrived home, she would have to pull Brady onto her lap and find some way to explain to him what was going to happen this morning.

It was normally a forty-five-minute drive from Bea's home in Mountainair to Interstate 25, half on Route 60 and the rest on 47. Randy made up for lost time, and they reached Route 47 in less than twenty minutes. At this rate, they'd reach the interstate by 7:20.

The railroad track was five minutes past the split of 47 and 60. Just as the track came into sight, the lights started flashing. The gates started their downward arc when their car was still a quarter of a mile away. "Shit," Randy muttered. The train was coming. It was slow. Kathy could read her husband's mind, knew he was thinking he could beat it to the crossing. She gave him a look she knew he couldn't misinterpret: *Don't try it.* He slowed and stopped just as the engine reached the highway.

It was a long train. The terrain was flat, and they could see for a long distance but could not see the end of the train. Kathy guessed its speed at twenty miles per hour, and slowing. She watched Randy seethe. Slower and slower. The train must have been about halfway through the crossing when it stopped. 7:10.

"*God damn it!*" Randy couldn't hold it in.

Kathy glanced back at Brady, who was watching the back of his daddy's head. "It's okay, honey," she said quietly to Brady. "We just want to get back to Megan." She placed her hand on Randy's arm and rubbed gently. "It's okay, honey," she whispered again.

They waited three minutes, which seemed like an eternity. The train didn't budge. Randy looked at Kathy. "I've gotta turn around and take 60 to the interstate. That'll cost us half an hour."

"I know. We'll still make it by about eight-thirty. Be safe. We're all right on time."

Randy squeezed her hand and turned the car around. They reached the interstate at 7:30. They had just under an hour's drive on the interstate, and then five minutes to their house. Randy punched it to ninety, watching both ahead and behind for troopers. *Surely*, Kathy thought, *they won't be looking for speeders this early on Sunday morning.*

They were – from the air. After ten minutes on the interstate, Randy looked in the rearview mirror and saw distant flashing lights racing toward them. He slammed on the brakes and slowed to seventy before the cruiser could get close enough to clock his speed. Kathy looked sharply at him when she felt the brakes grab, and, seeing him looking in the rearview mirror, turned and saw the cop closing.

"He can't *possibly* be after us," Randy said. As the cruiser pulled in behind them and turned on his siren, Randy blurted, "Shit! What else can go wrong?" Brady was quiet and looked worried in the back.

Kathy could feel her husband's frustration as he said, "I could tell him we're having a medical emergency."

"I think the fastest way out is to have everything ready, give him anything he wants, thank him, and get back on the road."

"God, I'm sorry, honey," Randy said.

Kathy could see him fighting tears, hysteria. She knew he felt like he was screwing up the biggest crisis of their lives. "It's going to turn out all right," she said, rubbing his arm again. "None of this is your fault."

He looked at her and said, "I love you, Kathy."

"I know. I love you, too."

The ticket was issued, and they were released, ten more minutes behind schedule. As they pulled into traffic and accelerated to seventy-two, Kathy smiled at Randy, searching for some way to lessen the tension. "You know, there *is* one bright side to that little stop." Randy looked blankly at her. "That's two hundred bucks the State of New Mexico is *never* going to see from us. At least that's *one* little satisfying victory in this crappy morning."

Randy forced a grin. It was 7:50 and, provided nothing else would go wrong, they would be home in fifty minutes. Kathy, feeling more in control than she had all morning, looked back at Brady and said, "Honey, we're going to break a rule this morning. We're going to unfasten you, and you're coming up here to sit on my lap."

"Okay, Mommy." In ten seconds, he was on her lap, with one arm around her neck.

"Brady, we're going on an adventure today, and I want to tell you about it."

"Are Woofis and Megan going, too?" he asked, looking worried.

"Yes, they are."

"What about John? You said John and Megan had a fight. Is it better now?"

"Honey, John and Megan didn't *really* have a fight. I *had* to tell Grandma that, so she wouldn't worry. Listen to me, and I'll explain. There are some really good people and some really bad people in the world."

"I know about the *bad* people, Mommy. We saw them at the mall, with Bernie. You showed them!"

"Yes, you did see some bad people. Well, some bad people like that went to John's house yesterday, and they took John away. Don't worry. We're going to get him back. But, I couldn't tell Grandma, because Grandma would have worried about us, and I didn't want her to worry anymore."

"Are the bad people after *us* again?"

"Not today. And our adventure today will get us away from them for *good*."

"How? What about John? Will *he* get away?"

"Yes. We're *all* going to get away to the good people "

"Where *are* the good people? Who are they?"

"Well, Brady, I'm going to tell you what I think is going to happen today. But, we aren't completely sure. We think we know, but if it doesn't work out like we think, we have another plan." Brady looked up at her questioningly. She took a deep breath and went on.

"You've seen things on television about space people. Well, it might be hard to believe, but we've been talking to some really *nice* space people on the Internet. They have a *wonderful* place to live, and they've asked *us* if we'd like to live with them." Kathy was surprised at how ridiculous she sounded to herself as she tried to explain this to her son. "All of us, your daddy and me and you, and John and Megan and Rufus.

"You've heard us talk about how bad things are getting here and how dangerous. *Lots* of people are getting attacked, like we did at the mall. So Daddy, John, Megan, and I decided we want to *all* go together and live with the space people. We weren't going to go for a few days, but now, because the bad people have John, we have to go right away. John left Megan a note saying we should all go today if he isn't back from the bad people."

"But, what about *John*?" Brady asked. "What if he isn't *back* when we go?"

"When we tell the space people – they're from a place called Bremo – when we tell them to take us, they'll get John, too, no matter *where* he is."

"How will we get there? We can't *drive* to space, can we?"

"No, we can't. It'll be different than any way we've ever travelled before. When your daddy and I tell you it's time, just close your eyes for a minute, and when you open them, we'll be there."

"Like *magic*?"

"Yes, honey, like magic."

"John, too?"

"Yes."

"Even *Woofis*?"

"Yes."

"Wow! Will Woofis live with us, then? What about our baby, and Megan's baby?"

"We will all go, and we'll all be together."

"What about *Grandma*? And Grandpa Jarrett and Grandma Jane?"

"They aren't coming right now," Kathy said, trying hard to sound strong and confident. "But, after a few months, we can invite them, and they can come then."

"Do they know we're doing this? They'll be scared for us. Can we call and tell them we're okay?"

"Honey, that's one of the really hard things. In order for them to be safe from the bad people here, we can't tell them right now. They'll be worried about us, and that bothers us a lot. As soon as it's safe for them to know, we can email them and tell them we're okay. And invite them to come, too."

"But, you're not *sure* we're going? Why *not*?"

"Well, we've never done this before. We believe the space people. And we've talked to other people who say they *have* already done it, and they love it. But, *we've* never done it ourselves, so we aren't completely sure."

"But we're *almost* sure? What if it doesn't work?"

"Yes, we're almost positive. If it doesn't work, then we're all going to move to a place far away from here, where we'll be safer."

"But, if it doesn't work, then who'll get *John*?"

"We don't know, yet." Kathy paused, trying not to think through that. "We'd have to figure that out."

"I hope it works," Brady said somberly.

Kathy pulled him to her tightly. "I do too, honey."

Kathy looked at Randy, who'd been listening. He half-smiled and squeezed her hand. They were almost to the Los Lunas exit. It was 8:05, and they'd be home in just over half an hour. Kathy worried about Megan. She would be expecting their arrival in ten minutes, and they had no way to call her. She saw Randy glance at the clock and knew he was thinking of Megan, too, and beating himself up again for leaving his cell phone at home. Well, at least they were going to make it.

Five miles past the Los Lunas exit, Kathy saw all the brake lights ahead of them light up. Within three minutes, they were at a dead stop, six miles beyond the last exit and four miles from the next one. It was 8:17. They couldn't turn around in the median, go back to the previous exit, and take the streets through Albuquerque, and still make it by 9:00. That would take well over an hour. They couldn't get out and walk cross-country to the nearest road and hitchhike or get a cab and make it by 9:00. Not even close. Traffic was stopped as far ahead as she could see. It had to be an accident. Their only hope was to drive up the berm to the next exit. If they could make the exit in ten minutes, they could drive straight up 47 to Alameda. If they pressed it and ignored speed limits, stop lights, and cops, they could make that drive in half an hour and still arrive with five minutes to spare. Randy and Kathy looked at each other.

"What time do we have to be home to go to the spacemen?" Brady asked his mother worriedly.

"We wanted to be there by nine o'clock."

"The clock says eight-eighteen," Brady said, looking at the digital clock in the car. "Can we still make it, Daddy?"

"We're gonna try." He eased the car onto the berm. They went a quarter of a mile before a tanker truck saw them coming in his rearview mirror, and pulled over to block their path. The roadside embankment was steep at that spot, so they couldn't pull around the truck. Randy looked at Kathy. "I could go talk to the guy, tell him we're having an emergency and *really* need to get to the exit."

"How many more times would we have to do that, and how long would it take us?" Kathy asked with calm resignation. "We're done. Everything's been against us this morning. Megan's a smart girl, and she's got a cool head. She'll do what it takes."

"Do we have to be home with Megan to go to the space people?" Brady asked.

"No, honey," Kathy answered. "They told us if any of us, Megan or John or your daddy or me, tells them to take us, they'll get us all, no matter *where* we are."

"So, Megan can tell them we want to go all by *herself*?"

"Yes, she can." Kathy wondered how difficult this morning had been for her best friend, and what kind of unforeseen problems of her own she'd had to deal with.

It was 8:30. Most of the drivers had shut off their motors. Randy received a few disapproving glares from nearby motorists seeing the awkward position of their car on the berm. Kathy had one arm wrapped around Brady. She placed her other on Randy's thigh palm up. "You might as well shut it off. Even if the jam started to move way up ahead, there's no way we can get home by nine, now. All we can do is wait and leave it in Megan's hands. There's nothing else to do."

Randy turned off the ignition and intertwined his fingers in his wife's. Brady laid his head on his mother's shoulder. They sat quietly and watched the minutes tick off the clock in ultra-slow-motion.

*   *   *

It was a long flight. John didn't have a clue where they were headed. He guessed somewhere on the east coast, but it could just as easily have been out of the country. He remained cuffed but was relieved that his hands were in front of him. The blindfold had not been removed. He sensed the continued presence of the stranger who had talked to Talbot, but the man didn't speak. John couldn't hear him stir or breathe. He assumed the man was either reading or sleeping, but he never heard either pages turning or deep breathing.

John didn't know how long they'd been in flight. It seemed like days but was probably three or four hours. After they landed, John, still blindfolded and with hands again cuffed behind his back, was escorted off the jet and placed into the backseat of a car. Then came a ride of what John guessed to be half an hour, followed by an escort into a building. He was led into a room where he was again belted into a chair and had ankle shackles applied. The handcuffs were removed and re-secured, with his hands again in front. No one had spoken to him since he'd boarded the plane, and he hadn't uttered a word. The only conversation he'd heard had been his captors talking brusquely with one another.

"Uncuff his leg."

"I'll lead him down the steps."

"Put him in the car."

"Take him to four-fifty-two and secure him."

"Give him some water." *That* had been a welcome command. He'd had nothing to eat all day, and nothing to drink since the three cups of morning coffee. A bottle of water was placed in his hands, and he savored it.

He had been assisted and guided, neither gently nor roughly, in moving from place to place. He had no idea what would happen next or how soon anything would happen. He guessed it was sometime Saturday night. Once seated in room 452, wherever that was, he was left alone for what seemed like hours but probably wasn't. He heard nothing except his own breathing but sensed he was being watched. He shifted in the seat from time to time in unsuccessful attempts to lessen his discomfort.

Eventually, he began to nod off, exhausted from the events and emotions of the day. The instant that sleep came, a heavy steel door clanked loudly as it was opened, and he heard a small group walk in. A man said, "Take the blindfold off." *Finally!* Its straps were tight and had cut into the skin of his head and ears. He closed his eyes as the blindfold was removed. Even with his eyes closed, the light from the room hurt his eyes. He opened them slowly, squinting to minimize the pain. The room was intensely bright. He was dead tired. His mouth was cotton, and his eyes were crusty. He had a throbbing headache. He made out three figures standing several feet from him, watching him. Two were in white lab coats. The third, standing behind them, wore a dark business suit.

"Do you want water?" The voice from before came from one of the white-robed figures.

John nodded his head slowly, and the other robed man walked to a refrigerator, extracted a bottle, brought it to John, and placed it in his hands. This time John drank greedily.

The man spoke again. "Do you need to use the bathroom?"

John nodded slowly.

"Just to urinate?"

He nodded again.

"Unfasten him."

The one who had brought the water released him and helped him stand. He said, "Bathroom's behind that door." He pointed to a door twenty feet from the chair. "Do you need help?"

John shook his head and mumbled lethargically, "No." He stood for a moment to steady himself, and then shuffled to the door. He came back out in a few minutes, becoming more alert. The man who had been doing most of the talking motioned for John to go back to the chair. He shuffled back, sat down, and was rebelted.

John looked at the three men staring at him. The talker said, "Mr. Resnic, I'm Lawrence Chirtle." Nodding toward the other, younger man, he said, "This is Duane Smith." Then looking back at the suit, who had been silently observing, he said, "And this is Brian Betz. We have some questions for you and we need you to give us your full cooperation. Do you understand?"

John spoke slowly. "Yes. May I also ask a few questions?"

Chirtle answered, "No, Mr. Resnic, this interview is one-way. You may not ask questions."

That's it? Not, 'We won't answer your questions,' but, 'You can't even ask any?' Whatever's going on here, there's nothing lawful about it. He decided to try anyway. "Mr. Chirtle, could you at least tell me what time it is?"

"Mr. Resnic, if you have difficulty comprehending or following instructions, this is quickly going to become an *extremely* unpleasant interview for you. You've been told you are not permitted to ask any questions. *None.* You do *not* get to ask the time. Now, do you understand that?"

"Yes."

"Good. Let's get on with it."

The thoughts were flowing faster through John's pounding head. It was possible he might *never* be allowed to leave this room. He had to prolong this interrogation for as long as he could and hope that, if he could last until 9:00 Sunday morning, Megan would save him. *If* Bremo was real. *If* Megan was still free. *If* Megan, Randy, and Kathy could bring themselves to send the message, knowing *nothing* of his whereabouts. He guessed it was now between midnight and 4:00

Sunday morning. He needed to seem cooperative but do everything he could to drag out the discussion. *And* protect Megan. Above all, *protect Megan.* And their child. *My second-chance child.*

Chirtle leaned against the desk in the middle of the huge room. Brian Betz stood farther back, motionless and silent, looking directly and continuously – *invasively* – at John. Smith sat on a chair beside the desk. All three watched John.

Chirtle began. "Mr. Resnic, what's your relationship with Megan Stanforth?"

John's heart thudded. He had not expected their first question to be about Megan. "We're engaged. She is carrying my child."

"Where is she right now?"

John gambled that she had not been apprehended and stuck with his earlier lie. "If this is Sunday morning or afternoon, she's probably still at her parents'. I didn't expect her home until Sunday evening." From the lack of reaction, John guessed his response hadn't conflicted with anything they already knew. He breathed an internal sigh of relief.

"Mr. Resnic, do you have any idea why you were seized?"

"The agents who abducted me told me I was suspected of being a subversive."

"Do you have any idea *why* the Government might have suspected that of you?"

"No."

"Come now, Resnic. You said Stanforth is carrying your child. Surely, you know human beings the world over are not currently fertile?"

"Yes."

"When did she become pregnant?"

"I believe on January 19, just before the infertility epidemic hit."

"Mr. Resnic, do you see any unusual coincidence in that?"

"No. We weren't trying to get pregnant. At the time, I didn't want a child. It just happened. It was just chance."

"So, you're saying you had no advance notice there'd be an action to strike the Earth with infertility?"

"No. How in the world could I have known *that*? Are you suggesting I have some kind of connection to the Nazi plot?"

"Resnic," Chirtle stated forcefully, "this is your *last* warning before it will get unpleasant. You just responded to my question with *two* of your own. *You* don't ask questions. You answer ours, and that's *it*! Give us the facts, and give them to us straight. This is the last time I'm explaining that. Now, do you *understand*, or do you need convincing?"

John couldn't help but glare at his inquisitor. "I understand."

"Did you have any advance warning the Earth would be struck with infertility?"

"No."

"Do you believe the Nazis are behind this infertility strike?" Chirtle continued.

John thought quickly and replied, "I don't know."

"You don't *know*? Have you listened to the *news* lately? Have you listened to the *President*?"

"Yes, I know what the media and the President say."

"Then why do you say you don't know?"

John spoke slowly, deliberately. "The news media blows things out of proportion. Things haven't always turned out to match the pictures they paint. And presidents have misrepresented facts to the public more than once. I'm not saying I believe that's happening now. All I'm saying is that these things have happened before. So, just because the media and the President say Nazis are behind everything, I'm not *completely* convinced that's so."

"Doesn't that sound subversive to you?"

Choosing his words carefully, John said, "No, it doesn't. The United States is a free country, full of intelligent people who think for themselves. Having a little doubt about the proclamations of the media and our political leaders is part of the American way of life."

"Well then, John, are you aware of any *other* plausible explanations for the infertility crisis? Have you heard of any other explanation that *you* think is more likely?"

"I've read dozens of opinions on-line. I can't say I think any of them are more plausible than the President's account.

But, how could I...?" He caught himself before he asked the question. "I mean, I can't be sure that *every* explanation I've read is wrong."

"Have you communicated electronically with anybody about these other explanations?"

Closing in. They probably have some of the emails to Liz and Ben. Better not lie. "I've had some communications that could probably be considered related to the infertility issue."

"With whom?"

"A couple who said they were Ben and Elizabeth."

"Who are they?"

Careful. "They're from Australia. At least, they said they are. With email, you're never sure if the people on the other end are who say they are."

"How recently have you communicated with them?"

"The last time was about a week and a half ago."

"Why did you stop emailing?"

"They told me they were closing their email account, and they didn't leave a way to contact them. I haven't heard from them since." *Keep saying "I" and "me", not "us" and "we." Keep Megan out of the picture.*

"Do you know where they are now?"

"No. Truthfully, I *never* knew for sure where they were. Only that they claimed to be in Australia."

"Did they claim to know who or what caused the infertility strike?"

"Yes."

"Who?"

"They thought aliens caused it." *They're testing me.*

"Did they identify the aliens? Did they have a *name* for them?"

"They said the aliens were from a planet called Bremo."

"Do you believe them? Did you believe them at the time?"

"I didn't know *what* to believe at the time, and I still don't."

"Have you ever contacted, tried to contact, or been contacted by these Bremo aliens?"

Concentrate! What did we say in the emails to Liz? "I had two or three emails go back and forth with someone on the Internet claiming to be Bremo."

"Mr. Resnic, was it *two* or *three?*"

"I think it was three."

"Three each way? Three from you to them, and three from them to you?"

"No, I think it was two each way, if I remember right. Four total."

"Did you *believe* what these supposed aliens were saying?"

"No, not really. It was too far-out. And, like I said before, with the Internet, you can never be sure *who* you're talking to."

"Was there anything unusual about their communications that made it seem to you like they might actually *be* aliens communicating with you?"

"They seemed to know a lot about me. More than I'd have thought any one person could know. But then, with electronic research at everybody's fingertips, it might be possible for somebody to find out a lot of personal information. I don't know."

"Anything else that that made you think they might be real?"

"It seemed uncanny how fast they could respond to questions."

"Like what?"

John tried harder to recall how far the emails to Ben and Liz had gone. "Well, some of it was kind of crazy. They said their travel method was instant teleportation. They said they could conjure up most anything from nothing. Sitting here trying to explain it, it all seems silly. I'm not sure why *anybody* would think it could be believable."

"Instant teleportation, huh? Did they give you any names of people they'd teleported?"

"Yes. Three names. I tried tracing them down but could only find one of them. I think her name was Patti Laurent, from Canada. When we checked her out, it turned out that a Patti Laurent had disappeared from Alberta a few days before. I guess that's another thing that made it seem more believable."

"What do you mean, when '*we*' checked her out? Who is '*we*'?"

John flinched, he was sure noticeably. He hesitated. "Ben and Liz and me. On the Internet." *Shit! Don't do that again.*

"What about this Ben and Liz? Did they communicate to you about any other contacts they'd made with other people about Bremo?"

"Yes. I think they said they'd been in contact with two other people, and they thought both of them had disappeared."

"Both teleported to Bremo?"

"They thought one was teleported and the other went to the police, but they lost contact with both of them."

"Has Bremo invited *you* to teleport?"

"Yes."

"Have you *accepted*?"

"No."

"Why not?"

"I can't believe it's real."

"Do you *plan* to accept?"

"No."

"Why not?"

"I can't believe it's real."

"Does this interview make it seem more real?" Chirtle's voice projected a touch of sarcasm.

"It makes me *want* it to be real," John replied, unable to refrain from returning the sentiment.

"Has Megan Stanforth been invited to teleport?"

"No. She thinks I'm crazy for ever having communicated about this on the Internet with *anybody*. She's completely convinced it's all a hoax."

"You say you communicated with whoever was claiming to be Bremo. How?"

"Email."

"What's their email address?"

"That's another strange thing that makes it more believable, or at least more inexplicable. They don't have one. The emails I received and the emails I sent contained no identification or addresses. And the emails wouldn't stay in my message bank. They disappeared. I tried to find where they might be stored in my computer, but never could find them."

"Did you print copies of the emails?"

"You're probably going to think I'm being evasive, but what really happened is that I tried. The problem was that any emails either to or from Bremo wouldn't print."

"So, you're saying there's *no* evidence you ever communicated with Bremo?"

"None that I know of. I mean, it'd be fine with me if you guys decided I'm making the whole thing up and let me go. If I'd been able to print any of the emails, I'd gladly give them to you. But, I couldn't. You've got my computer. I assume you've got somebody dissecting it right now. If *you* can find those emails in there, that'd be great. I'd like to have copies, if I could get them."

"Did Bremo give you a deadline for accepting their invitation?"

"Yes. Sometime around the end of this month."

"So, it still isn't too late for you to accept?"

"I don't think so. I think it's close though."

"You said Bremo claimed to be responsible for the infertility strike. How did they do it?"

"They didn't say."

"You didn't *ask*?"

"No."

"Mr. Resnic, how could you *not* ask so central a question that could've helped you decide if they were for real?"

"I don't know. I just didn't ask."

"All right. Then how do you *think* they did it?"

"I never said I thought they *did* do it. I told you before; I don't know *what* to believe. The government says Nazis did it. *That* seems more believable to me than aliens."

Chirtle looked over his shoulder at Brian Betz, as if to ask if there was anything else. Betz spoke for the first time, quietly, but precisely and directly. "John, did Bremo communicate any overall purpose to you?"

John had felt uncomfortable with Betz from the beginning. The eyes felt as if they bored right into his soul. "It's crazy," John responded slowly, "but they claimed their plan was to trade planets with us."

288

"Did they say why they hadn't just forcibly taken our planet?"

"They said they're committed to nonviolence. They also said they can be patient and just wait fifty years or so, until whatever's left of the human population stops resisting, if we refuse to cooperate on a trade now."

"All right. That's enough for now," Betz said to Chirtle. Then he added, and John was sure the comment was solely for his benefit, "We have enough from him to sort and evaluate his responses"

"We're going to leave the room for a while," Chirtle said. "You're probably exhausted. Feel free to get some sleep. We'll be back."

They walked out of the room but left the lights on. John thought they wanted him to get a good look at the room. He also assumed they wanted the brightness to make it difficult for him to sleep or rest. It did. He observed the room. It was big, about fifty feet square, with ceilings that looked twenty-five-feet high. He felt small in it. Everything gleamed, like a sterile clean room. The walls, floors, and ceilings were bright white. The room furnishings and accessories were stainless steel. The rear corner of the room to his left had a medical table large enough to secure an adult. It had straps to hold a body down.

He saw what he guessed were small, camouflaged cameras. Around the upper perimeter of the room were panels that were probably one-way glass. He assumed there were several pairs of eyes on him at all times and that every sound in the room was being recorded. John didn't like this room. Suddenly, he *hated* it. He hated his situation. Left alone and immobilized, he fought panic at the prospect of what the coming hours would hold in store. He exerted his full might against his restraints to see what would happen. Nothing.

Chirtle was right about one thing: John was thoroughly exhausted. His body desperately needed sleep, but it was too bright, he was too uncomfortable and too distraught, and his mind was fighting sleep. After what seemed like four more hours, he nodded off in spite of himself. Just as his awareness of his surroundings drifted away, the door reopened, its mechanisms clanking through John's brain, and the trio of Chirtle, Betz, and Smith intruded into hazy semi-reality.

"Did you have a good nap?" Chirtle boomed.

John snarled at him. He wanted to leap from his chair and strangle Chirtle. This appeared to be the desired reaction.

"Take it easy, Resnic," Chirtle said. "We've reviewed the tapes of our chat, and we don't like some of your answers. You're holding back, and we don't like that. Fact is, we're not going to accept that. Now, you've got one more chance to do this the easy way."

John desperately wanted to know the time. He guessed the latest possible was 7:00 a.m. Sunday, the earliest 3:00 a.m. He prayed it was nearer to 7:00. *Hold out for just a few more hours.*

"Where's Stanforth?"

Relief flooded through John. They still didn't have her. "She told me she was going to her parents' for the weekend."

"I didn't ask you what she told you. Where is she?"

"At her parents'."

"No, she isn't. Where is she?"

"If she isn't there, I don't know."

"Resnic, you're coming closer by the minute to experiencing hell. You'd better start providing some complete and truthful information. When we talked before, you made a reference to 'we.' Then you tried to say you were talking about Ben and Liz. That didn't make a lot of sense. You also said Stanforth is convinced that Bremo is a hoax. You lied about that. Have you and Stanforth discussed accepting the Bremo invitation?"

"No," John retorted strongly. Maybe too strongly, he thought.

"What deadline did Bremo give you?"

"Around the end of the month."

Chirtle exploded, spit flying from his lips as he stepped menacingly closer, hands clenched into fists, his harsh voice booming and reverberating off the hard surfaces of the room and within John's head. "You tell me the exact day, Resnic, and I mean right now!"

"I think they said April 30," John replied, trying to maintain control.

"How did Bremo say they initiated the infertility strike?"

"They didn't say!" John yelled. "What the hell do you want me to do, make up lies?" He felt himself losing it. He was dead tired. His situation was incomprehensible, and his fear of being unable to protect Megan was unbearable.

"Didn't I explain clearly enough that you *answer* the questions, not ask them?" Chirtle bellowed back at him. "We'll beat you so hard, your brains'll be splattered all over the floor around that chair! Answer the question! Now!"

Silence.

"All right." Betz spoke tranquilly after the brief standoff. "Let's all calm down. John, you're going to tell us everything you know. The entire truth. The only question is whether you'll do so willingly or by other means. There are certain things we know. We have transcripts of the emails transmitted between you and Ben and Elizabeth. It's evident from those transcripts that Megan was never convinced Bremo was a hoax. So, we know you've been lying to us. We also know you've been telling some of the truth. Where we're going to go now is away from the lies and to the whole truth. I'm going to ask you a question, and you're going to tell me the truth. Have you and Megan ever discussed the possibility of accepting the Bremo invitation?"

John sat silently, looking straight ahead.

"Look at me, John." Betz's eyes were riveted on his. John felt as though Betz was drilling into his mind, extracting whatever information he wanted. Betz said with more calm than John had ever heard in anyone's voice, "John, you will give us an answer."

"No," John whispered, summoning his willpower.

"No, what?" Betz asked. "No, you never discussed it, or no, you won't answer?"

"No!" John yelled, continuing to be plagued by erratic loss of self-control.

Betz turned away, glanced at Smith, and walked slowly to the back of the room. Smith walked over to John and, without a word, slammed into his jaw with a fist that felt like a rock. John thought his head was splitting. Blood spurted from his nose and flowed in his mouth from teeth digging into cheek. After allowing the pain to swell and radiate for a minute, Betz turned around and walked back toward him. "I'm going to ask you again, John. Did you and Megan ever discuss the two of you accepting the Bremo invitation?"

John looked straight into his eyes and glared hatred. He didn't speak.

"All right, John," Betz said calmly. "We're going to leave and let you consider your situation. Then we'll come back and get the full truth from you. You'd be wise to make this easy on yourself. In the end, you'll be unable to resist, anyway." They left, locking the massive door.

John's head slumped forward. He whispered, "Megan, please hurry. God, let it be nine." He was not able to focus. The vicious blow, added to his exhaustion and emotional strain, had taken a tremendous toll on his senses. He sat motionless, head hanging, dripping blood. Random, incomplete thoughts wafted through his mind. His comprehension of time passing was unreliable.

At some point, John became groggily aware of men back in the room. It seemed there were more of them. "John. John, do you hear me?" The calm, patient voice belonged to Betz. John didn't move. Through the fog, he heard Betz say, "Douse him." The utterance held no meaning to him.

Smith had a five-gallon bucket of iced water. "Wake up, Resnic!" Chirtle shouted as Smith tossed the icy mix on John's swollen, bloody, aching face and his torso. John jerked back in the chair, looked up with his one open eye, and saw Betz.

"Good, you're awake," Betz said pleasantly. "Can you hear me?"

John nodded almost imperceptibly.

"Can you speak?"

John nodded again.

"Speak, then."

"I can talk," John managed to grunt through his swollen mouth and broken jaw.

"Good. Now, answer. Did you and Megan Stanforth discuss going to Bremo?"

"No," John managed a clear response.

"Okay." Betz addressed the group around him: "Strap him down."

John saw three more huge men in addition to the original trio. Horror rose within him. They unfastened him from the chair and lifted him across the room to the examination table. As they pinned him down, he struggled, but it was useless against these beasts.

John was wide awake now. His arms, legs, head, and torso were cinched to the table. He couldn't believe how much his body hurt. The straps were so tight, they burned into his legs, arms, chest, and head. Out of the corner of his eye he saw Smith filling a syringe and blurted out, "What are you *doing*? Let me out of here, you *bastards!*"

"Calm down, John," Betz said with no emotion. "You aren't going anywhere. You will tell us the truth. This," he said, pointing to Smith's syringe, "is going to see to that. I can tell you there are some nasty side effects to this potion. Unfortunately, John, your life as you know it is over. However, it also has some amazing benefits. I guarantee you that you'll shortly be telling us the complete truth to anything we ask." Betz walked to the table and stood close to him. John began to shake. "Hold that arm still," Betz commanded one of the goons.

John couldn't move. From the corner of his eye, he saw the needle lowering to be inserted into his vein. He tensed his whole body, clenching his fists and gritting his teeth. His mind screamed, "Meeegaaaan!" His mouth made no sound.

*   *   *

Megan paced in the kitchen and watched the clock tick on 8:30. Kathy had said they'd be home fifteen minutes ago. Her panic intensified. *Keep your cool.* She walked past the computer and made sure it was still working. She had turned it on half an hour ago. The night had been terrible. She had been up and down out of bed twenty times. The TV had been on all night, providing background noise. When she had tried to watch it, her mind had swirled, and she had no clue what program was on. She had little control over her thoughts, which jumped from worry to worry. Rufus was tense and edgy, too, absorbing Megan's aura. Her world was unraveling. She ached to know where John was and what he was going through.

"Come on, Kathy. Where are you?" Megan said aloud. "Get here!" Without thinking she tuned the TV to local traffic and weather. *It's Sunday morning, idiot. There can't be a traffic jam.* She couldn't believe what she saw. There it was: an accident at the south edge of Albuquerque. The northbound lanes were stopped, traffic backed up for eight miles. "Oh, God," she whispered. "It can't be them." *No, they're just caught in traffic.* There were only a handful of people who could have been in the accident, and there were hundreds, probably thousands, in the backup. *They're just caught in traffic.*

"Oh, God," she said again. "They aren't gonna make it! It's just me. Nobody but me." She dropped her head down into her hands and closed her eyes. *I have to do it. By myself. Send us all off the Earth, away from everything .... Save John.* She wiped a tear and prayed he was alive. "Come here, Rufus," she said softly. Rufus sauntered to her and laid his head in her lap. She rubbed his head. "It's just you and me, boy. We can do it. Stay with me, Rufus, and we can do this." Rufus licked her hand.

Megan stared at the clock. 8:40. *What if the computer doesn't work? What if the power goes out? What if I can't open email? What if it doesn't send? What if I can't make myself do it?* She walked to the computer desk and sat. She brought up the email screen. *What am I supposed to type? Where's my purse? I need the CD!* She couldn't remember where she had put her purse, and her panic grew yet stronger. *Calm down, Megan, it's on the kitchen counter.* She got up, walked to the counter, and pulled the CD out of her purse. She went back to the computer, hesitated, inserted the CD, hesitated again, opened Word, clicked on the CD drive, and called up her documents. She found the one she needed and read the simple instruction. Then she clicked back to the email screen. It was 8:45.

She typed on the addressee line: "Bremo." She moved the cursor to the subject line and typed painstakingly: "Take us all." She flipped back to the Word document screen and reread the instruction. Then, back to the email screen – back and forth seven times before she made herself stop, convincing herself it was done right. She moved the mouse to position the cursor on the "send" button. 8:50.

She walked to the dining area, looked out the back window, and stared at the trees, the grass, the sky, the birds, the swing set, the sun. *Will I never see any of it again? Will I never see my dad again? My sister?* Tears streamed down her face. *Save John. Do it!* Back and forth between the computer and the window. 8:55. She stumbled twice, nearly falling the second time. "Kathy, please come home," she whispered.

Megan sat down in front of the computer. 8:56. Time crawled but continued to pass. Her mind went numb. She sat motionlessly, wondering vaguely whether she was able to move. 8:57. She had no thoughts at all. She stared at the computer screen with its digital clock in the lower right hand corner. She didn't move a muscle, didn't even blink, hands folded in her lap. 8:58. She read the lines without thinking or comprehending. *Bremo. Take us all. Bremo. Take us all. Bremo. Take us all.* A thought flitted through her head. *I'm not going.* She read, *Take us all.* She thought, *I'm staying here.* Read, *Take us all.* 8:59. Megan raised her hand, held her index finger a hair's breadth above the mouse button, and stared blankly at the finger.

*   *   *

The man looked over at his wife and said, "I wonder if we're going to sit here all morning." They were at a dead stop in a traffic jam on Interstate 25, on their way north to El Vado Lake to meet their best friends. They had decided it was time to talk with them about the dire state of affairs and to try to figure out whether there was anything they could do to protect their futures. "You'd think they'd get the problem cleared off to the side and let traffic pass. We should call Bob and Sally and tell them we're gonna be late. Is your cell phone in your purse?" He glanced past his wife, out the passenger window. "Hey, where's the idiot who thought he could pass everybody on the berm? Their impatience must have got the best of them." He smirked. "Are they walking?"

"What?" his wife turned and looked. "Why, they're gone ... even the little boy." She looked up and down the highway but saw no sign of them. "They must've gone down the hill on foot."

"Idiots," her husband said.

*   *   *

"What the *hell*?" Betz exclaimed in uncharacteristic surprise as Smith began to insert the needle into Resnic's arm. The other five men stood staring at the table, mouths gaping, speechless. "God *damn* it," Betz added softly. They were all staring at an empty table.

Chirtle said to himself as much as to the others, "If there was any doubt in your mind before, it should be gone now."

John Resnic had vaporized.

Betz couldn't recall the last time he had experienced failure. The feeling was surreal. He felt no anger, disappointment, or even fear of reprisal. After the brief moment of initial shock, he was conscious of nothing except the thought that his mission had failed. Inexplicably, he didn't care.

*　　*　　*

The Jarrett residence was empty. As the clock digits on the computer had changed to display 9:00, Megan's finger had descended and lightly pressed the left button on the mouse. She felt her finger touch it, but, after the first sensation of a surface pressing back on her skin, she saw and felt nothing more.

The computer screen was blank white. Megan and Rufus were no longer in the room.

Epilogue
Saturday, June 14

Kent and Linda Ballor sat talking on their back porch in Mountainair, New Mexico. They were worried about many things. Kent, at 59, was nearing what he had always thought would be his long-awaited and hard-earned retirement. For the last thirty-five years, he had worked his way up to second-tier management in a nationwide construction management company that specialized in design-build projects for real estate developers. Just one year ago, the future had looked bright.

Now, everything was tumbling down around him. Several of the company's clients had stopped paying their bills. Most had not declared bankruptcy; they had simply stopped paying. Yesterday, the company had called a meeting of managers to inform them that the firm's banking resources had reached their lending limits. If none of the late payments were received in the next two weeks, the company would not be able to make payroll. Wholesale layoffs were to begin Monday.

Kent thought the speed at which this had all happened was part of a knee-jerk reaction by the entire United States business community to the expiration of the thirty-day period of economic controls Jamison had forced on the country. A year ago, the demise of the company wouldn't have bothered Kent that much. Then, he'd had a large nest egg in his 401K retirement plan, most of it in stocks. January, February, and March had been hard on his account. Its net value had started to tank seriously after the first of April. On April 16, on his way home from work, he'd heard that the stock market had dropped ten percent that day.

He'd hated the thought of absorbing the huge loss his plan had accumulated over the first quarter by converting the whole shooting match into CDs, but he was too close to retirement to risk any further losses. The value of his portfolio was down almost thirty-five percent from its high point less than a year before. Enough was enough. He decided to pull the plug first thing Thursday. However, that night, the damned President had frozen everything. The salvaging of the Ballor retirement plan had to wait.

After the President's thirty-day no-trade period, when the markets had reopened, the limits on price drop imposed by Jamison's plan were reached quickly every day. Regardless of his efforts, Kent had been unable to get his assets transferred before his stocks reached their daily drop limit and were no longer permitted to trade. He couldn't transfer the assets himself. The agent for his plan had to initiate all transactions. Whenever he could get any response at all from his agent, it was never anything more than another excuse. Now, the value of his 401K stood at less than one-quarter of its maximum value. It was no longer a retirement plan.

The country was falling apart. The *world* was falling apart. From late April until late May, Jamison had made so many public addresses, one couldn't keep track of them all. However, by early June, it was becoming obvious that none of his grand schemes were working, and the speeches just stopped. The world economy was a catastrophe. Regardless of all the progress Jamison was claiming on the infertility crisis, nobody Kent and Linda knew could name anyone who was less than five or six months pregnant. Riots were occurring daily in all major cities around the world, and they were becoming more violent. Police and military presence was everywhere.

Kent and Linda were discussing what would happen if the Government and all semblance of law and order disintegrated. What would they do? How would they survive? Where was their American Government now? Where was the confident, committed leadership?

Linda looked across the yard to her neighbor's back porch. They had known Bea Bowerston's family all their lives. Bea, her husband Stephen, and their only child, Kathy, had moved from Mountainair to Los Alamos almost twenty years ago, when Stephen had been transferred. At that time, Kathy had been in grade school. A year after Kathy had gone to college,

Stephen had been killed in an automobile accident. Shortly after that, Bea had moved back to her family's hometown. Kent and Linda had been happy to have Bea as their neighbor eight years ago when she'd returned to Mountainair.

"I am worried about what will happen to us," Linda said, "but at least we have each other. Whatever happens, it'll happen to us together. But, I'm really worried about Bea. She lost Kathy and Brady, what, seven weeks ago? They were everything to her, the only family she had left – and they just disappeared. No word, no nothing. Their abandoned car on the interstate with no sign of them? Just gone. For a while, I was afraid Bea was going to wither up and die, too.

"Then she got hooked up with that laptop computer. Now, she's gone off the deep end. She's obsessed with it. I mean, I'd have bet money she'd never have any desire to go near a computer. But, she lives on it. And she's so secretive, always closing it if anybody gets near."

Kent and Linda had been sitting on their front porch on Memorial Day, when a car they had never seen before had pulled into Bea's drive. It had caught their attention because the woman who had gotten out had been carrying a baby. The infant had looked from their distance to be a newborn, which had become an unusual sight. The man had carried a laptop computer case. They had stayed in Bea's house for over two hours. When they'd walked out of the house, Kent and Linda had seen Bea, crying, hug the woman while the man had carried the baby back to the car. The laptop had been left with Bea. As the woman had turned to get into the car, they'd heard Bea say, "I can't tell you how happy this makes me. I'll never be able to thank you enough, Bernie."

"Yeah," Kent said slowly, shaking his head, "I'm worried about her, too. She's always been the nicest lady. Always so pleasant and friendly. Losing Kathy and Brady stole everything from her. You know, we haven't been over to visit her for almost a week. I don't know what we can do to help, but we have to keep trying. We still have some of your oatmeal-raisin cookies left. Bea loves them. Let's take a plate of 'em over."

"Good idea. I'll get them."

Two minutes later, they stepped down off their back porch, cookie dish in hand. They saw Bea sitting in the rocking chair on her screened-in back porch, head bent over the laptop. They saw her look up for a moment, and they smiled and waved to her. Bea looked straight at them, seemingly looking through them without seeing them. She made no acknowledgement that she had seen them wave, but just looked back down at her computer screen.

Linda felt an overpowering sense of pity for her. They slowed a bit but continued toward her house. They had just crossed into Bea's yard, when, as they were both looking directly at her, she just wasn't there anymore. She hadn't gotten up from the rocking chair. They could see the back of the laptop. They could see the chair, rocking from the loss of the weight that had been on it. But, Bea was gone. Kent and Linda stopped dead in their tracks, gaping at the creaking chair. Not thirty feet from them, Bea Bowerston had vanished before their eyes.

www.ingramcontent.com/pod-product-compliance
Lightning Source LLC
Chambersburg PA
CBHW071307200626
46813CB00015B/493

* 9 7 8 0 9 8 3 9 6 1 2 0 8 *